LAZARUS EFFECT

THE LAZARUS EFFECT

HJ Golakai

Abuja – London

Born in Frankfurt, Germany, Hawa Jande Golakai spent a vibrant childhood in Liberia. After the civil war in 1990 she bounced around the continent. Having lived in several countries she considers herself a modern-day nomad and cultural sponge. Hawa is currently a laureate of the Africa39 Project, celebrating 39 of the most promising contemporary authors under the age of 40 on the continent. She enjoys performing autopsies and investigating peculiar medical cases for her storylines. In addition to writing, she works as a medical immunologist and health consultant. She lives between Monrovia and anywhere else she finds herself.

First published in 2016 by Cassava Republic Press

Abuja – London

www.cassavarepublic.biz

A CIP catalogue record for this book is available from the British Library and the National Library of Nigeria.

Nigerian ISBN: 978-978-953-514-6

UK print ISBN: 978-1-911115-08-3

E-book ISBN: 978-1-911115-09-0

Printed and bound in Great Britain by Bell & Bain Ltd, Glasgow.

Distributed in Nigeria by Book River Ltd.

Distributed in the UK by Central Books Ltd.

To my family, who know me best and worst. And Miss Gloria Dunbar, for teaching me 'the difference'.

You will live by the sword and you will serve your brother.
But when you grow restless, you will throw his yoke from
off your neck.

Genesis 27:40
The Holy Bible
New International Version

Prologue

The teenager broke the bones of her neck and wrist and felt no pain. The core of her being, a vibrant girl who had loved the colour red and salty, vinegar-soaked chips, was gone – spirit and flesh had parted ways two years earlier. The husk left behind meandered through an underground drainpipe. The pipe traversed a field and wandered into a residential suburb with a brisk business imprint, its chambers swollen with rainwater. A torrent of filth – mud, plastic garbage, the effluent of other people's lives and carelessness – pushed the remains back and forth.

The girl's corpse had lain dry and undisturbed for over two summers, nestled in a storm drain protected from the elements by pipe failure in the drainage system. This year's rains were particularly brutal, disrupting the rest haven. Flooded, the concrete channel rolled and settled, shifting and releasing its contents. The corpse had knocked through kilometres of sub-city planning, bones breaking along the way. Now, it faced a battle of size versus mechanics: the larger channel diverted into smaller culverts and the force of the run-off was too weak to expel the unusually large cargo. The girl's corpse lay wedged between a fair-sized stone and the unyielding lip of a pipe – stuck, literally, between a rock and hard place, rocking gently in the current.

Braving the cold on a nearby footbridge, a solitary figure hopped from foot to foot, waiting for some sign of the body. After days of rain, the torrent should have released it, or a piece of it, by now. Nothing had appeared, meaning it had to be stuck in the system. Something like this had been bound to happen. The watcher had been quick to the scene within an hour of the first raindrops falling and had tried and failed to pull off a rescue mission. Trying to fight the strong current in a confined space, alone and on an empty stomach, was a mad idea. A death wish. Only the living could fight for the dead, and the watcher felt frozen between those two worlds most of the time.

So, the watcher watched. As the first to have seen the dead girl dumped in the storm drain and the last one to see her alive, the watcher's waiting was mixed with a strange sense of loss. She wasn't coming out. Eventually she would, but not today or tomorrow. And when she did, whatever terrible things had landed her under the city would pop out, too. Trouble was behind her; the watcher also waited with a sense of dread.

Breathe.

A few hundred metres away, a solo jogger zipping past the open expanse of Rondebosch Common grappled with the smaller but no less important issue of personal biology.

Voinjama Johnson grunted as her legs ate up asphalt. She had no objection at all to the principle of fitness; in fact, she'd missed – in a distant, offhand way – her university days as a star track and fielder. But this new 'taking back command' routine – forcing herself to do things like run at ungodly hours to prove to her body that she was mistress of it – was a pain in the ass. She sucked in lungfuls of air, eyes watering a little as it nipped around her nostrils. The rub of a Cape Town winter, a temperamental witch's brew of whipping winds and slanting rain and rolling fog and wan sunlight, wasn't much help either.

Vee cruised to a halt and bent double, hands gripping knees, appalled at how unfit she was. Her mind was definitely racing faster than her body; miraculous, considering how much more baggage it had. Thoughts to the tune of, *Please, by summertime, let it be over. Or let it be better, easier.* If things had improved, if 'it' had come under control by then, she'd fulfil every promise (lie) she'd made to God. Anything so that these absurd morning runs wouldn't be necessary any more. The running was meant to clear her head, but evidently the blockage up there was being cleverly circumvented. Doctors couldn't tell you everything …

'Can't tell you squat,' she wheezed, clenching her teeth against another stab of leg pain.

… but it was reasonable to assume that at least one of their remedies would've worked, either by blind luck or a process of elimination. Psychosomatic manifestation of pain. Hyperventilation. Periodic blackouts. Idiopathic illness, they said, shaking their heads. We can't diagnose if we can't pinpoint a causative agent. Apparently, no diagnosis was still reason enough to medicate every symptom to death. Take these pills to help you sleep. *No thanks, they carry me down too deep. Then I'm groggy all day.* These ones should work for the pain.

They knock out all my other senses, too. I zombiefy. Homeopathic medicine? *I can't afford it! And isn't that just white people's version of witchcraft?* Start a pastime then. Do something creative. *I have a job that pays me to do that. How much more creativity do I need?* No, not your job. For yourself. You need a hobby to take your mind off things.

To take a mind off a thing. So simple a principle, yet so mammoth an undertaking. Mind … thing … *flick of a switch* … off. If only life were so–

A series of spasms interrupted her thoughts, growing from flutters and trembles into agonising, involuntary clenches, and then rolling into one whole-body muscle seizure. Vee hunched and bit a howl down to a low groan. Bad, *bad* place and time. Making a spectacle of herself on the Common like an addict in the throes of a meltdown: terrible idea.

Through a prickling of sweat and tears, she flexed enough to catch sight of another jogger, bounding along with all the vim and vitality she would never have. Summoning all the strength she had, all she knew she'd have for the rest of the morning, Vee pulled herself upright. Her vision swam.

The mirage, a caterpillar-like blur of white sneakers in a streak of maroon, tightened focus into the figure of a dark-haired young woman in a velour tracksuit. You can't find those tracksuits anywhere now, Vee thought, arranging her features into a mask of affable exhaustion. Two, three years ago they were the rage in shops, from cheap to boutique. Finding one now was like looking for a kidney on the black market. The woman looked Vee over and began to slow down, concern creeping into her smile. Grinning, Vee flipped her a reassuring thumbs-up and dug her fingers into her waist under the strain of keeping her legs steady, letting the woman take in her sweaty face and heaving chest for good measure. They exchanged the 'you get it' nods and smiles of those who shared intimate knowledge of a gruelling activity and the woman jogged on, shiny ponytail swishing behind her.

Vee felt her legs buckle, welcomed the concrete embrace of the footpath as she collapsed near its grassy verge. She fought to keep her lids open and eyes in focus, to keep her chest from exploding. Her arms twitched at her sides.

She disappeared down the mouth of the monster, the sensation of being swallowed crushing down on her breastbone, squeezing sound out of the air around her. Her eyes were live coals, scorching holes towards the back of her skull. Everything shimmered.

Through the haze coating her eyes, another figure materialised and moved closer. The outline was familiar ... that of a teenage girl in a red woollen hat. Vee's scream disintegrated into a croak in the back of her throat. She scuttled away, oblivious to shards of gravel digging into her back until a particularly jagged edge forced her to a halt. Wheezing for air against the knot lodged in her throat, she closed her eyes and counted backwards from fifty-three. Why fifty-three she had no clue – it had worked once in the past.

Vee got to zero, took several deep drags of air and blinked at the dawn once more. The girl in the red beanie was still there. Vee released a shuddering breath, squeezed her eyes closed again and ran through another countdown. This time when she opened her eyes, the expression on the girl's face was a mixture of impatience and amusement, the smirk of someone who was in a hurry but wasn't above killing a few minutes to see how long Vee's silliness would continue. Once she had Vee's full attention, the girl proceeded to do what she always did: head cocked, she studied Vee from her superior vantage point, a hunter at the end of a kill, watching an animal thrash out its pitiable last. Then her eyes softened. She shot a look over her shoulder and back to Vee several times, motioning with one hand.

She's not misting.

Of course she wasn't. Because she wasn't there, wasn't real. As solid as the teenager *looked*, tangible as a tree or scurrying squirrel, one detail betrayed her. Her chest rose and fell, but the winter chill belied proof of life. Vee watched her own breath turn to white mist as it hit the air; her tormentor had none. She moaned. She was losing her mind. Her heart thudded against the roof of her mouth like a tiny, dying bird.

'Oh my God, are you all right?'

Vee peeped out from behind her hands, this time into a pair of eyes in a highly concerned and very real white face. She tried to answer and it came out a burble of gibberish running over her lips. Head lolling, she tried to relax and dug deep. *Try again. Use your words, Johnson. Stand up. Kick your own ass if you have to.*

Hovering, the woman patted down her pockets as her tiny, manic ruff of a dog bounced up and down, yipping.

'You saw her?' Vee managed at last. 'She was right over there, with the red hat. You saw her, too?'

'Who?' The woman brandished her cell phone and fumbled with the keypad, peering down at Vee and scanning the area, fearful. 'Saw who? Where? Were you mugged? Just hang on, young lady. I'm calling for help.'

Vee relinquished control of her neck muscles. Vomit spurted down her T-shirt and over her shoulder as she allowed her head to roll onto the pavement one final time. The dog licked the regurgitated breakfast off her face, while the owner struggled between pushing the animal away and yelling into the phone.

Vee closed her eyes against another really shitty morning.

ANATOMY OF A MURDER
Strawberry lips

Jacqui smoothed the duvet cover against the bed as flat as she could get it. Then she folded ... once ... twice ... tucked the edges in tight under the mattress, smoothing her hand along as she went. A well-made bed mattered to her mother, and these days what mattered to her mother mattered to Jacqui. The *kak* would hit the fan soon enough and the more she did to sweeten the inescapable journey through hell, the easier she'd make things on herself.

The floor she could never get clean enough. Besides that, it really ruined the whole room. It simply didn't match. She had no idea how something as concrete as a floor could be out of place, since all the other bits either had to work around it or ignore it completely. But *this* one did its best to piss her off. She didn't know much about styling yet, but one day she definitely would. One day, when she was an interior designer, or just a designer, period, knowing and being known for having cutting-edge information on such things would be her *effing biznas*! Cool would radiate from her in waves and people would envy her taste. She'd have closets bursting with top-notch stylish clothes that her friends could borrow without bothering to return. Her super-expensive convertible would have spinning rims and her mansion would be full of pimped-out shit–

'Sherbet,' Jacqui corrected herself out loud. 'Sherbet, sherbet, sherbet! Never say shit, say sherbet!' she ranted, scraping the broom over the ugly floor. No one would ever respect a designer with a foul mouth or covet her fashion advice. But then again, she knew for a fact that arty people were always pumped to the eyeballs with drugs and screwed around carelessly, swearing being one of their more normal habits. This new 'afterlife of her eternal soul' thing kept getting harder and harder to live up to.

Okay, fine, it wasn't too bad. The socialising part of being born again was actually kind of fun: the youth meetings, braais and parties, the study groups where they did more gossiping than homework. Later on, though, after she made it big, how would all of this conflict with her image? Separate and part of a personal life was one thing – it could be easily packaged as a no-go area and even lend a bit of mystique to a star personality. But part and parcel of a public image, unless you were a gospel icon, was plain uncool. It soured quickly and could end up looking like a cheap publicity stunt, and there wasn't much picking yourself up after that. She'd seen it happen too often: big break, the dazzling rise, media darling ... then poof! Some stink rose from the grave and there went all your hard work. Back to eating *pap en vleis* on your ouma's stoep. A girl had to be careful. Image was everything.

'Jacqueline!'

'Yes, Mum!'

'Don't shout at me when I call you! And that room had better be spotless before you even dream of going anywhere!'

Jacqui bit back a slew of curses and kept sweeping. She was practically out of the house; all she had to do was hold her tongue a little while longer. Once she was done, she turned her hand to finishing touches, adjusting the carpet in front of the door and lamps on the side tables, opening the curtains to let in the light. Her mother hated open windows and rudely gaping curtains, especially since the flimsy red material Jacqui had insisted on didn't hide much without the heavier ones drawn over them. A young woman undressing with nothing but saucy voile between her and the leering eyes of pervers-by, candles flicking their glow onto the windowpane, a soft breeze drifting past ...

A teasing smirk lifted Jacqui's lips. Okay, sometimes it was obvious she hadn't worked the poison of too many girlie movies out of her system. But if only they knew ... If only she could get it through to both of her parents, without actually having to tell and crush them, that it was too late to headache over spilt milk. All she could do now was stay on the mostly straight, annoyingly narrow and often boring. Well, she could do her best. No doubt her mother would be up here after she left, yanking the curtains shut, snooping through her things while trying not to leave obvious signs that she had, doing her best to preserve their humble home's dignity. It was worth a try.

Jacqui checked the time and threw the rest of her look together in the last few minutes. It was cool and cloudy outside, showers threatening to come through later, so she stuffed her hair under her favourite red knitted cap. Saturday tennis wasn't as big a deal as basketball training but still counted as an outing, and outings, thanks to her mum, were as rare and precious as gemstones these days. *Every* outing meant dressing up.

She zipped the tracksuit top of her school kit over a plain, loose T-shirt, liking how it worked with worn blue jeans and battered Bata *tekkies*. Saturday girl: scruffy chic, effortless. All her cool, new gear was zipped away, only to be worn during practice, and maybe after, depending on how brave she felt. No point inviting more questions when escape was so near.

Jacqui slung her gym bag over a shoulder and took one last look in the full-length mirror. She made a face. Too plain. She unzipped a side pouch of the tote and fished around until she found her make-up bag. Couldn't hurt if she dotted on just a bit of her favourite lip gloss. Fruity and rose-red, just the way she liked it. Her lips gleamed as she smeared them together. She pulled a few curls out of her ponytail, rounding off the cute messiness effect.

Much better. Jacqui lifted her index finger, licked the tip and then pressed it down onto her jutting bum, hissing air out of her teeth like the sound of a cigarette going out on something wet. A sway of hips and a giggle propelled her out the door.

Oh, behave.

1

The waiting room was an airless sinkhole of Monday-morning blues, its crisp décor struggling to lift the mood. Vee, an unrepentant fan of a brisk breeze, would've gotten up to crack a window, were her godson not sprawled across her lap. After twenty minutes of butt-hopping into any available seat to avoid the sun's glare, she didn't feel like bothering. To top it off, she was starving. Why did everything in this bloody city take so long?

The sit-in of glum faces around her didn't seem to know either, or care. A paediatric appointment in this joint was a gem not readily discarded, though Vee was considering it. Every few minutes, the man beside her fired a round of coughs too rich for Vee's liking, making her question whether it was the child he had in tow who needed to see a doctor. She kept her godson to her chest and leaned away, smiling politely. This was Cape Town and tuberculosis was real. You could never be too sure.

'Waiting still?' Soft brown eyes in a tiny face looked a question up at her.

Vee nuzzled Ikenna. 'Aay sugar, I know. But we got to wait like everybody else, okay? Just small more.' A new fit of coughing erupted at her shoulder; the man was bringing up hacked-up pieces of lung. She hopped to her feet.

'Or maybe,' she muttered, hoisting the toddler onto her hip, 'we ask some questions.'

The receptionist was serving the cocktail proffered by all gatekeepers: apathy and bullshit, garnished with feigned sympathy. She barely lifted her gaze to acknowledge Vee's questions. 'I'm really sorry ma'am, but the doctor can't see you yet. As you can see, it's gonna be a long wait for everyone. You just have to be patient.'

'Patience covers an extra twenty minutes. It's been over an hour,' Vee said. 'Come on, the patients here are *this big*.' She gave Ikenna a playful swing towards the desk and he giggled, waving his arms. 'How much time can it take to look one over and prescribe a cough syrup?'

The girl pursed her lips. 'Obviously, you're not his mother.'

Vee bristled. 'Not his m— *excuse me?* Whatchu tryin' to say, that I–' The receptionist crossed her arms and popped a hip, prepared for showdown. Vee took one look around the crowded room and sucked in the storm. One stupid move and she'd be back on the butt of the line. TB Hero would be the least of her worries; the kid on the end was covered in a rash and throwing up orange chunks.

'Pardon me,' she sugared, starting again. 'Please, okay, I really have to get to work. Can you check how much longer it'll be? I'd really appreciate it.'

The receptionist sighed. 'What name is it under?' she asked, flipping through the appointment book.

Vee supplied Ikenna's name and appointment time. 'I'm his godmother. It's under his mother's name, Connie Ade–'

'I see it, but there's nothing I can do.' The girl met her eyes and softened. 'Look, it usually isn't this crazy, but one of our paediatricians doesn't seem to be coming in today. Ten, fifteen more minutes, max. I'll make sure you're in the next batch called.'

Vee thanked her and turned away, then remembered her prescription. 'Where can I find a pharmacy in the building?'

The receptionist grimaced. 'Sorry man, there's no pharmacy on this floor. Used to be, but everything's been shuffled because of the renovations. Ground floor, west wing, oncology. Bit of a walk.'

Cursing under her breath, Vee left her cell number and set off.

There was trying too hard, and there was just right. The Wellness Institute was clearly aiming for a healthy mixture of both. It was clinically chic, if there was such a thing, but not so self-important as to have ditched the conventional hospital feel, which, gory or not, lent a weird kind of comfort. It was however, New Age-y enough to have opted for old parlance like 'institution', which did no harm when paired with taglines like 'a beacon of hope in health care' and all its other cutting-edge frills. Even under renovation, the place looked and felt good. The tastefully carpeted corridors and pastel waiting lounges were comfortable distractions from the construction work underway. Unsightly scaffolding and noise from an active building site were unwelcome additions to the muted plushness of the interior, but the WI had collared brisk business and was handling it well.

Vee didn't ask for much from hospitals. They were like jails and children's birthday parties – if you got out alive, count yourself lucky. Having spent most of her life in places where access to a proper doctor was a raffle win for most, hanging on to high expectations didn't feel right. Clean bed, capable staff, clear diagnosis; that would do her. But here … here you got that and a gushing fountain of more. She felt ashamed for surreptitiously eyeing the fresh paint and smiling staff, comparing them to the poky clinic in Kenilworth that would certainly never see her face or debit card ever again. Her last GP had been pleasant enough. Well, until her problems overwhelmed them both and threatened to reveal his ignorance in more specialised matters, which had resulted in a hurried referral. She was glad of it. The WI was hot property – if they didn't have someone who could fix her, nowhere would. Their bill was bound to be piping hot, too. The key was remembering that her health was important and worth paying for to preserve. She would keep singing that refrain and watch in mute dismay as the invoices filled up her postbox.

Her cell phone tinkled.

'Where the hell are you?' Chari hissed in her ear. Vee held the Nokia away to check the number. Of course: Charisma Mapondera, office busybody, using an office landline snoop. The woman would rather risk being overheard by half the staff than spend a cent of her own airtime calling in a more private spot. 'It's almost eleven. She's been stalking you all morning.'

'Uh. I'm running a little late,' Vee said. Portia Kruger, editor-in-chief and omnipotent 'She' could grind her bones to dust later – a task she always took on with rabid glee. 'You're supposed to be covering for me. I didn't know there'd be all this rigmarole. This place is more like a new nightclub than a hospital. Aaaay Lawd.' Ikenna's body clock was chiming his next nap session and from the lolling of his head, he wouldn't hold out for much longer. She relaxed her grip on him, forcing him to stay awake by clinging on to her.

'... know *exactly* how she can be. You don't even sound like you're at a doctor's appointment. Oh my God. You're not at a doctor's appointment, are you, you traitor! You're at a job interview. You're packing your bags to work for the *Mail & Guardian* and leaving the rest of us in this dust bowl. Don't even deny it.'

'You got me. In one morning, I'm taking a three-year-old to his check-up, hustling to mine ...' Vee mentally amended the second to 'postponing mine indefinitely', since something had to give or she'd be here until lunchtime. At the thought of another appointment missed, through no fault of hers, relief coursed through her. Guilt hunted relief down and ate it. Was she really trying or simply going through the motions? She *did* want to know what was wrong with her, dammit – she was pursuing every avenue and life kept getting in the way. 'Then I'm rushing home to throw on my power suit and speeding to town to knock out a brilliant interview at the *M&G*, all before twelve.'

Chari giggled. 'Okay, okay, you're at a doctor's office full of whinging kids, your life is sad and you don't need atto from me.' Vee had no doubt that Charisma was idling behind her desk, untroubled as she used her phone and pilfered snacks from her drawer. Chari hated anyone who was immersed in their own lives, leaving her smack alone in the middle of hers. Vee could hear her cogs turning, churning out ways to snoop. 'How come you have to take him, anyway? Why can't his mother do it? You do know you've got next to zero sick leave days left. And why are you at the doctor's so often these days? I know you're not preggers … you've actually lost weight. Your ass is turning white.'

Vee lowered Ikenna to the floor. He latched onto her leg and began a half-hearted whimper. 'Chari, I already told you: she's tied up.' Vee could only imagine what her best friend was up to her eyeballs in. New stock arrivals turned her into a monster, knee-deep in merchandise for her boutique and hollering at her staff. Connie Adebayo put nothing before her child, except on days she could happily prioritise being a businesswoman after bribing his loving godmother with discount clothing. 'Don't worry about me, I'm just … running some tests. Routine.'

'Isn't that just like these modern mothers? Inconsiderate. Always finding ways to foist their kids and their needs on single friends. Exactly what my cousin did! She wants to be here for the 2010 World Cup next year, right, so she packed up with her kids, left Harare and pitched up one clear blue—'

'Chari, I'll call you back,' Vee lied, and hung up.

Where the hell, she wondered, striding up to the nearest enquiries desk. The woman on a call behind the counter stalled Vee's question with a brusque 'one-minute' finger before she wrapped up and supplied directions to the makeshift pharmacy. Vee rounded the next corridor and ran into an impossibly long line. *Please Lord, don't let that be the pharmacy.*

It was the pharmacy.

Vee swore under her breath. The line was moving fast, but not fast enough. Close to three years in South Africa and their policy on lines, queues they called them, was still an amusingly annoying mystery. Everyone patiently waiting their turn, smiling completely inane and unnecessary smiles at one another as if in agreement about the absurdity of the wait, admiring the ceiling, taking ever-so mincing, obedient steps closer to their big moment. With the exception of a passport office, nonsense like this would cause a bust-up in West Africa. The hustle and flow of her kinfolk was as chaotic and yet as organised as a thumping bloodstream. Everybody got what they were after, some jostling and hackles raised, no mental gymnastics. This was asking too much, even for a Monday.

The bright, messy collage of bulletins on the board nearest to the pharmacy caught her eye. Vee quit the line and wandered over, keeping Ikenna, alert and at heel, in sight. In the years to come she would think back to that moment, scouring her memory for a reason, a jolt or inkling that had drawn her over, and would never be able to pinpoint one. What had made her move out of line and what would have happened if she'd stayed put. No reasons besides boredom and impatience ever presented themselves.

Vee scanned the wall-mounted board, one eye on the line (five more people to go, almost there). There was a farewell announcement − a much-loved specialist moving to greener pastures, good luck in California! − two postings for research nurses and a notice from admin apologising for any inconvenience caused by parking restrictions during the construction phase. The left section of the board dedicated itself to interesting times, chronicling through a splatter of photographs the happy moments between patients and the staff.

One snapshot stopped her mid-turn, pulled her in with such authority it felt as though it reached out with one hand and tilted her chin in its direction, then pressed pause on her entire day with the other. Vee froze. She blinked until her eyes started to water. The photo was still there. Her hand went up of its own free will and her fingertips traced its borders, confirming it was real. Not all of what she saw these days was.

Before her was an image of a birthday celebration in a hospital room.

A bunch of kids and two nurses, one middle-aged and the other dew-fresh, a huddle of grins around a huge cake propped on the lap of a bald, prepubescent boy. A few of the other children were bald too, but unlike the boy in the middle, they wore bandanas or caps. A girl stood near the boy's elbow, at the edge of the photo but somehow in the middle of it, as central as the boy himself. Her smile and stance were uncertain compared to the other kids, like she knew herself an outsider here – her hair too full and glossy, her complexion too rosy. As the girl crouched to fit into the frame, her hand rested on the boy's arm, fingers curled around his bony shoulder as if he were a reservoir of strength she hungrily drew on. Even without the knitted red hat and the knife of time to carve away the baby cheeks, the girl's face was unmistakable. An animal groan made Vee start and look around in surprise, until she realised the sound came from her own throat. A couple nearby looked up from their conversation and squinted in her direction.

'Teelinglingling. Teeleeeelingling,' sang Ikenna, tugging on her jeans. Dazed, Vee looked down as if she'd never seen him before in her life. It took a moment to sink in that he was mimicking a ringing cell phone. Hands shaking, she fished the Nokia out of her handbag.

'Miss Va … um, Viona … Vaija … uh, Miss Johnson,' spoke a hesitant voice. 'Tamsin here, the receptionist from upstairs. Dr Kingsley's almost done with the last patient, so he'll see you in ten minutes. That okay?'

'Yes, thank you,' Vee croaked. 'On my way.'

Her face was hot, melting, sliding off, the combo of plastic and glass of her phone icy against her skin. This Air Girl, this Smiling Everywhere Girl, she lived here, inside this picture, in this hospital. She'd been inside this building at one point. There was no mistaking it, no question about that smile. The girl in the photograph was the younger mould of the tormentor, but nonetheless it was her. The one Vee kept seeing when there was nothing to see. This face was the ambassador of last week's jogging meltdown and all the other unwelcome sightings. The force in the ominous undertow she sometimes felt when sitting alone, of being watched, hovered over, the one that pricked up tiny anthills on her skin.

Vee wiped a clammy slick of moisture off her forehead. Anxiety rolled, fogging her vision.

Not here. Not now.

God no no no no no no no …

2

Dr Ian Fourie lingered outside the front entrance of the Wellness Institute and sucked in the fresh morning air, enjoying a rare opportunity for introspection before his day began. He stood at his car, looking over the signs of progress. The place was almost finished. Almost ... but not quite. Active building sites were a blight, no matter how contained and low-key the forces involved tried to keep them. And builders never finished on schedule, ever. They were meant to have wrapped up in May, when winter kicked in, yet here they were still, staring down the barrel of October in a few weeks. Mercifully, most of it was confined to the back of the grounds, but the thought of people equating a chaotic exterior to shoddy service within made him sour.

He couldn't think of the WI as up and running until all the finishing touches were complete. Ian liked things *done*. Finality and full stops were reason to relax. Right now, he couldn't give in to any excitement bubbling under. It was unlucky to celebrate prematurely, or worse, to overstate one's abilities to complete a task and then fall sadly and pathetically short of it. A lasting stain of my pessimistic mother, he chided himself.

As if to taunt him, the wind picked up. Dust rose and the protective sheeting draped over the concrete lip of the roof billowed above his head. Ian stepped back and coughed, flicking dust off his coat. He looked up at the ledge above the double doors of the main entrance, where the institute's sign was being erected at last. The temporary wooden slats supporting the lettering groaned and shifted in the wind, sending more debris crumbling to the ground.

'What the—' He peered closer and blinked, lost for words. They were courting a lawsuit if a plank got loose and brained a prospective client on his or her way in.

Ian scanned the perimeter tape demarcating the edge of the site, spotted a cluster of builders under a jacaranda at the edge of the car park and headed towards them. 'Who's in charge here? You? Okay, come with me, please ... yes, you, come with me.' He drew the puzzled headman back to the entrance and jabbed a finger. 'Do you see that? Are you and your men responsible for erecting this sign?'

'Ja, sure.' The man frowned. 'But right now's our tea break.'

'Naturally. And in the meantime, this establishment poses a danger to all when in fact it's our duty to heal and protect. Do you not see the irony in that?'

The headman's expression replied an unequivocal no, he did not. 'Look man, no worries. *Ons sal dit later regmaak. Hoekom, is jy die hoof van die hospitaal?*' He looked Ian up and down, waiting for a reply, then repeated, slowly, as if speaking to a child, 'I said, we'll fix it later. Why, are you the head of the hospital?'

His lip curled as he flicked his eyes over Ian's cashmere coat and BMW keys. 'Don't you speak Afrikaans, man?'

Ian's keys dug into his fist, heat flooding his face. He wanted to scream at this lout that he practically ran the cardiology unit and was one of the finest specialists on the payroll. 'Yes, I do, of course,' he snarled. 'But right now, that's not the primary concern.'

The headman took a pointed sip from a steaming mug and flicked his eyes over the sign again. 'Ja, sorry, *sir*. We're working as fast as we can. We'll drop everything and get that fixed for you right away.' He walked back to his circle of brethren without a backward glance, and Ian watched them make a big show of amusement as the headman overplayed their encounter.

Ian grabbed his belongings from the BMW's front seat, glowering. He hadn't meant to grandstand like an ass, but appearances mattered. The WI couldn't afford to be a reminder of the establishment it used to be. The clientele they wooed wanted excellent care as much as a touch of grandeur. Under no circumstances could anything mar the facility's debut, not if he had anything to do with it. All the hours of ass-kissing and elbow-greasing had to even out to a substantial payoff, if his efforts hadn't been a waste.

Ian shut the door of the BMW X5, savouring its meaty sound. That was the sound of a good car as far as he was concerned, that thick, coming-together clunk of expensive doors. The car noises he remembered from his childhood were overly loud and metallic, a death rattle of abused doors and engines on the brink of collapse. Both of his daughters, conscientious as they were, thought the car a waste of money and murder on the environment, but their distinct lack of complaints at the BMW's comfort and legroom on long trips didn't escape his notice. His son was a simpler soul, bless him; grabbed the wheel at every available chance.

Ian strode up the path and through the automatic double doors, hoping to avoid any more encounters of the crass kind. Lingering and mingling was not on his agenda today.

'Good morning, Dr Fourie.'

He turned towards the deep voice. Behind the security desk a tall, dark-skinned man in uniform rose to his feet, his eyes warm. Patriotic as Ian was, he secretly believed that the best service in town was almost invariably provided by foreigners, his wife excluded. Etienne Matongo, a Congolese getting by in a job he wouldn't be doing in better times in his own country, always had a cheerful greeting every morning he was on duty. Matongo and the WI went way back. He'd stayed dedicated to the establishment from its infancy to the bloom it now enjoyed, and had earned the deputy of security and surveillance title. Ian spared the few minutes it took to exchange pleasantries about the weather and their families, and then hustled for the lift to the second floor before anyone else cornered him. He ducked past his personal assistant and the assault of morning messages, emails and appointments he knew she had waiting for him and snuck into his office. He hoped, in vain really, that none of the other PAs had seen him. The first moments of peace in the mornings were worth killing for.

It lasted about two minutes before the phone went. Let it ring, he thought as he reclined his chair, pressing thumbs into tired eyes. It didn't stop. Sighing, he reached over and answered. It was Tamsin from paediatrics, fraught and apologetic as she informed him they had only two doctors available and the place was a meat market. She knew it wasn't his responsibility to monitor his wife, but she'd tried the other Dr Fourie several times on her beeper, cell and home phone and still no answer. Could he perhaps …

Ian hung up. He didn't need to glance at the wall calendar or the smaller, flip-over version on the desk to know the date. No parent ever forgot the month that carried the anniversary of a child's death. Obviously that was why Carina wasn't at work yet, why he knew she had no intention of turning up at all. September had truly begun, and every year like clockwork, September rolled in like a cumulonimbus, dank, heavy presence that chewed up every scrap of joy in his heart and home. Every member of his family grew subdued, avoided eye contact and engaging conversation, not to mention the frequent, inexplicable absences from home. Having slept at a nearby bed-and-breakfast last night, he was hardly setting the best example.

Their well-coordinated, sombre dance around the unspoken was familiar – sickeningly comforting, in fact. All the same, he'd expected it to have petered out, if not through the passage of time then at least from how exhausting it had become for all of them. He couldn't help but conjure up an image of himself seated at his mother's kitchen table as she fussed over him, his attire and confidence changing over the years but a petulant, hangdog expression tattooed on his face. The years had yawned between them, and neither had been able to submit to the grief of losing a husband and father. Food and denial became substitutes for communication. Anything could petrify into tradition if people gave it enough respect. Now here he found himself again, decades later. Rinse, repeat. Superstitious he was not, but wondering if a curse hung over his head was beginning to sound plausible.

Ian picked up a framed photograph. The smiling face of his son looked back at him, a face so like his own that the resemblance threatened to splinter his ribcage. In a green shirt splashed with a jaunty print that made him look even younger than his fourteen years, Sean grinned as if he hadn't a care in the world. Wherever he was now, he likely had no cause for cares. Even with the barest of fuzz on his scalp and lighting that hardly compensated for a sallow complexion, it was hard to tell he was a sick child with precious moments left of his life.

Ian removed the frame and drew another snapshot from behind the first, peeling them apart. The heavy, gilded frame ensured no one ever guessed it was there. The hidden photo showed a young girl in a T-shirt and blue jeans, framed in a doorway with hands in pockets and shoulders raised as she laughed into the camera. Same smile, same-ish nose.

They could be brother and sister.

Absurd, seeing as they were, a bond they would've enjoyed more thoroughly had he allowed it in the short time they'd known each other. '2 September, 2002' was written on the back of the boy's photo, the same day as today, the memory captured mere weeks before he died. '17/03/07' was scrawled behind the girl's. Sean, who in a few weeks would have been dead for seven years, and Jacqueline, missing for nearly two.

Two of his children lost in less than a decade, frozen forever at ages fourteen and seventeen. Two grieving mothers hating his fucking guts for the rest of his life: one whose smouldering contempt he had to swallow every day, the other's leaden silence and ability to freeze him out of every line of communication more effective than any physical blow.

Ian picked up the phone. It felt like a boulder in his palm. The next number he dialled was his wife's.

The knife carved a slice off the carrot, nearly taking with it the tip of her finger. Carina swore and stuffed the digit in her mouth.

The metallic taste of blood coated her tongue and amplified, filling her mouth and nose. The smell brought back the operating theatres of her internship, of patients drugged and helpless, relying on her skill to see them through. It reminded her of many smells she couldn't face today: baby powder, full nappies or vomit. She couldn't handle the combined aroma or sight of babies living and *being,* no matter how much she was needed at the hospital. *I can't face much of anything right now.* She squeezed her eyelids together and sucked in gulps of air. *Today I see myself through.*

It was pointless. The tears would come no matter which way she played it.

Motherhood was a glum occupation, Carina thought. A dull, thankless stretch of heroism that some women, most, were born to shoulder. Others were self-made, morphing into the role as their bodies plumped and the realisation that they'd intended to do it at some point sealed their acceptance, even joy. Others were simply resigned to the prospect. She had no idea where, or if, she fitted into either of the latter two groups, but she definitely wasn't of the first. She'd never fancied the idea of mothering, mostly because she hadn't given it much thought, preferring to think of things only when they were immediately relevant. She had, though, very much liked the idea of being part of a couple. The better half of a pair. Significantly othered.

Once married, she'd had no clue why the first pregnancy had surprised her. She hadn't gone out of her way to prevent it, and the thought of a termination had repulsed her as soon as it sprung to mind. Not on any moral or religious grounds, but purely on the principle that she always completed anything she began. Her own mother wouldn't have been shocked to discover her daughter's first reaction to the news had not been unbridled delight. Carina made sure she didn't deliver the news until she wrapped her head around it herself. Not that her mother was someone she had a history of rushing to with tidings of any sort. The woman took judgemental way too far. Since childhood, Carina felt she'd been accused, too harshly in her view, of being too sleepy in her decision-making in some areas and too headstrong and impulsive in others. This from the woman who, after all these years, still doubted that her daughter's decisions – to study medicine, leave Germany to practice in Africa and marry a man who wasn't white – were all carefully considered. Which, of course, they had been.

Four pregnancies, though ... Carina herself hadn't seen that coming. After the trauma of Sean's birth, when they'd finally laid his perfect, downy head on her chest, she'd told herself she was done. One was enough. But like most modern women who thought themselves above the subservience of love, she hadn't made any allowance for how powerful would be her need to please her husband. Ian was absolutely besotted with Sean. In that sentiment she'd agreed with her husband wholeheartedly, as they joined forces in showering their eldest with the adulation he deserved.

She'd named him Heinrich, after her own beloved father, but as was usual resigned to having her authority undermined when he went by Sean, his middle, 'less stuffy' name. Regardless of what he was called, no child deserved spoiling with love and gifts as the first Fourie. Sean was as good and sweet-tempered in the flesh as he'd been *in utero*, not at all what she'd expected. Carina had looked on in quiet terror at the monstrous blue-veined stomachs, pimpled faces and oedemic legs of expectant mothers, the frightful carryings-on and tantrums of other people's offspring in public. How had she, a seasoned paediatrician, not noticed these things before? Which blinkers had shielded her eyes from the truth that these little balls of human, her primary clients, were hell-raisers? Without a second thought, she simply doled out the routine lines on childcare that parents craving sleep or time to themselves craved. Until it was her turn, but she'd gotten lucky.

At least with Sean she had. As her belly had swollen distastefully another three times, her attachment to her firstborn had grown disproportionately more intense. None of her children, Sean included, looked much like her. One of her girls, Rosie, even had the audacity to look like a reincarnation of one of Ian's overbearing, bearded great-aunts. But Sean had had enough of her in him to satisfy her, she reflected with a smile, something in the general way his features arranged themselves while he battled his emotions and fears. He'd got his strength and resolve from her and, combined with uncommon cheerfulness and maturity, his personality had served him well throughout the course of his illness.

Carina blinked against a hot welling of tears. All that self-sufficiency had driven her crazy. Throughout her medical career she'd seen her fair share of myths debunked. The one about the glowing angel that soldiered through chronic illness, uplifting others despite his or her own pain and hopelessness, was as rubbish as unicorns. Sick children were like sick adults: frightened, cranky, and downright impossible. The terminal ones were the worst.

Her Sean had been different. She'd waited desperately for the moment he'd become pathetic with need and fear, allowing her to be the pillar of maternal strength she needed to be. Until the bitter end, he was more a comfort to his family than they'd been to him, more so because every last one of them had failed him. It was almost as if Sean had been born to die nobly and show others how to do it. For heaven's sake, even that bastard of Ian's—

She shrieked as the knife sliced through the same finger again, deeper than before. Blood arced over the kitchen counter and the vegetables. Hissing and swearing under her breath, Carina wrapped the nearest piece of cloth, one of her favourite scarves, around the cut. On the tabletop, her Samsung cell phone began to buzz and vibrate like an irritating electronic animal, lifting and clattering back against the marble in miniature convulsions. With one hand she grabbed it, pressed a button and balanced it against an ear with a shoulder.

In the front garden, Serena Fourie peered through the kitchen window at her mother on a call. Her cascade of blonde hair shrouded the phone, while she bustled around with things unseen. Serena didn't need to be within earshot to know who was calling and what the call was about. It was almost midday and her mother, the workaholic, was at home. She watched her mother's posture change sharply: her fine-boned, slender frame, which none of them had inherited, stiffened and her face reddened as her head snapped up, nearly causing her to drop the phone. She uttered what looked like sharp words into it and turned her back to the window.

'Boo.' Two fingers poked her in the ribs and Serena jumped.

'Cut it out,' she said to her sister, not turning around. Her voice came sharper than she meant but she couldn't help it. Every word and every movement would be as barbed and poisonous today as it had been for weeks. By the look of it, the two likeliest contenders for a showdown were already squaring off. They'd held off for longer than last year, not bashing antlers until the actual day. Serena wondered if that was good or bad.

'That means you're jealous, if you jump when someone pokes you,' Rosie giggled, unbothered. Her chest against Serena's back, she draped her arms around Serena's shoulders. 'Or having *sex*.'

Rosie leaned into her neck, and Serena caught the waft of something sweet laced with peanuts on her illicit whisper. In silence they watched their mother, breathing almost in tandem. In the kitchen, Carina cut the call and flung the phone away from her, then began pointlessly shunting items around on the counter.

'What's she doing?'

'Making stew for supper.' It was eleven thirty in the morning.

'Was that Dad?' Rosie whispered.

Serena nodded.

Another pause. Then: 'What's the date today?'

Sighing, Serena disentangled herself and spun around. The exasperated look she shot Rosie said, You *know* what day it is today. The day Sean had begun what would prove to be his final bout of chemotherapy. They all knew, had been *raised* to know and remember every landmark of their brother's short life.

Rosie's face remained woefully blank for a few seconds, before dawn broke through the clouds and she nodded robotically and hung her head. Serena shook her head. Trust Rosie.

'I won't be here for it, though. Supper, I mean.' Serena hefted a gym bag of clean laundry. 'Got cell group tonight. Going back to campus.'

'Lemme come with you.'

A car crunched up the front driveway. It pulled to a stop outside the gate, and a young man slithered out of the driver's seat and craned his neck over the gate. His hopeful eyes searched those of his sisters. Serena gave her head a sad, slow shake, and Lucas Fourie slumped back behind the wheel and drove off. She walked through the gate to her own car, fighting the urge to look back at Rosie standing alone on the lawn, biting her nails and looking lost.

3

Vee hung her legs out the driver's side of her Toyota Corolla and polished off a Top Red apple. As lunches went, fatty steak rolls and unwashed fruit weren't the best she could do, but it worked on the move.

'On the move' had a nice ring, active with a predatory edge, which made a pretty good ripple on the stagnant pool she called her career these days. The shocking part was that she'd let it happen and hadn't cared much. Her recent blackouts told of a subconscious dissatisfaction, but her subconscious wasn't really her problem if it didn't speak up. True, making its presence felt by flipping all her switches with no provocation at the oddest times was not ideal, but that simply meant there'd have to be some new ground rules.

Reminded of one, Vee popped a foil tab of Cipralex and grimaced the pill down her throat. The previous plan, finding a specialist in her brand of issues ('psychiatrist' sounded so wrong and 'therapist' far worse), was canned. Popping pills for a so-called anxiety disorder was the size of it; a professional and meds combined she couldn't handle.

Vee flipped through a paperback, eyes skimming, mind wandering. Solo missions had their perks. Most of the staff at *Urban* magazine couldn't handle twiddling with their own thoughts to keep the hours from crushing their skulls in. Juggling the drudgery of being both investigator and part-time features editor meant she was well aware that she was looked upon with both awe and pity.

She gnawed on the apple core, relishing the mingling of the pips' bitterness with the film of medication on her tongue. Hard as it was to admit, 'investigator' was nothing but a title at this point. One more lame fashion feature, one more piece of junky prose slapped under a 'human interest' header, and she'd start collecting scalps. Now was the moment to poke the bear, or perish.

'This isn't how we operate.'

'Yeeessss, it kind of is. This,' Vee nodded at the manila envelope, every angle of her pitch outlined and cross-checked to the hilt, 'is what you expect of me. When last have I asked you to expect things of me?'

'A while, I'll admit,' Portia Kruger said. 'And I've not minded too much. You're stretched across two publications. If anything, I've been expecting you to announce that you were scraping together what's left of your leave and buggering off for a bit, not asking for more work. You're ill, anyone can see ...'

Vee dropped her arms and leaned her head, ever so slowly, to one side.

'That was …' Kruger raised exquisitely manicured hands in apology. 'You have asked that I not pry, and so far I've obliged. *So far*. But this is clear out of the blue sky, not to mention rather obscure an angle, even for you. Surely you don't think I'm so out of touch or poor at assessing human character that I'd miss the subtle traces of a personal agenda in here,' she tapped the edge of the folder.

'It's a good story,' Vee replied, flagging.

'Come now, there's more. Show your working as well as your sums. We're not doing the movie scene where I'm the bastard boss forcing the ingenious maverick to toe the line and throw away a great hunch. I don't know which journalism tactics the Americans taught you at the oh-so-prestigious Columbia University, but it's not how the cookie crumbles on the dark continent.'

Okay, so we are *doing this.* Vee steeled herself. Her CU credentials only popped up when Portia felt intimidated – which she had no reason to be, as an Oxford graduate running one of her father's newspapers at thirty-two – and when she wanted to sharpen her claws on a minion's bones. The editor-in-chief looked intrigued, and also piqued that she hadn't sent a writer to sniff out a story like this already.

'This breaks us out of our comfort zone, which we need. Badly.'

'Too hard core for a major feature. An article on the rising incidence of missing children sounds riveting, but where's the appeal? Our readership isn't chuffed when we go too dark.' Portia eyed her as she ran her palm over the back of her chignon, from which a few curls had tumbled loose.

Taking a different tack, Vee rallied. 'I haven't done investigative work in months. We're both wasting resources. That can't be what you want.' *Too whiny; turn it around.* 'Our readership needs pushing. Otherwise we're just adding to the growing pile of garbage that sets us back to last century.' *Johnson, come on! Predictably combative. Steer straight, for God's sake.* 'Look. This could be as big as the xenophobic violence piece ...' Vee levelled a challenge, but Portia refused to meet her gaze, looking away with a genteel cough. 'And *that* made waves, if memory serves.'

'Voinjama, there's no debating you've done some great features here, okay? Kudos for the violence thing.' Portia waved a hand. 'It's still on everyone's lips.'

'On lips, maybe, but not under our credits. My name was on it but it didn't even appear in *Urban*.'

Portia flinched and Vee stopped. Mentioning how often serious material got shifted to *City Chronicle*, how final decisions on content were beyond Portia's control, was suicidal.

Portia blinked thrice, slowly. 'Would you like to go over to *Chronicle*?' she asked, voice soft. 'We're family, after all, and you've collaborated with them before. It wouldn't even be like moving.'

Vee shook her head quickly. 'No.' Yes. Did she? They *were* all part of one media company; moving one building down the street wouldn't be like moving at all. Everyone looked so happy over there. She bet only corporate demons of the recognised variety hounded their heels – stress, deadlines, brutal competition – not dead teenagers.

Portia displayed her top row of pearliness in a rictus Vee could only assume was a smile. 'You know what they say about grass being greener. Now, I suggest you take the piece about the singer-slash-socialite from Joburg. Rehab, steamy French boyfriend, new album ... there's a lot of meat on those bones.' She slid another dossier over from the stack on her desk. 'Look, she gushes, you go through the motions. This isn't the worst idea.'

Vee kept her arms at her sides.

Portia sighed. 'Voinjama. As combative as our ... relationship has sometimes been ...'

'We have a relationship?'

'Don't be obtuse. It doesn't suit you.' Portia mulled a second more, measuring her words. 'I do, despite assumptions, take interest in my best people. I'd actually prefer that you coast the median, for now, instead of ... being you. So what's it to be? Missing urchins, or pop star?'

Vee reached over slowly, picked up her file and stowed it under her arm.

'Your own funeral.' Portia settled behind her desk. 'Oblige me and don't interpret that literally, which you have in the past. I have no intention ...'

Vee sighed. 'Portia, if we're not doing the movie scene, I'll just take the rest as implied. Deliver and don't screw up, or you'll take me off it and make me regret it for the rest of my time here.'

Portia cocked a brow. 'Same chapter, same page,' she said, and flicked her finger in a 'get out' gesture.

★

Vee put the magazine aside and checked her watch: well past 5 p.m. Where was Paulsen?

Portia was testing, or merely pitied, her. Whatever the cause, the effect landed her here, parked in Little Mowbray opposite the home of one Adele Paulsen, itching for the first face-to-face interview of what would hopefully become … what? Vee was after more than a soapbox article. 'Forces' had led her here – God, how precious and moronic that sounded! – and she knew, much as she cringed at the admission, that the force was strong within her indeed. Her maternal grandmother, a woman possessed of mystical powers of the 'African science' variety, had often warned Vee in whispers about her 'specialness'. Years later and Vee's take was that she was just especially sticky for weird shit.

Vee snickered, back of her hand over mouth, until she lost her breath a little. She was losing it. This was how the slip down the slope began.

That was neither here nor there now. She had to turn this around fast or have it taken away – no, snatched and burned and never spoken of again. Precisely why she hadn't been entirely transparent with Portia, who had no clue how flimsy a lead she truly had, or with Adele Paulsen, who'd chosen to believe she was in some way connected with the official investigation of her daughter's disappearance. The former she would deal with later. Portia was fond of giving her sufficient rope with which to hang herself. As for the interview, experience had taught her that lying would get you through the door and no further. If

Adele Paulsen smelled a rat early on, everything was dead in the water. Vee popped gum into her mouth and chewed. Coming clean was invariably harder than lying.

A boisterous group of bare-chested young men in shorts and sneakers jogged past. One caught her eye and whistled, calling out something in Afrikaans that made the rest burst into laughter. Vee hissed and turned away, dismayed as a familiar, unwelcome warmth spread below her navel. Lately, her mind was a cesspool of smut and, being somewhat single-minded, she knew it would affect her work. It was hard to give anything full focus when sex – the loss of it from her life, reacquiring it again with any decent regularity, how much of it other happy bastards were having – occupied a startling portion of her thoughts.

The unsettling part was that men were everywhere – statistically, miserably, half of the population. Ever since she'd been dropped ass-backwards into singlehood, she noticed that they were more everywhere than she'd ever known them to be. Their obliviousness to their sexual draw bordered on spiteful. Striding around displaying V-shaped torsos misted with sweat and bare, muscled legs ... it had to stop. Her last major assignment had propelled her into riots and neighbourhoods shredded by prejudice, and also into the arms of an Angolan photojournalist. No more mistakes of that kind.

A woman laden with bags of shopping began fiddling with a front gate two houses up from the car. Vee leapt out of her head and the driver's seat, clicking the alarm after her.

'Ms Paulsen? I'm Voinjama Johnson. We spoke yesterday morning.'

The older woman looked confused, then her eyes cleared. 'Yes, yes, of course. Miss Johnson …'

She trailed off and went back to fiddling with the clasp on the gate. Vee stepped in, unburdened her of two Shoprite grocery bags and followed her into the front yard when the gate finally swung open. It was a small, pale-blue house with a tiny but manicured front garden. The walkway leading up to the front stoop was a lattice of crumbling stone, swept free of dirt.

Vee watched in amused wonder as a black puppy under a tree produced its body weight in excrement. She thought of her own dog as the puppy bounded up, barking and weaving around their feet. Adele Paulsen gave it an affectionate rub with one foot and brushed it aside, climbing the stairs as she rummaged for her house keys in her handbag. She launched into a ramble about how being a teacher was very trying work, especially without the use of a car, which was in the garage. It meant she was always late for the appointments she hadn't forgotten. And she was really forgetful, especially now that there was no one around to hold things under her nose.

The woman was obviously house-proud. The entrance corridor was neat, and the wooden floors looked like they'd enjoyed a recent wax and buff. In the sitting room, rays of fading sunlight poured through windows trimmed with heavy floral curtains.

The bright tidiness kicked an unexpected swell of pity up Vee's throat, and she checked herself quickly. If she'd lost a child – which she had, but not in the pure sense – keeping a home spotless and welcoming would be a priority of the lowest order. Her own period of misfortune wasn't long buried in the basement of memory at all: unwashed body, swollen eyes, perfectly happy to marinate in her own stink and self-pity were it not for those who loved her. Society extolled the virtues of strength, but nobody ever gave any solid advice about how to break down properly. How long could a mother bustle about playing hostess, all the while wrestling the thought that her only child might be somewhere no mother would ever want her baby to see?

'I completely forgot the time,' Paulsen called from the kitchen. 'I hope you didn't have to wait too long.'

'Not at all,' Vee lied. Idly, she examined a large ornate cabinet filled with china plates, dusty mugs and tiny figurines. If there was one thing that crossed all cultural boundaries, it was the cabinet with the delicate glassware and precious silver. Jacqui, like all children, would likely never have touched its contents if she had valued her l–

'Ian gave most of those to me. Precious, they are.' Paulsen spoke up behind her, setting down the tea tray. 'From his travels during his university and postgrad days. Me, I haven't really travelled much. To Namibia once, before I got pregnant with Jacqueline, and once the two of us went to Zimbabwe in the good old days when it was such a nice country.'

Over the rim of the teacup, Vee dissected Adele. This woman devoted a daily portion of her energy to staying on the go. No one ever need see how miserable she was. Or how angry. The canned rage was hard to get at over the pain and armour of niceness, but it was unmistakably there. It had to be a struggle carrying on as a preschool teacher, seeing those eager eyes and candied smiles every day.

'And where are you from?' Paulsen probed, pushing short brown hair behind both ears. 'Your accent's very different.' She leaned over, deftly spooned three measures of white sugar into her tea, and leaned back in her armchair. Moving Adele. Still Adele. Vee swiftly cast a vote for Moving Adele. Still Adele looked ready to rise at any moment and slap the taste out her mouth for holding the cup the wrong way.

'I'm Liberian. From Liberia,' Vee added stupidly.

Adele 'ahhed' and raised her eyes ceiling-ward, snapping her fingers. In the measured cadence of an educator, she rattled off the capital city and two neighbouring countries before leaning into current politics since the end of the civil war. Vee jarred, pleasantly surprised and impressed. Most locals had little knowledge of other cultures 'further north', as they called it. The darker Africa, a realm devoid of ice cream or shopping malls.

'To be honest, I really didn't know what to expect after we spoke yesterday,' Adele said, wary as the small talk died. 'With a surname like Johnson ... but you're obviously not coloured. What does your first name mean?'

Vee's internal alarm beeped a warning. They were gliding into avoidance-tactic territory, and time was something she didn't have much of. 'I'm named after a trading city in the north. There was a mix-up on my birth certificate between place of birth and my intended name, so ... Voinjama stuck.'

'What name were you meant to have?'

'Ms Paulsen, I'm sorry to be abrupt, but ...' Adele tipped her head, understanding mixed with resignation that they had to buckle down to it eventually. 'I'll start by being upfront as to why I called. I mentioned looking into old missing persons cases, but ... it's actually for a magazine article. I'm an investigative journalist for *Urban* magazine. Maybe you've heard of it.'

Paulsen gave no response except to settle deeper into the sofa. Vee plunged on.

'I'm not connected with the police in any way, nor am I a private detective. But I do care about what happened to your daughter and others like her. Her story stood out and ... shall we say, led me here.'

Truth kept light. No way in hell could she explain to this woman that during her panic attacks she caught glimpses of what looked like the ghost of her missing child. The photograph she'd 'borrowed' from the bulletin board at the Wellness Institute would remain under wraps for now.

Vee squirmed under Adele's gaze. She was reminded of waiting outside the principal's office for punishment.

'So Ian, Dr Fourie, he didn't hire you to find Jacqueline? How'd you find me?'

'Um, no, he didn't,' replied Vee, taken aback. Had she gone that far in her misrepresentation? She was certain she hadn't. *Ignore the second question.*

Armed with the photograph and buckets of innocent charm, she'd managed to wrangle an identification out of the more talkative staff at the paediatric oncology unit. People were blabby if they thought there was a chance of seeing their names in print. It was easy enough to link Jacqueline to her mother, but suspicion sealed off communication beyond that. Otherwise, all she got was a very tenuous connection to a Dr Fourie; both an Ian and a Carina falling under that surname had refused to take her calls.

'I'm sorry if I led you to think otherwise,' she said. 'I hope you don't change your mind about speaking to me.' She cringed internally. Never give a source the option of shutting you down. Her sanity, more than her livelihood, depended on finding the truth behind Jacqueline's disappearance.

'How much do you want to know?' Adele Paulsen asked wearily. Vee wasn't fooled. Adele's eyes were heavy with words, heaving for release. Vee whipped out her Nokia, switched it to voice recording and got a mute nod from across the table, the go-ahead.

'Please,' said Vee, propping it on the table. 'Everything.'

4

At the age of sixteen, she had met Ian Fourie, Adele Paulsen began. They were two middle-class coloured teenagers growing up in Athlone, her family a few rungs further down the ladder of the class system than the Fouries. It was the early eighties and the winds of change were blowing through apartheid South Africa, but not hard enough to keep up with the tornado of ambition swirling inside Ian. His aura of 'more-ness' had him destined for greater things than what the restrictive government had mapped out for 'non-whites'. Bright herself, Adele was perfectly content with her horizon and vacillated between nursing and teaching. Highest on her list of priorities was to adore her secret boyfriend. Ian was immensely intelligent, but – like many talented men – lived under the thumb of an insufferable matriarch.

'It's amazing how powerful men can be such shrivelled assholes in their mothers' presence.'

Vee started a little at an expletive dropping so comfortably out of the mouth of such a collected, well-spoken woman.

'Ian's family didn't have much more than mine, but watching his mother carry on you'd think they were rolling in it. Every time I came by, that crabby old bat had her face scrunched up like I had come to steal something. In a way, I guess … I guess I had. We were both so young and didn't think for a second that we wouldn't end up together. Naïve first love.'

'What made you stop seeing each other?'

'We didn't. We never actually broke up, not formally. He left in December of '81. One day he was here in Cape Town, the next he wasn't. They had family abroad, in Europe. His mother hadn't wanted him to leave the country to study medicine, but once he'd started up with me, it became the best idea she'd ever heard. I knew Ian wouldn't pass up the chance in a million years. Not that our relationship didn't matter: Ian's just like that, always has been. He had a fire to climb, still does, nothing ever stood in his way. Personal relationships, love and the like, just have to work their way around his grand plans.'

Bitterness left her voice and she looked up with softer eyes. 'He isn't all cold, ambitious bastard. Ian's a good man, he truly is. He protects and provides. I think so much is expected of him by so many people that it gets hard balancing success and keeping everybody happy.'

She still loves him. Something, fear maybe, coiled around Vee's heart. Given time, would she deflate and petrify into an Adele, a woman blindly defending a man who had, for all intents and purposes, moved on with his life? What the hell was love worth, then, if you could be abandoned without a backward glance?

'We stayed in contact as much as we could. We didn't talk much about where our relationship was going, or whether it was going anywhere at all. Ian avoids confrontation when it matters most and being apart took a huge toll on his studies, so

I stopped asking. There was nothing either of us could do about it. After a while, we just grew up. I, for one, started feeling extremely stupid waiting for a man who'd be so different when he returned — that's if he ever did. He'd be a doctor and I'd be a teacher, you know? Politically, things were taking drastic turns. Apartheid was on its last legs and we were on the brink of new opportunities. But at the end of the day, he'd still be a doctor and me a teacher. I started thinking ...'

That his mother was right.

'Maybe his mother had a point, much as I hated to admit it. And you know how long-distance relationships can go and what men are like. Who knows what they get up to? I was young still, and if I didn't look forward, my whole life would pass me by. So ...'

Adele shrugged, an encyclopaedia of history in the movement of her shoulders. She'd done what she had to, and damned if she didn't look ashamed and apologetic about it. Her hunched posture spoke of a woman who believed, to her own bewilderment, in one true love in a lifetime.

'We fell out of touch eventually. It got easier. There were other men. Some were wonderful and I tried to take the relationship seriously. But ... have you ever been in love?'

Vee dropped her eyes to her boots.

'Then you know what I mean. You pretend to get over someone so well that you start to believe it. You remember all the history, everything they put you through, and tell yourself you can't forgive. Then you plan this new life, to hell with the past. And all the while, deep inside you know you're completely full of shit.'

Vee fidgeted. Dammit, was she looking at her own future here? 'What happened when Ian finally came home?'

Adele shrugged again, only this time it was more a lazy lifting and resigned dropping of the shoulders. As if gravity was too strong to encourage more.

'What I expected. We didn't just pick up where we'd left off. Too much time had passed for that. We danced around it. I heard talk in the old neighbourhood that he was home for good, but over a year passed before we saw each other. Cape Town's pretty small but you can avoid people if you want to. We finally ran into each other at a party at a mutual friend's place. He looked so much the same. Only difference, he was married.'

She looked over, clearly expecting reproach. Vee nodded, impassive.

'I knew – of course I knew. His wife wasn't with him that night. She was ready to pop by then, about to have their first. I only saw her in passing over the years, and not often. We ... met, much later on.'

'What was she like? When y'all finally did?'

'We didn't talk much that night. Wanting to pretend for a while,' Adele ploughed on, voice soft, a lover reminiscing aloud, alone in her sitting room. 'That's what grown-ups are meant to do, save face and moralise until they're not fooling anyone any more. Then we met up for drinks, just to catch up. How long does that last with a man you have a past with. We swapped old stories from back in the day and laughed ... It became a routine. More drinks, lunch, we're only talking, I was just in the neighbourhood, until ...'

She turned away, her expression a tempest of too many emotions for Vee to untangle.

'After Jacqui disappeared, I started thinking maybe it was God's way of punishing me, both of us, for the way we behaved. It's crazy superstition, thinking that a child is a necessary sacrifice to set things right again. But I can't help feeling that if we'd been more careful and she'd never been conceived, or if I'd been stricter and done more to keep her away from that pathetic family, none of this would've happened.'

'When *did* Jacqui get to know her father's other family? Was it your idea, or her father's, to be closer to them? Or Carina's?'

A sharp, bitter laugh broke from Adele's lips. 'Whose *idea* was it? My God, it wasn't anybody's grand *idea*. The three of us would never be that ridiculous, discussing things like mature adults. There was never a sit-down, no 'Hey, wouldn't it be fantastic if our families got to know each other and became one big, happy unit.' God. Imagine that happening.' She shook her head, chuckling again into her tea. A swift slurp and she set the cup down and fixed Vee with her full, grave attention. 'You really have no clue, do you?'

Adele's eyes drifted down again, this time to her feet, crossed at the ankles. 'You know, when you called wanting to talk, I thought, I *hoped*, that Ian was finally stepping up. That finally he wants to stop being macho and grieving alone, or expecting the police to work miracles after two years, and that he had hired someone. Looks like wishful thinking, as usual.'

Vee waited.

'Jacqui was born not long after Sean. In fact, Jacqui's close in age to the three eldest Fourie kids. She was born after Serena, same year. Carina did *not* waste time. She got pregnant right after they were married, and popped three more kids like it was going out of fashion. I assumed she'd be different, posh and what, being a doctor and white and all that. Maybe have only one. Maybe take some time to get to know his family, get used to our racial mess and whatnot. Ian might as well have stayed and married a coloured girl, another darkie like himself.'

'No love lost between you and the missus, then.'

'How could there be, considering the situation he put us in?' Adele snarled. 'Ian is no fool. He's brainy, but not lacking in social skills the way the clever ones are. Especially with women – he has a special way with women. Not just in *that sense*. He has a way of making you … obey him, somehow. No one ever discusses things with Ian, really, but somehow you find yourself swept along till you wash up somewhere with no idea how you got there. The unspoken rule concerning his two families: we were separate and would stay that way. You know how it goes.'

Vee knew the deal well enough, having grown up in a similar set-up. Big house, small house. As old as the hills, a virtually indestructible pillar of the African family structure.

'Of course, it was up to me to do most of the staying away, not that I had any intention of doing otherwise. They've always had that house out in Pinelands and I stayed in Athlone up until recently. Paths didn't need to cross.

'Then Sean developed cancer,' she murmured. 'Some form of juvenile leukaemia. Life plays the cruellest jokes, or then again maybe it's God. He was the sweetest of the lot. You couldn't find a better child. The terrible irony was that they were *both* gifted doctors who had to stand by, useless, and watch him die. No parent should have to go through that.'

'There have been major advances in cancer research,' Vee said, digging through her rudimentary archive. 'Especially for children. Surely there were more options?'

'You may be right,' Adele agreed, 'but the type Sean had was severe. I remember the first time Ian told me. It broke him, though he fought to stay optimistic and rational. That boy was the world to him. Sean was five or six then, two years older than Jacqui. Something about the treatment he got must've worked, because he went into remission. Then, eight or so years later the cancer came back, and this time it had claws. He was taken overseas, but still … So they started looking for bone marrow donors and … eventually Ian and Carina came to me.'

The room breathed for a few beats as Vee joined two and two.

'Jacqueline was Ian's, too. She and Sean were blood. The doctors always do family first, and they assumed they had a shopping list. It was the worst luck ever. Three siblings, and not one that was a good match for Sean – not even little Rosemary. Ian and Carina didn't come close either. They had no choice but to ask for my help. At first he demanded it, saying it was his fatherly right to use one child to help the other as he saw fit. I told him to adjust his attitude and come back when he had.'

She sighed. 'It wasn't the kindest thing to have done at the time, but Ian picks the wrong moment to aggravate me. He can't admit he's wrong or needs help. He adjusts terms to suit

– calling in a favour, keeping score, being entitled to this or that. He said the most utter bullshit, about doing so much to provide for Jacqui and whatnot, like that had obligated us to him. He even offered to pay me if she was a match.'

'What did you decide?'

'As in, did I let them 'compensate' me for using my kid? No, I didn't. I'm a mother! What pissed me off was his suggesting that it could all be kept quiet. Slide me some cash, take Jacqui to the hospital and stick her up with needles to help Sean. I don't know what that man had in mind, but he was willing to pull some dodgy stunts and risk losing his medical licence rather than be upfront with his wife about who the donor was.

'That's when I saw him for who he really was – someone who lived and breathed his bloody career and image. The great doctor was ashamed he'd made himself common by having a love child. He loved Carina but came to my bed when the fancy bloody well took him. Then he expected to snap his fingers, and I'd put my daughter through pain, for what? I knew then I'd never get any respect unless I demanded it, so I demanded it. No matter how afraid he was of throwing us all into the same messy pot, this time he was forced to consider *my* pride. He had to get his precious Carina's hands dirty too, as in they both had to come to my home and speak to me about it properly. And I won't lie – I wanted them to *beg*. Which they did. But it didn't end there.'

Vee read her body language. 'You were still apprehensive about the donation process.'

Adele nodded. 'The first round was only blood tests to see if they were compatible. With half-siblings, I thought it was a long shot. I could still feel like a good person who had cooperated even when nothing had panned out. But once a match was confirmed, it got real. Even after we explained it to her, Jacqui was brave and wanted to do it. She met Sean and they really hit it off. The procedure sounded straightforward, there'd be anaesthesia and everything, but it was too overwhelming. I'm not proud of it but I lost my nerve and backed out. I got Jacqui discharged from the hospital and took her home.'

In the leaden silence, Vee did some arithmetic. With Sean aged fourteen, Jacqui would have been twelve. Old enough to absorb the awkwardness of their parents' dilemma, but not old enough to understand every adult nuance, every undercurrent of friction. Vee pictured it: two families, subsets of each other, fighting and saving each other from drowning all at once. 'That couldn't have been easy for you. Didn't go down well with the Fouries either, I expect.'

'I'm not a monster. I knew I'd crack, but I needed time to digest it. Then Sean took a turn for the worse and it put things into perspective. It wasn't about me or Carina or any of us. I didn't need any more convincing, but Carina came to see me on her own, to beg me one more time to help save her son. Mother to mother. She wasn't the same cold, hateful woman who had sat in my lounge when we'd met face to face. I agreed to take Jacqui back in the next morning.'

'But the procedure didn't work, did it? Sean died.'

Adele nodded. 'It never even went ahead. In that short time, Sean developed an infection. They tried everything to save him. Infections are common before transplants, and his system was already too weak from everything else. He passed away around this time in September, not long after his birthday.'

Adele rummaged through her handbag for a pack of Stuyvesant Extra Mild and tipped it in Vee's direction. Vee shook her head. She had more than enough chipping away at her already.

'I warned Jacqui not to smoke,' Adele said, exhaling out of the nearest open window. 'I never used to. Disgusting habit. Told her it would lead to an early grave.' She shook her head bitterly. From her lips to God's ears.

'How did Jacqui take Sean's death?'

Adele knocked ash out of the window and walked out of the room. Minutes later, she returned with the squirming puppy in her arms. 'Sorry,' she said. 'He's not house-trained yet, but I never have the heart to leave him out in the cold.'

New cigarette between her fingers, she continued: 'My girl was so different from me. Sometimes I wondered whether they didn't hand me the wrong baby at the hospital. She took it so hard, because to her she'd messed up. She was like that, so protective and proud. When she loved someone, she made their well-being a personal responsibility. Something her father could've learned a lot from.'

Now came the hard part. Vee cleared her throat and sat straighter. 'Ms Paulsen, you speak about Jacqui in the past tense. I'm sorry to have to ask, but does that mean you don't believe she's still alive?'

Without hesitation, Adele shook her head. 'No,' she replied flatly. 'Wish I could say different, like 'I feel it in my gut' or 'Deep down a mother knows', but I can't. Jacqui was a handful. She was growing wild and I was essentially a struggling single parent. But one thing she wasn't was cruel or maliciously dishonest. Yes, she lied – which teenager hasn't? But she wouldn't run off without one word, not *one*, to tell me where she was or how she was doing. Nothing would make my girl do that to me. So, no, I don't think she's alive.'

She lowered her dejected weight back into the sofa. 'I told her to stay away from those Fouries. I knew nothing good could come out of it, but she wanted to be part of them so badly. By the time the madness of the transplant was over, the idea of them had taken root. She wanted a real family. I tried to be enough, but they had a draw on her I couldn't compete with.'

'You suspect they had something to do with her disappearance?'

'Don't know what to think. I've been over it a thousand times in my mind and it makes no sense. This city's dangerous, but no one wants to think what can happen to their own. I've learnt so much about missing children these past two years … Do you know how many go missing countrywide? Over one thousand six hundred per year. And three hundred of them are never heard from again.'

Her voice cracked. The burning circle of tobacco illuminated a film of liquid brilliance in her eyes, threatening to break over the rims. 'One thousand six hundred a year,' she whispered, 'and my baby's one of them.'

Vee switched off the recorder and let the silence chew at the edges of the room. Families and their lies and wars. If anything was familiar ... She refrained from rubbing her tired eyes. Outside, the light faded fast. 'Do you have a picture?' she asked.

Adele walked over to a dresser, and retrieved and handed over a thick envelope. A lot of thought had gone into cobbling it together. Among the papers were two photographs. The uppermost showed Jacqui on the beach, fully clothed and laughing as she held a Coke. She had a small face, framed by shoulder-length curly hair, and her mother's brown eyes. A pretty pixie of a girl. The second showed her decked out in full uniform, forcing an embarrassed smile for the camera on what looked like a momentous school day.

'Keep it,' Adele said, blowing smoke in Vee's direction. 'I don't need so many any more. Sometimes I think I'm the only one left in the world who still cares what she looked like.'

5

Cape Town doesn't really see men, Joshua Allen mused. It definitely wasn't a man's city, red-blooded, not the way Johannesburg or Rome felt, or parts of New York. Sure, people looked; their eyes rested on and made out the shape of a person representing the male gender, but somehow it didn't quite register. Weird, for a city with a markedly higher proportion of women than men. He would've thought the female majority would be … not exactly beating doors down with sticks, but a little more attentive. Husbands and fathers were the worst hit, trundling after their womenfolk everywhere. Their owners.

Joshua leaned against his car in a parking lot in Rondebosch, eating an ice cream cone. He felt ignored, and kind of lonely, if he was being honest. Which was nuts, since he was in the clutches of a draining situationship that left little time for feeling sorry for himself.

He stared through the glass-panelled entrance of the Pick n Pay supermarket across the way, making short work of identifying the pair of women's shoes he'd come with from among a stampede of others. Real leather boots, an ankle-length cut with a matching maroon handbag. Expensive stuff. He should know, since he'd paid for every stitch. The shoes met another pair before the till and began an animated exchange he knew of old: toes pointed at each other, heels clacking. He'd have to wait longer.

'Great,' he muttered. He was a dumb disciple too, just like all the other guys. Here he was, left to rot on the curb like an old banana peel, and he wasn't even put out. Wouldn't be surprising if women no longer registered his presence, either.

'Hey, gorgeous,' he ventured to passing potential, endless legs in a snug pair of jeans.

'Fuck off.' The girl eyed him up and down with lazy nastiness and swayed on.

Too young, anyway. Her hips dipped just a touch in his direction, though, he was sure of it. He pushed off the bonnet of the Jeep Cherokee, took a step in the direction of the supermarket, instantly concluded it was a bad idea. He would be eaten alive. He leaned back again. Five more minutes and that was it.

A solitary figure across the street caught his eye. A familiar outline loitered near the display window of an electronics store, watching Celine Dion in concert on a dozen stacked TV screens. Joshua hesitated, smoothed his hair down best he could and stepped off the curb, right into a tree trunk of a chest.

'How much per hour?' the guy in his way said, frowning.

'Uh …'

'Parking.' The man pointed to his car and dug through his pockets. 'How much?'

'Oh,' Joshua said. The man, stout and fair-haired, was a good two heads shorter, compensating with the brand of bravado that Joshua had come to expect from Mzansi's paler citizens. Joshua shrugged. 'Ten bucks … rand. Ten rand. Twenty if you take longer than half an hour.' He was acclimated to this shit. The Mother City played a remorseless game of favourites, cosseting some of her children and abusing others, a reality inescapable unless one chose to ignore it. This was hardly the first time some random had assumed he was a car guard, or a janitor, or a waiter, going on nothing more than skin colour. Might as well make some money off it. The man made a big show of his surprise before he paid up, muttering about the country going to the dogs as he walked off.

'Please man, some money for food.'

Joshua dropped his eyes, further down this time. A street kid, a skinny little thing in an oversized, battered tracksuit top and shorts – too short for a Cape Town winter, however mild Joshua considered it – stared a challenge up at him. The kid's eyes skimmed over Joshua's tatty attire, sizing up both his rank as a fellow homeless person and right to any money changing hands on that turf.

'Listen, kid, I scammed this money fair and square,' Joshua teased. 'How 'bout we split it?'

'*Ten rand?*' The boy snorted. 'And *that's* yours.' He pointed accusingly at the gleaming Jeep and then thrust out his hand. 'I saw you park.'

Joshua chuckled and handed over the note. 'Here's a bonus.' He pushed a KFC box with an unfinished three-piece meal in it at the boy. 'You need it more than I do.'

He struggled to keep himself from breaking into a run as he crossed the road. On the other side, Celine Dion's rapt audience hadn't moved, a bulging plastic bag of shopping clutched in her hand. His heart was going way too fast for half a minute's exertion, but that much was out of his control. He searched his mind for the perfect, coolest opener and the best he came up with was: 'I've asked you to stop following me around. I'm never gonna crack and sleep with you.'

The woman turned, and a huge smile lifted the most inviting mouth Joshua had ever pressed against his own.

'Joshua Allen! I do declare,' Voinjama Johnson rolled her eyes. 'You always know how to ruin my day with your presence.'

'V.J.'

She was competition, tall for a girl – a jibe she always hissed at. Joshua dragged her into a hug and she laughed and pretended to struggle, while he surreptitiously revelled in the smell of her hair and neck. A waft of baby soap, vanilla and something feminine and bespoke filled his nose, setting off an ooze of warmth under his breastbone. His arms made quick study through her navy pantsuit. She wasn't back to her usual weight since the surgery but she looked a lot more solid than she had when they'd last met. Her ass was still perfection; her smile touched her eyes.

'Stop groping me, New York City boy. Whetin you doin' heah? Dah nah even yor neighbourhood. And it too cold for dis kana nonsense.' She prised the ice cream cone he'd forgotten he had from his fingers. She took a large bite and made a series of throaty sounds he hoped, had long hoped, he'd hear one day in a less public, less clothed arena. 'Brain freeze, but so worth it. Yeah, so, I had no idea you were still in town, since you too hip to take anybody's calls. Whehplay you been hidin' so?'

Joshua grinned. She'd been a floater for two-thirds of her life, yet aside from a slight American affectation her accent was unharmed. 'For Chrissake, when are you gonna learn to speak English properly? You write for a living.'

Vee gave him the finger. 'When Celine Dion stops freaking me out. Why do *you* look like ...' she mussed her hand over his overgrown hair, the stubble on his face, the hole in his T-shirt, '... a homeless turd? You're supposed to be an expat, a high-powered finance exec. Have some pride.'

'I had some time off. I'm allowed to cut loose too, y'know.' Joshua shot an eye across the street and his heart dipped. Vee followed his gaze. Her eyebrows cocked at the sight of the pricey boots, prowling a hole into the concrete of the parking lot, a frown on the face of the wearer. 'Ohhh,' she smirked. 'Shopping with the missus, and she looks twitchy. My bad.'

Joshua grunted. 'Cut that out; she can wait. Let me walk you to your car. It's getting late and you're loitering around, enticing muggers ...'

'My car's two steps away. And the French Canadian songbird isn't finished ...'

'You hate this song. C'mon.' He steered her by the elbow, the back of his neck itching thanks to the laser of annoyance drilling into it from across the road. He'd patch that up later. 'You look good,' he said. 'Much better. Happier.'

'I'm working on something.'

He lifted his eyebrows.

'Good question. Time will tell.' She crunched the cone down to a nub, eyes planets away.

Oh, Jesus. Joshua studied what he could of her profile in the half light, the almost too-muchness in the slant of cheekbone and plumpness of mouth. Her mind was on the grind and the process was practically audible: shit unspooling, hacked and bashed to pieces and spliced back together in a digestible, Voinjama-approved format. 'What're you doing?'

'Nothing! Jeez. Why everybody always think I'm *doing* something?' He said nothing. 'Okay, not nothing. A small something. I'm still figuring out what, though.'

'Your somethings can derail into a series of weird, very bad other things.'

'That's because ... you know ... circumstances get away from me.'

'No, it's because your process is so moronic that it circles back on itself and just about manages to squeak under the door and turn out brilliant. Face it. You got a thing for starting fires when you've got no water on standby.'

'Msshw,' Vee sucked her teeth and poked a finger near his nose. 'Don't shrink me. Just because you know a few of my problems ...'

He quirked his eyebrows again. A few?

Vee pulled open the Corolla's door and eased in. 'Dickhead. I'll see you later.'

'I'll hold you to that,' he called after her.

ANATOMY OF A MURDER
Diamonds on the soles

The endless wait for the throng of sweaty health nuts to clear off before hitting the showers was worth it. Newlands Sports Club wasn't abuzz in the winter months, but now that spring was on the horizon, they couldn't get the place to themselves on a weekend.

'Hey, Tammy!' Jacqui yelled from a toilet stall. 'There's no toilet paper in here. Bring me some?'

Tamara blew an extravagant sigh. 'Remember the golden rule: scan before you squat? Drip dry, you're gonna have a shower right after, anyway.'

'Ag man, that's disgusting! Come on, pretty please, check one of the other stalls for me?'

Tamara clenched her fists. This was Jacqui all over, every time. Me, myself and I; everyone else – go die. Like during the tennis match … what had that been about? Jacqui being more Jacqui than she needed to be: super-competitive, grinding every winning set into the opposing side's face and haggling over every fault. Her cell rang in the middle of a deciding serve and when Jacqui called time to get it, which she never did, Tamara couldn't help her curiosity getting the better of her. Jacqui had turned into quite the secret agent with all the whispered phone calls. Secrecy drove Tamara bloody mad.

Jacqui had stepped off the court and, despite how accomplished an eavesdropper as she was, Tamara couldn't make out who the caller was.

Probably Jacqui's mother, who was *such* a stalker, checking up on them every flipping minute. Could've also been that airhead Bronwyn. Jacqui slipped into her 'special needs voice' several times, which she only put on when she was speaking to her Bible buddy or that dumb younger sister of hers, Rosie. It could just as well have been Ashwin, who took every shot he had at the championship medal for losers, grovelling every chance he got. Tamara couldn't believe she'd considered shagging him to piss her girl off. She had moved closer, pretending to put her visor cap back into her gym bag while she kept an ear cocked. Jacqui was agitated for sure, but all Tamara managed to pick up was, 'Look, I'll come, okay, I swear. I promised and I won't let you down.'

Jacqui's game had gone to hell after that and so had hers, Jacqui too distracted and she too absorbed in watching her lose her edge and wondering why. To top it off, she hadn't had the gall to retrieve the visor without feeling she'd need to explain why she'd put it away in the first place, and now her face was fried. Tamara rubbed the red surface of her forehead and hissed at the soreness. A sparkle of tears prickled in the back of her eyes. It looked majorly disgusting, and when it started peeling and make-up couldn't hide it, just forget it. Why the hell was she always obsessing over Jacqui? Why couldn't she learn to focus on her own bloody life?

'Tam-tam! You in the shower yet?' Silence. 'You still out there?'

Tamara sighed. 'Yeeeaaah, I'm heeere.'

'Well, jeez, what's up with the creepy silence? Hurry up loser, we're not gonna wait for you.' A moment passed, then: 'Don't get pissed but can you bring me a tampon from my bag, please, super-please? Nee, man, of all the days to start leaking.'

'Shit, Jacqui, I'm not your flippin' maid, you know! It's like you think I just jump at your say-so,' Tamara barked, instinctively reaching for Jacqui's satchel and working the zip. 'Anything else you need, madam?'

'Fine, bitch, I'll get it myself. No need for the aggro.'

The ridged soles of a pristine white pair of sneakers peeped out from under the jeans and T-shirt Jacqui had come wearing. Tamara threw a glance over her shoulder and wiggled them out. Nike, one of the latest designs. Brand new, expensive, *original* Nike. Daddy-bought, for sure.

'Hang on, I'm bringing it,' she murmured. Jacqui started to wail and Tamara made a fist, counted to five, and then called out that she was on her way. Jacqui answered with a perky '*Dankie, meisie!*' and the shower started up again, hissing over the sound of her singing.

We don't all have rich fathers. Tamara laid the shoes on top of the satchel and crossed her arms, staring at them. Jacqui's dad was a heart specialist who'd ditched her to keep up appearances with some white chick, true, but he was splashy enough to spend this kind of money on *tekkies* and that was a sweet deal. One that spoilt, stuck-up witch didn't deserve. Tamara looked around one last time, and before she could talk herself out of it, grabbed the shoes. She fumbled with the zip of her own bag for what felt like a lifetime, finally got it open and stuffed the sneakers inside as far down as they could go.

'Hurry up, I'm haemorrhaging!' Jacqui cackled gleefully.

Tamara rearranged the clothes and toiletries in Jacqui's gym bag, fluffing up the contents so the shoes wouldn't be missed immediately. Jacqui never checked her kit after a practice. Until today she'd never had reason to, so it wasn't likely she'd notice anything missing until she was home. Tamara bit her lip for a second. *She wouldn't care. She never cares.*

Tampon in her hand, she scuttled to the showers.

6

'You sure you don't want something to eat?'

Vee drained her cup of Ovaltine and ahh-ed in satisfaction. 'Nope. Can't stay. And don't give me that look.'

'Bheti whyyii?' Connie pouted. 'I'm coming to cook any minute now.'

'Yeah, you coming. Christmas coming. I only came for the ambiance, anyway.' Vee stretched her feet out. 'Y'all know how to make noise like market people round here.'

And it served her purposes. Connie's flat in Rondebosch was the antidote to the imperious silence of her own house that she wanted to avoid right now, the white noise she needed. Tonight had been no disappointment. Connie's younger sister Adesuwa's whining about her financial woes was tuned to the perfect pitch, warbling over the baseline of Ikenna jumping up and down on every surface that could support him, refusing to be put to bed. Connie worked the books with her two employees, deaf to the din, Napoleonic in her approach to success.

'Thanks again for taking Ikenna to the paed for that chest cold,' Connie said. The lounge had emptied, Suwa out getting takeaways and Ikenna asleep at last on Vee's lap. 'I waited two weeks for that appointment, and Suwa couldn't leave classes to do it. If I'd lost it, haaay!' She pushed out her mouth at the prospect. 'That WI not funny. No sympathy for the plight of those with no lives.'

'You tellin' me,' Vee said. Before Connie pounced on the loose thread and started grilling her about whether she'd made her appointment, which would no doubt be followed by a cuss-out that she hadn't, she hurried on: 'Speaking of the walking dead, guess who I bumped into this evening at Pick n Pay, looking like a shoeshine boy?'

It took a second. Connie put down her wine glass. 'Oh-o-o-o! And so we begin. Again. What did he say? Did he do that sleepy-eyed smiling thing? Did you tingle?'

'*What?* No. We didn't talk much. Don't start your fwehn-fwehn noise about—'

'Laaa-yah! Lies. You know what your problem is? You're ungrateful.' She popped a hand up over Vee's protest. 'Shut up. America don waste plenti moni on your jagajaga country and you still refuse to aid one of their citizens. That man's been massaging your ego forever, and you won't give him some ass. Give the man some ass, please. At least, let him lick something. This is bordering on animal cruelty.'

'Jesus be a fence …' Vee scooped Ikenna up and headed for the bedrooms. 'You somebody Ma, o!' she hissed.

'I know, right. Pregnancy arrived by bus.' Connie winked and made a lewd gesture. 'Old-fashioned stress relief. You can't say you don't need it. Stretch those long legs.'

'Ikenna, dis your Ma get mouf like street walker,' Vee whispered to her sleeping godson. 'Shameless.'

'Msshw. Shame is for lonely people. Like me.' Connie drained her glass and smacked it down. 'Abeg, leave my house.'

Vee complied, hitting the road for home soon afterwards. A quiet evening and a full belly were all she now craved, preferably in a dark room where she could zone out uninterrupted.

Till then …

Running into Joshua Allen on the street wasn't the surprise. Her *reaction* to seeing him was the thing. She'd almost forgotten how uplifting it was seeing another friendly face, one that knew her unfriendly past. In the four years they'd known each other, his exterior hadn't changed at all. Height and build perfect for swimming or track, but wasted on a joker who refused to take any sport seriously for long. Heavy, sloe eyes that rescued his face from being too sharp and odd. That infuriating shit-eating grin when he could be bothered. Their meet-and-greet had typified Allen's ambience: materialise looking like a soggy pile of crap, rattle her chains with some nameless beauty hating on the sidelines, then disappear.

Wow, he's thirty, Vee thought suddenly. About five weeks ago. Time was growing him up. It was depressing how their lives had been, and would continue to be, careening down paths unpaved, both of them as unprepared as children. Broken dolls. Joshua had come to Cape Town on a quest for the Holy Grail, the perfect family. She'd come to follow her heart. Fat lot of good that pursuit had done them.

He was the product of an African-American history professor who'd fallen for a Hindu anti-apartheid activist exiled in the US. When the democratic tide had turned against the apartheid regime, exiles had begun to trickle home. His old man had returned and married respectably within the Indian community, letting time wither the American connection. Joshua had been six when his father had returned for good, never looking back.

Nearly twenty years later, Joshua had boarded a plane. The reception he'd received had been far from rosy. The final slap in the face had come when an uninterested family on the African continent had refused to acknowledge his existence and a loving one in America had kindly advised that he bury the past for peace of mind. Older and wiser, he now called Cape Town home away from home. He'd never admit it, but Vee knew he drew an illicit thrill from the proximity to his old man. The hovering nightmare, the illegitimate pin itching to burst the well-constructed bubble of a traditional paterfamilias. Lazy vengeance was right up his alley.

Vee idled at a red traffic light. She hadn't seen Joshua in a while; his reappearance had dredged up a lot that she would much rather forget. If she was being completely unfair – and what was driving alone on a mild winter evening, back to an empty house, if not a green light to do whatever the hell she wanted? – then it could be said that her predicament was all Joshua Allen's fault. He was friends with Titus Wreh, and Titus Wreh had torn her heart out and pissed on it. Had Joshua not been living here, maybe neither she nor Titus would've had the bright idea to leave New York, which spelled the beginning of their end.

Fine, it was a stretch, and even she knew it. Titus had been hunting for a change of scene, preferably one on the continent and, like many in the know, to avoid the worst of the global economic crash. She'd hardly wanted to say it to his face but her ex, a Liberian–American hybrid who'd lived three quarters of his life abroad, tended to paint his expectations with an overly rosy finish. Before long, the empty romance of 'returning to the Motherland' had become reality, one she should've put brakes on. But … a woman in love was not a well-reasoning organism. She had a commendable master's degree from a fine institution in hand, the world was her oyster, fortune favours the brave and love would find a way, and all that. She'd landed a temporary position with an independent news agency to complement Titus's new job with Deloitte, and they'd packed their bags.

Now, here she was. From engaged, employed and happy to a mess, drowning in the fulminant fuckery that was her new normal.

The ghost of an ache, surely a phantom sensation, started up in her abdomen. Vee sneaked a hand under her sweater and rubbed the tiny ridge of a scar, one hand on the wheel. Wisdom and self-awareness had come at an astronomically high price. Waking up in a hospital post-op, minus an ovary and a foetus she'd had no idea she was nourishing. Signing on full time with a goddamn fashion magazine because she was out of job options. Being miserable, broke, abandoned … or, to put it another way, unceremoniously un-fiancéed, if there was such a thing. A blizzard of blows.

'What am I s'posed to say when I'm all choked up and you're okay? I'm falling to piiieeeces yeah,' crooned Danny O'Donoghue of The Script, his heart breaking unevenly all over 5FM radio.

'I hear you, o,' Vee muttered, switching it off.

Not since she was maybe ten years old had she anticipated a birthday, but turning twenty-nine in a month's time held the promise of a new beginning. Twenty-nine felt like the last phase of a painfully drawn-out ripening. It would be wiser. Lonelier, more bitter, more sexually frustrated. Definitely poorer. But fuck it, she was ready.

She taxied into the garage and slammed the door as she got out, a noise bound to bring her dog running. Having her own place was the best and she didn't miss having a roommate. The last one, Mia, had been lovely, wild of hair and brimming with spiritual guru-ism, but time had exposed that she was about ninety degrees short of a right angle. Never had Vee met a person less suited to the sane, regular rules of cohabitation. Her snobby cats Ginger and Wasabi, strict sushi diet and unrelenting peppiness had pushed Vee over the edge. Luckily, Mia was a peaceful soul who shunned confrontation. She'd moved to Observatory, where her kookiness was appreciated.

Vee plucked a wad from the post box, not bothering to look them over. Bills and takeaway menus, it only ever was. Through force of habit, she scanned the dark street as she closed the gate after her. A fat-cat vehicle, luxurious in shine, hulked a tad too close to her driveway. Must be her neighbour's, the one constantly into new toys; she'd have a word with him about boundaries tomorrow.

Vee dumped her handbag and laptop on the kitchen counter and, without switching on any of the lights, opened the fridge. Milk. Mineral water. Leftover fragments of fish gravy, jollof rice and boiled sweet potatoes. Bread and Windhoek lager. Fresh salad ingredients. Vee scratched her nose and popped the freezer compartment. Free-range chicken and prime beef cuts. She closed the fridge. Bottle of wine on the kitchen counter. She paused, and then sniffed. Asian food. No dog.

'You want another beer?' she called out.

'Nah, I'm good, just opened this one,' a male voice called back.

She grabbed the wine and headed for the lounge, still not flipping any switches. Criminals were best confronted in the dark.

'Didn't I warn you to stop breaking into my house? Don't you see how creepy this has got?'

Joshua waved. 'I took your concerns under advisement. See, I opened the curtains. So it wouldn't be, like, evil villain skulking in the dark when you walked in.' Light from the streetlamps filtered through the windows. The onyx-black, ice-blue-eyed husky near Joshua's feet didn't budge, simply swished his tail in welcome. Treachery and deceit in her own home. Males always stuck together.

'Come on, you're glad I dropped by. Besides, breaking and entering's a skill I learnt from the best.' Joshua tipped his beer at her in salute. 'Like all skills, if you don't use it, you lose it. Hungry? Dig in, please.'

Vee made a grateful sound through a mouthful of Thai noodles. It was very good. Too good to be a cheap takeaway. Wiser not to ask.

'I don't taste any meat in this.' She stirred the veggie-laden mix with the chopsticks. 'There's no meat? It's meat-free?'

'That's mine. Yours is in the microwave.'

Vee got up, zapped the carton of pad thai and sat back down. Blowing on it to cool it, she said, 'Throwing money around doesn't impress me, negro. For your information, I don't keep bread in the fridge. Or buy pinot noir. And free-range chicken? What's wrong with normal chicken?'

'That's an excellent pinot from a grateful client, you refugee. Don't refrigerate it. And learn to buy better food for the sake of your health.' He looked severe as she rolled her eyes. 'Remember, you've only got one ovary, cripple.'

'Whatever,' Vee said. She scarfed noodles down until the snarl of hunger was gone, before slowing to leisurely bites. She looked him over: he hadn't even gone home first to change out of his bum wear before he'd sneaked in. This was their thing and he'd missed it; she'd missed it, hugely. She stretched her legs until they reached his and tapped her boots against his loafers. A smile darted over his eyes, barely lifting the corners of his mouth. He tapped back. Vee cleared her throat. 'How's the girlfriend?'

'Here we go.'

'What? You can take a cheap shot at my ovaries, but I can't ask questions?'

He folded his arms. 'I don't have a girlfriend. I'm saving the spot. You know that. So stop asking.'

She rolled her eyes, appalled at the heat tickling her cheeks.

Unsafe ground. Their … whatever this was … was built on it. Grudging respect, liberal scoops of abuse, a tacit flicker of something that tiptoed ever closer over the years. Titus had been their referee. Now that he was gone and they were left to their own devices, they found their friendship its own trajectory. Joshua had introduced her to the dark web, a place she never wanted to revisit, and to the underworld of finance, showed her how extortion and tax evasion worked. She had schooled him in shoplifting and housebreaking. He'd explained the nuances of male anatomy, including the precise international units of small, medium and large penis sizes, and given an impressive live demonstration. She'd ignored his women, until he'd passed her the responsibility of dumping the insipid ones by email when he couldn't be bothered. At her lowest, he'd given her a place to stay, a bank card with no limit and a shoulder. She hadn't deserved it, was too up her own ass at the time to appreciate it. Yet, and still. Here they were.

He smiled, a real one. 'We done?' Banter-wise, he meant.

Vee flexed her neck and put her head back, stress seeping out of her like tiny, invisible insects squirming out of her skin and jumping off her shoulders. She felt better. In less than half an hour, she felt markedly better.

'Are we ever?' she answered.

7

'So, what's this something you're working on?'

'Come on. I can't talk about my cases. It's unprofessional.'

He hooted. 'You work at what's barely a newspaper, not at the Pentagon. Spit it out.'

She threw a used serviette at his head. Then she told him, omitting the part about apparitions and anxiety attacks. That was all hers for now.

'This kid's been missing for *two years* and you wanna revive the case. And solve it. What've you been smoking?'

'No, the story's too twisted to walk away from. As dysfunctional goes, this family's textbook material. The strangest part? Paulsen hates their guts but won't go as far as outright accusing them – not of murder, at least. She's pretty torn up, seeing as the better part of this is her fault. As she sees it, between a lot of careless whispers and screwing around she and Ian managed to *chakla* two families till everlasting. She wants the case closed but not to cause any more pain, which is the dumbest, most passive-aggressive shit I ever heard. Her kid goes AWOL and is most likely dead, and she acts like her biggest decision is whether to flip out on them like an avenging angel or just stay self-righteously pissed in her corner.'

'Maybe there's your mystery solved. She did it and can't come right with herself. Ever watched *Snapped: Women Who Kill*? Half of those crazies are kid killers.'

'Nah.' Joshua cocked his head and Vee did an adamant flip-flop of her hand. 'I'm telling you, no. I don't *know* that she didn't kill her own daughter but ... yeah. I know. If she's after anything, I'd say it's money. You know that fancy health-care facility that's still under renovation, the Wellness Institute?'

Joshua flashed all his teeth. Employees at JPMorgan Chase were bred to run like thoroughbreds, his grin said. Illness was a luxury he couldn't afford, not on his bonuses.

'Well,' she said, 'some of us are still human enough to get sick once in a while. We can't all crash-land from Krypton in perfect health and Gucci shirts.'

'This old thing? Mr Price all the way.'

She shook her head. 'That glass and chrome building in Claremont. They're adding a physio unit, mega swimming pool, gym and spa. The works. It's got everybody lining up.'

'Since when are you everybody? You'd never see a doctor even if you had an extra pair of eyes. Everything okay?' He levelled a squint and Vee mumbled something, avoiding his eyes. He shrugged, let it drop. 'Why in tarnation does a hospital need a pool and spa?'

'It's an 'institute'. Apparently, nobody wants to be openly confronted with the fact they're diseased and mortal, precisely what hospitals are good at. They say they're promoting a spiritual and holistic combination. New Age evasiveness is all the rage now.'

'My point is the Fouries are far from starving. They're both senior staff at WI. They've offered Paulsen money for her 'cooperation' before, when it involved saving their son's life, but ever since her daughter went missing she's felt a distinct lack of support on their part. She may've changed her mind about recompense.'

She found and spread out the contents of Jacqui's case envelope: copies of the official police report, statements from everyone questioned, newspaper clippings, hotline numbers for missing children sightings. She pushed the second photograph in the pile towards Joshua.

'That's the basket she's put all her eggs in,' she said, tapping the image of a man in the snapshot. 'Ashwin Venter, the boyfriend. Twenty-five, auto mechanic, bit of a bad boy with a record. Obviously, Mommy didn't approve. She demanded that Jacqui end the relationship; they quarrelled and Jacqui took to sneaking around behind her back. When Adele found out that her precious was still running around with him, grinding gonads no less, well, you can imagine how that went down. Typical mother–daughter stuff.

'But Adele swears that Venter has the perfect motive for murder. She suspects Jacqui was pregnant from the way she was acting before she disappeared, and that Ashwin found out and flipped. She heard them fight a couple of times just before Jacqui disappeared, but couldn't really pick out what it was about. Jacqui even came home with bruises one time, wouldn't talk about how she got them. She just told her mom that she hoped she was happy now, because she'd broken up with him. He obviously didn't take it well. Came by their house a few times making threats and causing a ruckus. They had to call the neighbours to get him off their property.'

Joshua eyed the photograph, his expression sceptical. Venter had a protective arm draped around his girl, the look on his face one of overplayed bravado. He was pale and freckled, well-muscled but kind of short. Hardly the toughest stud on the block. 'I guess bad boys come in all flavours,' he muttered. 'What, he offed her when he found out she was having his baby? Doesn't sound like your average male reaction.'

'My thoughts exactly. But according to Adele, this guy's typical coloured trash – her words, not mine. In his teens he was part of a gang. When his father died he inherited the business, which he couldn't manage, and it started losing money. To top it off, he's got two kids with other women. He'd been hauled into court for child maintenance and was seriously struggling to make ends meet. Basically, he wouldn't have been over the moon about baby number three. He probably saw Jacqui as a soft option. Naïve schoolgirl star-struck by a big-time player. The way Adele tells it, he begged Jacqui to get rid of the baby, she refused and it went downhill fast.'

'Dang, she really has it in for this guy. She knows all this how?'

'Oh, she's gunning for him all right, but her gun's not loaded. Sure, he confessed under interrogation that they'd argued and even fought physically before, and had a huge bust-up on the day she disappeared. But other than that, there's no proof.

The cops pegged him as their main suspect, especially when it turned out he was the last person to see her alive and he couldn't produce an alibi other than his sister. They brought him in for questioning a number of times, even held him in custody for two days without a formal charge, but with no evidence they eventually had to let him go. No body, no crime.'

Joshua frowned. 'So, what, the cops hound one guy without much to go on, then suddenly the case goes cold? They didn't have a body, but surely they had *some* evidence to build a case. When people go missing, they tend to leave a trace. Girl leaves home …'

'Girl leaves home on September twenty-second, 2007. It's a Saturday morning, just after ten.' Vee took the reins, steering from memory. One thing her brain was good at: spooling facts, running playback. The flipside: glitching out in the face of overwhelming levels of choice or visual input, typically in malls and supermarket aisles.

'She cleans her room and takes off for tennis practice at Newlands Sports Club with her friends, or so she tells her mom. That part of the story holds up. After that, holes. Just before midday, Adele called to find out where she was, got told they were on their way to lunch in Rondebosch. Like most teenagers, Jacqui was a great white liar, so her mother was in the habit of checking on her a lot, particularly on weekends. Didn't do much good, because Jacqui still managed to give her the slip. She ditched her girlfriends and went to Ashwin's garage in Athlone. According to him, it was simply to talk about their relationship, but it escalated into a screaming match. He wanted her back and she wasn't havin' it. Later, he swore up and down that the subject of pregnancy never came up. The prospect of having another child, this time with his beloved, wouldn't have scared him but would have made him the happiest man alive.

'*That's* when the trail goes cold,' Vee flung her hands up. 'By about four in the afternoon, Ashwin gave up the bended-knee act and Jacqui left. He swore he never laid a hand on her that day. Nobody admitted to seeing her again. Everybody who tried calling her once they started to get really worried said her cell was switched off. Wherever she ended up, I'm guessing that phone ended up there with her.'

'Not necessarily,' Joshua countered. 'She could've lost it or it could've been stolen.'

'True, possible. Too many possibles at this stage.'

'Whatever you do, you've got to roll out with it like a boss. 'Cause I bet your boss's given you this much,' he held two fingers an inch apart, 'wiggle room.'

'Oh, my inner bitch is so poised.' Vee sat up. She let silence bounce around the room for a minute. Then, 'Sorry I forgot your birthday.' She reached across the table and covered his hand with hers. 'I meant to send you a male stripper for the big three-oh.'

'Shucks, guess I missed out.' He stroked her fingers. 'Don't worry about it. I wasn't here, anyway. New York.'

'I'll make it up to you.' She side-eyed him, testing the air with her feelers, wondering if it was safe just to spit out what she'd wanted to get off her chest from the second she'd run into him. Screw it – she was going to ask. He looked so relaxed, though.

Why ruin the mood? No, she would see him on the weekend and bring it up then.

'So, how's your friend doing? Where he at?' she blurted.

Joshua drew his hand away. He didn't meet her eyes, but his shoulders and the corners of his mouth spasmed. 'Haven't heard from him,' he replied when he did look up, holding her gaze steadily. 'You know I wouldn't hide it from you if I had.'

'Well, does he know how *I've* been doing? Does he give a righteous shit?'

Joshua dragged his hands up and down his face and over his head, messing his bramble of hair even more. 'Uggghh. Vee …'

'Y'know what's funny?' She chuckled. 'I'll tell you what's the final word in hilarity. Filling out a new form at the WI the other day and getting to the section on contact details for next of kin. Ti was mine. He's been my go-to all the time I've been here. So, I'm sitting there with my pen hovering over this piece of paper–'

'Stop. Don't do this.'

'–poised to write who the hell knows what, at a complete loss. He took pride in that position, especially since we weren't linked by marriage yet but since I knew we would be, I relinquished control. He sure didn't have a problem with telling some doctor to slice me open and chop off a vital organ; he signed that consent form pretty willy-nilly. Then, because he had to play nursemaid for a few months afterwards when I lost it, suddenly behaving like my kin was too much to handle. He fucks off to …' she flapped her hands, 'wherever, and I'm left here dealing with …'

'V.J.' Joshua stayed quiet for a full minute. 'This was too much on both of you. You were unconscious from an ectopic pregnancy gone rogue. He had to make a call. No guy wants to be the one to call his fiancée's parents, like, 'Hey, your daughter's dead by the way, 'cause I kept my thumb up my ass too long deciding what to do.' And he took care of you afterwards, while you blamed yourself and him and the entire world. You were a mess.' He made a move towards her and she got up and walked to the sliding glass doors feeding out onto the patio and backyard. 'And I say 'were', because though you're still pretty shitty now, you're in much better shape.' Pause. 'He loves you. He didn't abandon you.'

Vee snorted. '*Six months* and no word. How the hell d'you know?'

'I know what it is to love you.'

Vee stared at her lawn. It was easy to forget, in the throes of her egocentric rages, that she wasn't the only one dealing with the fallout. Joshua had stuck it out, for his own quasi-selfish reasons, true, but he had, never once railing against his friend. Whatever Code Amongst Men Titus had broken, Joshua hadn't broken rank and had kept it together for her sake. She wanted her pound of flesh; as much as she loathed to admit it, her ex still had a hold on her. An ever-slackening hold – barring a sprinkle of bad days, Titus now crossed her mind with lazy frequency – but a complete exorcism was in order.

She blinked back the film of sting in her eyes. Other than Connie, Joshua was the size of it in her realm of ride-or-die allies in Cape Town. Titus got the friends after Armageddon.

It'd probably be to her benefit to come clean about the anxiety attacks. Joshua had borne far more than his share of the weight for their friendship, but he deserved honesty. He was a staunch advocate of facing oneself in all things, and the frightening magnitude of her symptoms indicated there could be something concrete to his theory.

Joshua said: 'Back to your thing. It's strange, but it made me …' He stopped. 'What? You were about to say something.'

'Hehn? No. Just a random thought.' She waved it away. 'What's strange?'

He squinted at her for a long time. 'The story sounds familiar. I dunno, something you said in the beginning …'

'Well, you were here two years ago. Jacqueline Paulsen's disappearance didn't make headlines, but it got local media coverage. I'm sure you read or heard about it.'

'No, that's not it. More recent … Anyway, it's gone now. But it'll come back to me.' He rose.

She walked him to the front door, a pang knocking round her chest. She didn't want to be alone just yet. Monro tottered after them, nudging the back of Joshua's legs, and settled on his haunches at the door. 'When're you planning to take your dog back?'

'Next week,' Joshua lied promptly. 'Saturday. Next week Saturday, bright and early.'

Vee sniggered and gave a thumbs-up. 'Next week' was a year-old excuse. An attack in childhood left her terrified of dogs until Joshua had dumped the husky on her for a couple of weeks, which had turned into, well. And he went on enjoying his spacious Sea Point apartment while Monro tore around her tiny yard.

'Your eyes look like a horror movie. Get some rest. Don't stay up all night chasing clues down that black hole between your ears,' he said. 'And eat something. Fatten up a little. Your ass used to be thorough.'

He dawdled; he always did. Vee dawdled with him. It felt good, smelled good, having a man this close. He gave his customary goodbye, a graze at the edge of her mouth, a little too protracted as always but quite safe. She didn't expect it when he pulled back, turned her inside out with a look, and kissed her full on without pause or caution. Soft, incredibly warm, right amount of pressure. Vee leaned into it for longer than she should have. She caught herself and pulled away.

Joshua cleared his throat. 'Right.' He stepped out of the doorway and crossed the path, walking backwards to his car. 'Are we done, Voinjama Johnson?' he called.

'Are we ever, Joshua Allen?'

Vee latched the door, biting into a smile. Monro looked up at her and issued two sharp barks.

'Don't you dare judge me,' she said.

8

On Monday evening, Chlöe Bishop perched on the edge of an expensive oak desk and tried not to look uncomfortable as it dug into her backside. The inner flesh of a woman's upper thigh was incredibly sensitive to touch, and no one knew this better than she. She shifted hers away from the man's clammy fingers with a nervous titter, but it only succeeded in shifting his focus to another spot under her skirt.

She didn't need to check the time to confirm what she already knew, that she was horribly late for a date. It didn't matter how late she was, or whether she showed up at all. She and her ex would only go around in circles. It was time she accepted that she'd been dumped, and begging was only crushing the market value of her self-esteem.

What choice did she have, though? Her living situation had gone from loving and financially supportive to broke and hugely uncomfortable, since two people who'd been romantically entwined couldn't carry on living under the same roof without friction. Not when one of them (*Not me*, she thought bitterly) kept bringing random losers home for casual sex and calling it 'processing heartbreak'. This was how she found herself putting in a little extra something into her job search, seeing as how a killer CV wasn't getting her anywhere.

'So ...' She slid off her tank top to reveal a lacy bra, thrusting her breasts into his chest. This creep was old enough to be her father. Nope, no father thoughts right now. Her parents were disappointed enough in her. She pressed herself into his chest and turned a flinch into a light kiss on his neck. Did women really do this; did it truly work for men? It seemed so. Mr Cohen was practically panting.

'Am I in, or not?'

'Oh, you're in, Miss Bishop,' he breathed into her ear, flicking his tongue around the cavity. Chlöe summoned the willpower not to retch. 'You're definitely in. I've already made the call and sent the email. You can start at the beginning of next month.'

Chlöe did her charming laugh, casting her tinkle around the massive office and hoping the edge of desperation she picked up on was perceptible to her ears only. Never mind that it was well past 7 p.m. and no one else was in the building to hear or witness her performance. She slid off the desk.

'End of the month isn't good enough,' she said, keeping her back to Cohen as her top went back on. 'I need to start as soon as possible. You said there was a good chance of an opening, the only thing was to apply pressure in the right places. Thought you could make that happen.'

He chuckled into her hair, his lips and breath tickling her scalp. 'What do you want, my blood? I said–'

Chlöe turned and cupped the swollen front of his pants, the sugar in her smile letting him know his prize handful was all she was after. 'I'll take something in writing, too,' she whispered, lips brushing his.

'Oh, you'll certainly get it in writing,' Cohen said in her ear. 'But first …'

Five minutes later, Chlöe lay on the floor, divested of everything except the skirt. She averted her eyes in horror from his erect penis, glad its latex sheath gave her one fewer thing to worry about. No one warned girls like her strenuously enough about heterosexual encounters, and for that she was grateful. Prior knowledge would have made soldiering through impossible. Her sentiments on phalluses – revulsion – had been cemented early on in life and weren't likely, ever, to change. Cohen held her panties to his nose and inhaled with reverence before entering her. Chlöe shuddered and tried not to clench up, turning gags into soft moans. She would keep her eyes closed the whole way through; there was nothing else for it.

Now I get why it's called a carpet interview, she thought, stealing a peek at the pricey carpet under her head. At least she wasn't on her knees. The weather was hobbling towards spring and she had to protect her knees if she wanted to show them off. She adored pencil skirts.

9

On Wednesday morning, Vee peeked through the blinds of Portia's office at the girl sitting across the hall. Shiny, fox-red hair, clumsily flat-ironed – it was naturally curly, the ends gave it away – but professionally layered down to the shoulders. Clear, pale skin; pretty expert make-up for someone that young. Peach cashmere sweater and tartan pencil skirt followed enviable curves for a white girl; a lot of bustiness on top, zero butt below. Vee released the slats and the blinds snapped back into place.

'Tell me she's for the style team,' Vee said.

'She's for you. Chlöe Bishop, your new assistant. Well, our new intern.'

'Our new intern or my new assistant? She can't be both. And when did we start getting new interns? I thought you terminated the whole programme after last year's fiasco. They cost us too much money and weren't worth the trouble. They barely pulled their weight. The whole thing did nothing but give you grief and be a pain in our collective ass.'

'No, I didn't terminate the programme. I put it on the back-burner.' Portia sat. 'Look.' She put her heels on her desk. She was the sort who looked like she would never put her feet on tables anywhere and then looked amazing when she did it. 'This girl is a fresh graduate ... well, fresh enough. She came for an interview a couple of months ago and I told her I'd think about it. Frankly, I forgot her the second she left. We're not hiring right now, economic downturn, blah blah blah. Then a higher-up called in a favour and that favour trickled down to me ...' She shrugged. 'She's desperate. And I am quite drawn to desperation.' The tint of nostalgia in Portia's smile brought up the memory of their first interview together like a smack to Vee's face. 'I've reconsidered. Give her a chance. One month probation. Enough time for your ... thing to pan out.

'Why her? She can't need this job. She looks like the whitest girl in the universe.'

'Racism,' Portia chastised wearily. 'Remember sensitivity training and how much you enjoyed it last time? And don't forget, I'm half white. The person with the power to fire you.'

Vee gritted her teeth, took a calming breath and squinted through the shutters again. 'This case is frozen solid, Portia. It's going to defrost really slowly, and it won't need much heavy lifting. I can't be dealing with a newbie's disappointment that this isn't racing along like some TV mystery.'

'Not true. You need an extra pair of limbs running around and handling the grunt work on your opus. Let's not forget the strings I've pulled here.'

'Right. The strings,' Vee deflated. Portia's myriad pulleys. This time she'd pulled some golden ones indeed, likely through her father the media mogul, and now a substantial chunk of the official Paulsen case docket was at Vee's disposal. There had to be payback.

Portia waved stapled pages headed 'Curriculum Vitae: Chlöe J. Bishop' at Vee. 'What doesn't kill you ... If you think about it, getting an assistant is like a promotion.'

'How about a promotion with a pay raise?' Vee grouched en route to her office. She rolled the CV into a scroll, debating whether to toss it into the nearest bin. She wasn't wasting her time on a catalogue of white lies. CVs never told you what you needed to know – like how much abuse someone could take before they snapped and quit. If the grunt had balls, she'd be able to tell how large soon enough.

Vee neared the tearoom, and the redhead sitting in the row of visitors' chairs outside it rose to her feet. She didn't spring up with annoying eagerness, nor did she unfold her legs with the languid grace of the entitled and take her time. She just got up, and smiled. A fine spray of freckles dusted her nose, and a tooth on one side of her mouth was slightly crooked. Not so perfect after all.

She shook hands well. Vee didn't hold any store in the idea that firm handshakes conveyed strength of character in either gender, but she was, at least, pleased that Chlöe Bishop's fingers weren't sweaty or cold. Her nails were neat ovals and painted a cloudy, neutral colour. A few locks fell carelessly across her forehead. They looked deliberate.

Vee narrowed her eyes. Chlöe Bishop looked laid back, but was she really? Vee hated babysitting empty, well-dressed surprises, which new hires too often turned out to be. She waved Chlöe into her office.

'How old are you?'

'Twenty-three.'

Vee winced. *Jeez, she had her first period yesterday?* 'Politics and languages, ehn. I see you didn't study journalism or any form of media, or even creative writing.' She pushed the CV aside. 'Seems odd you'd be so hot to take this job. Enlighten me as to why.'

'Well, I've always been fascinated by the magazine industry. Must be every girl's dream to be this close to the action. I love a challenge ...'

Vee dropped her forehead onto the desk and pretended to snore.

Chlöe stifled a giggle with the back of her hand, then snapped under control. Vee felt a soul-baring ramble coming on. She wasn't disappointed.

'Umm,' said Chlöe, 'I don't know what I could possibly say here that won't sound dodgy. I can imagine if I were you, sitting on the other side of that desk, looking at my experience and all that and wondering why I'm fooling myself. To be perfectly honest, I'm ... kind of desperate.' She winced at her own words. 'And very aware of how that makes me look but I swear I'm not a chancer. I truly am passionate about working in media. Okay, okay, sorry ...' She pumped her hands at the curdling of Vee's expression. 'Never say passionate, it's old and overplayed and we all hate it. No more passion. But I do love media and social networking. It's ... not easy to get into if you don't exactly have the qualifications.' She blanched, bit her lips and looked down as if she'd reminded herself of something. 'So I appreciate both you and Ms Kruger for letting me through the door.'

Vee was certain she caught the quivering of Bishop's bottom lip, but dismissed it as a trick of the light. 'How early can you be here to kick-start the day? Start working on layouts, do some copy-editing, minor stuff.'

Chlöe perked up. 'I'm an early riser. Let me know what time you usually get here and I'll beat it by an hour. I also make excellent coffee.'

'Good for you. Time management and multitasking. Learn to be a wizard at both because you're going to be everybody's Girl Friday for a while.'

'Middle child,' Chlöe smiled, pointing a slender alabaster finger at her chest. 'I'm used to abuse, believe me. I'd feel lost without it, actually. Point me to the work pile and I'll put myself to shame.'

'Can you type fast? And research – are you any good at fact-checking and digging up background? I hope you have your own car, because there's a lot of running around involved.'

'Great at the first two. And yes, I have my own transport.' She crossed stockinged legs. 'Why, will you be needing a driver as well?'

Vee fought a smile. Cool and milky as marble, just fractured enough to show she was genuine but not a flake. And a smartass. Nice hybrid. Hazing over.

She spent the next few minutes going over the general workflow and duties in Bishop's future. Halfway through outlining the Paulsen file, Charisma strolled in, lancing Chlöe a snooty, quizzical eye.

Vee blew out a breath. 'Chlöe, this is Charisma Mapondera. She's–'

'We share the office. Call me Chari,' Charisma instructed. 'I pronounce it 'Carrie'. Like in Sex and the City. But Africanised.'

'–the other token foreigner on the team,' Vee continued, ignoring Chlöe's what-the-hell look. 'Ex-editor at a political newspaper in Zimbabwe that was a huge pain in the government's backside. When they tried to blow up their building, she ran like a coward and here she is, lighting up our lives. Chari, Chlöe Bishop. She doesn't answer to you in any way, only to me. Take it up with Portia.'

Charisma snarled a few choice words and left to do just that. Vee kept her eyes on Chlöe, frowning slightly as she noticed how her eyes danced over Chari's outfit and how she wore her curves. This one was an unrepentant fashionista. Or was there more to it ... 'Are you done?'

'Sorry.' Chlöe blushed and fidgeted. 'Those are some really great pants she's wearing. And your jacket too, wow.'

'Uh-huh. Word of advice: avoid Chari. She's a terrible person. Meaning she's fun, but also the absolute worst. Especially for careers. I can be an asshole too, but I'll watch your back. As to my general style, I make a lot of this up as I go because we don't have a budget for standard procedures. Broad strokes: be really observant and extremely tenacious. Take no for an answer but find a way to turn it into a yes. Be ever ready to piss people off. A lot.'

'I've managed that extremely well in the past.'

'I'm also obliged to warn you that things can get ...' Vee balked at saying 'dangerous', '... weird. Don't bother asking

Portia permission for anything; she'll only shut you down. Me first, always. I'll handle Kruger.' Vee pushed over a stack of papers. 'Your copies of all things Paulsen, what I know so far. I drew up a to-do list. We need to cover most of that ground by the start of next week. Feel free to add to it as time goes on.'

Chlöe scrutinised the inventory, barely arching her eyebrows. 'Hhhmm. This much,' she murmured, running an index finger halfway down the page, 'I can cover today, tomorrow afternoon at the most. How …' she drummed two fingers over her lips, eyes narrowed. 'How strictly do I have to colour inside the lines, legal-wise? Say I want stuff done fast but the usual route doesn't cut it. Not all channels are created equal.'

Vee fought the urge to hug her. 'The more upfront you are with me, the better I'm able to lie to our fearless leader.' She stood. 'Any questions? And no, you don't get a gas – smh, petrol – allowance for your car. Early days yet. We'll talk to Portia about it.'

'No, no questions.'

'Perfect. Chlöe Bishop, welcome aboard the Titanic. May you perish in interesting times. I'm headed out now and you won't see me until much later.' Vee shouldered into an extra cardigan before throwing her jacket over. 'Got people to pester, starting with a bereaved mother.' She waited, expecting Bishop to whinny like a foal, adrift without a nanny this early on. Last chance to find a flaw in the gemstone.

Instead, Chlöe said: 'I thought you said this girl was a missing person. Are we already assuming she's dead? Is this a murder case?'

'We assume a lot to start.' Vee stepped through the door. 'We add, subtract, divide as we go along, till we get it in focus. Frequent updates.' She raised thumb and pinkie to her ear: call me.

At last, Vee allowed herself a grin. Chlöe. Let's see how she gets on. On her way past Portia's open door, Vee threw on a scowl for show. Kruger could smell happiness like a bloodhound and annihilate it like a Rottweiler.

10

Days that started out well often didn't stay that way for long. Upstairs in Jacqui Paulsen's bedroom, Vee sifted through her most precious possessions, things the girl would never touch or value again. Jacqui had been a nice, normal kid, and her stuff confirmed that. Vee chided herself for thinking in past tense and gloomy absolutes like 'she was a good girl who was never coming home again', but she had to concur with Adele and her instinct on that point. Jacqueline Paulsen was gone for good.

And she'd left a lot of junk behind. There were masses of clothes in the cupboard, some folded, others still wrapped in transparent plastic, collecting dust in closet hidey-holes. There was an alarming predilection for the tools of beauty, especially high-sheen lip gloss, of which there were several tubes, some unused with the sticky white barcode still attached. Most were in red and hot pink shades, complementing the room's colour scheme. A Nike shoebox of odds and ends was tucked at the back of the topmost tier of the built-in cupboards. Vee hoped it would yield something more interesting, but after opening it she wasn't sure.

Feeling bad, Vee twiddled a condom packet, flicking it back and forth between the fingers of one hand like a casino chip. She didn't have any qualms about rooting through a stranger's belongings, and a teenager who brazenly kept condoms in a shoebox wouldn't exactly be falling apart over the threat of discovery.

Vee was far more worried about the shrunken woman downstairs, drowning her sorrows in a relay of tea and menthol cigarettes. Rekindled interest in the case had let mayhem loose, and the little house in Little Mowbray was overrun with invisible demons. Though Adele insisted to the contrary, she'd most likely taken some comfort in the lull that followed the hysteria of Jacqui's disappearance and allowed herself a life – one tempered by loss, but normal. Now the bandage had been ripped off before the healing process was complete, and the wound was seeping.

Grief deflated its victims. Adele, wrapped in a dressing gown and shrivelled to half the woman she'd been two days before, had greeted Vee at the door and granted her free reign in her daughter's room. 'The police went through everything countless times. Nothing up there surprises me any more,' she said, triumphant, daring the new challenger to bring on a fresh gush of anguish. Vee would've preferred to do her ferreting in the evening but arguing proved useless. Adele had already taken leave for the day and that was that.

Vee turned the condom over in her palm. It was the cheap variety, encased in foil so thick and crunchy you half-expected to find a baked potato rather than a contraceptive inside. 'Make-Me-A-Daddy condoms', standard fare at free clinics and university campuses. Reliable, some of the time. Maybe Jacqui had been knocked up after all.

Vee tossed it back into the box. In her book, seventeen was a little young to jump from heavy petting to going pro. She'd waited a couple more years herself, and ended up taking the plunge with a dullard who hadn't deserved it. Jacqui had clearly opened her eyeballs to life sooner. But condoms in the house, though – you wouldn't pull that if you weren't courting trouble. The back of a closet wouldn't throw off any mother worth her salt. This shoebox was giant middle finger in the rule of law's face: 'Up yours, I'm doing me and you can't stop it.'

'Did you find anything?' Adele asked from the doorway. Vee jumped. Adele looked like Sisyphus, lugging the unbearable sum of her sins up the hill of daily life, only to have to haul it up again the next. For all her burdens, the woman moved like a ghost.

'I knew about those,' Adele dismissed the contents of the box with a wave of a hand, 'like I knew about Ashwin and boys before him. Don't take it the wrong way, she wasn't all over the place with anyone who winked at her. She wasn't that kind of girl. But kids these days, they get there so much faster than we used to when I was young. It's a scary reality. You can't stop it.'

'So she flouted your authority a lot, then?'

Adele gave a dry chuckle. 'Yeah. Sometimes it felt like all she did.'

She stayed in the doorway, clutching the front of her robe and looking lost. Her eyes scanned the room for a place to sit, somewhere she would cause the least disturbance, preserving the shrine as it had always been. Vee drew out the chair behind the desk but Adele chose the bed instead, perching so close to the edge it looked like she might fall off. Her skill and ease holding the pose told of many visits to the room, probably staring into space for hours or crying her heart out. Vee settled down beside her.

'How did she meet Ashwin?' Vee said gently. 'Y'all had been living here for years and she had a healthy social life. Athlone's a long way for a popular girl to go for romance.'

'I told you, she was nothing if not dogged in her loyalty. There was no reason to hide away after Sean passed on. The dirty secret was out. I needed a change from the old neighbourhood; schools were better here and Ian made a contribution for her sake. But Athlone always had a hold on her. That's where she spent her childhood and some of her best friends still lived there. They met because she hung out there from time to time.'

'Did you put her on the pill when you found out about their relationship?'

Adele sniffed and shook her head. 'No. That would've made it painfully real, that she wasn't a child any more.' Her breath wafted stale from sleep and heavy with the sweet smell of alcohol – brandy or rum, Vee couldn't tell. So, not just tea in the tea, then.

'I told her to be careful and I'm sure she was,' Adele continued. 'She swore she was, but I didn't know exactly how she was going about it. We did talk about sex and things like that, but ...'

She shook her head more vigorously as she looked down at her hands. 'God, I have so much to answer for.'

'What about her father? Were they close enough for her to confide in him? Maybe she felt more comfortable talking to a doctor who also happened to be her dad.'

Adele flinched like she'd been slapped. 'Jacqui had her secrets but she was close to *me*. She wouldn't hide major things from me, because I respected that she was too old for me just to punish her. Ian just *spoiled her*,' she hissed, tears welling up. 'The older she got, the less time he could spare. At least he was consistent and ignored all his kids. Whenever he did manage to drag himself over here, he compensated by buying things she didn't need or giving her money to do just that.'

She flapped her hands around at random objects – the clothes, computer, cosmetics – to illustrate. 'Useless junk to make up for being a lousy father. Jacqui was too naïve and good-hearted to see through it, but I knew that once she got older she would. She wanted to be one of his 'real children'. Like if he filled her life with the same material things, it would be the same as living in a fancy house with them and being a fucking Fourie. She was desperate for that status to make her life meaningful. It made me sick.'

Or maybe Jacqui was just a carefree girl who took her good fortune where she found it, and didn't sweat the small stuff like most hormonal teenagers, Vee thought. Doting parents who lavished gifts and overlooked bad behaviour were thin on the ground in adolescence. Jacqui sounded like a skilful sweet-talker.

'Was she close to her half-siblings? You told me they knew about each other, but how well? Did they spend time together?'

'I suppose.' Adele sounded reluctant to answer. Her shoulders sagged. 'From the outside it seemed she got along with all three of them all right, but I sensed some underlying friction. Maybe it was just the normal tension between young adults, but I got the feeling there was more. Ian and Carina run their home like they do their careers – by the book. Those kids should be much more individual and aggressive, but somehow they haven't fully matured. You'll notice it when you meet them. They follow their parents' orders, and I'm sure their instructions went along the lines of 'don't get too chummy with your bastard sister'. Not that Jacqui didn't manage to win them over. Her personality was impossible to resist.'

'Did she ever say anything specific to you about it?'

'Kids need their secrets. And anyway, how bad could it be? They got along well enough for children who hadn't grown up together, who had only found out about each other's existence when the eldest was dying. Under the circumstances, they had taken to each other better than any of us adults would've expected. Lemons into lemonade. If something more serious had been bothering Jacqui, she would've told me.'

Kids need their secrets and parents need their lies. Or they needed to tell themselves something even when they knew or suspected differently. Adele didn't quite meet her eyes, so Vee tried another tack.

'She, Serena and Lucas were all in their late teens. Did they share interests, was she closer to either one of them? I'll be speaking to both of them, of course, but it would really help if I had a clearer picture of how your daughter spent most of her time and with whom.' Vee still needed to chase down Bronwyn Abrams and Tamara Daniels, two of Jacqui's closest friends and the most hopeful leads about how her final day had played out.

'Lucas, more in the beginning,' Adele said. 'Jacqui had problems with other girls, even from a young age. They either got along great immediately, or they couldn't stand each other at first sight. After Sean died, it was easier to turn to her other brother. I didn't see what they had in common, personally. Lucas was a bit awkward, though I haven't seen him for some years now. I did get the impression that something changed between them after a while, because she got into Serena more, and then the little one.'

'Did she give any specifics?'

Adele shook her head for the hundredth time. Vee suppressed a sigh. Too many gaps.

'Well, I know they went to church together. She and Serena, and sometimes Rosemary,' Adele elaborated. 'Jacqui took it as a pastime in the beginning, a way to spend more and more time at that house. After school, on Sundays. But she actually became born again, to my disbelief. I didn't buy it at first, knowing my daughter and her flights of fancy. It was too cute to be taken seriously. Then she started to live up to it and I had to accept it for what it was. What mother would complain? She didn't become an angel overnight, but there was a big difference.'

That explains the 'hidden' condoms, Vee thought. Vestiges of an old life, squirrelled out of sight and mind but not discarded. 'Difference how, exactly?'

'Just different, in every way. Her life ... her *soul*, it just changed. I ... I don't see how any of this is important. It didn't save her in the end.'

Adele hunched, chin drooping to her chest, as if attempting to fold into her own body and implode. Touched to an uncomfortable degree, Vee stopped and let the silence spin out. She hugged her arms close, partly to ease the chill in the air and partly to prevent herself from reaching out and touching the woman. Not every grieving person received touch in a comforting way; she'd learnt that from past experience.

Adele started to shake, a series of minute tremors undulating through her, threatening to jar her completely off the bed. 'You have to help me,' she choked. She repeated the words as if in prayer, voice barely audible. Vee heard her tears before they came.

'I'll do everything I can,' Vee heard her mouth promise. 'But you ... we need to be patient. It takes time–'

From the towelling of her gown, Adele produced a thick brown envelope. Her hands shook as she held it out, her face contorted like the thing would spring to life and bite her. 'I can pay you,' she said, nodding hard, reassuring them both. 'If money's the problem, if it makes the process faster ...'

'Ms Paulsen,' Vee murmured, backing away from the bed. She couldn't remember getting to her feet.

'It's twenty-five thousand. Take it,' Adele said, thrusting out the packet. Vee gently pushed her hands away. 'Please, *please* take it.' Adele tried to stand, and, like a very old lady, shuddered back onto the mattress. Her shoulders quaked as she held her head in her hands and sobbed. Against her better judgement, Vee opened her arms and drew in the grieving mother.

Back on the street, Vee fumbled with her car door and a vibrating handbag. The air outside was cooler and much fresher. Away from Adele, everything felt less dour and stale. She dug out the Nokia. Blocked caller ID. She answered anyway.

'I know how to help you *and* get you to go out with me.'

Vee sucked her laughter back in shock as she watched her breath puff white. A few days and September was over – how the hell was it still so cold? She yanked the door open and scrunched into the driver's seat. 'Dah whah dey white pipo payin' yor good money for, Joshua Allen, to harass other pipo during working hours?'

'Hear me out. Before you say no.'

'No.' She snickered and pressed the 'end call' button. She had hardly got the car's engine pumping when her phone started tinkling again.

'Are you sitting down?' Chlöe breathed in her ear.

Vee switched the engine off. The blast of the heater was so loud she couldn't hear a damn thing. 'In a sense.'

'Then check this out. First of all, I'm still tracing Jacqui's steps. As in, making every stop exactly as she did that day, hazarding a guess about how much time she'd have spent at each place. I'm about to leave Newlands Sports Club, headed for Athlone, but I'm nearly done, which doesn't work with our timeline. Either I'm moving way faster, which I'm not, or she must've gone somewhere or met someone, another stop that wasn't recorded in the police report or any of the statements. Which makes me wonder: if she did make another stop, why didn't whoever she met come forward to inform the police?'

'That's what we find out. I like the way your mind works. You did great, taking the initiative to physically trace her steps.' Vee could practically see the tendrils of Chlöe's gingerific blush wafting down the receiver. Bishop was clever but pampered; she needed her pats on the head. As long as she walked the walk, Vee saw no reason to withhold.

'Next, I traced her cell,' Chlöe said. 'By some miracle – I guess because after she went missing no one considered it was the most pressing thing to do – the phone wasn't blacklisted. It's still in use somewhere in town. Actually, it was last used early this morning in Gardens, only it's under a different number now.'

'Gardens? How'd you swing that?'

'Well,' Chlöe yelled above what sounded like a pack of tennis enthusiasts trash-talking about their last match, 'all cell phones have this chip thingy embedded in them to give them a specific identity. It's called the International Mobile Equipment Identity, or IMEI number. If the phone gets blocked that should render it useless, but nowadays any dodgy Nigerian shop can unblock it for you for, like, a hundred, two hundred rand.'

Vee cleared her throat pointedly.

'Oops, er, sorry. Not that I'm implying that all Nigerians are shady, or that dodgy cell phone shops are only run by Nigerians. No offence to your people. Uh, no wait, sorry you're *Liberian*, so–'

'Bishop.'

'Right, um … so you can pay to have a stolen phone unblocked by anyone with the smarts. It's done by duplicating or changing the IMEI number so it's not accessible to being traced any more. Phone goes off the grid as stolen, somebody else can use it. But Jacqui's phone wasn't reported, and whoever this moron is, they didn't bother to change the IMEI as a precaution. They just got a new SIM card. So technically it could be traced, but nobody's looking for it. I've got records for this cell on the old line when Jacqui had it *and* on the new one the thief's using. Do we care who the thief is? Are we tracking him or her down?'

'Whoa, li'l missy! Gimme a minute.' Vee fired the ignition again and blasted the heater. She couldn't remember if running a car's engine was only dangerous in enclosed spaces, but screw it. 'How do you know this stuff, anyway? I've never had to track a cell. I just hunt the owner. And how'd you get IMEI tracking and phone records and all that? Surely you need permission from the cell phone company.'

This time, tendrils of guilt filtered down the line into her ear.

'I have this friend, this guy who knows a lot about technology and gadgets. He's a wizard and a hugely useful contact to have. Let's just call him The Guy to keep it simple. He can—'

'Was any of this legal?'

'Well …' This time Vee pictured Chlöe's masterful pout. Of course she'd be a pouter; had to be. 'Look, no offence, but we're not lawyers looking for admissible evidence; we're looking for a story. Of course legal is best, but you *agreed* it's not the quickest, most innovative way to meet a deadline. Which is looming. And again, I really need this job and appreciate you taking time to mentor me, so if it looks like I'm doing anything and everything to impress you right now, I am.'

Chlöe Bishop: both charmer and snake. 'Okay, okay,' Vee conceded. A few hours ago she'd championed all wayward means of getting information as long as they were circumspect; now here she was sounding like a hypocrite. 'I did give the go-ahead to bend the rules a bit, so you're off the hook. And stop calling me a mentor, I'm not that old.' She rubbed her forehead. 'I don't know if we need to worry yet about tracking down stolen phones. It may be important, it may not. For now it's on a back-burner. What else you got?'

'As far as the records go, I haven't looked at them too closely yet. But it *does* show that on the twenty-second, the day Jacqui went poof, the phone was switched off at about 4:30 p.m. – hang on … 4:43 p.m. exactly. The last incoming calls were from another cell and a landline, both belonging to her mum. She did try calling her, like she told the police, to find out where Jacqui was and tell her to come straight home.'

'Adele had her on lockdown. She could only go out for practices and sometimes on weekends, provided she kept in touch. I guess she took that day to go on her own mission and give Adele the slip for a few hours.'

'I can relate. That's all I've got on that score. I also tried to find Tamara and Bronwyn. Tamara works for a fancy dress shop called Bella Blues in Claremont, but she's on leave until tomorrow so I'll have to try her again. Bronwyn I can't get hold of at all. I keep getting her voicemail and I haven't had time to check if her address is still the same.'

'Consider me impressed, Chlöe. One more thing: can your computer guy extract hidden or encrypted files? Jacqui's desktop may need an expert eye. He's trustworthy, right?'

'Hundred per cent. Free ... noooo, but don't worry about that. He owes me one. He'll need to see it himself. Either bring the entire hard drive or copy it onto an external.'

Vee exhaled. 'I was afraid you'd say that,' she said, looking through the windscreen at the Paulsen's blue-and-white house. There was nothing for it; she'd have to go back in. The already squally sky lurking over the house's lifeless outline doubled in gloom.

11

The two schoolgirls in front bopped with confidence, while two more flanked at their elbows and one lone girl trailed like a forgotten piece of string. Their black stockings in leather lace-ups made a tiered line as they exited the grounds of Pinelands High, blue blazers flapping as they escaped into a nippy afternoon's freedom. Vee watched them. She didn't need to be near enough to hear their animated conversation, since it was bound to run along universal, predictable lines – boys, where to shop, accursed assignments, more on boys, the weekend.

Wind surged past the narrow lane, lifting curlicues of debris and leaf fragments into the air. The girl in the lead tilted her head, a tumble of blonde curls, into the wind, trying to catch a leaf in her mouth. Something went up her nose instead, and even from a distance Vee could tell the sneeze she gave was the cute kind associated with all pretty young things.

This teenager was not the one Vee sought. The formation of girls dissolved as more students hurried past, and then Vee spotted her target. The straggler. Unlike the sneezing Pre-Raphaelite blonde, Rosemary Fourie was far from delicate. Bulky and broad-shouldered for a girl of fifteen, she lumbered, shoulders hunched like she knew she was working with more than the other girls, and not in a good way. Cut off her ponytail and she could have been a pubescent boy with a bright future in rugby. A member of the posse gave her a punch on the shoulder and Rosemary gave a friendly shove back, sending the girl flying into another friend, who caught and steadied her. The group erupted into laughter, a self-conscious Rosemary joining in reluctantly, her arms crossed over her chest. She looked like a baby bear among china dolls.

Vee trailed from a measured distance, keeping Rosemary in her crosshairs as she crossed the sidewalk outside the school and strolled down the road towards the petrol station. Vee kept one eye on Rosemary and the other on general alert. She wasn't a fan of blindsiding kids, candy from a baby and all that, nor did she want to get stopped for being some kind of pervert. These schools tended to be quite strict about who they allowed around their impressionable students. Or maybe her conscience was growing back.

She'd dawdled outside the gate for what felt like forever, watching child after child either take off for home on foot or get picked up. Much to her relief, no car opened its doors to swallow the solitary teenager and Rosemary's amble was clearly aimless, not to mention that her size made her easy enough to pick out from among the other schoolkids.

Rosie dropped to one knee, tied her laces, popped to her feet and swung around with a scowl. 'Are you following me?' she yelled. A pair of strong, brown eyes set in a square, heavy-boned face bored into Vee's. Rosemary looked scared, and curious, but she had a pre-adult air of learning to stand up for oneself about her.

Vee shrugged. 'Uh, yes. Yes, I am. Sorry. Are you Rosemary Fourie?'

Shrug. 'Yeah. Just Rosie.' The girl waited.

'I'm Vee Johnson. I'm a journalist. I'd like to talk with you privately for a minute, if you don't mind.'

Rosie's curiosity faded and her fear went up several notches. 'Ja, okay, so you're *that* journalist. So I *do* mind, 'cause I'm not supposed to talk to you.'

Wonderful. So the family, dysfunctional or not, did actually communicate. Vee expected Rosie's parents to have told their children that a member of the press was poking around, had called them multiple times for information. She just didn't think they'd have told them right away, giving her an opening for a clean sabotage. Whatever happened to protecting kids from the truth?

'Come on, it'll only take—'

Rosie broke into a lumbering run, her schoolbag bouncing around on her back. She squirmed through the door of a white minibus taxi idling for customers at the roadside. 'I'm not supposed to talk to you! Stop harassing my family!' she shouted. The *gaatjie* slammed the minibus's door, cutting off the rest of Rosie's words. Vee couldn't hear what she said but whatever it was made every head in the taxi turn a look of disgust in her direction. The taxi pulled off Forest Drive.

Suddenly everybody in this goddamn city's an advocate for children's rights. Vee started her car, wondering whether she had the speed and crazies to match that of a taxi driver. As far as white taxis went, Main Road supported a string of indistinguishable pearls at all times, more during peak hours, so keeping a tail was a nightmare. She managed to maintain a three-car distance and for one absurd moment considered driving alongside and shouting 'Her sister was murdered! Ask her about that!' She tossed that plan immediately, envisioning the driver flicking his crooked cigarette into her car and setting her ablaze in traffic. Rosie was strong and surprisingly fast for her size. If the taxi stopped and she bolted, Vee doubted there'd be enough time to track her down.

She needn't have worried. Passengers disembarked and boarded along numerous stops but not one was Rosie. Once they hit Claremont, Vee breathed easier. How would any teenager in a halfway decent town want to kill a few hours after school, if not hang out in a mall? Cavendish Square was the best place to get swallowed in when you were fifteen with an allowance to blow.

Vee scrambled for parking down a side street next to Adult World and pressed a clutch of coins into the palm of a parking marshal. She broke into a jog, elbowing through the lunchtime crowd, in time to spot Rosie jumping out of the minivan. Just follow the blue blazer, Vee thought.

It worked until a hive of taxis zoomed into the designated drop in front of Shoprite supermarket, disgorging school blazers in a Picasso of colours, scattering adolescents to the wind like butterflies. Vee swore and craned her neck over the throng of after-school specials.

12

Chlöe cooled her heels outside Bella Blues, unaware that less than half a kilometre away Vee was being besieged by harried commuters and shoppers. The boutique's display window was inviting, decorated with the sort of mouth-watering items Chlöe had a weakness for. It took all of her self-restraint not to go in. She knew too well what she'd find: gushing assistants (at those prices, what couldn't be faked?), plush couches for the weary and credit card machines that were never out of order. Willpower could only be tested so far. She had to face it: her days of relaxing after an exhausting but rewarding expedition, surrounded by a sluttery of shopping, were over. That lifestyle of indulgence was on ice indefinitely. Meanwhile, she was fighting to embrace an inner career girl who stood on her own two feet. In far less expensive shoes.

Chlöe checked her phone again for time. Not that she had anywhere else to be, for heaven's sake. Driving back to town from Athlone, the manager at Bella Blues called her to say Tamara Daniels was around. Daniels was technically on leave but she was one of their best; committed, liked to pop in from time to time even when she was off. Today was one such lucky day.

Tamara agreed to a chat, as long as it was a quickie and Chlöe could pitch up pronto.

Irksome, then, to turn up only to find Tamara had run out to grab a munchie in Cavendish Square across the road. Chlöe sighed, dragging her eyes from the display windows. The only safe place to poke around in was a lingerie shop. Impervious to the siren call of lacy cups and boudoir knickers, she browsed in fascination. Thank God she'd never had a partner who needed impressing with this kind of stuff. Well, excepting the most recent occasion a couple of days ago, but the Neanderthal in question barely counted as humanoid, much less a consensual sexual partner. Chlöe shuddered. She'd done his memory justice and burned those knickers he'd sniffed without a second thought.

'Hey!'

Chlöe turned, pasting on a smile. The leggy, cookie-coloured girl, boosted by a pair of weapon-toed boots, eyed her up and down, a box of confectionery and coffee cup from Mugg & Bean in hand. For the second time that day, Chlöe Bishop felt too short and too white.

'Are you the reporter wanting to talk to me? Don't know why we couldn't do this over the phone.' Tamara Daniels sported a heavy Cape Flats accent, a Model C school inflection in the undertow. Probably came with a big chip on the shoulder, too. Chlöe braced herself.

'I'm on leave, you know. But I'm curious to know what this is about.' Tamara perched on a nearby bench with the fluidity of the tall and dextrous, not once jostling her parcels or exquisite handbag. 'Lenora,' she indicated her colleague with a nod in the direction of the boutique, 'only said you wanted to ask about my old friend, Jacqui Paulsen. Haven't heard that name in … hoo-oo, it's been a while.'

'How well did you know each other?' Chlöe fought to maintain a professional air and not stare at the doughnuts being devoured. Had she had breakfast? Yes, an age ago. Tamara ate with witchy daintiness, pinching off pieces of doughnut with red fingernails and cramming them down a corner of her mouth so as not to disturb her lipstick. She caught Chlöe's stare and offered one up, which Chlöe gratefully accepted.

'We were best friends. We met in high school after I moved to the neighbourhood. My parents relocated from Bellville and I finished my last two years at Rhodes High. Jacqui had already been there a year before me, had a head start in popularity.'

'What was she like?'

Tamara's laugh was empty of genuine amusement. 'Jacqui was Jacqui, you know. Flashy, talkative, tendency to think she was better than everyone else. Her dad was a big deal but she still lived pretty common like the rest of us, so I don't know what that was about. And he bought her lots of nice things, and didn't we always have to listen to her talk about it? But we got along well enough, though. She was mostly okay. Just sometimes she really pissed me off. Like, Jacqui just loved being the centre of attention. When she was alive, that was all she was about, and now she's dead I'm not surprised it still is.'

'You think she's dead, not missing? Maybe she left to strike it big somewhere else.'

Tamara snorted sugar. 'Where else would she be? Jacqui used to go on and on about how she was gonna make it big one day. First she was gonna be a designer, then an interior decorator, then it was theatre and drama. Trust me, if Jacqui ran off somewhere and made it on her own, she'd contact everybody to boast about how well she was doing and what losers the rest of us were for staying behind. If she *hadn't* made it, she'd be moaning about how horrible her life was, but at least she was trying and who're the rest of us to talk.'

Chlöe nodded, rearranging her preconceptions. So, this wasn't a friend – this was a Frenemy. A creature many loathed to admit was central to female companionship, frolicking in its natural habitat. Carried on like a comrade, backstabbed like a burglar. Tamara had more than likely coveted the position her friend had occupied – top dog – but had settled for being as close to the limelight as possible and nurtured some pretty bitter feelings while she was there.

'What can you tell me about the day you last saw her?'

'*That* day.' Tamara shook her head. 'I don't know how many times I've relived *that day* and told the same story to the police. They harassed me, they harassed my family, they turned the whole neighbourhood upside down and still didn't find anything. You wanna hear it again?

'Well, here it is, the long and short of it,' she replied to Chlöe's nod. 'Me and Jacqui went to Newlands Sports Club at around eleven in the morning. We were both on the girls' basketball team at school, so we liked to play something different on the weekend, mix it up. Tennis was our thing, sometimes we'd mess around in the pool. Few other girls used to join us. Newlands has great facilities and students get in for free, and we could dump our parents for a while, which was perfect. We played until one o'clock.

'On the spur of the moment, we decided to go watch a movie at Cavendish, but Jacqui bailed and left the group. She made up some lie about having stuff to do for her mum, blah blah, but we all knew it was that Ashwin idiot she was going to see. She swore she'd dumped him but she was being really shifty that day, so I knew he was somewhere in the mix. We were close, but you know how girls are: we hide our drama when we can't deal with all the judgement. Anyway, she took off and the rest of us went to the movies, and the next thing I hear she's missing and Mr Ash is denying everything. But I swear to God, I didn't see or hear from her again after that.'

'What time was it exactly when she left you?'

Tamara pondered, shoving another pinch of doughnut into her mouth. 'We wanted to grab some food and still have time to make the two-thirty show, so we had an hour to hustle. I'd say we got a taxi and left her in Newlands at around one-thirty.'

Chlöe was stumped. Was there something she was missing, a question she was leaving unasked? There were over three hours lost in the ether in between tennis and the last time Jacqui's missing phone had been on. 'So she, like, didn't call you even once for the rest of the day?' she pressed, hating how lame she sounded. Tamara was already on her feet, impatient to push off.

'No, not once.' Tamara spoke quickly, but then she paused, allowing some unspoken thought to knock around in her head a bit. 'Like I said, I really didn't trust or like that Ashwin of hers, but maybe he wasn't lying about everything. Jacqui had loads of friends and liked being liked, but strangely enough she could keep a secret. Who knew what else she was up to? If anybody can help you out more, try Bronwyn Abrams. In some ways she was closer to Jacqui than me.'

Chlöe explained they were well aware of Bronwyn's existence but were having trouble getting in touch with her. She reeled off an address and contact number hoping for a nod of confirmation, but all Tamara did was shrug.

'If you already know about Bronwyn, I can't really help beyond that. She wasn't with us that day. Don't know her number or where she stays or nothin'. She wasn't my friend per se; she mostly hung out with Jacqui. They used to be tight from their old 'hood when they were kids, then Jacqui moved away, or she moved ...' Tamara arched her shoulders again and shook her hair to indicate the tale was muddled and uninteresting. 'Some long story. Anyway, we had Jacqui in common, but not much beyond that.'

'That sounds like an intriguing dynamic.' Chlöe knew stalling wouldn't work for much longer and she couldn't stomach the sound of her fake 'investigator voice'. 'Why was it, exactly, that you guys weren't all that close despite having a best friend in common?'

Tamara looked pained. 'Look, who knows why some people get along like a house on fire and others can't stand each other's guts? Don't get me wrong; we weren't enemies, far from it. We just ... didn't gel. Bronwyn had a very sweet, insecure personality. Lots of handholding. I *really* don't rub shoulders too well with chicks like that. Sucks up too much energy. Jacqui was great with her. She was always wonderful with that kinda stuff.'

Chlöe wondered how Tamara's temperament worked in a sales environment where delivery was crucial. But from the look of Tamara's outfit, the girl clearly let nothing mess with her money. 'You said Jacqui was good with secrets. Is it possible that that played a part in her disappearance? Maybe she was pregnant, or in some other kind of trouble that led to something worse?'

This time, Tamara's laugh was a short bark of incredulous scorn. 'That's *way* more than unlikely! The only thing Jacqui was better at than starting shit was getting out of it, so no way would I believe she'd let any situation get that far out of control. Okay, I'm not saying she was superhuman or anything, but Jacqui was dead clever. If she was in too deep, she definitely would've told me, or her mother, or *someone*, y'know. She wasn't some stupid *girl*, to go drink bleach or whatever. Pregnancy is so not on. No, she would've told me. Jacqui was majorly ambitious, and she wouldn't be careless enough to screw up all her magnificent dreams on one mistake. Not for Ashwin.'

Chlöe arched her eyebrows, massaging for more.

'Ag, man,' Tamara continued, 'her mum was all worried that they were 'doing it' and, sure, I didn't like his ass, but that whole Ashwin thing was nothing but a high-school fling. A major man upgrade was gonna happen after that. Jacqui liked guys and fooled around as much as the next girl, but unlike the next girl she was no bubble-headed romantic. Beemers and Gucci don't mix with an old-school coloured guy who wants a goody-goody wife and lots of kids. Like, hello.'

Hello, indeed. So heart-throb wasn't quite the centre of the universe he was painted to be. Or as much as he'd *believed* himself to be? How confused would he have been about that? Or had Dad found out and taken matters into his own hands?

'I really have to go.' Tamara shuffled, looking uncomfortable for the first time. 'Not that I don't wanna help you out, but ...'

Chlöe nodded, jostling titbits into the right slots between her ears. Maybe she should've written stuff down in case Voinjama asked for specifics later. Journalists were supposed to write things down. *Crap*.

'Look, this isn't easy for me. I'm not some bitch,' Tamara said. Her guard dropped for the first time, and sadness and anger frothed to the surface. 'I really, really do miss her. We both wanted to move on to greater things and leave our old lives behind; that's all we ever talked about. All this time I just couldn't believe she'd just pack up and leave without me. Piss off for a *jol* in a new city and not care who she left behind.' Tamara gulped. 'It was easier to assume she was selfish and left without saying goodbye. I could be angry with her for that. It was better than ... thinking the worst.'

Chlöe nodded some more, unsure of what to say. Tamara would work through things in her own way and time, with or without platitudes from a stranger. Instead, she promised she'd be in touch if there were any more questions.

'Whatever you find out, can you gimme a shout? So I finally know what happened to her.' Tamara waved half-heartedly and walked away.

13

The security guard hardly spared them a look as they passed through the doorway swaddled in a clutch of other shoppers. Vee hung back as the girl behind the parcel counter slid Rosie's school satchel into a free slot and handed her a beaten, numbered cardboard disc in exchange. The bargain bin store was crowded but Vee wasn't worried about keeping up in here. Rosie looked intent on being as idle and oblivious as an afternoon would allow. She draped a shopping basket noncommittally over her elbow and meandered through the aisles of bins.

Crunching on an apple, Vee kept the schoolgirl in sight. Dogging people's footsteps involved a lot more watching than pursuing. The trick lay in maintaining a line of sight at all times, which was easy with so few of the aisles blocking her vision. She retained a wide angle of rotation around Rosie, keeping several warm bodies between them, making sure she was never more than a profile in peripheral vision.

The guard was in plainclothes, which was a relief. Vee didn't have the energy to deal with a uniformed, walkie-talkie tough guy, should things go sideways. The guard's attention and hands were thankfully engaged by the giggling parcel-counter attendant. Burrowing through mounds of 'Made in China' with harried mothers, Vee kept one eye on him and the other out for Rosie, sharp elbows and scampering kids.

She held up a ladies' white tank top, played the fabric around in her fingers. The quality was appalling. Nevertheless, it sang of warm days in clean jeans, of Sunday shenanigans. Her thoughts stole her away for a moment, as some fantasy man caressed the small of her back and murmured in her ear. As Joshua ...

Vee tossed the tank top back into the bin and brushed her fingertips over her forehead. She needed to get a grip. She was a little lonely, fine, no shame in that. But there was truth to the saying that shopping (for men) while hungry (desperate? She wasn't *desperate*) was a bad idea. And with Joshua? Inviting, persistent as hell, but off limits. *Extremely* off. Like, miles offshore of sanity's dominion to even be flirting with one of her ex's best friends.

She snapped out of her head and scanned the floor for Rosie. She was gone. Vee's heart somersaulted. *Shit, woman, focus.* Her head was meant to be in the game and here she was, in heat and trying to drive heavy machinery. She tiptoed to the next aisle, peeped, and exhaled when she saw Rosie, jammed up against a garment rack, her eyes vacant.

Why the hell won't she just leave? This dump didn't have much to offer. Vee frowned. The twitchy look on Rosie's face was suspicious, and the girl had one hand behind her back like she was hiding something. The arm behind her back darted to a shelf and a flash of colour disappeared up the sleeve of her school jersey. Rosie pressed her arm against the side of the display shelf, flattening her 'purchase' so it didn't stick out so much.

Well, I'll be damned, she *is* shopping, Vee snickered. Shop*lifting*, and doing a horrible job of it. Vee switched her phone to video record and angled her palm, filming as Rosie spirited more merchandise into her knee high socks by pretending to tie her laces. The shoelace thing was clearly her go-to ninja move.

It didn't go unnoticed. The Asian woman behind the till yelped and pointed, sending a male counterpart muscling over. A scamper of children dashed across his path and the sharp-featured man fell, grabbed on to a metal bin and overturned it. The Asian woman bellowed in Mandarin in the direction of the security guard, jabbing her finger at Rosie.

Rosie's eyes flicked back and forth. Her face folded into childlike confusion and she shot up and stumbled past the other quizzical shoppers. The security guard grabbed her, shoved her against a wall and started to pat her down.

Vee jostled the nearest rack of clothes and the metal rail of print dresses toppled onto a pile of boxes. Everyone turned.

At last, Rosie seized the day. She drove her elbow into the guard's stomach and sprinted. Vee ghosted in the commotion and slipped out too, before the doors were barricaded, stopping long enough to stretch over the parcel counter and snatch Rosie's schoolbag while the attendant wasn't looking.

'Hey, whoa! Wait up, let me talk to you.'

Out of breath, Rosie turned around and nearly tripped over her feet trying to run faster. 'I told you to piss off! Don't you get it? I'm not talking to you!'

'Hey, hang on, look … Rosie, all I want … hey, will you just *slow the hell down* for one second?' Vee stopped, and took off running again when the security guard from the shop poked his head through the entrance. She grabbed Rosie's arm and hauled her around the nearest corner. 'Jesus. All I need–'

'I DO NOT HAVE ANYTHING TO SAY TO YOU,' Rosie spat. 'So fuck off!'

Vee plucked her cell out of her pocket. 'Cool. If that's your stance, watch this.' The muscles in Rosie's face did a comic plunge as she watched the video.

'Aaaand … there.' Vee hit pause and held the Nokia right under Rosie's nose, making sure she got a good look at herself, limbs flailing in a mad dash for the door, sleeve stuffed with stolen goods. 'That's definitely you. Is it enough to press charges? Who knows? The shop owners might be forgiving. But I know it's enough to convince your parents that their daughter gets up to no good after school instead of going straight home like she's supposed to.'

A whimper trickled out of Rosie.

'Oh, and …' Vee held up the satchel. 'Yours, I believe? Now we can have a civil conversation, or we can make this bigger than it needs to be. What d'you say? It won't take long.'

'I have to get home.'

'All right, then. I'll give you a ride back to Pinelands.'

Rosie nailed her eyes out of the passenger window as Vee drove, determined not to make eye contact or speak.

She'd allowed herself to be led down the street like Marie Antoinette on her way to the guillotine. Vee undid the central locking and pulled her side open. Rosie didn't budge.

'What?' Vee said. Rosie looked stricken, as if she was about to be sick. 'Look, I know you know the drill about stranger danger and whatnot, and I should know better than to offer lifts to a minor. But hand to God,' Vee raised her right, 'I have no intention—'

'Is this your car?' Rosie squeaked.

Vee threw up a shrug, kicked a tyre. 'Yeah. My A to B. Nothing fancy like you're used to but it'll get you home.' Rosie's expression didn't change and Vee sighed. 'If you'd rather …'

'It's nothing. I … it reminds me of a model someone I knew used to have. I never liked it.' Rosie flicked the door open like the handle had teeth, scoured the interior, exhaled and climbed inside.

Now, they worked the highway in silence. Vee felt sorry for the kid — her heart was practically thumping through her blouse like a cartoon. Rosie looked the part of a fighter but wouldn't say boo to a mouse. Vee decided to go easy on her. Thieving kids were right up her alley, seeing as she used to be one. She'd had flair and lightness of touch to spare, though, laughably lacking in Rosie's case. A girl her size trying to be deft and inconspicuous at anything was a joke.

'You did all right back there,' she lied, easing conversation open. 'You went wrong trying to take too much. Always gets you noticed.'

Silence.

'D'you do this a lot? How many stores do you hit in a week?'

Money shot. Rosie whipped around, mouth twitching. 'No, I don't 'do this a lot', okay? I'm not some fucking thief or something.'

Of course not. You just steal, which is totally different. 'Hey, I'm not judging you. For real. And I told you already, don't worry about me telling your parents about any of this. I was only bluffing to get you to open up.'

'Yeah, right. And if I don't?'

'I know strong-arming you won't work, Rosemary. But help me out here, for your sister's sake. This story could go a long way to improving how missing persons cases are handled. It would mean a lot to families like yours, who've lost someone. Don't you care about that?' Vee stopped. Preaching froze people up.

'I do care. Why wouldn't I?' Rosie said, barely audible. Head bowed, she looked like she did care, deeply, but couldn't summon the muster to do anything about it.

Vee let her marinate. It would take or it wouldn't. She could afford to be a little patient.

'She taught me how to,' Rosie mumbled at last.

'Hhhmm?'

'Jacqui. She showed me how to shoplift. That's how we used to spend time together sometimes, after school or on the weekends.'

'Okay.' Vee straightened behind the wheel. 'How did it start?'

'The way things *always* started with Jacqui. We got bored one afternoon and starting messing around to kill time. One of us walked out of a supermarket with a chocolate we hadn't paid for, and it turned into a thing. We started getting better at it, practising only in small, stupid places, like the one we were just in. They don't have cameras or sensors at the doors, or real security or anything. If there was a guard, Jacqui would flirt with him while I took something, but usually she did the lifting 'cause I wasn't that good at it. I get confused if people look at me, start worrying that they know and it throws me off. We got caught a coupla times, but Jacqui was a sweet-talker. Or she'd pay guys off to not call the cops.'

'Your parents never found out?'

Rosie shook her head. 'Don't think so. We only did it *sometimes*, when it was just the two of us. Lucas and Serena would never go along with it. And anyway, we stopped after a while … least I did. The smaller shops got too easy and Jacqui said the security was way too good in the malls for us to try it there. You ask me, she got bored with it. She got bored with things easily. People, too.'

Rosie released a huge breath and settled more comfortably into the seat, unburdened.

'Y'all didn't need the stuff, or money to buy it. It was for fun.'

'Why not? Jacqui got off on thrills. She'd be into something crazy for a while and then just get over it. My sister Serena says she had a deficit disorder on top of her daddy issues, like, she *really* needed to be the centre of attention so Dad could always be focused on her. Which is nuts, 'cause Dad only pays attention to old, rich guys with dodgy hearts.'

'And what do you think?'

'She was cool and fun and she paid attention to me, which no one else ever did. *I think* the real reason Serena got all churchy and dragged Jacqui along was because she got jealous we were spending so much time together and leaving her out of everything.' Rosie crossed her arms and made a click in her throat. 'Like if *they* were hanging out together, Jacqui would have less time for me.'

'So if Serena brought Jacqui into the born-again circle, why was she still bunking school and stealing?' And buying condoms to wear out with her gangster boyfriend. Church had really worked its magic. 'According to Ms Paulsen, Jacqui changed a lot once she got the spirit. You saying it was all an act? Why'd she go that far to lie to her mother?'

'No, man!' Rosie rolled her eyes like she was talking to the biggest dunce on the planet. 'Jacqui really was saved … well, kinda. She used to be full of it but that was all *before*, when we first met her. And the only reason we found out she existed was because the Sean thing happened … don't know if you know about *that* part …' Her voice caught. Her eyes strayed out of the window again.

Vee nodded. Act One of the Fourie tragedy had largely played out before a child too young to comprehend much, but Vee assumed Rosie was every bit as affected. Pain and sorrow tended to die hard in families, petrifying into bitter, heritable legacies instead. Rosie likely knew Sean the legend better than the flesh-and-blood brother, but it was clear she cherished him nonetheless.

'Do you remember him at all?' Vee asked gently. She had experience with lost brothers, too.

Rosie pulled a contemptuous face. 'Ja, of course! I was eight when he died.' She worked her lips around like her words made her mouth sour, as if she had better practice keeping her memories of Sean in than running her mouth. 'He was sick most of the time, though. I can hardly remember him not being sick, and doing normal stuff with us.' She slammed a knuckle to her lips and attacked her nails. 'It drove Mum crazy,' she whispered.

Vee changed tack. 'Go back to how you kids got to know each other.'

'After the secret of Jacqui being our sister came out, she started coming around to hang out more. Not right away, but gradually, until we got used to her. Mum hated it, but whatever, Dad said it was okay. Jacqui took her time getting close to us, like she needed to make up her mind if any of us could replace Sean. She loved him best of all, even though they knew each other for five minutes, but that was our parents' fault. Her mum included. The three of them lied to all of us. So anyway, Lucas was her first pick, but, Lucas being Lucas, that didn't last. Then Serena—'

'Wait. What's 'Lucas being Lucas' mean?' This was the second time someone had skirted around Jacqui's weird relationship with her half-brother.

Rosie looked pained and embarrassed. 'Look, Miss Johnson, I don't wanna say something I'm not supposed to. I'm not even meant to be talking to you. All I mean is my brother's a little strange. He gets … intense. People can take it the wrong way.'

'Intense *how*, Rosemary? Spell it out for me.'

'Long as you know I'm not saying my brother's crazy, or anything else to incriminate him in whatever happened to Jacqui!' Colour exploded on Rosie's cheeks and forehead, emphasising an unflattering smattering of acne.

Vee took a deep breath, mentally cursing television crime shows. 'I'm not a cop, remember? I just need you to clear up a few things so I've got a clear picture.'

Rosie fidgeted. 'Lucas can't play it cool when he cares for someone, especially female someones. He tends to form unhealthy emotional attachments to the women in his life, especially the role models that are important in his development as a man. Some can go on for quite a while; others he just abandons when he finds another target to obsess over.'

Vee bit the inside of her cheek to hold in a spray of laughter. Oblivious, Rosie banged on with her recital: 'I think Lucas has Freudian issues, but I'm not sure which ones. But it always centres around women; he's very scared and docile around male authority. He's kind of confrontational with other men, like with Dad, but it's usually hot air, and he ends up backing down. I imagine the seat of all that misplaced emotion is Mum. Because it starts with mothers in most cases. I mean, even the way he *looks* at her. It's the way you look at a mother, but like … not really, at the same time.'

Vee cleared her throat. 'That's really something, Rosie, it truly is. Tell me, did any of you kids ever go for therapy? You know what therapy is?'

'Duh. I'm not stupid.' Rosie crossed her arms, pouting. 'Yeah, we went. It was useless, but we had to.' She shook her head, looking adult for the first time. 'Grief counselling and some kinda child therapy, and my parents did marriage counselling one time. That didn't last.' She snorted. 'Now they take each other down in the open and everyone gets pissed off at everyone else for no reason. That's our new therapy.' She looked Vee up and down with a frown. 'Why d'you ask? I read a lot about this stuff too. Does it show?'

'Nope. Never mind. Tell me more about Lucas and Jacqui. What happened?'

Rosie fired a round of shifty looks, slunk deeper into her seat, opened her mouth, closed it. The sight of the conifer-lined streets of Pinelands brought her agitation back in full swing. Her legs started to bop up and down in anticipation of escape.

'You better tell me, 'cause it makes a big difference if this comes from you. I'm gonna find out anyway, and if I have to hear it off your parents, hehn! You know how that'll go,' Vee said. 'They'll paint themselves like heroes and dump all the mess on you kids, mainly because they have no idea what this has been like for y'all. Girl, you do not want to hear what you sound like coming out of your parents' mouths.'

Rosie chewed her lip, stalling. Vee considered central-locking all the doors and forcing her to live off potpourri until she got an answer.

'I'll tell you if you stop here,' Rosie said as they veered off Forest Drive deeper into suburbia. 'Don't take me all the way home. I can walk.'

'It's no problem. We're almost there.'

'No!'

For the first time, Vee was close enough to notice that Rosie's hazel eyes, wild and boring into hers, were rimmed and flecked with green. They were undoubtedly her most striking asset, one of few she could take pride in.

'Nobody should see us together. I don't want any questions.'

Vee pulled over and drew up the handbrake. She flipped down the sun visor to keep the glare out of her face and shifted around in her seat so Rosie had her full attention.

'Lucas started acting weird around Jacqui.' Rosie hugged her schoolbag to her chest as if it was all the comfort she had left. 'He started having feelings for her. Y'know, *very* non-brotherly feelings.' She gulped. 'Everyone thinks I'm too young to notice anything and find out stuff, but I do. Well, I don't know how far it actually went but I knew something was up. Jacqui went cold and stopped wanting to be around him. I tried to bring it up but she shut me down. But I think they... you know, that, like ...' Her fingers harassed her socks, pulling strips of elastic loose. 'They maybe *did it* with each other or something.'

'As in ...'

Rosie's blush went nuclear. 'You know. As in, *that*.'

14

'Oi! Stop being anti-social over there!' Charisma shouted.

Vee flapped a hand over her shoulder to shush her and went back to the view.

The rooftop of *Urban's* office building was her headspace. The CBD was one hell of an impressive spreadsheet; the throb of traffic and a strong south-easterly fluting past her ears made for a brilliant lunchtime soundtrack. Throw in the phallic magnificence of the Absa building towering over the downtown hustle, and decompression was instant. Vee looked down, fighting that visceral urge to spread her arms and launch herself over the edge.

'Voinjama Johnson!' a chorus of voices screamed.

'Give me strength and succour.' Vee covered her face with her hands, breathed, and meandered back to the group. The terrace wasn't big enough for destressing one person, let alone five. Chari and Chlöe, along with Lebo Khumalo from layout and design and photographer Tallulah MacArthur, and it was a bit much.

'Puff?'

Vee pushed away the smoking butt in Chari's hand. '*No. Jeez.*' Chari held it pinched between her thumb and forefinger, meaning it was no ordinary cigarette. 'How can you smoke that and be coherent later?'

'One hit is for great creative energy,' Chari grinned hazily. 'Well, let's say two hits …'

Vee tuned out the volley of office gossip between the four and grabbed a lawn chair. The battered furniture was a gift from Portia, cast-offs from her last redecoration. Portia wasn't a fan of her staff shooting the breeze up here but didn't see the point in banning it. Vee faced her chair in the other direction, overlooking the ledge, and let her thoughts sail out.

They were screwed. Well, *she* was screwed; Chlöe didn't matter yet. She wasn't *completely* screwed, not yet, but she couldn't see a way to backpedal out of this. It wasn't at all like her to lose heart so quickly but she felt exhausted already. Illegitimate thieving daughters, thuggish boyfriends, coital congress between siblings. How did each slippery thread weave together with the others? What was the backbone of her piece, if she couldn't even see an outline? The police had given up – who the hell did she think she was? Not to mention that sweet incentive of twenty-five grand Adele had pushed at her. A heft of bills she'd held in her hand, seriously debated pocketing – journalists danced over the line all the time, what was twenty-five really, and who would know – until common sense slapped her and she'd refused. Her palm still itched with the memory of it, though. Adele wasn't quite compos mentis right now, but Vee didn't intend telling Portia a thing, not even to win a few points for moral fortitude. If Portia found out anyone connected with the case had so much as waved a hundred rand note under her journalist's nose, that would be it – story axed, welcome to reassignment. All Vee needed to do now–

Chlöe coughed at her shoulder.

Vee smiled up at her. 'Those bitches too over the top? You get used to it. They sound like maniacs but they're not. Not fully, anyway.'

'Uh, no, it's not that,' Chloe hissed. 'We've got company.'

'Shit, hide the joint!' Portia never came up here, nor did anyone else. Vee swung her legs down and got up. She blinked. 'Whuhh … Joshua? What're you doing here … and what's that nonsense in your hand? You bought *flowers*?'

Joshua thrust out the bunch of poppies. He was back at work; the haircut, clean-shaven face and crisp shirt was all there was to say about that. 'If Mohammed won't come to the mountain …' he shrugged, leaning over to brush a kiss on her cheek.

'This is a cheap and dirty stunt,' Vee said in his ear. She didn't have to turn around to know their exchange was being devoured by the intrigued collective: the stares lasering into the back of her neck were evidence enough. 'You know our rule: no workplace antics, no showing up to offices. You think this is funny?'

'LOL! What care I for rules? You should've taken my calls. You know I only play dirty when you don't take my calls.' He dropped another kiss near her ear. 'You smell incredible, by the way.'

'Mssh, pervert.' Vee nudged him away, but it was too late. The coven advanced.

'Hey, no penises allowed up here. No funny business either.' Tallulah folded her arms. 'Who might you be and who are you to her?'

'He has no name, and we're just fr–'

'Joshua Allen. We used to fool around in college, till she started catching feelings. I was the best she ever had.' Vee's jaw dropped. 'I apologise for the intrusion, but this young lady promised to meet me for lunch and then stood me up. My hand was forced,' Joshua said.

'We *never* … I *never* …' Vee took a deep breath. Charm and deception were Joshua's forte. The girls were already staring at her as if she'd burnt down an orphanage.

'But I know how she can make it up to me. Let's walk, shall we?'

'Yes, dickhead, *let's*!' Vee grabbed his arm and pulled him towards the stairs. Out of the corner of her eye, she caught the lewd movement of Chari licking her fingers.

'Please don't slap me. I couldn't resist,' Joshua laughed.

'Slap? More like–'

'That's great.' He bounded a few steps ahead and blocked her path. 'But before we get kinky, listen to my proposition. Last time I came over …'

'You mean the night you broke in against my express wishes.'

'To-may-to, to-mah-to. You mentioned the Wellness Institute and this Dr Fourie, and it rang a bell. Long story short, how'd you like to hit a swank party tomorrow night in Constantia?'

'Pertinent to the WI and the Fouries, how?'

'Rich people, free food, an evening of my delightful company...'

Vee made a bored face.

'All right, fine, but it's related. The reference rang a bell because, naturally, our firm is connected to those who live a lush life and, naturally, those folks like to throw their weight around. Sometimes they put their muscle into charity, other times into private and lucrative business ventures, something that makes them look philanthropic but will also make even more money.'

Vee leaned against the staircase and amplified her bored stare. Joshua brokered in corporate finance, a world that, shameful as it was to admit, was more arcane and complex than her intelligence had command of. He'd been at JPMorgan Chase for years and still wasn't completely transparent about what exactly he did for a pay cheque. Terms like 'mergers and acquisitions', 'liquidity risk' and 'derivatives' he bandied about with aplomb. Vee hated it. She could explain her job in a few sentences, while his version took hours and several glasses of wine. Whenever she had trouble sleeping, she only had to call on him to explain his work one more time. Every time she felt troubled that he was a capitalist demon working against the very causes she stood for, he did something to reaffirm her faith in him.

'How long and complicated is this gonna be?' she said.

'I'll keep to the sidewalk for the pedestrians,' he promised. 'The WI is a breakaway from another private hospital that tanked about five years ago: Claremont Life and Medicare Clinic – CLM. Capital issues. One of their backers must've seen the recession coming and cashed in their chips early. Some of the doctors left, but others stayed and did the legwork to get a private clinic off the ground. Well, the guy who's throwing the party is a shareholder in the WI venture. He knows how to spot money and make it, so he didn't just put his name behind this so the public would thank him for having a big heart. Well, yeah, ass-kissing is a form of currency, too. But the money he sank into the WI is set to make him an even prettier penny.'

'Isn't that like laundering?'

'Half of how you make money is like laundering. How d'you think banks work? The other half is like …' Joshua flip-flopped a hand, '… lying or stealing. So basically, like life. Depressing, I know. I need to give you the tutorial on laundering again, because I don't think you got it.'

'Can't wait.'

'Anyway. Philemon Mtetwa. Our Midas in question. Soirée at his mansion tomorrow evening. A little birdie told me that half the board of directors and senior staff will be there, including …'

'The Fouries.'

'Bingo. I'm invited and I need a date. Who better than one who snoops, eavesdrops and asks awkward questions over the entrées? See, I'm always looking out for you.'

It was true; he always was. There was no snappy answer for that.

'What happened to Bitch in Boots?'

He shrugged. Flapped a hand like a bird taking off in flight. 'It wasn't meant to be. She couldn't hold an escargot fork.'

'Pssh. Because everybody who got sense knows you eat snails with your fingers.' She searched his eyes and his eyes smiled back, teasing. It was a dangerous premise for a date, which was what it would be; they both knew it. An evening in make-up and heels, knocking back bubbly, snuffling for gold like a truffle pig on the other … so tempting. She badly needed to get out of the house. But bad things could end up happening, very bad things.

'How did you get invited, anyway?' she grunted. They trudged into the main hub, where the din was overwhelming. They lingered at the stairwell door. 'Are you one of the hotshots handling this guy's investment holdings, or what?'

'Wow. That's not even in the ballpark of what I do, little one.' He gave her nose a tweak, then made eyes at his watch. 'Okay, I'm out. But tomorrow evening, seven, are we on? Please.'

'Fine, I'll be your date to the rich pipo party. Now …' She pointed to the elevators and he tipped an invisible hat in farewell and headed towards them.

'Who was that?'

Vee jumped. The doors of the lift had barely closed in Joshua's face and here Portia was, barking at her shoulder.

'Nobody. Damn. Is privacy a pipe dream when you work with women?'

'Of course. What did Nobody want? Aside from aggravating my hayfever.' Portia cut her eyes at the flowers. 'Is he a source on the case?'

'Absolutely not.'

'Hhmm,' was all Portia said. For an absurd moment before she walked away, Vee thought she caught a glimmer of respect.

15

A spray of sparks arced off a beat-up Honda as a new exhaust pipe was soldered in place. In another corner of the workshop floor, a mechanic gunned the engine of a no-hoper while another two celebrated with greasy high-fives.

On days like these, Marieke Venter barely felt female. She had to squeeze a boob or sneak into the loo to check down her knickers if her creases and crevices were still there. On the days she was on her cycle there was no need to: the crew, who knew her too well, let her know she was persona non grata. On those days, every word she said (she had to admit, she did snipe a bit) got taken out of context or ignored. It would help if there were another woman around. Unfortunately, the downside of working in a garage – or in the auto-mechanical industry, as her father had insisted on calling it – was that birds of her feather were rare.

'Where's Ashwin?' she asked one of the mechanics.

Pieter shrugged, wiping a spanner on his blue jumpsuit. 'Thought he was in your office. Typical. If you find him, tell him I need him working on the Golf's suspension. That lady wants her car today and if he doesn't want *kak* like last time …'

Marieke clenched her jaw and muttered something crude, low enough to stay under the racket. Pieter gave her a look and she flushed. She never griped openly about her and Ashwin's problems. It stirred up chatter, and the guys sure knew how to gossip like hens. Being the only woman at Venter's Auto and Electrical Garage was one thing, but it would help to no end if she didn't have to run the place more or less single-handed while Ashwin farted around.

She slipped into their cramped office, the only place on the premises besides the toilet that had any privacy. She groaned as she put her feet up.

I need another job, Marieke thought. Which was crazy. She was the administrator, head of finance, roster organiser and competent under the hood; she had several jobs already. Besides, Venter's was family, and you didn't bail on family.

She knew full well what Pieter's look had been about. Despite all her efforts, Ashwin didn't show her enough respect. The boys on the workshop floor gave her her due, but not her own brother. Some had worked for her father and were proud to see at least one of his children remained dedicated to the garage's survival. Surgery on automobiles had been her dad's passion, and busting her ass to keep his business afloat was hers. Ashwin had other ideas, but he would, seeing as the old man's will favoured him and he owned the shop.

Marieke tapped piles of bills and orders against the desk and put them to one side, getting grouchier by the minute. She knew she was no genius and her talents were few, but she knew what she was about. She was great at doing what she was told, getting things in order and keeping them that way. Maybe that made her a simpleton to some, but it was her fussing that kept Venter's out of quicksand time and time again. *She* had done it, and still did. In the pinch of crisis, she—

A loud tap sounded on the glass panel separating the office from the chaos of the floor. For the thousandth time, Marieke wished the partition was one-way and soundproof. She wished it was bulletproof too, not so much for her sake as for that of the idiots on the other side.

It was Pieter again. He gestured wildly, hand to one ear in the shape of a phone receiver as he mouthed something. She frowned and waved him in. Did he want to use the phone?

He shook his head vigorously and stabbed a finger at the office landline, moving his lips slowly. Come one, come all, was that what he was saying? She threw her hands up. He rolled his eyes and came round to poke his head in.

'Yassis, Marieke, you suck at charades. I was saying, *someone called*. The same woman that called before, asking for Ashwin. I figured she wouldn't mind speaking to you instead, but you were out.'

'What woman?'

'She's called before, even stopped by and waited around on Tuesday morning. I took a message.' Pieter pointed to the Post-it stuck to the edge of the desk and closed the door behind him.

Marieke spent a long time deciphering the Khoisan rock painting that was Pieter's handwriting. Afterwards, she contemplated. Her grey cells were shuffling down a road and she didn't like where they going. An investigator was looking into an old missing persons case and wanted a word with her big brother.

For all Ashwin's past shenanigans, there was only one thing that hovered in the background of their lives, the ghost that wouldn't move on and leave them in peace. He'd said nothing to her of calls and drop-ins by investigators, but it went a long way towards explaining his volatile mood and unexplained absences that week. He was avoiding the unavoidable. After everything that had happened back then, with everything that she knew, he was still running and still shutting her out.

'*Nie meer nie,*' Marieke whispered and stuffed the scrap of yellow paper with a scrawled number on it in her jeans. No more.

16

'Where do we start?' Chlöe asked as she and Vee climbed into her VW Polo.

Vee scratched her nose. Two strike-outs at Venter's Auto: neither of the eponymous owners was present to give her the time of day. She'd let it slide for now. Ashwin Venter would surface eventually, and when he did she would be there to roast his slippery behind. It was Friday – no harm in switching to go-slow mode for the rest of the day. Chlöe was aglow after her first interview with Daniels and chomping at the bit to tackle Serena Fourie on her own. Vee wanted to ease her in; best not to push it.

'You know what, let's handle your errands first, whatever they are. I doubt Serena is on campus right now, and if she is she's probably in a lecture.'

Chlöe twitched and fidgeted. 'Forget I mentioned that. My stuff's not urgent at all. Let's try to catch her now before she disappears for an early weekend. You know what students are like.' She started the engine. The radio blasted on, staccato rhymes backed by a crunk beat rattling the doors. She fiddled the dial to low.

'Lil Wayne?' Vee turned the CD case over several times and squinted at Chlöe. 'You look more like a Taylor Swift typa gal.'

'White people can't love hip-hop, ha ha.' Shaking her head, Chlöe tucked a curl behind an ear and backed out of the underground lot. 'How prejudiced of you, bosslady. I'm shocked.'

'Just drive,' Vee chuckled, reclining the seat. *Bosslady*. It brought to mind a buxom authority figure dressed in colourful *lappa*, multitasking like an octopus and beating people's ears with wooden spoons when they dared to idle in her presence. Had a nice ring to it. She ought to act more like it, now that she had her own personal slave.

*

'What now?' Vee swirled her tongue around the Steers vanilla cone and stared down the street. There was no 'what now' that she could think of.

They were on University of Cape Town's Lower Campus, Tugwell residence. On the other side of the road, déjà vu to the scene outside Rosie's school. Another group of girls, older this time, less awkward, or better at pretending not to be. Far brighter feathers on these birds; the confines of school uniform were buried in their nightmares.

'Pink tights in the twenty-first century. Booty hanging out of ripped jeans. Ugh, it's like the sidewalk threw up a fruit salad,' Chlöe drawled. 'Can't believe I was ever that duh. What d'you call a display of youth and hotness that no one cares to see?'

'Unrepentant foxismonitism.'

Chlöe looked at Vee long and hard. 'Rhetorical question, but okay. Show-off.'

Vee shrugged and turned her attention back across the street. The foxes shared a laugh as they waited for the campus shuttle service, passing a one-litre Coke between them. One of them was trying too hard to come off casual and upbeat. Serena Fourie was a poor actress and looked visibly shaken.

'She won't talk to us,' Chlöe said.

'She will. Give it a minute,' Vee replied. 'It's been, what,' she checked her watch, 'fifteen minutes since I tried to corner her and she blew me off. She's rattled *and* she has no idea I'm still around. Let it soak in.'

'Then what? You planning to make me wait in the car again while you go over there and snatch her out of the group, or hang around till she comes back from wherever she's going now and ambush her outside her room? I mean, we can't just faff around here all day.'

'Shhh.' Vee waved Chlöe quiet.

Earlier, when she'd walked up to Serena as she came out of her residence hall and tried to massage her into answering a few questions, two things were clear during their brief exchange. One, that Serena had been genuinely caught off guard. Nothing in her manner suggested that Rosie had breathed a word to her about Vee and their encounter. Two, that Serena's body language ran several shades deeper than skittish – she was frightened, and not just a little. Serena was prissy and cautious: her ponytail was too severe, she was dressed for the rare burst of sunshine yet still had a cardigan in case the weather flipped again; she wiped the mouth of the Coke bottle with a tissue every time it came around to her for a swig. Serena Fourie was the type to consider all surprises a slap in the face. She was thinking, and thinking fast. If she had anything to defend – or hide, for that matter – they had to act before she regrouped.

'Hide.'

Chlöe scrunched her nose. 'What?'

'Hide, or hiding, is what I'm going to do. Not you – you stay put,' Vee said, dropping to a crouch behind the Polo's bonnet. 'She never saw us together so it's perfect. Now, look over there and tell me what you see.'

'Uhhh. Four girls … terrible fashion sense, very troubled hair. They've got satchels and books, they're laughing, pretending they're not checking out those guys standing–'

'Not what's in front of you, what you *see*. What kind of girls are you looking at? What stands out about the picture?'

'I don't get it,' Chlöe said, after a long pause.

'Four girls, yes, but what flavour? Three vanillas, one …?'

'Café latte?'

Vee flipped a thumbs-up. Maybe Adele's snide observations had some weight to them. *Ian thinks he's better than his upbringing … those kids were raised to respect only one side of their background.* Meaning, by heavy inference, the side that wasn't coloured. Every friend Vee had seen Rosie with was white. Coincidence, maybe, but her high school had a diverse profile. Why then, didn't she hang out with a more mixed group of people? Watching Serena with her posse made Vee wonder if she'd found a nugget to mine.

'No offence, bosslady, but either you're mentally unstable or *really* racist,' Chlöe said, leaning over the hood to talk to Vee. 'Having white friends doesn't mean she's any more likely to open up to me than to you. That's ridiculous. This is the new Mzansi, for heaven's sake.'

'Then hustle over there and prove me wrong. I bet you a hundred rand you can get her to meet us ... you ... somewhere we can talk.'

'What angle could I *possibly* deploy that you haven't already?'

'You're a smart girl, Bishop. Surprise me. Hundred bucks.' Vee pulled up her trouser legs and got comfortable with her ice cream on the pavement.

★

'I take it you're both feeling terribly clever and pleased with yourselves right now?' Serena glared.

Chlöe shifted in her seat and muttered an apology under her breath. Across the table, Vee's smugness was in high beam. The trio took up a booth in a campus bistro, slow on an afternoon that opened onto a Friday night.

Vee gloated in silence. Serena had followed the rap-loving redhead like a lamb, giving Vee the opportunity to sidle up minutes later and 'bump into them'.

Other than winning the bet, there was little to rejoice over, for Serena was proving the antithesis of her awkward younger sister. After five minutes of empty talk and stonewalling, it was clear she was the spokesperson for the Fourie offspring. If Serena wasn't already using her abilities of deflecting, obfuscating and flat-out lying to her advantage in her law studies, then she wouldn't be worth her salt as an attorney in years to come. Because lying she was. She kept an eerily cool head for a girl so young but there was a lie in the mix, and she wasn't giving away specifics to trip herself up.

'None of what I, or any member of my family, have to say has any relevance whatsoever to what happened to Jacqui. If at all something has happened to her, which you or the police have no proof of.'

'Relax, Serena. We're having a normal conversation.' Vee shook her head like she was appalled.

'You have absolutely no right to harass us this way.'

'This isn't harassment. We simply need information, backstory, a quote or two. The family's always the best source to approach. Why not help us out?' Chlöe said.

Now for bad cop. 'Just information,' Vee reiterated, hardening her eyes. 'How can we be fair and objective if we go to print without the family's viewpoint, without allowing them to tell their side of the story? This is your chance to make sure that happens.'

'I don't give a damn what you write.'

'Ah, then, I guess you don't give a damn about what became of your sister.'

Serena's eyes lit. *Fuck off.*

Vee waited for her to hurl the insult in her face and nothing came. Serena's eyes screamed it and her mouth twisted furiously with a desperate need to do the same, but she couldn't bring herself to surrender. Vee didn't blame her. It would be a travesty hearing expletives come out of a mouth that pretty.

'I do give a damn! I *loved* Jacqui. We all did!' Chin trembling, Serena glared at the wall and absently swept her hair over one shoulder. It had likely taken ages to blow-dry to a silky fall of burnt umber, and the ends wisped into sweet curls. Vee felt sorry for poor, gauche Rosie. Next to her sister, she probably resembled her father in a bad weave.

'Then?' Vee shrugged like it was a no-brainer. 'We're here to respect whatever you can share with us, and it'll go a long way.'

Serena's throat worked, her eyelids flickering at the appeal a less stressful option held. It was easy to guess what the thoughts whizzing inside her brain were: the press were relentless and vicious, and once a stench got up their nose, they'd follow at a snarl until they dug up an entire cemetery looking for buried bodies. On the other hand, willingness to cooperate had its merits.

Serena mulled it over and shook her head. 'No. Sorry. Have nothing to add to what you already know, and I doubt anyone else in my family can.' Serena grabbed her tote and got up. The only time her cool slipped was when she turned and added: 'If you have another story, follow that and let this go. Please.'

★

'*This* was your secret errand?' Vee gaped. The only word befitting the house in front of her was 'mansion'. The Cape Dutch-style home was concealed from view by a tidy cluster of oak trees, their new spring leaves popping in. The skirts of the lawn were plush and verdant. A cobbled spine of a walkway snaked up to a veranda creeping with vine and rustic appeal. Vee resisted the urge to press her nose through the wrought-iron bars of the gate and beg the residents within for a crust of bread and a farthing.

'*This* is your house?' she spluttered. 'Why the hell are you doing this job if you live like this? You're out of your mind.'

'How do you know I don't need it?'

Vee jabbed a finger at the house. 'Bish, please.'

Chlöe groaned long and loud. 'I'm not trying to prove anything, all right? This is not my home any more. Trust me, it's a really long story. Just picking up a few things and we'll be out of here.' Chlöe went back to pressing the intercom buzzer over and over.

'And who's that?' Vee asked. A tall, light-haired man strolled down the drive towards them.

'My older brother, Jasper.'

Vee snorted.

'Yes, yes, I know, Jasper Cole … Chlöe Jasmine … we're rich and white. Sue me.' Chlöe put a hand on her hip and pulled a pout Vee would come to know with great affection. 'This isn't as simple as it looks. Please, *please*, can you wait in the car? I won't be longer than ten minutes, promise.'

Vee put her hands up and kicked rocks. Drama download for the work week was over. Bring on the weekend.

17

The teenager's skull smashed into the metal grate. The impact caused the foci of cracks in the bone to splay into hairline fractures. As sewer water emptied out of the underground pipe, dead weight stayed behind: garbage, driftwood, the carcasses of pigeons and one unfortunate cat. On a cement level close to the Black River and the N2 highway, the battered skeleton finally came to rest. Hours passed in a silence broken only by the chatter of vermin. Once again, the surface of the remains began to dry.

Skeletonisation, the decomposition of soft tissue that leaves behind only bone material, is a sure and steady process dependent on temperature, moisture and the action of micro-organisms. If a dead body is left undisturbed. The traveller in the drainpipe was up against much more than structural damage. Its early stages of putrefaction, the process in which the body disintegrates on a molecular and physical level, had begun in a very dry, aerated setting. Due to the constant blast of air rushing past it for several months, the usual destruction caused by bacteria had been impeded. Instead, mummification had begun. Skin and muscle that should have rotted away desiccated into a leathery parchment that hugged the bones. After being submerged for days, the remains were somewhat rehydrated, and the hitchhiking microbes on its surface resumed their busy task.

A rat wandered close for a nibble, flinched and pushed off, disgusted by the tough flesh and layer of dark slime covering the corpse. Some things even rats won't do.

★

Years killed love.

No one ever imagined it happening to their relationship, yet it happened far too often. Maybe time annihilated objectivity, too, for surely not all or even half of married couples were always unhappy. Carina Fourie couldn't care less. If the years had turned her into a graceless bitch, then so be it. She was willing to admit to her part in the saga. If she was a hag, then she had a fine accomplice in her spouse. Ian had a heavy hand when it came to bludgeoning their marriage, but again, she was also responsible. When had she stopped being a supple, fresh-faced young woman who took on life with zest, career with resolve and men with a wanton sparkle in her eye? At forty-seven she was no spring chicken, but by no definition was she washed-up. So when, exactly, had the apathy set in? When had the naked body of a man, her own man, in good shape and appealing to any red-blooded woman, become the pathetic shape of another human being, unalluring?

Since I lost my son. Since we lost our son and this man I call my husband refused to look me in my face and tell me anything but lies.

'What're you thinking, Carina?' Ian moved around the bedroom with the easy prowl of a man in comforting, familiar surroundings.

Comfort he had dedicated intellect and sweat to providing for them, but familiarity he was drifting farther away from on a daily basis.

'You know how much I hate that question.'

A three-piece suit lay on the bed next to her jade silk gown. He leaned over and peeled away the white starched shirt, not bothering as the towel gradually loosened around his waist. Ian had hardly bothered to cover his nakedness in the fresher days of their union. It used to titillate her senseless the way he used to emerge from a shower, tall, brown and glistening. Spread himself along the mattress to air-dry, waiting with a knowing smile for his European temptress to lust him up. To moisten her lips and lashes and face with the droplets on his skin—

That woman was dead. Carina put her powder brush down, deciding to forgo any make-up tonight. Another thing she needn't feel obliged to care about – being sexy, licking dew off horny husbands, or anything else that fell inside that wide circle. She wasn't worried that there might be another pair of willing lips seeing to Ian's dermis outside the confines of their bedroom. There could be one; there might be many; there may be none. There had been Adele, and that was all that would ever matter.

His hair was still wet from the shower, curling and releasing trickles of water down his neck. *Kroes hare.* Kinky hair. Enough black in it to point firmly at his bloodline. The blood her elder daughter secretly wanted out of her as much as those kinks she spent hours blowing and flattening out. The same hair her son had inherited, that all her children had. No nods to her influence.

Her son. It used to be her *sons*; now it was singular. The dead must give way to the living. Her mind was betraying her more often over the years, as it was doing again now, scrambling for reason in fluff. Her eyes met her husband's in the dresser mirror and held them until she broke the moment in cowardice.

'I don't know where to start with you any more, Carina. I don't know what more to say.'

'Then go with your instinct and say nothing,' she snapped. She dropped the hairbrush with trembling fingers. 'Isn't that what we *as a family* have agreed to: silence?'

He flinched slightly, no more than that. The sting behind her oft-repeated accusation that Ian *was* the family, that they only functioned as a successful unit as long as all were in service to him, didn't affect him any longer.

Ian rubbed the bone close to his eyebrows, a sign he was struggling to control his irritation. 'We can't talk to that journalist. We can't live through this again. You know that.'

Who's we?! Carina wanted to scream. Instead, she swept into their en suite bathroom and slammed the door.

Bitterness. Bitterness killed love, and she'd embraced it. Flushed with shame and a giddy sense of triumph, Carina said to herself, *I am bitterness, and rage and regret, and I've killed the love in more ways than one.* She couldn't bring herself to look at the reflection in the mirror as the thought warped through her mind again and again.

I killed the love and happiness in my home. She forced a tiny smile. Well, then, there was nothing like vengeance to light a flame under a rotting carcass.

18

'Lawd' ha mercy,' Vee whispered.

The fir-lined gravel driveway snaking up to the house in front of her was so long you could starve to death trying to walk it. An elegant foyer with marble arches overlooked an immaculate garden, tastefully lit for the evening's festivities. If Chlöe's house was a mansion, the grandeur of this one had no name. A stately sprawl, that was it. The owners were clearly members of the club where champagne flowed with little restraint.

'Hhmm, mah pipo, dey even sef got wata fountain,' she marvelled. 'Lookah dah fat li'l boy playin' harp insah it.'

'Stop acting country and stick to boardroom English,' Joshua said sternly. 'That's a boy *made of stone* with a harp. Although, they are rich enough to pay for a real child to stand in a freezing fountain all night.'

'Now I feel underdressed for all these champagne wishes and caviar dreams.' She fussed with her hair, and caught him watching her with disturbing intensity out of the corner of her eye. 'What? Don't start. I've had a shitty day.'

She'd spent most of it waiting for news on the data on Jacqui's computer. At last 'The Guy', dexterous hacker into private records and acquirer of internet gems, had emailed his findings, and it had crushed her: forty gigabytes of uninspiring junk that any sprite in tune with the times would have on her PC. The one folder Vee had hoped would be pay dirt turned out to be nothing of the sort, just pages of initials, dates and what looked like rand value amounts. It made no sense. What had Jacqui been up to? Running some kind of extortion scam?

'I wasn't. Christ. I was just thinking you clean up pretty good.'

'I clean up exceedingly well. Boardroom English.' Vee snapped her vanity mirror closed. 'And that wasn't what you were thinking.'

'Well, since you're forcing my hand ...' Joshua's mouth turned up a little, 'I was imagining you with just the shoes on, nothing else ...'

Vee slammed the car door. 'Dammit, Allen, you promised me good behaviour, so if you're gonna be carryin' on like this all night—'

'Aww, don't be like that. That's the last one, I swear. Hey, wait up, will you slow down ... Haha, you can't run in heels, can you? Now you better put on your best smile and don't forget I brought you here, ungrateful wench. Ow, shit Vee, you hit like a guy!'

Inside, Vee did her best to keep her lips tightly pressed so her open mouth didn't catch flies. It wasn't like she hadn't seen wealth before, but no two displays were alike, and some display this was. Joshua steered her away from the sparkling decorations towards a waiter with a tray of bubbly flutes. 'I know you have a problem with focus, but that's what you need to be doing right now. That's the host over there: Philemon Jabulani Mtetwa.'

She snorted effervescence. Joshua's Yankee pronunciations never failed to make her feel better about her own awkward attempts. 'You're pathetic. This country's your second home – learn the lingua franca. Any one of the eleven.'

'Bite me, I'm half Indian not Zulu. He's a major player in the investment game. I'm talking millions upon millions.'

'How many did he put into the WI?'

He held up far too many fingers. 'Not him alone, through his satellite companies and co-investors. But let's just say somebody's getting fired if a wing isn't named after him.'

'How does he know the Fouries?'

'They're right over there. Go ask them.'

The couple was certainly not what Vee had imagined. The man was no short, overbearing dictator, but tall and not at all hard on the eye. He was doing a fine job of working the room and making nice, laughing in all the right places and pumping hands with ease and pride. His axis of rotation centred round the squat, speckle-haired Mtetwa, casually dressed himself, and a few other men in expensive, semi-formal attire. Tied to Ian by an invisible string was a fair woman, on the thin side, clad in an unsuitable shade of green that worked up her pallor. Carina was trying far too hard to look flat and uninterested; she resembled her daughter Serena as she did it. Vee narrowed her eyes. Anytime someone went that long without blinking, gremlins were hatching evil inside their skull.

'She looks so … plain.' Vee felt superficial for saying it, but the Carina of her imagination was grander than her husband.

'So plain and … small.' She turned to her date for thoughts and Joshua was gone.

★

Hours later, her nerves were tissue-thin. The buffet was excellent, but there was only so much that mustard-encrusted beef, artisanal bread and spicy prawns could do. Inserting herself into random conversations was easy enough, but extracting useful information was like pulling teeth. Whispers about Mtetwa barely graduated beyond the good ol' Zulu boy made golden on a British education and a passion for business solutions for rural communities. Vee couldn't keep her eyes off Carina, how deadpan she looked, yet her eyes kept flitting around and narrowing, especially in Ian's direction. Any minute now she'd rip an arm off the ice sculpture and take it to her husband's head.

Liquor oiled up the crowd. Vee flitted from one faux-intellectual conversation to the next, soaking up garbled nonsense.

'—problem is that Malema reflects the rotten core of the government! If the crown prince can prance around accusing Anglo American of *raping* the country—'

'—then she of all people shouldn't be living in a dreamland. That's what marriage is, not romance and excitement or even happiness for God's sake, but years and years of—'

'—gay pride. I'm sorry, but not getting on a soapbox for sexual freedom doesn't make me *any* less of a liberal than not having black friends makes me a racist—'

'–tiger! Then this little Japanese guy pops outta the boot, and there's this part with the Mike Tyson punch … Can't explain it, man, you need to just watch *The Hangover*. Best movie *ever*!'

Who are *these people?* Vee sucked in fresh air on the gilded balcony onto which she had escaped. Why couldn't she have been a gossip columnist? They adored these awful parties steeped in chocolate gateaux and the toxic lives of others. And where the hell was Joshua? Ah, yes, of course, her beady eye observed, laughing it up with some hottie in a backless dress. Useless punk.

'Do you mind if I sit here?'

She turned, and nodded at the man who had appeared at her shoulder. She took her dessert plate from the chair.

'Sorry to disturb. I'm not a smoker, but I can't take the drivel in there any longer.' His smile was the first genuine one of the evening. He held out his hand, pulled it back and looked at it with a crinkle of his nose, then wiped it on the front of his shirt. He offered it again. 'Sorry, barbecue sauce there. Marcus Neethling. You work with the hospital?'

Vee shook her head. 'Just a lowly layperson. Who diagnoses all her medical problems using Google, like everyone else.'

'Ha. Really. I find that hard to believe. A lovely woman like yourself looks far too intelligent to trust the internet for reliable medical information.'

Vee smiled. Okay, so the good doctor was angling for more than innocent conversation and fresh air. 'What kind of doctor are you?'

'Psychiatrist. The psych ward staffers are the underdogs at WI. Probably why most of us didn't show up. We weren't even allocated our own wing, yet we're coping with a huge influx of referrals …'

A bell rang in the back of her mind. Psychotherapy plus Neethling. Shit. This was the guy she should've been paying regular visits to, the doctor to whom her old GP had referred her to get to the bottom of her … stuff. The very same she'd been on her way to see on the fateful morning that Jacqui Paulsen's photograph dragged her into a vortex.

'Are you okay? You look like you've just seen a ghost.'

Vee threw her head back and laughed. 'You wouldn't believe it if I told you,' she muttered. Then again … As her mother often said, there were lessons in chance encounters. 'Actually, there *is* something that's been knocking around my brain for a while. A friend of mine is in a psychological quagmire, if you can call it that. I know you're off the clock, but …'

He was open and engrossed as she talked of this fictitious young woman her age, in great health and full of promise. His eyes flicked to high beam when she got to the interesting part: say this woman began, *spontaneously*, to suffer from brief, unexpected and crippling attacks for no apparent reason.

Neethling cocked his head. 'Muscle spasms? Nausea? Dizziness? A paralysing fear that this is the final gong, the world's about to end?'

'Exactly! I mean, yes, come to think of it my friend mentioned those very symptoms.'

'It's a typical panic or anxiety attack, or chronic anxiety disorder if it's been going on for a while.' Neethling was a little hesitant in the beginning about embarking on what was clearly a consultation, but was leaning into it. 'In my opinion, and I deal with more serious mental disorders, but others would agree–'

'*Mental disorder?*'

He laughed and held up his hands. 'Hold on. That sounds too scary. Let's call it a psychosomatic event. It stems from our normal fight or flight response, but because the trigger is sudden and unprovoked, there're a lot of theories as to what causes it. But in a healthy person with no history of drug abuse, other mental conditions or a genetic predisposition … then a good place to start would be here.' He tapped a finger on the side of his head.

Vee hugged her arms to her body. 'What … How would that matter?'

'The body and the psyche express trauma in different ways. All our systems communicate, even when we set up mind-blocks. I guess you could say the body reacts against a conscious effort to suppress the anxiety. Unfortunately, the experience is like having a meltdown.'

'What if …' Vee dropped her arms. They felt naked and useless by her sides, so she grabbed her glass with both hands to hide the tremor in her hands. 'What about hallucinations?'

'Like what, lucid dreaming? Sleep paralysis?'

'No.' God, how she wished. 'A real manifestation of … shapes. Things you could touch if you weren't completely paralysed.'

'Visions of what, exactly?' Neethling looked uneasy.

Vee waved a hand. 'Ahhh. I can't believe I'm about to ask this. What the hell. Can one of these attacks … can they open doors to the other side? Like, make things that aren't real come out of nowhere and … menace you?'

Neethling rubbed the bridge of his nose. Yep, Vee thought. He's going to call the guys in white to drag me away. 'I won't give you a neurology lecture, but anxiety attacks stimulate many areas of the brain. They're intense and can imitate a highly spiritual experience. Joan of Arc? Paul on the road to Damascus?'

'Oh-h-o-o! I thought the reigning scientific theory debunking all that was schizophrenia. Or bipolar disorder. Or boring, Christian nuttery.'

Neethling laughed and put his hands up. 'No comment, on any of that. All I'm saying is brain chemistry is complex. Don't let it fool you – your friend, I mean – into thinking the supernatural is a possibility here. Consider the obvious. Has she ever gone through a huge trauma, physical or emotional? Something she never fully processed or let go of?'

'It depends. I'd have to ask her what she considers traumatic,' Vee said. 'She's seen a lot. Her definition's pretty wide.'

'There you go, then. Examine the past. Panic attacks and PTSD go hand in hand. Death, major life changes, horrific experiences like war–'

The flute stem snapped and slashed her thumb, and the glass tinkled to delicate bits on the balcony floor. A waiter materialised to clean up the mess. Mark Neethling rose to help, but Vee squeezed past him and scuttled off the balcony, leaving him staring after her with a frown.

19

___

'I saw this medical series once,' Vee mused aloud, taking her thumb out of her mouth, 'about horrifying ways to die. This woman cut herself. A small knife cut, and flesh-eating bacteria got in her system and started eating her up and they had to chop her arm off to stop it.'

Joshua examined the cut. 'Nothing's going to dissolve your arm off,' he said. 'While we're on the subject of honesty …'

'We very much weren't.'

'Lately you've been very shady. You're hiding something. Don't forget you already have the talent for theft. Throw that in and you're well on your way to turning into a full-blown criminal.'

Vee put her finger back in her mouth and looked away. She was in no mood to be psychoanalysed twice in one night. She felt stupid enough for giving a virtual stranger access to poke around her life, her guarded hurts. What had she been expecting – that Neethling could magic up a cure in one sitting? 'You should get better friends. The open-book kind, who don't lie or keep secrets.'

He cussed the air blue. 'Why don't you just talk to me? What could be so terrible? And before you answer that, weigh in everything else I already know about you. And you about me.'

This is different. This time I'm being haunted, or I'm possessed, or I'm certifiable. I'm terrified and I don't want you laughing at me. No ... I couldn't bear it if you gave up on me. Quilting together the patches of Jacqui's story was her problem, and the process was much more convoluted than it looked in the movies. Movie ghosts introduced themselves, and then went about sprinkling helpful clues for the intrepid heroine to find. Jacqui was a lazy, taciturn diva.

'I ever told you the story about my Grammah?'

'You've told me a hundred stories about your grandmother. She practically raised you.'

'The other one. The one I never talk about.'

Joshua's eyebrows jumped to his hairline. 'The one that throws bones and shit?'

'She's a *zo*, like a spirit medium ... cleanser, not a witch doctor.' She folded her hands on her lap. 'When I was born, she told my mother I was her 'gift'. That I had a wonder about me, and she would teach me all the *zo* intricacies. There was going to be a ceremony and everything when I got to a certain age.' Vee looked up at Joshua and saw she had his full, horrified attention. 'That's why my mother fell out with her mother and they barely speak to this day. That's why even when I go home I rarely visit her, though she's reformed and not in the spirit business any more.'

Joshua's irises were two onyx planets swimming in an ever-widening ocean of white. 'Are you saying she made you into a witch?'

Vee put her hands over her face and laughed. 'No, dummy. My parents are Anglican snobs, they'd never let shit like that happen. I'm saying ...' What *was* she saying? 'I don't always know what I'm about, what all the things in me are reaching for. I don't want you getting swept up in my mess again. I can handle it.'

'Everything isn't always about you and what you want.'

Vee put her head on his shoulder. 'Of course it is. That doesn't even make sense.' She plucked the tissue that had been wrapped around her thumb out of his hand and tucked it back around. 'I'm ravishing and intense and highly complex. But I'm not myself right now. So don't get all up in your feelings.' She gave him a peck at the corner of his mouth.

'You're right.' He kissed her, briefly, on the lips.

'This is inappropriate.' Vee kissed him back.

It would never go any further.

The mood threw a curve ball, shooting tingles up the back and between her legs. He nipped her bottom lip and she gave a little shudder. She linked both hands around his neck; he dragged her onto his lap; she ran her fingers over his buzz of curls; he moved a hand up her thigh, smoothing her dress aside–

'Whoa!' Vee pulled away.

'What?'

'Sshhhh!' Her mouth dropped open. '*Oh my God, how did I miss that?*'

Joshua sagged. 'Jesus wept.'

Vee barely heard. She called up a blank page in her mind's eye, a table much like the ones she'd used in secondary-school bookkeeping. A clear, nondescript sheet with a line down the middle to separate a credit and debit side. Basic accounting, no mess, no fuss. But suppose that was exactly what Jacqui *hadn't* wanted? What if the files had looked disappointing because they were meant to? If anyone snooped around in Jacqui's room hunting for proof of mischief, for something that looked out of place, all they'd uncover was–

'Absolutely nothing,' she said to herself. She snatched her clutch handbag on the edge of the bench and took out her cell, gave Joshua an apologetic grimace, and dialled. In seconds, the other end picked up. 'Chlöe, finegeh, listen. Remember the mystery folder The Guy sent us today? Yeah, I know, useless. But what if it wasn't?'

She rattled off her theory: the files were a track record of a little informal business. One side was an inventory of all Jacqui's merchandise, and the initial typed next to it was simply the name of the person who'd made the order. A crossed out name meant money and goods had changed hands – transaction sorted.

'I was waaay overthinking it. We know Jacqui liked being up in things. Things cost money; she had to be getting the mah from somewhere. Now I thought about all the ways a clever girl could go about getting spare cash and none of them added up. Adele, forget it. Her pa spoilt her all right, but from what we saw in her room, her acquisition dysfunction was worse than yours, something Ian wouldn't enable. She couldn't have been twisting her oliver for some sugardaddy so he'd pimp her lifestyle. Her best friend would've told us, and Jacqui doesn't strike me as the type. Why be with a cretin like Ashwin if you weren't a romantic deep down?'

'Then what was she up to?' Chlöe replied.

'The obvious. Rosie *handed me* the answer and I didn't get it. Every kid tries their hand at enterprise at some point, right. Rosie said they shoplifted for a while and lost interest. But Jacqui didn't, she just went wholesale on her own. Those bales of clothes in her room, that was it! She was hawking what she was stealing. What better way to make money off other fashion-crazy gossip girls.' Vee chortled. 'Jacqui fuckin' Paulsen. This li'l girl was a mafia market woman.'

Now it all computed, what the brand new clothes in those three plastic bundles were for. Jacqueline had contrived her own ingenious shortcut to the pocket money dilemma.

'Okay, hmmm … I see your reasoning …' Chlöe mulled. Vee pictured her pinching her bottom lip. 'If that *is* the case, she must've been at it for months, pssh, maybe even a year. That was quite a printout we got. Where the hell was the money going?'

'I've got a few ideas. I'm sending you pictures of the things she had lying around in her room; our answer's bound to be in there. I know it's late, but go online if you can, check if any of it was pricey. I'm in the middle of something.' Vee hung up.

Joshua said, 'You're a fantastic date, by the way. In case you were wondering.'

'Sorry.' She kissed his cheek. 'Tell me, what kind of kid were you? I mean, at seventeen? You've told me plenty about your childhood but you do get cagey with the details around high school.'

'Because my teens were weird and stupid. Everyone's are, they're supposed to be. I have little trust or respect for anyone who peaked early. What was *I* like?' He slouched, stretching his arms along the backrest of the bench. 'Horny.' He shrugged. 'Impatient, brooding, obnoxious. Excited that high school, the most confining place ever, was almost behind me. Scared shitless about the concept of 'the rest of my life'.' He paused. '*Super* horny, and obsessed with obsessing over all the action I missed out on.'

'You were still unblemished at seventeen? How did I not know this?' Vee gasped in mock horror. He looked like he'd been fiddling with people's daughters since the first grade. 'But you look like such a ho.'

He shook his head. 'Nah. Learnt on the job. I had a lot to work through … awkward, gangly, a smile to frighten small children.' He flashed a sharky grimace and ran a finger over his teeth. She understood the gesture: braces. So the shit-eating grin was, in part, the flourish of a talented dentist. 'Every girl I wanted was taken, half the time by one of my friends. Wasted a shitload of time on stupid crushes.' He pressed an index finger to his temple. 'Huh. Breakthrough moment. I may have a thing for unavailable women.'

Her Nokia interrupted. 'No need to go online,' Chlöe said. 'These products are all dead expensive. I recognise the brand names: REN, Dr Hauschka, Sisley. La Mer facial moisturiser

– that's liquid gold in a jar, bosslady. If our girl was buying herself status, she fucking knew how to shop for it.'

'How could her own mother have missed all this?'

'No offence, but did *you* recognise REN's mayblossom and blue cypress cleansing gel?'

'Point taken. We'll go through that file again on Monday. I now pronounce you free to enjoy the rest of your weekend. Where are you, by the way?' The clamour in the background was outrageous.

'Joburg,' Chlöe said.

'You *flew* to Johannesburg for the weekend?'

'No, Grandma. Joburg the club. Long Street.' Chlöe ruptured into giggles and whispered, 'Gotta go, someone's writing their number on my boobs.'

Vee hung up and gave Joshua a pained look. 'Can we please leave, before I lose it again?'

20

Vee got her notes in order as, once again, she waited in the paediatric unit's reception, this time to be ushered into Carina Fourie's consulting room.

The last thing she'd expected come Monday morning when she got to her desk was a call from either of the Fouries, so Carina's genial summons to meet at the WI came as a surprise. Vee had listened with no interruption, agreed to the meet Carina at ten-thirty and thanked her for offering an interview. She hung up and sat at her desk, letting the encounter boomerang around her brain. Either the Fouries were up to something – as a rule, people loved the idea of a successful pre-emptive strike and it rarely worked out that way in reality – or they had decided to play it straight.

Vee kept an eye on Carina's door and took advantage of the half-hour of free wifi to browse emails. Things were taking shape. Chlöe had checked in to report that the Sticky Fingers theory was holding up. Several old classmates of Jacqui's had confirmed buying her wares on school grounds at knock-off prices. The headmaster eventually cottoned on to the enterprise and called in Jacqui's parents, threatening immediate expulsion. Adele and

Ian had pleaded ignorance and moderation, and after a lot of negotiation Jacqui's punishment was shaved down: suspension if the goods were returned, and counselling. Her disappearance meant neither had transpired and Jacqui had at least been spared one minor embarrassment.

Why hadn't Adele considered it important enough to mention? Better yet, why not avoid the possibility of meddling questions altogether by getting rid of the evidence? Adele clearly had an unhealthy relationship with her daughter's room, but an oversight like that was just plain sloppy. Vee wondered what Adele had told the case officers who'd examined Jacqui's belongings, that's if they'd caught it at all and questioned her. What Vee was most interested in knowing was how the good doctor had handled his daughter's disgrace. Ian would hardly let something like that go unpunished.

Vee looked up to find Carina standing over her, for how long she had no idea. She closed her laptop quickly, rose and followed Carina into her comfortable, east-facing office.

'My husband will be joining us. I'm sure it'll be more convenient if we both speak to you. More practical, right? We're all busy people.'

Germans and their efficiency. Vee wondered a little guiltily if that was a racist thought to have. Within minutes she was comfortably seated, sipping on an overly strong cup of Jacobs Krönung blend and studying the husband and wife in the sofas across from her as they presented a united and creepily frosty front.

The quick clench and release motions of Carina's right fist were a dead giveaway that wifey was highly tense. Vee had an inkling that Carina called her on her own gumption but that plans had changed. Either she'd chickened out of riding solo through the interview, or Ian had found out and wedged himself in to monitor the proceedings. Vee leaned heavily towards the latter.

Adele had described him well. Ian Fourie commanded devotion, obedience, admiration, the spectrum. Vee didn't go so far as to call it magnetic – there was something warmer and more pleasant about that energy – but Ian did have a pull just by being in the room. In a blue shirt and slacks, shoulders relaxed as he made direct eye contact, he looked the picture of a man at ease, yet his eyes were guarded. He reached to his left and took hold of his wife's hand, but her body language didn't change. Eyes dead ahead, back straight, knees together. Her pale hand looked like a dead fish in his.

'I will start by talking about Heinrich. I'm sure you will want to begin at the beginning,' Carina said. There was a soothing cadence to the trace of German in her accent. She instantly began to look relaxed and strangely happy now she was on the topic of her son. It took a second for Vee to recall that Heinrich had been Sean's proper first name.

'He had acute lymphocytic leukaemia, or ALL. It's a common type of cancer in children and the survival rate is encouragingly high. Sadly for us, he had a very aggressive sub-type, which changes the treatment strategy substantially. He was diagnosed when he was five–'

'Five and a half,' Ian interjected, his voice gruff. Head bent, he cleared his throat and managed to look up, embarrassed. He issued a low murmur and nod for Carina to continue.

'Over the years, he went into remission but the outlook wasn't good. The cancer returned with full force in late 2001. We agreed with his specialists that since he wasn't responding to standard therapy, we would focus our energy on allogenic stem cell transplantation.'

Carina gave a wry smile at Vee's blank expression. ' 'Allogenic' simply means the transplant material would come from a donor who was a genetic tissue match. The stem cells they transfuse can either be from the blood or bone marrow. The best shot at improving our chances was to try both, but first we had to find a good HLA match.'

Vee settled back for a biology brush-up. In short, sufferers needed transplants from donors who matched their human leucocyte antigen, or HLA, type. The HLA complex was made of surface proteins found on white blood cells, the gatekeepers of transplant outcome. The lymphocytes had a search-and-destroy system for killing foreign cells entering the body. It made sense, then, that a high level of genetic similarity between the donor and recipient was critical, otherwise the transplanted cells would be hunted as 'enemies' and annihilated. HLA types were inherited, with parts of the gene coming from both parents. In theory, the odds were good that a child with many siblings would find a match.

'But that's only the science on paper. In reality, it's difficult to find a suitable match, and unfortunately Sean was unlucky. None of the kids was even remotely a possibility.'

Until Jacqui.

The unspoken hung over them like a cloud of napalm.

'Aren't patients commonly put onto transplant waiting lists in case the family angle falls through? Surely Sean was on one, to up his chances?' Vee asked.

The doctors exchanged a weighted look. For a brief second, Ian looked at his wife like a vulnerable, frightened man and Carina looked back with the deer-softness of an understanding wife.

Like a magic trick, they snapped back into formation.

'Yes, he was on the national registry. We even went abroad for a short while to explore options. But, as I said, nothing's guaranteed. Once you venture outside, the likelihood of finding a match drops and riskiness of the procedure goes up. The waiting lists are long, and with Sean's prognosis it could've been too late before we found a donor. In any case, it was then that I found out … I was made aware of …'

Carina swallowed and tried again. 'The option of testing Jacqueline presented itself,' she managed to choke out. Vee refrained from openly arching her brows. 'An option presenting itself' – now there was a euphemism to describe the crash landing of the Paulsens.

The walls flew up after that. Any question that demanded more than a one-word reply, the Fouries covered in minimal, often monosyllabic detail. Had they at any point offered Ms Paulsen compensation for her daughter's donation? How had Jacqui got along with the other children in the years following Sean's death? Could they shed any new light on her disappearance, and had they been fully transparent with the police?

Blank stares and muttered responses.

Vee kept jotting in her notepad, her voice recorder still rolling. *Is it me or does this whole family have a very disturbing vibe?* 'One final question,' she added, lancing a forced smile in the direction of Ian's pointed glance at his watch. Seriously? If anyone's morning had been wasted, it was hers. 'You explained how Sean's body had to be prepped to receive bone marrow cells from his sister.' Every time she pointedly substituted Jacqui's name for 'their sister', she got a response. Ian stayed deadpan but his jaw would clench, and there would be an involuntary jerk of the shoulder or quiver in the hand from Carina.

'Myeloablation, it's called,' Ian nodded. 'As much of his diseased marrow had to be destroyed beforehand. After transfusion, Jacqui's healthy cells would multiply and replenish his supply, like jump-starting his immune system.'

Vee nodded that she understood. 'So Adele had agreed. Sean had been prepped and so had Jacqui. Doctors were standing by. And then, out of nowhere, Adele has a change of heart and takes her daughter home. Right before the operation. What made her do an about-face?'

After an hour of smoke and mirrors, she'd found one loose thread to pull at. Carina dug the fingers of one hand so deep into the back of the other that half-moons of white formed under her nails.

'Adele was scared,' Ian interjected, just as his wife opened her mouth. 'We'd put a lot on her plate and expected an immediate answer. There's never any accounting for how a mother will react in a situation like this, how *any* parent would.'

'The transplant … it never happened, then?' Vee knew the answer but watching them narrate was infinitely more telling than working from notes.

Ian shook his head. 'Jacqui was home for a couple of days as we tried to talk sense into Adele. But like, overnight, Sean got an infection, or maybe the bug had taken hold already and we had missed it. In any case, his immunity was depleted and the doctors couldn't fight it. There was nothing anyone could've done.'

'She could've let her daughter stay in the hospital.' Carina was a statue with moving lips, her shoulders so taut they were nearly brushing her ears. 'She could've allowed Jacqui to stay. The transplant would've gone ahead and Sean might still …' She choked, breathing deeply to collect herself. She turned to Ian. Vee could only see her in profile, and felt a rush of gratitude she didn't have to be the one facing that level of contempt every day. 'That woman had no right to decide my son's fate. You gave her the power to let my son die.'

'Carina, please,' Ian quavered. 'It could've happened at any time. The risk of a fatal infection is always high in–'

Carina stood up, opened the door and walked out.

Interview over.

21

The *slap* chips on the plastic plate did a waltz under the aimless manoeuvring of Marieke Venter's fork. Across the table, Vee joyfully fed her face with a mutton bunny chow. She adored street food – the cultural nuances, the brazen messiness and flirtation with questionable hygiene, how you needed to tuck into it with both hands. Best dining experience ever. After years of boarding-school slop and refugee rations, nothing beat the sidewalk for grab and go's.

Gravy dribbled down her wrist and she licked at it joyfully.

'It's good, right?' Marieke preened. The food kiosk was her special place, one of a few close to the garage at which she could get great food. It was packed, but Marieke had said a few words to management and got a table outside under the striped awning. 'People say this lady makes the best curries and fish and chips in Cape Town. I'm always here on my break.'

Vee took a swallow of beer and managed a ladylike burp. 'They sure ain't lyin'.' Lunch out of the office was a welcome change.

She wiped her mouth on a napkin and waited for Marieke to work around to the conversation she was itching to have. Twenty minutes into lunch and the voice recorder had gathered nothing but small talk. But Marieke had called, so the ball was in her court. Vee was on a streak today, what with all the verbal diarrhoea and people calling her up to act as the commode.

'You're not what I expected.' Pale eyes gave Vee a once-over and skittered away. Marieke mashed a chip with her fork and ate it. 'How come your name's Johnson?'

'It's a long story.' Vee stretched and fumbled under the table, trying to undo the button of her jeans undercover. She was definitely getting a takeaway, mutton curry with rice this time. 'In a nutshell, I'm related to the president of my country. We're descended from a royal tribe, so we automatically get to rule.'

Marieke's eyebrows reached for her hairline. 'Tjo, really! So how come you're living here instead of rolling in it at home?'

Bless. Here was an unspoilt soul. Marieke looked about Chlöe's age, but aside from the perkiness they couldn't have been more different. Vee grinned and did a comical shrug.

The joke finally sank in and Marieke burst out laughing. 'Oi, you're messing with me! Of course you're not related to a *president*.' She stirred the mess on her plate. 'That's what I mean by you're not what I expected. Especially since you called so many times. I thought you'd be one of those reporter types, following us home with cameras and harassing us by the door. Or like cops do, grab you off the streets and beat you up till you talk.'

'I'm not allowed to kick ass any more. My boss made me go for sensitivity training.'

Marieke gasped. 'Oh my word, you mean you actually used to –' She caught on quickly this time. She giggled and wagged a finger at Vee. 'You do that a lot.'

Marieke relaxed. Vee soaked in the hum of the restaurant, letting ambient conversation and the beat of Afro-pop music from the speakers envelop their table.

Marieke cleared her throat. 'I need you to understand my brother. To really get him, so you get where he's coming from in all this. Ashwin's a good guy. He's had his moments over the years, but he's always been there for us.'

Ashwin was the eldest of three, Marieke explained, and she was in the middle. From problems in school to minor run-ins with the cops, he'd made a name for himself as the black sheep of the family. Carousing with a bad lot had blossomed into gang-level exploits. Their father had battled for years with diabetes until he'd lost. Shunted into man-sized shoes, Ashwin had taken over the garage. Vee read between the lines easily enough: putting bread on the household table was more Marieke's responsibility than her brother's.

'Is it true that he's got two children with former girlfriends?'

Marieke nodded a curly head. 'He pays full maintenance. I see to it.' She rushed on, 'Not that he wouldn't if I didn't; of course he would. He loves his boys. I'm not even sure if they're both his. One of the mothers is such a bloody gold-digger, but he does the right thing.'

'Which gang did he run with back in the day?'

'It wasn't even a real gang. They broke off from this other group of losers and started calling themselves The Lynxes. Then they weren't sure if 'lynxes' was the right word so they cut it down to just Lynx … They had these horrible tattoos that looked like a dodgy ostrich. Shem man, no wonder nobody took them seriously.'

Riled up now, Marieke dished the dirt on Ashwin's tempestuous relationship with Jacqui, none of which was news. Vee waited her out. This one was a distance runner; she liked to warm up to the meaty stuff.

'After Jacqui went missing, everyone assumed Ashwin was behind it. The way they were always fighting, making up and breaking up … I couldn't blame them. But I know him. He's done some stupid things, but he's not that stupid to commit murder because he got dumped.'

'But imagine how bad it looked to the police. He had a record, and he was jealous and hot-tempered. Jacqui ended the relationship, and people knew he'd hit her before—'

'She asked for it,' Marieke said.

'The cops basically had to hold him for questioning. As far as they knew, he was the last one to have seen her alive.'

'What they did was illegal! They dragged him in *three times*! They let him rot in a holding cell for an entire weekend. Do you know what happens in holding cells in this country?'

She gripped the edge of the picnic table and stuck her chin out over the table. 'No one asks questions in a holding cell. They don't care what you're in for. They did things to him that no one would wish on their worst enemy, that no man would *ever* talk about even with a gun to his head. Ashwin screamed and called for help …'

She swallowed hard and looked away. 'If he wasn't fucked up enough before Jacqui, he definitely was after that.'

Vee tried with great difficulty to phrase her question with delicacy. 'Are you saying—'

'*Yes!*' Marieke's hand shot out as if to cover Vee's mouth. She caught herself and dropped her arm. The agony in her eyes and mottling of her cheeks made it clear she had no intention of entertaining a conversation about her brother's ordeal. 'That's exactly what I'm saying.'

22

A white Opel Astra sat across the street from the cosy house with an orange picket fence. The driver had been sitting in the vehicle for close to three hours, working through bags of junk food and recycling his own stale air. A faint smell of farts hung over him.

At about 8 p.m., the tenant of the house drove up in a Toyota Corolla and idled in front of the remote-operated garage door. The man in the Opel imagined the driver stamping her finger on the button of the garage remote, irritation growing at its unresponsiveness. He knew the door wouldn't open, because he'd disconnected the wires. Eventually, the driver plunged from her car's warmth into the evening drizzle. She held a magazine over her hair and yanked at the hinge mechanism, trying to operate the gate manually. It was a clumsy struggle, what with a laptop bag strapped across her chest and only one free hand, but finally it gave. Unaware she was being watched, Voinjama Johnson scrambled for shelter and drove inside.

She hurried back out to shut the gate and jumped. There was a kid in the driveway.

The boy was anywhere from nine to twelve, so small and thin it was hard to tell his age, and dressed in a shabby tracksuit top. He shivered under the open garage door, cowering, one hand outstretched for small change. Opel Man watched with interest, waiting for the tall woman to shrink in fear and drive the street kid away. Instead, she pulled him out of the wet and said something to him. The boy kept his head down and shuffled his feet. There was a language barrier, it seemed. She used her hands a lot, and the boy didn't say much in response.

A dog emerged from the house, jumped off the back porch and pushed open the gate of the picket fence. Neither the woman nor the boy saw it, or they were too engrossed in their exchange to pay it any mind. The dog padded across the road, stopped right in the middle of it and stared, oblivious to the rain. It was a huge animal, more like a wolf than a dog. One of those sled-pulling breeds from snowy lands. Its coat was jet black, with smaller tufts of pure white around the ears and underside. Something about the way it didn't bark, growl or advance made the creature a lot more threatening.

The dog's blue eyes were questioning. They asked the Opel driver what the fuck he was doing skulking around, and how a very different kind of conversation would be had if he didn't push off. The Opel driver stared back into the dog's eyes, a little mesmerised. As if to stress the point, the dog took a step closer. The Opel burst into life and ground into gear. The last thing the driver saw before he sped off was the woman crossing the road and trying to peer into the car, a curious frown on her face.

*

Vee gave the shivering child a warm blanket, sandwiches and a hot drink. The damp magnified his body odour to an unbearable hum, but he refused to remove anything other than his old sneakers. He didn't say much, having sussed out by now that her Afrikaans was non-existent. He muttered a thank you for the ten rand note, and finished the sandwiches and hot chocolate in silence.

Vee left him and retreated to the veranda with a cup of Ovaltine, where Monro crouched on the stairs, staring out into the rain. Vee leaned against his warm fur. The strange car was gone but Monro would play sentry all night, radiating stern disapproval. It was his job to protect their home from harm, and she had no business interfering.

'You jeh comin' sit down heah de whole night?' she said. Monro snuffled, never taking his eyes off the street. She squinted into the night, straining to catch a glimpse of whatever it was, if there was indeed anything, that his canine senses were picking up. 'Nobody's trying to kill us in our sleep.'

Being away at work all day was hard on both of them. Part Siberian husky and part timber wolf, the husky was an intelligent breed of working, running dogs. On weekends, he could streak to his heart's content in open fields, but evening walks and a backyard littered with chew toys were not enough. Circumstances like these, sprinkled with excitement, were few and far between. Monro gave her a long look, surprisingly human in its condescension, licked her face and resumed his lookout.

'Ehn. Dah yor biznis o,' Vee gave up, and went back inside.

The kid was gone. The lounge and kitchen were empty, as were the plate and mug on the table. Vee checked upstairs. For all she knew, he was lying in wait for her with a weapon. She hadn't checked his pockets. The possibility of a boy that skinny leaping out of a closet with a butcher knife didn't fill her with dread, but safe was better than dead.

In the end, all that was missing were the blanket and a bulb from a lamp in the lounge. Her computer, handbag, cell phone and wallet were still there. Vee felt bad. She'd wanted to give him some new sneakers; not that anything she had would fit, but it was better than what he was relying on now. The blanket, at least, would add some extra comfort to whichever rough spot he laid his head on at night. She looked over her pile of work things on the lounge table and noticed that the Paulsen case file wasn't where or how she'd left it. A streak cut across the smiling picture of Jacqui stapled to the front of the folder, likely dirt from the boy's fingers when he was nosing through it. He had also splashed some cocoa, and the photo was soaking it up and turning opaque. Vee sighed and got a cloth to mop it up.

Parked well out of sight of Vee's front walk was another car, a BMW this time. A different, braver man languished against the door of the driver's side, hands in his pockets, watching and imagining Vee's movements within the house.

He pictured her eating, much too quickly and standing up, rifling through her unfinished assignments. She would watch the news with the top button of her pants undone, the sound on mute. She preferred newspapers; if she had to follow reports of a world falling to ruin, the printed page was less depressing than live images. She'd brush her teeth sitting on the toilet, or decide sleeping alone meant she didn't have to bother. She'd make plaits in her hair to protect it during the night and finger-comb the waves out in the morning. It was unlikely she missed his presence or still dreamt about him, and the thought hurt like hell.

The man considered going up the walk and knocking on the door. He chewed on the odds of making it further than a few feet from his car, contemplating the very real presence of Monro as much as he knew the dog contemplated his. It was late; showing his face could wait another day. He had wasted enough valuable time, anyway. Titus Wreh blew out a breath, got back in his car and drove on.

23

The wall ran into Marieke Venter. Hard.

At twenty-two, Marieke knew there were many perfectly innocent sayings that had lost meaning, thanks to society's perversion. 'We're just friends', for instance. She and Ryan from the garage were 'just friends', although very little of what they did together could be qualified as friendship, much less innocent.

'Walking into a wall' was another example. Lots of people, through their own clumsiness, walked into walls. Accidents happened. She was making a conscious choice that she wasn't having her ass kicked by her own brother, but rather that one of the four walls of the house they shared had chosen to forcefully run into her. By tomorrow, she would have come up with a better excuse for her swollen face.

Ashwin rammed into her from behind, using the full weight of his body to shove hers into the cold cement. Marieke choked on a scream, her jaw crunching into the wall. She tried to wriggle and felt something hard, probably his knee, digging into the small of her back.

'Ashwin, please …' she moaned, gulping down the bloody saliva pooling near a loose tooth. 'Please, I didn't tell her anything!'

He laughed in her ear. There was no alcohol on his breath, and Marieke's heart sank. Ashwin sober was a lot more dangerous.

'Lying bitch,' he growled, striking her head with the flat of his hand.

Ten minutes earlier, he had walked in on her having supper. The look on his face had made her mouth go dry. He knows about Ryan, her first thought had been. The rule was never mess with other employees, although she suspected Ashwin meant for her never to get involved with any man at all.

When he'd asked what she'd done over lunch that afternoon, she'd known that he knew. Pieter must've told him. She'd forgotten to cover her tracks by telling Pieter to forget Miss Johnson completely.

She had opened her mouth to lie and he had slapped her so hard the chair had almost toppled. She had grabbed the table to steady herself. Ashwin had made a grab for her, too. At first she'd thought he was reaching out to help, that his anger had immediately dissolved and he'd come to his senses.

But he'd gripped her by the shirt and dragged her to her feet, shaking her and shouting. What the fuck did she say to the journalist? How dare she talk to the press about their private family business? Marieke had started to cry, blubbering that she hadn't said anything and Voinjama Johnson wasn't from the press, she worked for a fashion magazine. Ashwin had shaken her harder and she'd spilled: they'd met for lunch, she was trying to help him, to make sure it was absolutely clear he hadn't done anything wrong to Jacqui.

His irises had turned to chips of dirty ice at the mention of that name. 'You made it worse!' he'd bellowed, and slapped her again. Marieke had screamed as she had gone down, her chin connecting with the edge of the couch, cutting her cries short. She had rolled onto the floor, dizzy and panting as the warm taste of iron had rushed onto her tongue.

Someone had banged on the front door, one of the neighbours. A woman's voice had shouted a frightened question and Ashwin had scuttled to the door and locked it. He had stridden back and yanked Marieke up, demanding to know what else her stupid mouth had said. Marieke had known he only wanted to know one thing. But never in a thousand hells would she admit to sharing his private shame, to confessing to another soul about the rape in police custody that was still eating him up inside.

'You lying bitch.' Ashwin's voice clogged with tears. His body shook with sobs and he put his cheek against the back of her head, disappointed at what she had made him do. 'You women are all the same, all lying bitches.'

Ashwin crushed the back of her neck with his forearm. Marieke gurgled and writhed against the wall as her head started to balloon, her vision blossoming red. The last thing she heard before she slumped out of consciousness was Ashwin's voice telling her over and over again that she was the bitch. Women were the bitches, not him – never, ever him.

24

'It was for tik,' Chlöe said sagely. 'The light bulb that street kid took. You hear about these addicts breaking into houses and not stealing anything but bulbs. They smoke tik out of them.'

'Oh, wow. That's *news* to me,' Vee said, rolling her eyes.

Chlöe pursed her lips.

'Oh, come off it, Bishop. Every journalist in the Western Cape has covered some story or other on meth and street junkies. Where to get it, how they cut it, how they use it. Hell, for one assignment this lady of publicly traded pleasures ...'

'A what now?' Chlöe frowned.

'A public woman. Dammit, Princess Di – a prostitute. She described, *graphically*, how they insert crystals up the brown corridors of their clients to get them off. Please don't make me explain–'

'I get it, I get it, stop,' Chlöe said quickly. 'I just thought, erroneously I now see, that *you* didn't get why the kid did it. You've been staring into space since you told the story. It's creepy.'

Vee left the window and eased into her swivel chair. The office was shrinking; *that* was creepy. They'd been going at it since morning and nothing was tying up.

Like where Philemon Mtetwa fitted in, for instance. Vee knew there had to be more going on under the gloss of nouveau riche entrepreneurship, so she took it upon herself to root around in his backyard. Zilch. Nothing germane anyway, though some of it would've made riveting headlines elsewhere. Investment-wise, Mtetwa dabbled in shades of grey closer to black, not to mention a few women his wife wouldn't be overjoyed to learn about. The climb to the top was steep, and victors seldom made it purely on talent, resolve and integrity. Mtetwa was no exception. For their purposes, they had nothing.

One small detail stood out, though. Eight years ago, Mtetwa had undergone a major cardiac operation at the then Claremont Life and Medicare Clinic. During the same period, one Sean Fourie had been at the butt end of the national transplant registry. Strangely enough, his name had shot to the top during the months preceding his death. Philemon Mtetwa had a revamped heart that was clearly thumping fit. Ian Fourie was an excellent cardiologist whose clients included some of the richest men in the country. It was hardly a huge leap.

'I'm saying it *is* a leap,' Chlöe said.

'It's too much of a coincidence to be nothing. You're new at this. Don't dismiss what's right under your nose because it looks easy. Oftentimes the thing we think happened, is the thing that happened. This shows that the WI isn't the only link between these two, and by this afternoon we'll have proof.'

At that very moment, The Guy was skulking through cyberland, hacking through walls with his prying, nimble phalanges. Getting into the WI's old patient records would be like picking his teeth. It wouldn't be long before he emailed scans of Mtetwa's medical file from 2002, detailing everything from which drug regimen he'd been on to how many times a day he'd squatted over the toilet.

'I bet you eight years ago Ian was Mtetwa's doctor, and he probably made the diagnosis that saved his life. Working that kinda magic can buy a lot of gratitude,' said Vee. She recalled Rosie's words to the effect that her father only had time to spare on rich, diseased old men. Someone that dedicated was bound to have buddies with clout.

'How could a man who gets handed a new lease on life stand by and do nothing a year later when he hears your son is terminal and desperately needs a transplant? That he has to wait his turn on some list with a thousand other nobodies? Mtetwa's got the power to bump a kid to the top of a registry.'

'Fine, let's say I buy that.' Chlöe spread her palms, and Vee noticed they were covered to the wrists in inky scribbles, personal notes she'd been taking all day. Vee warmed with pride. Her protégé was turning into a real newswoman. 'Let's say Ian and Mtetwa have more than a business relationship. If he owes Ian a debt of gratitude, then yes, making some calls would be a great way to pay it back. But Sean got a match *before* his spot on the registry even came into play, so that's a grand gesture totally wasted. And, more importantly, what does it matter? If these two men were playing 'scratch my back and I'll scratch yours', what does it have to do with Jacqui?'

Vee rubbed her temples hard, trying to defy anatomical barriers and massage her overheated brain. 'All right, I haven't thought that far yet. But I know whatever the Fouries needed to do to keep their boy alive, they did. And it ties in with Jacqui's disappearance.' For heaven's sake, Carina, the embodiment of feminism and modern education, sacrificed her pride and approached the mistress for help. 'It all comes back to Sean one way or the other. We just need to find the connection.'

She scrawled on the list on the wall-mounted chalkboard: find the connection. Medical connection number one: find Rachelle Duthie. The nurse's involvement with Sean's therapy had been key. She was still practising and living in the city, but they hadn't fixed a time to speak with her. Vee tossed the stub of blue chalk, noting a few other points were yet to be crossed off. Why the hell couldn't anyone locate Bronwyn Abrams, for a start?

Chlöe licked melted chocolate off a KitKat wrapper. 'Why d'you keep pushing the Ian angle? Arrogant, career-advancing jerk he may be, but Jacqui was still his child. Kids drive parents crazy all the time, but you gotta be one hell of a psychopath to actually kill them.'

Vee nodded grudgingly. 'He knows something, though,' she muttered. Ian had the most powerful hand, and that spelled motive. The rest were a pack of scrambling jokers in comparison.

'I'm liking Ashwin for this, big time,' Chlöe went on. 'As you said, the most obvious scenario tends to be the truth. He has a violent history and sounds immature. I say Jacqui tried to end it one final time, they had a huge argument and things got out of hand. Accidents like that happen every day.' She shook her head, eyes adrift. 'Women are evil, twisted sirens. They love you one minute and then flip their shit, blame you for it and crush you like a cockroach.'

Vee cocked her head.

'Ahem. Crime of passion is what I'm getting at.'

'Where did it take place? Yes, the mechanics saw them get into it at the garage on the day she disappeared, but they also saw her leave. He wouldn't be stupid enough to go ballistic in broad daylight in front of half a dozen witnesses.'

'He was stupid enough to slap her around in public before, so methinks that makes him contender number one for murder.' Chlöe puffed her cheeks. 'Let's say she left and he followed her. He followed her by car, they made nice, she got in … they fight again, and this time he kills her.'

'What did he do with the body, Bishop? A human body doesn't just vanish. The police searched his car and house; they practically went up his butt crack with a microscope.' Vee flinched. 'Poor choice of words.'

'You think?' Chlöe sniggered. 'Okay, maybe he didn't kill her right away. Say he held her captive for a few days, just to scare her. But after the hell he'd been through with the police, and with the whole community ready to torch him with no proof, he started blaming Jacqui for everything and snapped. Or maybe he meant to let her go, but by then it had got so out of control that he had to keep her quiet.'

'And maybe he smuggled her through the Underground Railroad and set her free in Canada. That's too many maybes, Chlöe.' Vee plonked back down and put her feet up on the desk. No matter which way she squirmed, the twinge in her lower back wasn't letting up. They'd been at it for too long; they needed a recess. 'Ashwin doesn't have the smarts to've kept a mami peppe like Jacqui hostage for long, especially not with all those eyes on his every move. Somebody would've noticed a false move.'

The cobalt blue of Chlöe's eyes sharpened to azure. She took the chocolate-smeared pacifier out of her mouth. 'Oooh, what's a mami peppe? Sounds sexy.'

'It's ...' Vee flapped a hand. How would one describe it in the Queen's language? 'Like a hot-blooded woman, a feisty geh.'

'Geh meaning girl?' Vee nodded. Chlöe murmured the phrase to herself a few times, doing her best to mimic the right accent. 'I like it,' she tittered. 'It does sound hot. Hey, am I a mami peppe?'

'No,' Vee snapped. 'And if you don't take that goddamn wrapper outta your mouth, I swear to God ...'

'But I'm huuuuungry ...'

Like a winged messenger from heaven, a colleague stuck his head in. 'You guys ordered the pizza? The delivery guy wants to leave it in the foyer. You better get out there before the vultures descend.'

Chlöe smiled coquettishly at Vee, raising and lowering her lashes like a lost puppy. The look wasn't new. She was broke, too broke to chip in for lunch. Vee sighed and got up. The tin of petty cash in the receptionist's office had better have enough in it. She damn sure wasn't paying for a communal meal out of her own pocket. If Portia wanted a stellar output, it was her duty to feed the hungry slaves that made the magic happen.

25

The line of cars waiting for the lights to flick 'go' blocked Lucas Fourie's line of vision. He squinted at the brick high-rise of brown and cream that his Garmin satnav had led him to, not sure what he was watching for. He needed to be in a spot with a better vantage point, but the thought of making an illegal U-ie in traffic and parallel parking in an available slot closer to the building made his armpits moisten. Traffic officers loved to bust fools who made stupid moves like that in the centre of town. Lucas liked to believe he was a guy who enjoyed a touch of predictable peril, if there was such a thing, and no more.

A woman pushed through the glass double doors, holding what looked like a pizza box. She paused on the sidewalk and looked directly across the street, her hand a visor against the sun. Lucas held his breath. He needn't be any closer to recognise the woman he'd been shadowing, the proud owner of the black wolf-monster. Had she spotted him? Not likely; he'd been too careful. He decided to sit tight.

Vee threw caution to the wind and jogged across the busy road, forgetting that lunch was still in her hand and Chlöe would be mewling with indignation back inside. She was paying for the delivery when the white Opel Astra caught her eye. True, the city was awash with white budget buys, and shabby Opels made up a significant proportion of that number. But twice in fewer than twenty-four hours couldn't be a coincidence, not when the first two numbers on the licence plate matched what she'd managed to see last night.

She sidled closer, expecting the car to burst to life and spin into the traffic, knocking her down. It didn't move. She peered through the windscreen at the man in the driver's seat, sitting as still as could be. In fact, it almost looked like he was trying to *think* himself invisible, the way small children did when they were in big trouble or playing a game. He was chubby, sweaty and kitted out from head to toe in black, except for a khaki cargo jacket. Covering half his face was a baseball cap and pair of tinted sunglasses.

I'm officially in the worst movie ever, Vee thought.

The journalist tapped on the window and made a beckoning motion. Lucas remained immobile but fluttered internally, unsure what to do. How had she seen him? Maybe she'd go away eventually. Instead, she leaned close to the glass and mouthed, 'Get out of the car, please.'

He complied. He had no choice. When they were face to face, she stood about a head over him, but he also noted she was wearing a pair of modestly heeled shoes.

'Who are you and what do you want?' She didn't look at all frightened. He'd expected her to be more shaken up.

'Lucas,' he muttered, then repeated with more confidence: 'I'm Lucas Fourie and I wanted to, um, talk with you.'

Her expression cleared and her shoulders relaxed. Murmuring a long 'ohhhh,' she looked him over. He knew what was going through her mind: that he wasn't as tall as his father, or as attractive, despite the resemblance. That he was less a man and more a boy encased in stubborn baby fat. That he was a terrible stalker.

'So.' She placed her box on the hood of the car. 'You know where I live *and* where I work. Did it occur to you at any point to walk up to one of those doors, knock and introduce yourself? To avoid having to do all this?' She fluttered her hands on this last point, indicating the mild insanity of having to confront strange guys in parked cars outside her job.

'Sorry,' he said. 'I thought you'd come looking for me, and when you didn't, well ... I sort of decided to come looking for you.'

'*Why* would I be looking for you?'

Lucas's head snapped back and he narrowed his eyes. 'Because,' he said, then stopped, floored that his motives weren't obvious. Didn't this woman investigate things for a living? 'Because you went looking for everybody else. You know, to ask all those questions about Jacqui and the police case and the past and everything. Don't you wanna ask me stuff, too?'

The chubby boy looked hurt and kind of flabbergasted, like a kid unfairly passed over during a schoolyard pick. It was hard to believe he was older than Serena. Vee mashed her lips together, keeping her laugh under her ribs. This family was intent on driving her batshit.

'As it turns out, I've gathered all the relevant information I need. And I'm sure your family will be happy to hear that, for now at least, I won't be harassing any of you. So thanks for dropping by and offering your help, but it really isn't necessary.'

The dig worked. Blood rushed to his cheeks and curled around the tips of his ears.

'What d'you mean, my help isn't necessary? I *knew* Jacqui. She was my sister, too! I had as much to do with her vanishing act as anybody else!'

Vee raised her eyebrows. Vanishing act. So Lucas was on the team of those who believed Jacqui had ditched the humdrum for bright lights somewhere more exciting. The outrage on Lucas's face was near impossible to fake. It convinced her they'd been right to exclude him from their enquiries. This guileless man-child didn't have a hand in murder and a cover-up.

He misread her expression as an accusation. 'No, no, I didn't mean it like that. I don't mean I *helped* her bugger off or do something stupid. Or ...' he gulped, 'that *I* did something horrible to her. I'm saying we were close. I could help with information.'

Vee crossed her arms. Cool, if he insisted on playing. 'All right. There is one thing that keeps running around in my head, and you'd be the best person to clear it up. When you say y'all were close, how close do you mean?'

Lucas looked blank.

'Were you having a sexual relationship with your sister?'

He took a step back and his chin dropped to his neck, a hundred twitches zipping across his face. Vee did a quick read on him. He was genuinely appalled and disgusted by the idea, but she sniffed something else lurking in the background. So Rosie was right: most of the lusting *had* come from his side. The fantasy hadn't been realised, but Lucas had certainly thought about it in shameful, wanton detail. Vee automatically had little doubt that if Jacqui had allowed it – and there was no question she'd held all the power – the line into the unthinkable would have been crossed. A highly unlikely pairing, though; Lucas wasn't in her league and a girl like Jacqueline would've made sure he'd known it.

Lucas nearly swallowed his tongue in his jumbled spew of denials. His heart was thumping so hard he was certain it was audible above the downtown grind. Rosie, that miserable moron, and her stupid mouth. But nothing had ever happened, *nothing*.

The Johnson woman sliced him up with her eyes all the while he babbled. It appeared she believed him, because finally she placed a hand on his arm and squeezed. Her skin was a deep, burnished brown next to his.

'Go home, man. Really, I don't need you for anything.' The smile she flashed was kind and lightly teasing, but he knew pity when he saw it. Her teeth were small and white, like those plaster casts the dentist used for demonstrations on proper oral care. She wrote his number down on the lid of the pizza box and promised to reach out if circumstances changed. With that, he was dismissed.

Lucas got back in his car and hyperventilated after she walked away. He watched her all the way to the other side of the street, where she stopped to open the pizza box. He continued watching as a man came out of nowhere and jumped her from behind.

ANATOMY OF A MURDER
Call me

The train was packed. Jacqui reached the station in good time and sprung for the extra one rand fifty that separated first class from third. This time of day, a ticket was no guarantee of a seat but managing to elbow out a standing spot was good enough. Much as she was ashamed of thinking so, smell was a deal-breaker. If it made her a snob that she found the air in the first-class cars more pleasant, then so be it.

A pregnant woman boarded as soon as Jacqui plopped into a seat. Jacqui tried ignoring her and pretending to fixate on the view outside the window, but couldn't do it. The dark-skinned woman gave her a bright, grateful smile as she lowered herself into Jacqui's seat.

More and more people filled the compartment, until bodies were mashed skin on skin. Sporting team colours, one group started up a catchy song while others tried blowing their vuvuzelas up at the ceiling. Jacqui groaned, remembering that Ajax Cape Town and Orlando Pirates had a league match at Newlands Stadium that day. It must've just let out, and this mob of *domkops* was heading to the central station in town.

Jacqui let her mind wander over the noise. The call she'd got during the tennis match with the girls was still eating her up. The whole point of today was to offload stress and have fun. To stop feeling like a liar and a fraud who was stretched in a hundred different directions. Picking up her cell had poured cold water over all of that.

Absent-mindedly, she reached for an ear and fondled the silver hoop piercing with a cross attached. It drove her mum crazy that she hadn't outgrown the habit, but the squashy feel of her earlobe was comforting, especially when she ran her finger over the outline of the cross.

Being born again made it easier to ditch more and more of her old self and embrace the new. It wasn't *always* easy, but she was catching on. Shoplifting, for instance – over and done. She'd miss all the cool treats and comforts she could buy with the stuff she sold, but it wasn't a path the Lord wanted her to continue on. And Tamara. Lord Almighty. How much more difficult did it have to get to stay friends with her, to remember why they'd even *become* friends? They used to be inseparable, and now they couldn't have a decent conversation without Miss Judgemental taking the piss out of her choices.

Tamara was stupid if she thought Jacqui didn't know she'd stolen her Nikes after tennis, just like she knew Tamara had made a play for Ashwin. The sneakers were ill-gotten gains, the finest sporting footwear she possessed, but Jacqui felt she could let it go. And she could let Ashwin go, too, but not to her girl. If Tam wanted to stay a bitch forever that was her own lookout, but friends didn't stand by and let stupid mistakes get repeated. This time that shit might actually stick and Tam could end up being his *wife* and baby mama number three. They weren't cool like back in the old days, but Jacqui wasn't going to idle by and let that happen.

And you're still saying words like 'shit', she scolded herself. Old habits died hard. The phone conversation pushed a nagging finger at her conscience, like a curious child toying with a rotting animal. It was going to be difficult, but she had one more slightly dirty deed to commit before she hung up her boots. It was a case of doing wrong to do right, and she hoped to God that He could forgive her. And–

The train squealed to a stop. Car doors squeaked open and passengers nudged and muscled out. In the bustle of bodies, Jacqui barely managed to hang on to her gym tote. At last, the doors suctioned closed and there were a few seats available.

Jacqui slid into one, thinking it was time to return the call and check how things were going at the other end. She went through her tracksuit pockets and came up empty. Where had she put her cell phone? Minutes later, she was in a mild panic as she turned the bag and all its compartments inside out onto the empty seat next to her.

She'd boarded the train with a phone. Now it was gone.

26

Chlöe came through the foyer just in time to see the attack. A man she didn't recognise rocketed out of a parked car with such ferocity that Vee didn't have time to react. The pizza box went flying as she stumbled, arms out to brace her fall. She came down rough on her knees and skidded face first into the pizza, smearing her white top and the side of her face.

The guy wasn't finished. He sank both hands into her hair and tried to drag her back up. Vee screamed and socked a punch into his stomach. The man bent double and let out a sound like air draining out of a balloon. Vee had time to gather her wits. Only just. Screaming an incomprehensible war cry, the man lunged again and they almost went down together. Punches, scratches and grunts flew.

'Stop!' Chlöe screeched. It struck her that an assault was going down right in front of her, less that a fortnight into her job, and she wasn't doing anything to stop it. She bobbed around the scrabble, not sure how to get in and separate them. Vee's body kept blocking her. The man created an opening by grabbing Vee by the neck and letting loose another roar as he shoved her. Chlöe flinched at the sound of bone connecting with the base of a nearby streetlamp.

The commotion brought people out of the building. Chlöe nearly burst into tears when she saw Chris, one of the security guards, burst through the front entrance at a run. Vee was slumped over, keeping her balance by holding on to the streetlamp. The man made for her again. She kicked out with as much energy as she had left and got him in the crotch. He crumbled to his knees and Vee collared him and slammed his head into the concrete.

'No!' Chlöe grabbed Vee around the waist and hauled her off. Judging from the manic glint in her eyes she wouldn't rest until her attacker's head was a bloody mess. Shaking, Chlöe held on to her as best she could. Onlookers gathered and rubbernecked as Chris and another guard pulled the assailant up, keeping a good grip on his arms and a wary eye on Vee. As they radioed for backup, the receptionist rushed back inside to phone the police.

'Oh my God,' Chlöe whispered. One side of Vee's face was ballooning. The metal imprint ran along the edge of her forehead, and Chlöe touched her hot flesh. 'Shit, that looks bad!'

'Who the hell …' Vee mumbled through a mouthful of blood.

Chlöe helped her to her feet. Chris and Guard Two had taken command of ushering the staff back inside and breaking up the crowd. Vee hobbled over to them. The guy they restrained, or rather whose weight they supported as his feet dangled inches off the ground, was still rambling and muttering in Afrikaans. Vee tilted his chin and let it drop.

She exchanged looks with Chlöe. It was Ashwin Venter.

★

On Portia's orders, they took the rest of the day off after giving the cops a statement and hanging around to see Venter carted away. Chlöe drove Vee's car to the nearest emergency room, where a doctor confirmed a mild concussion but nothing serious. He pushed some strong pain pills at them, stressing caution: Vee had to stay awake through the night, in case the damage was worse than it looked.

Chlöe couldn't stop trembling. Just getting them into Vee's house had been a mission: Vee steadying her jittery hand and guiding the key into the lock.

'I'm not dying.'

Chlöe jumped a foot. 'Huh?'

Vee eyed her over the top of a steaming cup of tea. Chlöe wasn't sure why she made it – force of habit, really – and Vee complained that her head felt too hot to bear even putting it near her mouth. 'Calm down. You've draped this blanket over me like I'm dying.'

'Sorry. White people are easily shaken by open aggression.' Chlöe sat down sheepishly. 'What a total loser. How could he attack you in broad daylight like that? This time I hope he gets buggered so much in jail he has to order a new rectum online.'

Vee tried to laugh and cringed. The medication had only dulled the pain. Chlöe pressed her and she admitted that everything had gone from strobing out of focus to a dark mass with a flickering orange halo. Chlöe watched her pass her tongue around her mouth for the dozenth time, feeling for damage. She reported that her inner cheek was bleeding a bit, but no teeth were chipped or loose.

'That was some show, by the way. Where'd you learn to fight like that?' Chlöe asked. A Mona Lisa smile was all the reply she got. Chlöe smiled back and let it go. Vee didn't have secrets as much as a whole other underground life.

She kept an eye on the dog sitting at Vee's side and it kept an eye on her. Since she had crossed the threshold the dog had kept her in sight, whether out of menace or mere curiosity Chlöe couldn't tell. Neither, she hoped. Monro weighed as much as she did, and her nerves were so frayed she was sure she'd pass out cold if the dog tried anything. Monro had howled and whined at the state his mistress was in, and Vee cuddled his head on her knee and murmured in a lyrical tongue Chlöe had never heard her use. So that was what Kpelle, the tribe she was from, sounded like.

'Is he gonna keep eyeballing me like that all day? It's very unnerving.'

'Don't mind him.' Vee stroked Monro. 'He's working out whether you're responsible for this or not. He'll make a decision soon.'

'Haha, very funny. How come he doesn't bark?'

'Huskies tend to howl more than bark. All that wolf blood.'

'Why Monro? Is he named after some famous person?'

'Monrovia.'

Chlöe chewed on it for a second. 'So you named your dog after the capital city of your country?'

'Not me. His real owner.'

'Who's his real owner? Is that him over there?' Chlöe tipped her chin in the direction of a photograph on the bookcase. It had to have been taken some time ago. A younger Voinjama and an even taller man had their arms around each other, grinning at the camera. 'He looks a lot like you. Oi, wait, is that your brother? I didn't know you had a brother. Is he older? Older brothers suck so bad. What's his name? Where is he?'

Vee caressed the lump on her head. 'His name is Quincy. Yes, he is older, and I don't know where he is. I'm not sure.'

'What d'you mean you're not sure? How can you *not know* where your own brother is?'

'Bishop, please.' Looking worn and strangely sad, Vee angled a nod towards the kitchen. 'Keep your mouth busy and get something to eat. You must be starving. Right now our lunch is rotting in a trash can.'

Chlöe microwaved rice and a savoury mix of greens with chicken from the fridge and barely made it past three mouthfuls. She sprinted back to the kitchen.

'Flip, that was hot! What's in there, devil's blood?' she called as she made herself a sandwich. 'No wonder you kick ass so well. You eat live coals.'

When she came out of the kitchen, Vee was asleep. Chlöe had to keep nudging her every twenty minutes. By five o'clock, she couldn't keep her eyes from drifting to the clock on the wall.

'You should go. I'll be fine. Connie will babysit me tonight,' Vee said.

'She should already be here. How many fingers do you see?'

'Get out, Bish.'

Chlöe rooted through her bag. 'Take these. They're my mum's. They'll help with the pain ... and, y'know, bringing down the intensity of all your feels. *Only take one.*'

Vee examined the pill bottle with a highly suspicious look in the one orbital that wasn't swollen. 'What you doin' with your Ma's drugs, Chlöe?'

'You left your brains on the sidewalk, bosslady. Don't question shit you can't understand right now.' Chlöe hugged her, feeling guilty for leaving. She didn't dare offer to stay. Today was evidence that beneath Vee's mellow exterior lay a molten reservoir of otherness she wasn't equipped to handle. Best she did as she was told.

'I'm really sorry that I didn't help you more today. I really tried,' she said on her way out.

'I'm sorry I didn't let you. Next time.' Vee gave her the most pathetic version of a wink Chlöe had ever seen.

27

Serena watched the couple in the parking lot. It was obvious they were eviscerating each other. Five minutes in each other's company was all it took to set them off. They had begun with that rubbish couples did in public, whisper-fighting and cold-shouldering. Now the gloves were off. The woman was half out of her coat, the brown sleeve that had no arm in it flapping in the wind like an injured bird. Her colouring was high and hair whipped about her face; every now and again she had to stop flailing her hands as she shouted to yank her hair behind her ears.

The man was struggling to keep calm. He said something that made her turn away. He kept talking to her back, and then made the mistake of laying a hand on it. She whipped around and yelled in his face, jabbing her finger at his chest, her face crumbling.

'I hate it when they do this in public. They don't even try to hide it any more.' Serena turned away from the window, a fist forming in her breast.

Etienne Matongo, the deputy head of security, dropped a hand on her shoulder and squeezed. Serena watched her father try to pull her sobbing mother into his arms as she fought him off.

Good thing it was after 8 p.m., when the car park was all but empty and most of WI's night staff was inside. So much for a peaceful evening at home, everyone pretending to be marginally sane. She'd ditched her friends and left campus so she could surprise her parents after work, spend quality time with them like a good daughter. Now there was this to look forward to instead, an atmosphere stuck through with razor blades.

'This time of year is hard for them,' said Etienne. His bass sunk his voice extra deep and at times Serena struggled to follow the strong lilt of French and Congolese. 'They must come inside this place every day, a place that reminds them of their love for your brother. It is not easy.'

Serena hung her head. It was true. Sean's charm had marinated into every part of their lives. A lot of people at the WI, the likes of Etienne who had known him too, remembered how great her brother had been.

'We don't talk about him any more. We either fight or keep our mouths closed so that the wrong thing doesn't come out. Nothing gets *said*.' Tearful rage snagged at her words. 'Sometimes I just want to talk about it, to *scream* out everything once and for all.'

She stared into Etienne's eyes, eyes that were, like hers, heavy with worry and fear. 'Do you ever feel like that? That you can't hold things in for one more second, that you have to let it out or it'll kill you?'

'The heart is a big place, but it cannot hold everything forever. Even big hearts must put down the load and rest one day.'

They both turned to the window and gazed out at the lot, unable to look at each other.

'Do people in your country believe the truth will set you free?'

Etienne sighed. 'I have seen many bad things in my country, Serena, as I am sure many have seen in other places. Bad things can happen anywhere, but it is up to one person to choose how the future will go. So, yes, *ma petite*, I think all over this world people believe the truth can make you go free. If you don't trust it, you can never trust yourself.'

Hot tears spilled over Serena's lids. She swiped at her face angrily with the sleeve of her biker jacket. 'How do you know … when do you feel it's right to let go?'

'I do not know that,' he replied. A muscular arm reached over and gave her more pats on the shoulder. 'But when *you* know it is time, come to me. I can help.'

He produced one of the paper towels that came from the dispensers all around the hospital and passed it to her. 'Now, please, take your parents home.'

28

Joshua looked furious.

Vee ignored him and carried on with her rant.

'At first I kept asking myself, why did he attack me? Then it hit me,' she snapped her fingers, 'like smh, of course, he found out I met with his sister. It hit me, ha ha, get it …'

'I see what you did there,' Joshua said.

'Uggh, stop trying to laugh, Voinjama. Hurts so bad.' She touched her head gingerly. 'My main concern's for Marieke and what shape she's in. Chlöe called me and told me about the other beating he dished out last night. Marieke finally stood up to him and reported it. So I get it, Ashwin's got a short fuse, but he still doesn't square with the murderer vibe. Jacqui's disappearance has got a clever feel to it. Smart but clumsy. Planned but unplanned, you get what I'm saying?

'That shifts Ian back to front and centre. Hehn, I do *not* like that guy. He's shifty, and he and that wife of his are hiding something. And those kids? Ho-o-o-o-o, talk about wackos. This is damn near Jackson family typa crazy, only it's the parents who got all the talent. And shit, did I tell you Adele tried to bribe me?'

'Several times.'

'It's only sinking in now that I've been too easy on her 'cause she's *the mother*. She could've done this; mothers aren't fountains of endless patience. Killers do that shit, tangle themselves in the investigation and drop all kinds of mess in the case to deflect attention from themselves. Maybe I'm looking right at her elaborate self-destructive scheme and I don't even know it.' Vee growled in frustration. 'It's not *fitting*! Somewhere it *doesn't fit* ...'

Joshua said nothing. He hadn't made himself a drink or got comfortable. The coat of his suit wasn't slung over the back of the chair. He reached over and laid his hand on her cheek like he'd done twice already since he arrived. He frowned and leaned closer, tipping her chin to the light and examining her pupils. 'Wait, are you *high*?'

Vee gently pushed his hand away. 'Jeez, drama queen. No, I'm not high. Not like Ice Cube and Chris Tucker in *Friday* high. I'm ... cruising.' She fluttered her fingers. 'Pain meds. And sumn' else Chlöe gave me. Makes you mellow and buzzy at the same time.'

'Yeah, but how much does it hurt? Look at this ... You have a partial imprint of a streetlamp on your face.' His fingers were cool on her skin. Vee suppressed a shudder, or what could have been a shudder; sensation was a little hard to process under the spell of Chlöe's pill.

She pushed his hand away again. The contact hadn't broken the skin and she was overjoyed to have avoided stitches. Hours of ice and some sweet medicine later and she was feeling close to dandy. 'Eh. It's not as bad as it looks.'

Joshua muttered inaudibly and got to his feet. 'Well. Guess that's me done, then.' He got up, dropped a quick peck on the top of her head and strode out of the lounge. Vee kept her seat for a full minute, heard the sound of a car engine hum to life before she shuffled up after him. The blanket around her shoulders was falling off by the time she made it outside.

She grabbed his arm at the door. 'Hey. Where the hell you going? I can't be alone. I just told Chloe that Connie was coming over because she wouldn't let me breathe. But seriously, somebody's got to help me stay awake.'

'I get the feeling you'll be just peachy by tomorrow without my help. And the day after, and the next after that,' Joshua replied. 'And to answer your question, home is where I'm going. Happen to have one of those, too, along with a job and a social life ...'

Vee flinched, mouth open. She closed it slowly and let go of his arm. He started down the walk and she sprinted ahead of him, her head yowling in protest, and yanked the door of the Jeep open.

'Allow me, your majesty. I'm *so* sorry I disturbed your evening.'

Joshua gave a low laugh and shook his head. 'Very mature.' He pushed the door open, crouched to slide in, then straightened up. 'Why do you need me here?' The frost in his voice and eyes made her take a step back. 'Why, of everyone you know, did you call me over?'

Vee looked away.

'Exactly right. You have a perfect reason why every single one of those people can't or shouldn't have to be here. But not me.'

'Is that what this is about? That you've done sooo much for me and kept the receipts for all your feelings so you can rub my nose in it when it suits you? That I don't *need* you, Joshua, that I don't *want* you? Grow up.'

He snapped his fingers. 'Bravo, Sherlock. Because after months, no wait, *years* of being more than happy to drink your bathwater, I chose today … the day you look like a bus ran your ass over, to wake up and say I've had enough.' Hurt and disappointment etched his features. 'When did you become so fucking selfish? What's happening to you?'

'Well, if that's not the reason, then what is it? You think my work's too dangerous? I should give it up and stick to safer material?'

It was grossly unfair and ridiculous, and she knew it. For both of them, the job was more need than conscious choice. Part of her wished she could take back the words, but the other half had taken the wheel and gone dark, steering her out of control. More than anything, she wished he was Ashwin. She wished to high heaven he was Ashwin Venter so she could drive through the flames at full throttle.

His expression changed like seasons in fast forward, going from pained to livid to sad in microseconds. Then it iced over, making it plain he didn't intend to get drawn any further. He dragged the car door open the furthest it could go, until the hinges squalled.

'Go inside,' he said. 'Call me tomorrow morning.'

'Msshw, dah nah all!'

Her eyes weren't quick enough to register him move. One second he was sliding into the driver's seat, and in one lithe shift he was close, practically in her face. He didn't tower over her, at least she had that, but she could feel how tight the reins were on his emotions. Pride all but streaming like smoke through her nostrils, Vee fought against her whimpering inner female, fought against being intimidated on her own doorstep. All the same, she quickly decided on a more moderate stance and retreated a couple of paces.

'You've already been surprised by one man today, Voinjama. Don't make that mistake again, because I'm that close ...' Inches from her face, he held his fingers millimetres apart to illustrate how far the live wires were from touching. 'Get back inside. Lock the doors. Have a hot bath and think things over. Turn up the volume on the TV to keep yourself awake. We'll talk tomorrow.'

He got in. 'Don't make me make the first call,' he warned. The Jeep swung off the drive and into the road. In a moment it was out of sight.

Vee stayed in her spot for a few more minutes, mouth dry and heart thumping.

'Bastard,' she croaked.

29

Vee swept inside and locked all the doors. She made herself a cup of coffee that sat neglected until it went cold. She wandered upstairs to the bedroom and switched on the television, trying to focus on the aimless jostling of contestants on a reality show on DStv. Eventually she gave up and went into the bathroom, switching the light off beforehand. The last thing she needed was the sight of her banged-up face in the mirror. She brushed her teeth, ran a hot bath, lowered herself into it and closed her eyes, making a concerted effort to relax. Her buzz had worn off and her brain needed powering down.

Joshua Allen was full of bullshit, her brain said. He had absolutely no right to flip out on her this way, none whatsoever. How dare he just show up at her front door—

You called him.

—show up unannounced in the middle of the night and cuss her out for no reason on one of her worst days ever. A crazed man, a suspect in a murder investigation, with a criminal record no less, had jumped her in the street and Joshua refused to react like a true friend. She winced at the memory of Ashwin seizing her head and ramming it like a jar he was trying to force open.

She was no stranger to violence or surprises. The uncomfortable truth was that the dark and unknown were enticing and she was drawn. Her relationship with the filth of humankind was far from healthy, but she'd been poisoned too early and the damage was done. Everyone had a drug, a secret and a line they had to cross when they were out of options. She knew where she stood with all three; the luxury of playing dumb had flown the coop ages ago. Those choices amounted to one and the same a very long time ago—

Vee broke off her thoughts, reshuffled the lot and put the pack away. Under no circumstances was she venturing into that zone of turbulence – not tonight. The Johnson buffet had more than its share of delights to nibble on. Ashwin Venter, Adele Paulsen, the entire spectrum of Fourie fuckery – gone.

Joshua Allen was a crafty, tenacious bugger though, and wouldn't piss off. The problem was that their relationship was fully out of hand. She'd leaned on him too hard when she was in crisis and now he'd taken how deeply she relied on his friendship out of context. He was taking advantage—

Is he, now? Is friendship all it is?

—twisting what they had into shapes that suited him. She was sorry she didn't have feelings for him in that way but she couldn't force it. He was like a brother, for God's sake. Fine, not *exactly* like Quincy, but Joshua was a good stand-in for the brother she sorely missed. So what if every so often the lines blurred and her mind wandered to how great he looked in a pair of jeans or mussed up after a long day with his sleeves rolled up. Or how good he smelled, or the way his arms felt around her, warm, strong arms with a thrilling edge.

In the darkness, Vee's hands acquired a life of their own. One moved slowly over her wet stomach to the sensitive skin under her armpits, working over to her breasts. Gentle circles teased at the ache in the hardened tips. Eyes closed, she drew a leg up and shivered as the warm water crested the exposed upper half of her body. The other hand slid down between her thighs.

She closed her eyes and reworked the evening's altercation. Joshua cornered her and growled an insult in her face. Exhilarated and flustered by his nearness, her heart pounded in her ears. She swore and pushed him in the chest, but he grabbed her by the arms and pressed her—

Pushed her roughly.

—up against the wall. Her flimsy act dissolved and she found herself trying to kiss him, struggling against the hold he had on her wrists. He chuckled, released his grip and lifted her by the hips in one smooth move, wrapping her legs around his waist. Their tongues clashed. He wrenched her skirt up and his fingers traced the length of her inner thigh. Vee trembled and sucked in her breath as his touch inched towards its target, pausing to caress her through her underwear. He bit her earlobe and pulled the material aside. Her breath caught; she felt the first stroke—

'Mtsssshw,' Vee snapped her eyes open. She climbed out of the tub, reaching for a towel. Ridiculous fantasy or wanton indulgence, seeing it through to its natural end would be of zero help in staying awake.

I need to watch a movie, she decided. Anything with a silly, nonsexual plot would do the trick.

★

He answered the door in a white T-shirt and a pair of boxer shorts. The harshest Cape Town winter never topped a mere weather tantrum for Joshua, with that Brooklyn ice in his veins.

Vee rubbed the goosebumps rising on her arms through her sweater. Perhaps her tropical blood was appalled at his choice of sleepwear or perhaps the outline of his upper body through the light cotton was that titillating.

Pull yourself together.

He shouldn't be a tease, then; she had eyes after all. And he did have a nice body, lean and sculpted, the sort that would wear well into and even after middle age. One end of his rumpled T-shirt was raised, showing just a flash of skin below his navel before the rest ducked into his shorts. She throbbed, the tingle turning into a growl.

Joshua cursed and rubbed his eyes, holding the door halfway open as a sign she wasn't a welcome sight. 'It's almost midnight.'

'I know what time it is. And I know you couldn't sleep either, so ...' She shuffled her feet. Scenarios like these were far easier to enact in your head than to play out in real life. 'I needed to clear the air by letting you know that you had absolutely no right speaking to me like that. It was out of line.'

'Duly noted, air officially cleared,' he grumbled. 'I get the impression I have no rights at all when it comes to you, so no surprises there.' He shrugged. 'Is that all?'

'Yes,' Vee said. 'No.' She swallowed. 'I was wrong and I'm sorry. You're not a houseboy to be summoned whenever I feel like it. That's not what I intended you to think when I called tonight, or *any* of the times I've called on you. It's just ... things keep happening ... it's too much and I get so ...'

A trail of smug lazed across his lips. He planned on having fun watching her bungle through an apology. He crossed his arms and leaned against the door, giving a barely perceptible nod to continue.

'There's no one else,' she finished. He raised his eyebrows. 'I mean, yes, there *are* other people I can call. But ... it's not the same.'

You've ruined other people's company for me. The words tried to worm their way out but she wouldn't let them. It wasn't necessary. Joshua's posture softened and with wordless resignation, he pushed the door open and stepped aside. They would go through the motions as always. He'd get her a blanket and cups of excellent coffee. He'd listen patiently as she dogged the steps of every harebrained theory she had, following streaks of light down endless tunnels as they swirled out of sight and left her frustrated. She would nod off in the middle of a sentence, and he would roll her into his bed and eke out a few hours of sleep on the couch. His car would be gone by the time she woke up.

Vee opted out of the usual scenario. Instead of heading for the lounge, she laced her arms around his neck and kissed him long and hard. She pulled back, breathing heavily, studying his face. Joshua blinked in shock, and then his eyes went from charcoal to well past midnight. He covered her mouth with his and dragged her over the threshold by the waist, using her butt to bump the door shut.

She kissed every part of his face she could get at, aggravated that he kept slowing things down by pulling away every now and again to nibble at her lips and throat. Vee pulled his lips back on hers and used her teeth with more force, almost biting through the soft inner flesh. Joshua swore and tightened his arms around her. Vee winced and hissed, her muscles twanging a sore reminder.

He stopped. 'You okay?' She nodded. He studied her with jarring tenderness, tracing cool fingers against her cheeks and nose. Then, slowly, he slid both hands past the waistband of her tracksuit pants and stroked her bare skin. His fingers edged into her panties, cupping her butt as he pressed her against the swollen front of his shorts. Vee felt her head empty and redirect all her blood flow to below her navel.

They made it as far as the carpeted floor of the dimly lit lounge, stripping each other of everything save her underwear. Joshua took his time to admire her satin finery, restraining her hands when she got impatient to strip.

'Wow, did you put this on for me? Is all this premeditated?' He dipped his head between her breasts and drew a deep breath. 'Devious,' he murmured, running his lips over the bra. Vee felt his surge of appreciation as she snuggled deeper into his lap, and she whimpered in response, loving the tease. He took her by the hips and smoothed her onto her back, and soon the caress of his mouth and tickle of his breath over the skin between her legs had her arching her back. The gentle lap of heat in her belly swelled into a tsunami that threatened to put an abrupt, unsatisfying end to ages of anticipation.

'No, Joshua … no, stop it, don't start nothin' fancy.' Her craving was too intense for frills.

Vee pushed him down and straddled his hips. She undid the front clasp of her bra, releasing her breasts and the condom she'd snuggled inside the cups. Joshua laughed in wonder, laid back and put his arms behind his head, outmanoeuvred into compliance. For the first time, she went slow as she did the honours, watching with pleasure as he closed his eyes, her breath quickening with his at every stroke of her hand. Once sheathed, he held her by the waist and together they eased into one another. Vee made a sound she barely recognised as her own. She paused, savouring the intensity and completeness of him inside her, then began to move. The rhythm she ground her hips to was rough and fast. Sweat hit her in the chest and burst. She kept rocking until she climaxed again and so did he.

Afterwards, they sprawled on the carpet in breathless silence.

'Exactly how hard did you hit your head?' Joshua asked huskily.

'Shut up,' Vee moaned. Months of repressed urges joined forces with pain, pleasure and exhaustion, unleashing hormonal fury. A boot was stamping down on the front of her skull, trying to kick a way out through the bone. Darkness sucked her down and under.

'Whoa-ho-o-o there, champ. C'mon, stay with me …' Joshua scooped her up and rocked her gently. He talked to her to keep her lucid and awake. They played the TV at full blast and he made excellent cups of coffee. Then they wrestled a second round, where he asserted his rights more firmly than before. Not that she had any complaints either way.

30

It was well past nine when Vee pried her lids open. She hefted a pillow off her head to find the sun up and the rest of the bed empty. So much for facing consequences of the night in the harsh light of day. If there was an uncomfortable, regretful conversation on the cards, it would have to wait. Joshua was on his grind and she had a day pass, thanks to Portia. Joshua had kept her awake all night long and not in the way she'd been hoping for. He'd worried that she really would slip into a coma and he'd be left with a body to explain. If she never had to play another game of chess or splash under a freezing shower again, it would be too soon.

She tottered to the bathroom, peed and scrutinised the damage in the mirror. The swelling was down, but her face was going for gold in the bruising category. A red splotch tainted the white of one eye. She sighed and poked it gingerly with a finger. It didn't look too bad, and thank God she was a fast healer.

She slipped back into her clothes and wandered to the kitchen. Fresh coffee was in the pot, and on the counter a red apple lay on top of an envelope. She grinned and sank her teeth into the crispy, sweet flesh, grateful she didn't have to trudge to the shops to buy her own.

She opened the envelope. 'I've had better, but thanks,' read Joshua's note. Next to it, a hundred rand note.

'Asshole,' Vee giggled, and tucked the cash in her pocket. Even if bread money was all her passionate efforts were worth, she wasn't going to turn it down. Times were hard.

After a huge sandwich, she tracked down her phone. A missed call from the office and an email from Chlöe. The latter bore positive news: Rachelle Duthie, the nurse acquainted with Sean's case, had returned their call. She could squeeze in a quick chat over tea or lunch as her shifts were less hectic this week. Vee checked her watch. If she made for home now to freshen up she wouldn't make tea, but she would just about make the lunch option. It was time to call on Nurse Duthie.

★

'There was some talk.'

The view through the window was depressing. It looked out onto the WI's west-facing lot, the centre of the construction work. The misshapen hole in the ground – it wasn't a swimming pool yet, though that appeared to be the objective – looked like the site of a meteor crash. It was half finished, the aqua tiles rimming the circumference in stark contrast with the basin, sloshing with muddy water and debris. Flimsy metal fencing and strips of orange plastic mesh cordoned off the perimeter. Either the WI's construction team had forgotten how unpredictable the weather was or time was pressing and they'd chosen to hedge their bets. Vee's eyes hurt looking at it, and they'd had their share of pain to deal with already.

She turned her attention back to Rachelle. 'Sorry, you were saying?'

They were sunning themselves on the terrace of a second floor café, the café itself tucked into a building dwarfed by the glittering WI across the road. Vee knew this area was an enclave for private hospitals and practices, for some odd reason; Kingsbury Hospital was a stone's throw away. Looking around, it was obvious that the café was making change from its prime location. Vee estimated that half the customers sipping lattes and munching chicken wraps were in the healing business. Doctors were as easy to spot as cops: billboards on foreheads.

Rachelle eyed Vee's blueberry muffin, so she pushed it towards her. Duthie wasn't much older than Vee, but her chubbiness indicated it had been many kilos and a significantly lowered restraint since she'd been the slim nurse in the old photograph.

'You said there was talk going around. What kind of talk?' Vee asked. Duthie hadn't told her anything new yet, recycling the Ian–Carina–Adele saga that had been an open secret on the ward, fully wrung of all its juices by now.

'The medical community here isn't so big. We know each other's business. Dr Ian's a prominent guy and whispers can take a long time to die down. Years ago, there was an incident when I was still at Claremont L&M.' Rachelle took her time to finish the muffin, pausing for dramatic effect, then wiped her mouth. 'Not long after Sean passed on, questions started flying around about how he climbed the transplant list so quickly.

It usually takes months, years even, so naturally it drew some attention. CLM was tanking fast by then, so a lot of doctors were under fire or investigation for something or other. Most of it was bogus, noise generated in the panic. We were bleeding money and clients, and administration needed to point fingers.'

'What exactly was Dr Fourie accused of?'

'Oh, no, no, no,' Rachelle pumped her hands, slow down. 'He never got *accused* of anything, not formally. I'm talking rumours. Admin started a witch-hunt, saying it was quote unquote 'highly questionable and unethical that a doctor would use his power or connections to turn favours for next of kin.' Hospital policy.' She shrugged. 'It died down. Far as I know they had no hard evidence and there were bigger issues – who had time to chase whispers? The staff thought it was bloody cruel and we let them know. They'd just buried their child, where was the harm in dropping it?'

Vee took a sip of carrot and orange juice. The Fouries were well respected; only a mob of monsters would've harassed them until they got their pound of flesh. CLM had made the sensible choice. Or … Vee cocked her head. The heat from the peanut gallery may have died a natural death, or someone may have pissed all over it. Damning allegations didn't disappear magically. Who, again, had the power to kick the legs out from under a thoroughbred, make it all appear groundless? Philemon 'The Man' Mtetwa, no less.

'They've put all that behind them now. They're both doing fantastic at WI. Ian's aiming for head of the cardio unit, and from what I hear, and *know*, he deserves it. When the rest of us bolted from CLM, he broke his back to build it up again.'

'You sure he'll be the lucky man for the job?'

'If ever there's a man, he's it. Though it might be a woman,' Rachelle smiled at her gaffe. 'That's possible, too. It's a brave new world, Miss Johnson. Women are up for everything now. Except maybe the things we used to be up for before, which are now suddenly beneath us.' She gave a cynical turn of the mouth before picking up her chai tea. 'Sorry, recent divorce. I find myself quoting my ex-arsehole too often.' She sipped and cleared her throat. 'But Ian's the prime candidate, no question. He'd have to really mess up this time to get passed over.'

Vee leaned closer. Maybe there was an angle there. 'So he doesn't automatically get the division head appointment? He has to work for it.' *And make sure he doesn't work against himself. Keep that past in the past.*

'Oh, yes. WI rounded up the finest staff and the competition's *hectic.* Ian's a shoo-in, he's local and all that, but it's not a given. The selection process involves a CV assessment, board review and performance evaluations. Colleagues can weigh in … You don't want a black mark on your record, even in your private life.'

Sounds like a presidential race, Vee mused. For a man so upwardly mobile, Ian's children were weights around his ankles. The rumours surrounding his son's death, his extramarital affair, Jacqui's disappearance … A lot of bad luck haunting one guy. No wonder he looked fit to pop a blood vessel every time he saw her. How far would a type-A achiever go to protect everything he'd worked for? And compared to that, what was Carina willing to do to save her family?

31

'Please wait, my sister.'

Etienne Matongo read uncertainty on the young woman's face as she broke her stride. He also saw curiosity and weariness. Girls like her had men pestering them all the time and he knew the look well. He could tell she was different, though, because curiosity was winning out. Her eyes flicked over his security uniform, and instead of hissing her teeth and walking off, she paused and studied him. He imagined she was deciding if his age and bearing excluded him from chasing young skirts. She seemed to relax a little.

'How are you?' He extended a hand. 'I am Etienne Matongo. I work with security.'

'Yes, I can see. Afternoon, Mr Matongo. I'm Vee.' She shook his hand, dipping one knee slightly as a sign of respect. He smiled, moved by the gesture.

'I want us to talk. Please sit with me,' he urged.

They walked and perched under the metal canopy of a bus shelter situated on a stretch of no-man's land between the hospitals and the highway. The cavernous mud pit that was soon to be a pool assaulted their eyes through the chain-link fence. Workmen knotted together over lunch near the makeshift plywood sheds. Vee scrunched up her nose at the sight of the sprawl of dirt and gravel.

'It is very dangerous,' Etienne said, voicing her thoughts. 'They must cover it. Someone could fall inside.'

Vee nodded. 'Very true.'

Etienne kept his gaze fixed ahead. 'You have been asking many questions.'

'Yes.'

'What are you trying to find out?' She smiled and didn't reply, so he added: 'Are you working with the police?'

'No.'

'Are you sure? You behave like the police. So many questions.'

'Do I? You askin' plenty questions yourself.'

'I have a reason for my questions and a right to ask them. I am in charge of security.'

The wind whipped a section of hair across her cheek. Vee turned her gaze towards the WI grounds, looking past the work site. Her eyes came to rest on the front entrance of the institute, where another guard stepped out of the cubicle at the gate to point directions and usher a visitor's BMW onto the grounds. Etienne understood the point she was wordlessly making: close as they were to the WI, they were not actually on its premises. Therefore the deputy chief of security was a few steps out of his jurisdiction, so to speak, to press her for answers.

'I'm not police. I'm a journalist, working on an investigation.'

This time it was he who wrinkled his nose. This was just as bad, if not worse.

'What are you investigating?' She answered with another smile, this time of disappointment, and he bristled. 'The Fouries are good people. They've done nothing wrong.'

'Even good people can do wrong. It happens every day. Anything is possible.'

'Anything is possible.'

She looked at him. 'Can you help me?'

'I have no information.' He stood. 'I can't help you.'

She went through her bag and brought out a business card. 'If you change your mind or think of anything you might know, please call me. No one will ever hear about it if you talk to me.'

'What I know is my job,' Etienne replied. 'And I know the Fouries. They are good doctors. You bother the wrong people.' He scratched the fleshy lid under his eyebrow with a finger. 'Your job is dangerous, no? It's a bad job for a woman.'

He touched his eye again, then his forehead. Her expression cleared; she understood he was pointing out her bruises. Dangerous jobs led to injuries, unacceptable in an upright woman. He noted with pleasure that her smile was gone. Her eyes grew dark.

'Can I ask you not to come here again? You bring bad trouble when you come here to ask your questions.' He delivered the advice with resignation, knowing full well she wouldn't listen. He had a young daughter like this one.

'What kind of bad trouble?' she said.

'Enjoy your day, *mademoiselle*.' He squeezed her hand quickly and walked away.

32

A seizure gripped her right hand and shook it, making it wobble like a boneless thing. Vee squeezed her eyes shut, willing the spasms to stop. The wave undulated through her arm and crashed into her chest, setting her pectorals off in involuntary jerks. Keeping her eyes closed, she sucked in huge breaths and focused on the finger clamped on her pulse. Ninety-five beats per minute and climbing. One hundred and five. She kept breathing, forcing her mind to drown out the soft patter of rain outside, the music coming from the stereo and whir of the fan heater circulating warmth in the bedroom.

Ten minutes and she eased closer to normal again. I can't have a seizure now, she thought, going back to folding clothes out of her closet. It had been weeks since so much as a whisper of the fits. Her confidence in the workings of her body was back and she'd got slack with the medication. In truth, she'd stopped altogether. A brain on drugs wasn't for everyone.

The white box of Cipralex taunted from the night table. Vee shuddered at the strip of blue-and-orange-striped pills. She'd done her homework on the vile concoction: prescribed for forms of major depression, in her case it targeted generalised anxiety disorders. Two genial chats with a doctor was apparently enough to write her off as a moody head case. She thought of the sweet Dr Neethling and wondered if he still had an opening. After her performance at the party, probably not.

I will not *have a seizure today.* She folded another shirt, fighting to keep her hands steady, and flung it into the box designated for charity. Her body replied with a jolt that had her swaying like a drunk for several painful minutes. The fit unclenched, and she hobbled to the dresser and snatched the box. Fingers shaking, she grappled with the pills. Just one for today, before the fury rolled in and swallowed her whole.

The doorbell screamed, its chime a stab in her ear. She started and her finger popped a tablet out of its foil casing. Ripples tap-danced down the back of her neck and shoulders as she watched the pill arc into the air, spin and roll under the dresser. Vee groaned and got to her feet, relieved the lower half of her body was still functional. Visitors weren't welcome on Sundays, but she didn't have the energy to pretend to be out.

'Hi,' Joshua said cheerfully.

'Hey.' *Can't deal with this right now.*

It had been almost a week. She hadn't called or made any plans with him, and he hadn't forced the issue. Vee smoothed a hand through her hair, a huge, soft pouf of frizz she hadn't bothered to blow-dry after she'd washed it. Her jeans weren't the cleanest pair she could've thrown on either. Her breasts tightened and prickled as the chill in the air nipped through her sweater, reminding her she was braless. She crossed her arms over her chest, glad she'd at least showered and cleaned her teeth.

'Thought I'd pass by and check on you,' he ventured after a spell. 'The new you. Y'know, the one who practically raped me and then vanished. Really classy.'

'It wasn't like that. I didn't ...' Tendons in her neck and shoulders spasmed. 'I thought it was best if I made myself scarce for a while. I didn't want to make it weird.'

'Nothing's weird.' She said nothing and Joshua chuckled. 'Can I come in, at least?' Drizzle as fine as icing sugar settled like drift onto his coat and shaved head. She noticed a bag of shopping in his hand. She bit her lip. He said, 'That's not what I came for. Give me some credit.'

Vee unlocked the security gate. 'What's all that?'

'Food.' He dumped the shopping bag on the kitchen counter and started unloading. 'We went about things in the wrong order. First, you share a nice meal together, and *then*–' He stared. 'What's up with your face?'

Her hand flew up to cover the twitching. The skin was burning. 'Sometimes it does that. I don't think it healed properly,' she lied. A hundred, maybe a hundred and ten beats per minute, without having to take a pulse. Any louder and her heart would drown out the thunder.

'You got hit on the left side.' He narrowed his eyes and walked over, held her chin and tilted it up to the light. 'That doesn't look good. You're blinking like a Christmas tree. You talk to a doctor about this?'

Vee wriggled away and rushed to the door. 'Gimme one minute,' she called.

She closed the bedroom door, eyes watering as she scanned the room. The Cipralex box was nowhere to be seen. It had grown legs and walked away. She struggled to her knees, legs shaking uncontrollably. Where the hell was it? Was the box in her hand when she went to answer the door? Was Joshua picking it up now, reading the insert with mounting horror? Breath frantic, she gave up on the box and focused on the single runaway pill, peering and stretching her fingers under furniture as far as they could go. Nothing.

Shit. The attack was in full swing. Sweat ran into her eyes and stung. She wrapped her arms around her body and fell against the charity box, taking deep lungfuls of air. The room reeked of male cologne. The muscles of her throat clenched violently and pain pummelled her chest. Cowering on the floor, Vee groaned long and low. The air thickened and closed in.

It felt like the agony and disorientation of being born. Minutes passed unmeasured. Or perhaps hours – she had no clue. Sounds were squashed and far away, two-dimensional. The sound of frying – had to be rain. Whirring of the fan heater. Footsteps and a knock. Arms around her, trying to lift her. Words, no sense.

A flash of silver and black came to Joshua's ear. As he dialled emergency, Vee took a swig from the dregs of her energy reserve and lunged for his cell phone. She missed, tried again and missed again, her fingers slippery sticks of butter brushing his.

'What're you doing?!' Joshua asked. 'I'm calling an ambulance.'
'Don't. Please,' Vee begged.

★

'You're right. You shouldn't have told me. You should've taken this to your grave.'

Vee buried her face deeper in her palms. 'I really don't feel like playing right now, Joshua Allen ...'

'Great, because I'm not. Hearing you've been dealing with these attacks all by yourself, thinking unicorn dust once a day and wishful thinking's gonna make it stop? And oh, ha ha, my favourite part, hearing you're being, what ... fuck, I can't believe I'm actually gonna say this ...' He scrubbed his hands over his face. '*Haunted*? Stalked by the dead? What're we going with here?'

'Do you think this is easy? I heard myself say it. I watched your face as I heard myself say it. And ...' She hugged her arms round her midriff. 'I'm glad I did. I feel like a fucking fly in a closed jar. I haven't been able to breathe, in every sense of the word.' She lifted her head. 'Do you believe me?'

He gave a long, aggravated grunt. 'Of course I believe you. I have to. This is the part in the horror movie where the hot girl's, like, "Do you believe me, Billy?!" and it goes one of two ways. Billy's crazy about her so naturally he says yes, and they fight the dark forces together and live to see the end credits. Or he's a loser and laughs in her face, and in the next scene the evil shitmonster rips his face off. I'd like to see our end credits.' He smiled. Vee drilled him with a glare of diamond. 'Yes, Voinjama Johnson, I believe you! You're quite the imaginarian but even you're not this preposterous.'

Vee sagged, the stone rolled away. She kissed his shoulder and leaned on him for a few minutes, then moved back to the dresser where her plate was. Pancakes, bacon, sausages, eggs. The skidmark of hormones left behind by an episode made the comedown less than pleasant. She'd zonked out and woken up to food and more tenderness than she was used to getting from Joshua. Breakfast in the afternoon and sandwiches were his specialty ... more like the only things he knew how to make.

He watched her eat, the furrow between his eyebrows deepening with every passing minute. The silence got creepy. Vee finally put the utensils down.

'I'm listening.'

'Four months, Vee. You sat on this for that long. You need to see a therapist. Some kinda professional. You're carrying a lot of crap around that you need to unload ...'

'Joshua ...'

'You can't really think that glossing it over is healthy. You got caught in a civil war when you were ten, for Chrissake. You had to fight for your life, you had to pick up a weapon and–'

'STOP!'

'All right. Okay, okay, no more.' He raised his hands and slapped them down on his thighs. They glared at each other some more. Vee pushed the plate away, not that there was much on it, and came back to sit on the bed beside him. 'You scared the shit outta me, okay. I thought you were having a heart attack,' he said.

She twisted her fingers around in her lap. 'That's what it feels like,' she said quietly.

'There has to be a trigger. What's the first thing you feel?'

'Nothing. I've stopped writing it down because I couldn't see any connection. They come on anywhere.'

Joshua looked around the bedroom. He rose and walked over to the box of old clothes, lifted out a T-shirt. 'Men's extra large. Yours?'

Vee snatched it, tossed it back into the box, and kicked it away. 'That's Titus's junk. He's had enough time to pick it up, so I'm donating it to charity. Should've burnt it all.'

'Bitter much?' Joshua shook his head. 'How can you *not* see a link here? When else?'

Vee froze. Their favourite music, the food he loved, wearing his cologne to work. She'd packed and unpacked these clothes a hundred times under the pretence of throwing them out. They used to jog on Rondebosch Common together and he'd teased her by zipping ahead, leave her laughing and panting in his dust. A myriad ways she subconsciously attempted to recreate her old life with Titus. Every single one of those incidents had preceded a seizure. It was a punch in the gut.

'Well. There were other times that had nothing to do with that. It's a terrifying feeling, don't think I haven't been fighting it. I've fought so hard to stop it coming back and every time …'

'Then don't. Don't fight it. Just let it happen.'

She reeled. 'It feels like I'm being murdered. How do I not fight that?'

Joshua shrugged. 'If you know it's inevitable, then let it happen. Struggling and pushing back hasn't worked, so flip the script. Go with it. Sounds crazy, but what've you got to lose?' He gave her one of his sage looks. 'Fighting isn't the only way to win.'

'Where'd you hear nonsense like that?'

'I dunno. *Kung Fu Panda*. Point is, it's poignant and true.'

Vee mumbled under her breath but didn't press the point. She wasn't always a fan of Serious Joshua. Serious Joshua held her feet to the flames, got a bit too wise and intense.

'So …' she said. By this time their chitchat would wind down and he would do his flirtation bit and head out. They had crossed the veil now, and she wasn't sure how their thing worked on the other side. Did he want to leave? She didn't want him to. He knew everything there was to know. He'd fed her and changed her music from the 'depressing garbage' she'd had on to a playlist on his phone. Kings of Leon belted out a bluesy-rock ballad she hadn't heard before.

'So …' He kissed her. Vee kissed him back.

'Wait.' She pushed him away. 'This isn't what you came for, remember.'

'Screw that. You just shaved a decade off my life, jitterbug. You owe me.'

'Smh, I'hn owe you nuttin,' she laughed.

'We'll see.'

33

The Mercedes-Benz E class rolled to a halt behind a cluster of bushes. The driver tapped the accelerator and the engine replied with an alarmingly throaty rumble. The driver's foot slipped off the pedals and skittered to regain hold. The driver put the car in park with a trembling hand and muttered a prayer for courage.

Minutes ticked past.

After eleven of them, a woman rounded the far corner at a jog. She wore a chocolate jogging suit with acid pink trim and paid no attention to the car, if she saw it at all. The driver started the engine and crawled forward, trying to follow without being spotted.

The driver of the Merc was in luck. The woman hadn't heard the engine, nor did she notice the pursuit. She was in her own world.

Vee pumped her legs at top speed. She closed her eyes every now and again and imagined the top of her head gone and the wind whipping over her exposed brain, cooling and clearing it of every care and grief. The days of running for fitness were over. Now she was in it solely for peace of mind and the sense of freedom.

After an unbroken fifteen-minute spurt, her legs gave out. She thundered to a stop and slumped onto the asphalt, heaving. No morning breeze was strong enough to blow all her troubles away. She drew her knees up to meet her forehead as she caught her breath, powerless to stop her thoughts from eating away at her.

She had failed. The one-month anniversary of the day she was handed the Paulsen case had passed her by, smirking, and had nothing to say for itself. She'd had to face Portia with the truth – the Fourie frontier had gone from quiet to a barren wasteland, and she and Chlöe had nothing to run in an issue. Both doctors had gone from making excuses to making threats, and finally to avoiding her altogether. Portia dumped her back on features, shunting her onto the most boring assignment available.

'If you give me more time, like two more weeks, even one, I know we're about to break something. I've been talking to Rosie ...' Vee angled.

'*Rosie*? The spastic one?' Portia's expression said she couldn't even summon the energy to be disgusted. 'Come on. Don't be this person.'

'She might not be as entrenched in all of it as the others, but she's my in. If I can massage her into getting me solid information that'll break her father's alibi, like a copy of his schedule from two years ago or solid proof that he, or his wife, weren't at the hospital the night Jacqui disappeared, we've got enough for an opportunity.'

'So basically you're harassing a child, the least common denominator, because you think she'll snitch on her father.' Portia sighed. 'When you said this case was frozen solid, what you *should've* said was it couldn't be defrosted at all,' she said, the pity in her tone cutting deeper than any reprimand. 'Forget it, Voinjama. No more sand in the hourglass.'

Too embarrassed and confused at her failure to argue any further, Vee dutifully pressed her nose to the grindstone.

The one highlight of October was her twenty-ninth birthday. Connie threw her a party that turned into a raucous affair. It was fun, but Joshua didn't make it thanks to work. He called sounding tired and faraway, boxed in by walls of documents overrun with ones and zeroes. Other people's millions.

'This is so unfair.' She hated wheedling in a quiet corner at her own party. Worst of all, she detested the thrill she got in feeling like a woman entitled to pry and make demands. It stank of high school. Vee cringed. The older she got, the deeper she regressed in her dating habits.

Joshua had promised to make it up by picking her up in the evening for a surprise outing, at seven-thirty.

By 7:45 p.m., her glow had vinegared. Dressed to dazzle, she sat in a darkened lounge, worried and pissed off in equal proportions. It was not like Joshua to be late and not call.

She moved to the window and looked out. Two figures loitered on the sidewalk outside her driveway. She let the curtains drop, a rattle of unease in her chest. For several days now, the sensation of being followed nagged at her, an invisible hand trailing down her spine. Maybe it was residual paranoia from the Lucas Fourie–Ashwin Venter tag team event. Shadows loomed everywhere.

Vee peeped again and her throat clenched. The figures took shape in the half-light. She stepped away from the window and thought long and hard. She took her heels off, opened the front door and pattered down the front walk.

'What the hell's going on?'

She looked from Titus to Joshua. So different and so alike. Titus was more ripped than she remembered, the cut of his biceps defined under his sweater. Had he been bodybuilding in his spare time instead of pining over her? Had he got wind of her adventures and gone on an ironman regimen to beat down any rivals he caught on his turf? She wasn't his turf any more.

'Yor better not start nuttin. There will be no ghetto shit in front of my house, so my white neighbours can judge me,' she warned.

They tossed an amused look between them and her face warmed. Ah. They intended to play this civilised. She didn't know whether to feel relieved or undervalued.

'Can we talk?' Titus asked.

She had an ear for his nuances and picked up the faintest quiver in his voice. Titus waited. Vee turned to Joshua and he looked away, eyes at half mast as his force field of inscrutability went up. She cursed him silently.

'Yeah. Go in and make yourself comfortable. I need a minute.' She waited for Titus to flinch or flare up at her tone, demand a 'please'. He was screwing up her evening and she wanted blood. He tipped a nod, no more. He shared an exchange with Joshua before walking away: a locking of eyes, the fractal arrangement of bodies at cryptic angles, a barely perceptible nod. Male language.

Vee breathed when he was gone. 'I'm sorry.'

'Ahh. The best laid plans ...' Joshua said.

They couldn't go anywhere now. If he asked her, she'd run back inside and toss Titus out on his ass. They could turn this thing around. If only he asked ...

'He had his reasons.' The wind flapped his overcoat at the lapels and threatened to upend her dress. 'For what it's worth.'

So he wasn't going to ask. Instead, one more shithead had jumped on the bandwagon hurtling towards certain death. 'You fuckin' jokin' me? You making his excuses now?'

'No. It's the truth.' He lifted and dropped his shoulders. 'You two need to work this out ...'

Vee climbed out of her head and brought herself back to the street. The wind stung her face, whistling down the street of whichever neighbourhood she had stopped in to catch her breath. Her muscles had dumped all the lactic acid and settled into a dull throb.

She touched the lapis lazuli necklace round her neck, the birthday present Joshua had given her that night. The night he had left her alone to do her own adulting, forced her to face Titus on the very day she had been least prepared for it. Laying low was the strategy Serious Joshua had adopted, fighting by not fighting. What she was meant to do or decide in the meantime, she still had no idea. It was funny in an achingly unfunny way. Never had she had two men she cared for this fiercely in her life at the same time, and yet, at her own choosing, her arms were empty. She didn't enjoy being alone. Her appetites left little room for singleton heroics, and she was a master at messing with her own head, whether or not she had romantic company. On the other hand, the solution for one man was seldom a second one. The situation needed to breathe. Or there would be no pieces to pick up afterwards.

Her watch read 4:46 a.m. Sunrise was about an hour away and she needed to get a move on. Vee wobbled to her feet, using the rubbish bin outside someone's gate to steady herself. She looked down the closed lane, surprised how far she'd come. Her legs hurt too much to even dream of running home. She started the stroll to the top of the road.

She heard the crunch of loose tarmac under car tyres behind her and veered out of the way of whoever was driving by. She frowned. No lights. Who would be driving before day broke without their headlights on? She glanced over her shoulder. The Mercedes on her tail echoed a shade of grey deeper than the street in twilight, an obese beast of a vehicle. Its glossy body came equipped with the trendy layering of lights that looked like cat's eyes stacked on top of each other. None were on.

Vee clicked up her speed. The engine pumped and the crackle of tyres grew louder. Her heart started to hammer. Okay, she was being followed. And not by someone on foot, where she stood a chance. She stopped and turned, slowly. The Merc rolled to a halt. The rasp of her breathing versus the gentle hum of German technology was all she could hear. She could just about make out the outline of the person behind the wheel, nothing more. The driver had dressed for the occasion and kept it dark.

Vee ran.

The engine rumbled and in seconds the sheer weight of all that metal was at her back, eating up the road. She burst onto the top of the road and rounded the corner, buying a few more seconds. The car lurched to the top of the road, made a wide, clumsy swing and rolled back, before turning the corner. It steered to the right, the headlights popped on and it squealed towards her.

Vee couldn't find the air to scream. At 5 a.m. on a deserted street, screaming would probably be useless. Crime had desensitised the nation; the neighbours would fasten their locks and send her a prayer.

The car ate up her thundering footfalls and Vee faked a right, yelping as the bonnet grazed her hip. She leapt behind a tree on the sidewalk, and the Merc swerved and smashed into the Durawall of someone's house. At last she found her breath, her scream mingling with the crunch of metal and glass into concrete. The headlights on one side were completely smashed. The Merc reversed down the verge of the pavement, its headlights obliterated on one side. The tyres wrenched around as it turned to get back on the road.

Who the fuck is this maniac?! Vee shot from behind the tree.

She thundered down the tree-lined avenue until she spotted a single lit driveway. Hope flared in her heart. In the millisecond it took to zoom past the house with its security lights ablaze, time slowed down. Out of the corner of her eye, Vee saw a woman with dreadlocks wearing an impeccable wool coat and idling next to an open car door, cell phone pressed to her ear. The woman jerked her head up and caught sight of Vee ducking and weaving with a swerving vehicle in pursuit. The woman's frown morphed into horror as the car made contact.

Vee heard and felt every second of the impact like she was having an out-of-body experience: the whump as the bonnet glanced off her glutes, the nip of air on her skin as her body flew, thumped onto the ground and rolled. She heard and felt muscles and bones shift in ways they shouldn't. Lava coursed up and down her side.

Cradling her arm, she hoisted herself up and tried to crawl away. The Merc zipped down the street and overshot the next corner, reversed, did a seven-point turn and roared off. Vee slumped onto the ground for the third time in seven weeks. Someone else finally started to scream.

34

Chlöe knew she was playing with fire, stopping to grab coffee and muffins in Rondebosch instead of hitting the road, and the risk wasn't paying off. If she ... if they didn't get going in about ten minutes, she'd be late. She'd vowed that Voinjama would never enter the building and find her assistant had yet to show up.

So far she'd kept her word. So far she'd kept her word about a lot of things, at least until last night ... when once again she'd been sucked in, chewed up and spat out like old, flavourless gum.

In a bakery on the other side of the street, Chlöe watched her ex-girlfriend fritter around the confectionery display, picking out the choicest bits. The sight made Chlöe's throat clench a little. She'd been handpicked like that, plucked from an array of supple beauties, set aside for carnal delights until her usefulness expired. *Am I really such a gullible hedonist?* she thought. Was she that much of a blind slave to her baser passions that she couldn't let go, or *be* let go, gracefully?

'Hey, I know you.'

Chlöe turned around, the devious itch that came on every time she heard a pretty voice tickling the back of her neck. The stone-grey eyes smiling into hers were needled with amber and framed with batwings of shoulder-length hair. Her pulse skipped. She'd wanted to be disappointed.

'Um, sorry, I don't think so.' She huddled deeper into her coat.

'Yeah, I do know you. Well, I've seen you, at least. We weren't formally introduced.' Three dark moles on the girl's neck did a fetching dance as she spoke. It was all Chlöe could do to keep her eyes off the inviting slope down the V-front of the girl's sweater.

'Remember, a couple of weeks ago? You came to UCT campus to hustle Serena away for a scary chat. You were with a tall black girl, the one with the lips and all that neck.'

Transfixed, Chlöe watched the girl's mouth move. Now this was a lovely pout, natural, and none of that sticky gloss rubbish. It matched her aura of home-grown, farm freshness. Free State, probably; Chlöe had hard evidence that the girls were hot out there. The wind whipped the girl's cascade of onyx hair into a frenzy, and she casually twisted it into a ponytail at the nape of her neck and swept the lot over one shoulder.

Chlöe gulped. *Pay attention and stop perving.* Of course, she remembered now. This was one of Serena Fourie's friends. A member of the flock she was with the day they came to campus.

'How's your investigation going?' the Farm Beauty said.

Chlöe's eyes narrowed.

The girl gave a short laugh. 'Sorry, am I not meant to ask? Is it a big secret? Serena plays it quite close to the chest when it comes to her family. Thinks they lower her prestige or something. Whose family doesn't?' Farm Beauty sighed. 'But she's not very good at hiding her emotions. She was really shaken up after you guys left.'

'Did she have reason to be?'

Farm Beauty smiled scornfully. 'Well, no offence, but you guys did ambush her in the middle of her day. You could've been more graceful and considerate about it. Serena's really sensitive.' She softened. 'Look, I'm sorry. I've known Serena since we started first-year Law together. It was really tough when her sister went missing. I get a bit overprotective when I see how much it still affects her.'

Chlöe felt a wrench of jealousy and longing. At most, she could count on two fingers the female friends invested in her life. Whether Vee liked it or not, she was now number three. It had been two years since Chlöe herself had prowled UCT grounds, and since then her social circle had become no less shallow. She wasn't good with women friends, and they tended to not be cool about her sexual preferences.

'What were you guys questioning her about?' the girl said.

Chlöe crossed her arms. For real? Did this chick think she could pump her for information? *Even* you *are not that hot, my love.*

'I only ask because,' Farm Beauty plunged on, 'I was there around the time when Jacqueline went missing. I … I think I was somehow involved.'

'What? Involved how?' Chlöe perked up.

It was FB's turn to swallow and look uncomfortable. She shivered and drew her trench coat tighter around her waist. 'Like I said, me and Serena have been friends since first year. We were roommates in Tugwell. The night her sister disappeared was so strange. It took me a while to remember this.' FB scratched her forehead. 'Serena got a call. It wasn't late; we'd just had supper, round seven-ish. She took the call in the bathroom for privacy 'cause those rooms were like prison cells. She got so weird after she answered, and then she went in the loo and locked the door. Didn't come out for, like, fifteen minutes.'

'Did you hear what the conversation was about?'

'You mean, did I eavesdrop? No. I don't do stuff like that.' FB looked offended. 'Anyway, afterwards she left the room for a while and when she came back her face was like ...' She shook her head and pursed her lips. 'Serena goes calm and freaky when there's trouble. She gets this aura like she's thinking really hard. She told me, in a very quiet way, that she had an urgent errand to run and asked if she could borrow my car.'

'To go where? Did you ask?'

The black waterfall shook from side to side. 'Couldn't. I wanted to, but the look on her face was like, tjo, don't dare. I asked if she wanted me to come along but she said no. So I gave her the keys. I was really worried about her, but also about my car. It was a new, blue Toyota Corolla I got from my parents for doing so well in matric. The new-look ones, not the old granny type. But it cost too much to run it, you know how student life is. You have a car and all your friends turn into bloody mooches and expect you to drive them everywhere, then they never chip in for petrol. I needed hard cash a lot more than I did a car so I decided to sell. I'd advertised it and had a buyer who was gonna pick it up in two days, so I really didn't want anything

happening to it to bring the price down. But I trusted Serena.
I had to, she begged me.' FB took a deep breath and stopped.

'Then what happened?' Chlöe prompted.

'Nothing.' FB shrugged. 'That was kinda it. She took the keys
and left, was gone for hours. I tried to wait up for her, but I
kinda had other commitments ...' A blush livened her cheeks.
She dropped her gaze demurely. 'I was meeting this girl, and
we ... hung out until pretty late.'

She 'hangs out' with girls! She likes girls! Chlöe bit down on a
grin of triumph.

'I got back to the room after midnight. Serena was already
in bed and the car was fine. Next day, I tried to ask what had
happened, but she insisted everything was cool and stonewalled
me, so I dropped it.'

'Do you remember what day this was? It was ages ago, but–'

'Twenty-second of September,' FB replied immediately. 'A
Saturday. I remember because I was really freaked out, seeing as
I'd never sold something as big as a car before. Afterwards I felt
like a baller; I kept counting all that money and looking at the
receipt. I have it somewhere, the receipt. The guy, the buyer,
was a car dealer. He was supposed to pick it up on Monday
and pay in cash, but he couldn't make the full amount by then
so we pushed it to Tuesday.' FB rubbed her hands together to
warm them. 'By Monday, rumours were already circulating
about Jacqueline Paulsen and by the end of the week it was
in the paper. They said she had last been seen on Saturday. I
couldn't help wondering ...'

Chlöe did the maths: by Monday the twenty-fourth, Jacqui was officially a missing person. Last seen at about 5 p.m. on Saturday. The very evening her half-sister got a mysterious call and then sped off all cloak and dagger.

'It had to have crossed your mind that Serena took your car for something dodgy. You suspected it or you wouldn't have brought any of this up. Why didn't you go to the cops?'

The girl bristled. Chlöe couldn't help but lust over how the amber splinters of her irises glowed when her blood went up. 'I said I thought I was *involved*, not that I was an *accessory*! And I only remembered the incident long after it happened and didn't think it was significant. Even now it sounds so thin. I want to help. When I saw you across the street and remembered who you were ...' Colour spread across her cheeks again and Chlöe felt gratified that it wasn't the only reason she'd felt compelled to strike up a conversation.

FB collected herself. 'Look, not for one minute did I think Serena did anything ... criminal. It's just not her way. She always said her sister Jacqui was, like, low-class and a loose cannon, she needed to get her life together. I figured she helped her to leave. Start over somewhere, like in the movies.' She shrugged. 'It's mad, but that's all I could come up with.'

Chlöe considered. It did indeed sound like madness; another loose end jangling around. And it went quite a way to letting Ashwin Venter off the hook, which she really didn't like. Venter was guilty – proof was all they needed.

'I have to go.' FB wrote on a piece of paper from her pocket and handed it over with a bashful smile. 'In case you wanna ask me more questions. Or y'know, hang out.'

'Isabella' was scribbled above a cell number. Definitely looks like an Isabella, thought Chlöe, watching her walk away. Moves like an Isabella, too. Her phone's ringtone snapped her out of it. Chlöe quaked when she saw the caller identity.

'Where are you?' Portia Kruger demanded. Her voice sounded strained to breaking point.

'Uh, Ms Kruger, I just–'

'Get to Kingsbury Hospital right now. Voinjama's been run over.'

'*What?* Oh my God!'

'I think it was deliberate. Whatever you two have got mixed up in …' There was a shaky intake of breath and muttered curses. 'Kingsbury. Know where it is? Take Main into Claremont, turn into Wilderness Road–'

'Y-y-yes, I know it, I know it!' Chlöe jumped behind the wheel and gunned the engine. She sped past two traffic lights before remembering she'd left behind breakfast, a bewildered ex-girlfriend, and quite likely the ashes of a toxic relationship. Chlöe realised she didn't have the stomach for any of it. By the time she reached Claremont, her encounter with the gorgeous third-year Law student had faded to a nagging red blip flashing in the basement of her memory.

35

Vee snapped the folder on the desk in front of her shut with her good arm.

'I don't buy it,' she said. 'And I'll tell you why I don't buy it.'

'I'm sure you will, and I cannot wait to hear it,' Sergeant Mthobeli said wearily. He was fed up with this woman, with her singsong accent and arm bundled in an unsightly sling. Violence against one's person tended to deter other people, make them re-examine their priorities. No such luck here. Journalists.

Ezra Mthobeli felt some admiration too, despite himself. In addition to single-handedly rejuvenating a long-abandoned case and pushing it further than any officer had, this journalist appeared to be getting help. He didn't know from where, but she was privy to a lot of information concerning the Paulsen enquiry that the press wouldn't be in possession of. Moreover, she'd been allowed to take a quick look at the docket against her assailant. Orders dribbled down from the top, and all he could do was obey.

'I can't wait to hear why you don't believe Carina Fourie is the one who tried to kill you. She has already turned herself in. On top of that, she has confessed to murdering Jacqueline

Paulsen. I've heard about this so-called investigation you've been running.' He wagged his finger under Vee's nose and resumed stamping the reports piled on his desk. 'You got lucky, young lady. After all this time and trouble, the case is solved. Your murderer has walked in and confessed, and you are still alive. Heh-heh, maybe you should come work for us!'

'I don't believe it because it doesn't make sense.'

'What doesn't make sense?' Sergeant Mthobeli banged his stamp one last time and put it to bed on a worn ink cushion. 'The hit and run? We took statements from you and the one witness who saw everything, and your stories tally. Both you and, er ... Mrs ...' He reached for Vee's accident docket.

'Mrs Pearl Nyathi,' Vee chipped in. The angel who'd seen the attack and called the ambulance and police. Thank the sweet Lord for corporate jobs that required late nights and early mornings, otherwise she would've lain in the street for a long while. She had a lot to be grateful for: battered arm and ribs, bruises everywhere but no broken bones or internal injuries. This couldn't become a habit.

'Yes. Both of you saw the licence plate number. In fact, Mrs Nyathi remembered all of it. But then–'

Mthobeli slammed his hand on the desk and Vee jumped. The sergeant smiled beatifically and spread his palms. 'A miracle happens! Before a case file is even opened, a woman walks into Pinelands police station and confesses to two crimes. Two!' He brandished two fingers and wiggled them close to her face, in case the significance of such incredible fortune was lost on her.

'This doctor claims to have killed a teenage girl, her husband's love child. She also admits to using her Mercedes-Benz in an attempt to flatten a nosy journalist who was making her life miserable. That would be you, by the way. So,' he waggled the docket chronicling Carina Fourie's escapades, 'we check out her story and guess what? It all holds water. She even drove the car with the smashed headlight to the station. Imagine that!'

'Which brings us here.' He smiled and waved his arm around the central police station, the squat building on the corner of Buitenkant and Caledon. Carina had been booked in Pinelands and transferred there. The mandatory two-day wait for a court appearance had passed and she was still in custody. Her lawyer was kicking up a fuss. The first hearing was scheduled for two thirty that afternoon. Mthobeli was looking forward to attending.

'So, please tell me which part of this wonderful tale displeases you.'

Vee smiled. Let the sergeant have his fun. 'Her story doesn't add up.'

'Where is your adding not adding up?'

Vee held her peace. She couldn't mention that her boss rewarded heroic endeavours, that Portia had ways and means. Vee now had copies of the original police docket, as well as the full case file on the Paulsen disappearance. 'There are holes in her story.'

'There are holes in my shoes, but I still wear them,' Mthobeli replied. 'I don't know if you are refusing to accept this and laying a formal complaint of culpable homicide. It is your right.'

Vee rubbed her arm. 'I told you, I didn't see the attacker.' Which was the truth. She hadn't even been able tell if the driver was male or female.

'Then we have to wait until the good doctor gives us a more detailed confession,' Mthobeli shrugged. 'Until then, all we have is what she's told us. Carina claims that Jacqueline went to their home late in the evening to speak with her father and found the house empty. Carina was the only person at home. Jacqui had always been rude to her and that night had been no different. Carina was facing the fifth anniversary of her son's death and she didn't want to deal with this child whom she wished did not exist. They had a heated argument that got out of hand and she killed Jacqui in a fit of rage. We have search warrants for their home but, to be honest, we are not optimistic.'

'That's the flimsiest confession I've heard,' Vee snorted. 'Killed her in a 'fit of rage', what is that? *How* did she do it? Where's the body? Why has she refused to let her family visit her?'

The sergeant shook his head and picked up another stack of papers. He didn't want to be rude, but he couldn't spend his whole day on this young woman and her questions. 'You can ask her yourself when you get the chance.'

A constable came in and made a silent signal to his superior. Sergeant Mthobeli turned to Vee, his forehead furrowed. 'This is a huge favour we're doing for you. I hope you know that.'

'I do. Thank you so much.' Vee got up. 'Won't take long.'

'Ten minutes. In and out.' Mthobeli picked up the stamp.

★

'I know you didn't do this.'

'You know nothing.'

'I know more than you do. That's why your confession doesn't line up and you're buying time until you work out the details. It's always the details that let you down, isn't it?'

'My story is airtight, my dear. I've made my peace with what I've done, and I'm willing to face the consequences. I'm actually at peace with putting my cards on the table.' Carina held Vee's gaze and hadn't flinched once.

She's *willing* to face the consequences, Vee repeated to herself. Martyr language, like she was taking the fall for someone else. 'Lies are exhausting, Carina.'

'Yes, they are. As I'm sure you well know.' A smile flitted over Carina's lips and was gone.

'What do you mean by that?'

Carina shrugged with her mouth. 'You are no innocent. You don't look like one. I'm sure you've done your fair share of manipulation to get where you are today.'

Vee straightened up. 'I have no secrets from anyone. And this isn't about me, is it?'

Carina's cackled. 'All women are liars, my dear. It's the bedrock of all our relationships. But you're right; this isn't about you.'

The room they were in was nothing more than four walls, ceiling and floor. They sat at a bare table with four decrepit chairs, space for lawyers and clients to confer. It was drab and featureless, like Carina had become. Her grey-blue eyes were washed out, like they'd been held under a running tap to leach out their colour and vitality.

'What did you do to her? Where's the body?' Vee pressed.

Carina stared past her.

'If you murdered her, you should know.'

'You shouldn't even be here.'

'True, but you were the one who agreed to speak with me. They only allow lawyers and immediate family in here, but you gave your consent to let me in. Why?'

Carina shrugged. 'Intelligent conversation, perhaps. You have been as invested in this ...' she waved a hand noncommittally, '*affair*, as if you are part of my family. I never bothered to ask you why. Why does this matter to you so much? Why would the death of this one girl make you so driven?'

Vee squirmed. 'Stop deflecting. You won't give specifics on what happened because you can't. You probably weren't even there. You have no clue if Jacqui's dead or alive, any more than the rest of us do.'

'Oh, she's dead,' Carina whispered. 'She's dead.'

Vee felt a chill race through her. Weeks of chasing testimony and stitching clues together, and here was her answer. If no supporting evidence ever surfaced that Jacqueline Paulsen was no longer of this earth, the look on Carina's face would suffice.

Carina's facial muscles contorted. 'She took my child, took my *life*. So I took hers in return.'

Adele. These two women had climbed over Ian, the orchestrator of their suffering, to annihilate each other. 'Talk to me, then. Let me tell your side of the story and make things easier for you.'

Carina scoffed. 'You can't help me. You know nothing. You're nobody. You couldn't even help yourself.' Her grey eyes burned as she looked at Vee's injuries. 'I'm fine where I am.' Carina went back to staring at the peeling paint on the walls.

Vee got up and knocked on the door for the guard to open up. The hinges whined as it opened. 'Good luck,' Vee said, and walked through.

36

Vee groaned. A headache was ripening and it felt epic. She mashed her fingers into her temples. 'Why won't it make sense … things are not sticking together, why, why, *why*?'

'Stop aggravating yourself. You should be resting.' Chlöe eyed her over the top of *Elle* magazine. 'I'm assigned to make sure you stay out of trouble.'

'You're assigned to assist me no matter what. I'll rest when I'm dead.'

'That's so not funny, considering what you've gone through. Take that back before it turns into a real jinx.' Chlöe looked scandalised.

Vee swung her legs off the couch. 'Resting' for the past three days had been driving her insane, and she felt like bolting. The end was near, she could feel it. She needed to be out there, chasing it. Chlöe would take some convincing, though. 'It's all these bits and pieces I can't make sense of,' she insisted. 'I hate loose ends.'

'At least now you can give up on Philemon Mtetwa.'

Vee nodded. Dirty or not, Mtetwa was in the clear. He had no real or imagined motive to harm Jacqui. As to means, they had confirmation he'd been in Denmark on business for three weeks around the time of her disappearance.

'Don't be smug. Ashwin's out, too. He's still locked up. There's no way he tried to kill me,' Vee shot back. Venter would be let out on bail soon but two assault charges weren't going away.

Chlöe blew air out of pursed lips. She put the mag down in her lap, finger on her page. 'Okay, let's do this *one more time.* Who's left?'

Vee raised her index. 'Adele …'

'A woman who, unless she's a raging psychopath, has no reason to murder her only child. Come off it. Then we've got the Three Stooges, Rosie, Lucas and Serena.' Chlöe counted them off on her hand and rolled her eyes. 'Whom I won't even dignify with reasons. Which of those three would make a likely candidate for murder?'

'Serena.'

Chlöe dipped her head from side to side. 'Eh. She wouldn't get her hands dirty unless she absolutely had to. And I don't want to hear one more word about it being Ian. You've *made it* make sense because you're gunning for him so bad. One afternoon with nurse Duthie and you were sold. And yet the prime suspect and self-confessed murderer, Carina, who all but painted you a picture when you saw her yesterday, you always put at the bottom of the list.'

'She didn't *confess.* Like, how would she even–'

'This theory-thrashing game sucks and I'm not playing it any more. Jacqui Paulsen committed suicide. She drowned herself at Camps Bay and we'll never know what happened to the body. Carina will unfortunately pay for a crime she didn't commit and everyone else will move on with their existence. Here endeth our fruitless foray into the inner lives of a warped cross-section of the Western Cape middle class. Amen.' Chlöe reopened the magazine. 'You really should get some rest. When you're back at work for real, you'll kick yourself for not taking advantage of this.'

Vee nodded absently. 'Maybe later. What I need right now is to check up on something medical. I hope you won't mind dropping me off, seeing as I can't drive.'

'What, *now?* It's nine o'clock at night, it's raining and the doctor who attended to you at Kingsbury won't be there.' Chlöe meshed her eyebrows. 'What're you up to?'

'Hospitals are open all night, and I didn't mean Kingsbury.' Vee locked eyes with Chlöe, watching slowly as it dawned on her.

'Oh, come on! Right now, at this flippin' hour, you want us to chase Ian down for what reason?'

'Ian? Who said anything about Ian?' Vee flexed her slung limb and winced for effect. 'My arm hurts. A doctor needs to take a look at it.' She laughed at the incredulity and disgust on Chlöe's face. 'Oh, stop. We'll swing by, poke around, rattle him a little, be back here in forty-five. Nothing too intense. Haven't you ever played detective?'

'This,' Chlöe touched Vee's sling, 'and this,' she pressed her bruised ribs, and Vee yelped and slapped her hand, 'don't look like playing. They look like trying to die.' Chlöe put her hands over her face and grunted. 'You're unbelievable. I want it on record that I'm thoroughly opposed to this craziness, and I feel it in my bones that nothing good can come of it. I say we sleep on it and approach everything with a fresh mind tomorrow morning.'

'Duly noted and overruled,' Vee said and tossed her the car keys.

★

It took forever convincing Chlöe to leave, but eventually Vee managed it. Chlöe delivered a stern lecture on the link between destructive behavioural patterns and early death, gave her an impressive list of reliable night-time cab services, and drove off looking deeply concerned.

Directionless, Vee lingered in the WI's reception for a quarter of an hour. An arm in a sling was perfect cover; people took one pitying look at it and assumed she belonged. She had no idea what she wanted to do, or how she'd go about doing whatever it was once she figured it out, but she felt imbued with purpose. Something would nose her on the right path, and it could happen at any moment.

The ebb and flow of humanity's afflicted trickled past the front desk. Television dramas had the world fooled, for not every medical facility was a battleground strewn with blood and pierced with screams twenty-four-seven. The skeleton crew manning reception was taking it pretty easy. Vee deflated a little. The ambience didn't feel like the penny was about to drop at any moment.

She wandered up two floors and over to the specialist units. There wouldn't be a cardiologist working this late, not unless there was an emergency, but it was worth a shot. If she so happened to chance upon Ian in the halls …

Her phone beeped as a text came in. She scrolled through it and her heart pattered:

Hi its Bronwyn Abrams. Sorry it took so long 2 get bak 2 u, been away in Worcester. Free 2 meet 2morow @ lunch or b4 I leav 4 my eveng shift. Call me, chat soon.

'How now, brown cow?' Vee murmured.

Bronwyn Abrams was back in the mix! Jacqui's long-lost friend had risen, and the wait had better be worth it. It could mean everything to talk with her, or it could mean absolutely nothing. She already had a healthy serving of zilch on her plate, so what harm would it do? If Abrams–

'What the hell are you doing here?'

Ian Fourie came towards her in angry strides. Apparently, consultants did work late, especially when the announcement for unit chief hadn't been made yet.

Vee tilted her slung limb in response. 'I'm a patient,' she replied, more calmly than she felt. 'Just thought I'd pass by and …' She let it hang, executing a frantic yet surreptitious recon of the floor. Two nurses poring over files … one random-looking person in a dark hoodie messing with a cell phone … a busy cleaner. Not fantastic odds, but good enough. She wasn't alone with a possible murderer.

'You're enjoying this, aren't you?' Ian fumed.

'No. That's where you're completely wrong. I'm not.' She turned to go and stopped. It was worth a shot. 'Do you know a Bronwyn Abrams, by any chance? Close friend of your daughter's.'

Ian ground his teeth so hard that muscle stippled at his jawline.

'She has information about Jacqui. I'm meeting her tomorrow to hear what she has to say. Might be the stroke of luck we need, right?'

He glared, then tipped the barest of nods and marched off.

★

'So you saw Ian and pissed him off *again*,' Chlöe said.

Vee juggled her phone to the other ear and took a breather, resting her sore hip against the wall of the corridor. 'I didn't piss him off. We talked. Gimme a minute,' she panted.

The longest hallway in the history of hallways sneered at her bruised body, and she still had two-thirds of the way to go. *What was it about the construction of hospitals that brought out the sadistic bastard gene in architects?* she wondered.

She'd been hopped up to get here, now all she wanted was to get out of this place. She must have taken a wrong turn somewhere. Vee tried to remember the baffling directions to the ground-floor exit that the night-shift cleaner on the second floor had given her. Some parts of the building were closed off and the lifts were under maintenance, the cleaner had said. *Sisi, just take the stairs down, neh, then walk all the way down down down that long corridor, then take a left when you see the blue door, don't use the orange one …*

The labyrinth of passages and the odorous medley of faeces, stale boiled potatoes and industrial-strength cleaner weren't the only things giving her the creeps. Her radar was bouncing off the walls. Vee wasn't sure who or what it was, but underneath her breathing and the rhythm of her heart, she imagined she could feel someone else's. In which direction, she couldn't tell. She scanned the corridor and each doorway that fed into it. The only passing stragglers were nurses and other unfortunates looking for a way out of the facility.

The feeling persisted, pulling taut the hairs on her arms and the back of her neck.

Calm yourself, woman.

'What's going on? Are you still there?' Chlöe's voice warbled and squawked, fading in and out.

'The reception's terrible down here. And I think I'm being followed.'

'What d'you mean, *followed*? If you're trying to freak me out, it's not funny. Vee? Vee?!'

Vee pushed open the double doors below the exit sign and a chilly breeze hit her in the face. The rain had slowed to a mist that swirled and spun around the orange haloes of the streetlights. She was in a semi-covered parking area, empty. To her right, a concrete fence demarcated the edge of the WI premises. She found her bearings and her heart sank. She was at the back of the premises – it was either turn back or walk all the way around to the main entrance to get a taxi. Why the hell had she forced Chlöe to leave?

Especially when there was that other pulse riding the wind, disguising itself in the dark.

'Somebody's here,' Vee whispered.

She lowered the cell but didn't cut the call. A streak of black dipped past her blind spot. She lifted her arms and spun. Two blows landed on the back of her neck and brought her down.

37

'Richie! Richie!! *Richie!!!*'

'Urrmgnghnshssh ...'

'Get up, right now!'

A long, unintelligible grumble and rustle of bedclothes came down the microphone of Chlöe's phone. 'It's so flippin' late, CC. What's so important that it can't wait till tomorrow morning? Always gotta be so dramatic.'

Chlöe closed her eyes and wrested her wits and temper under control. CC – short for cotton candy, strawberry of course, which her dear primary school friend had used to describe her then frothy mass of hair. How time flew. Not fast enough, if Richie was still hanging on to that stupid nickname. Well, time moved differently for Richie. The same kid she'd known all her life had regressed from a pretty respectable person into a mole rat, burrowed so deep under so many shadows he bordered on a spook. A spook who was on every hacker watch list locally and probably a few internationally.

'Richie, if you don't wake up right now, I swear to God ...'

'Hey, hey, whoa. I told you *never* to use my real name when you call me on a cell. What're you playing at?'

Chlöe swore long and loud. She didn't know much about computers but she did know Richie possessed every firewall and IT gizmo countermeasure invented. Security was no problem for him. She also knew that if the cowboys of cyberspace were actually paying him half the attention he thought he deserved, he'd have a lot less free time on his hands. It was a game he liked to play with himself – one of the few Chlöe was comfortable thinking about – that of the misunderstood whiz on the run from The Man.

She heard more rustling, exaggerated yawning and lip-smacking. Somehow he'd managed to link a cell phone, motherboards and a sound system into a symbiotic animal of wires, humming metal and blinking lights. It was a twisted thing of beauty. He could answer calls without having to touch a keypad, and every sound he made amplified fivefold as it came down the line. Chlöe pictured him, bleary-eyed, face creased, crawling off a mattress on the floor and probably tripping over a piece of cable in the search for a light. She wondered if his current digs, or rather his revolting sinkhole, was still the mess it had always been. Computer geeks were such a cliché.

'Right.' Heavy breathing, the sound of switches flipping, the hum of an engine being highly productive moved even closer. 'What can I do for you?'

'Two things. Check your phone first. I sent you a recording of a call I was just on. I need a trace on the phone I was connected to, like yesterday.'

He was silent as he listened to the playback. Fear bubbled in Chlöe's throat when the thumps and clattering and a sharp cry from Vee reverberated in her ear.

'Jesus, CC. Sounds pretty hectic. Who was that and what the hell are you mixed up in?' Richie laughed in wonder, alert now. 'How can you be having a *jol* this *lekker* without me? You're faking being a fashion blogger.'

'Journalist. And I'm not faking, so take this seriously and move faster than you're moving at whatever it is you're doing!'

The comforting patter of fingers flying across a keyboard filled her ear. 'You should know this isn't an exact science. I can't just magically give you an exact fix on where a person's using a cellphone. It's not a satellite tracking system. Calls bounce around between network towers depending on how close the caller is to one.' More tapping and distracted murmuring. 'And don't forget this isn't exactly legal. I have to stay a ghost in the system or my whole existence could blow up in my face.'

'Shut up and fix this, Richie, *please*,' she breathed.

At last, he chirped: 'Okay, got it. The phone is still on—'

'It's still on?!'

'Yup, active and bouncing a signal off a tower in Claremont, near Lansdowne Road. It went back and forth between that and a Wynberg tower a few times … hang on … twenty minutes ago. Now seems it's stationary, somewhere in the Claremont area.'

Chlöe didn't know whether to exhale in relief or tremble even more. 'Stationary in the area' could mean Vee had fought off her attacker. She could be injured but safe, grumpily wandering through the WI seeking help for a fresh set of injuries. Or far worse: there could be a dead or unconscious body lying in a parking basement with a blood-spattered cell phone next to it. Chlöe chewed her lip, tasting the sweat lining it.

'Where are you?' Richie asked.

Chlöe's heart did a pirouette as she peered through the windshield. For a second, she imagined movement darting near the empty parking lot. Maybe it was only a cat.

She should've gone home like Vee had told her, instead of sticking around and trying to be brave. She was *so* not brave, not even a little. Vee was good at daring plans on the fly; Chlöe liked her plans measured and easy to wriggle out of. But she was tired of obeying orders like a boring kiss-ass, which she suspected was the image she was cementing of herself in Vee's mind.

All she had to do was drive away, to the nearest police station. Yet she couldn't bring herself to do it.

'I'm home in bed,' she told Richie. 'Safe and sound.' The wind howled and her pulse fluttered. Another shadow that seemed a little too solid for her liking hurtled past.

'CC …' Richie sang his disappointment. Of course – how could she forget who she was talking to? He'd had her position locked before he'd even started working on Vee's.

'Listen, I said there were two things I needed from you.' She swallowed. He was never going to forgive her for this. 'I need you to call central station. Tell them what's happening. Insist on speaking to a Sergeant Ezra Mthobeli.'

'CC …' This time his voice was leaden. 'You know I can't–'

'Just do it, Richie. This is literally a matter of life and death.'

Chlöe took the phone from her ear and pushed it down between the cushion and the handbrake, careful not to press the 'end call' button. She managed it in time. A figure in black rushed out of the shadows, and in one swift motion yanked the door open and dragged her out by the hair. The last thought Chlöe Bishop had before her screams were cut off by a chokehold was, *Shit, forgot to lock the door.*

38

Voinjama Johnson was on her knees, the top half of her chest slumped over something hard and wooden. The smell of rust, mildew and new plastic mingled with that of fresh dirt. Her senses were, in a rudimentary way, attuned to her unfamiliar and uncomfortable surroundings, although her mind was not. She was conscious, but operating on a much-altered cerebral plane. Her breath condensed into vapour as she exhaled; her eyes were wide open, rolled back to the whites. On the monitor in her mind's eye, a sequence of events played out. It was a memory dulled by time, one nearly two decades old, that had squirrelled itself away in a recess she couldn't storm, hoping to destroy it. It surfaced when it chose.

The little girl shivered, legs crossed in front of her as she sat on the ground. The cold was coming from inside her bones. Fear danced in her bloodstream. There were people on the ground next to her. Some of them were dead. She couldn't see how many. She didn't want to see. But she could hear the buzz of flies and feel the foggy stench that came off their bodies, building like a raincloud over her head.

The ones who were still alive had a frightening heat coming off their skin, and they groaned and coughed and vomited on themselves. Every now and again they would twist like snakes or lift their arms up, as if reaching for an invisible force to help them. Some whispered, but the child couldn't hear what they were saying. But she knew they were talking to God.

So was she. She wasn't very big, and neither was her voice, but her Sunday school teacher said God could hear everybody, fish of the sea and ants on the ground alike. She wanted her mother and brother back, wanted to find them or for them to find her. But for now she couldn't hope for that. She would pray for one thing at a time, because God's hands were full with everybody's problems coming in one big rush. Now all she wanted was to get out of this place alive. The room was dark and stank with the smell of dead and dying human beings. Worst of all, it stank of fear.

All of them had walked as a group for miles across the city to cross into the 'safe zone', the side where the rebels didn't threaten and shoot civilians. She didn't know a single person in the group, but being with others made her feel safe. They walked and walked, and more people running from the shooting joined them. Some were carrying loads on their heads and sick children on their backs. Others had bundled their injured onto cloth or wooden stretchers. The crowd got bigger and easier to see.

By afternoon they came upon armed men, more like boys, who stopped them and told them to line up. They were asked their names, their tribes, what language they spoke and which part of upcountry their village was in. Some answered and others were too scared to talk. Some tried to run and were shot. The boys with weapons larger than their bodies got bored with harassing them, gathered them into their truck and drove back to a camp.

The camp looked like it had been a nice neighbourhood not long ago. Now it was just a spread of deserted houses. The people who used to live there were gone, and the walls were full of holes made by bullets and mortars. The rebels had kept the big houses for themselves and parked their trucks in a clearing in the middle of the compound. They separated the males from everyone else and said the men would join their forces. They said nothing about the women and girls and sick people. All the people they didn't need they pushed into one room with a small window high up on the wall and no air.

No one brought food or water. People wailed and prayed loudly. Hours passed, and soon they gave up and kept quiet. More time passed. The girl watched through the window as daylight faded and disappeared. There were sounds of vomiting and people going to the toilet on themselves. A woman screamed over and over, forever, that her baby was sick and dying. After a while she also kept still, and so did the baby. The young girl was too tired to keep her ears covered, but she kept her eyes away from it all, doing what her mother had told her. She sat with her knees drawn up and her head resting between them.

Through the window, daylight reappeared and faded once more.

The girl had gotten used to her hunger and walking for long periods. It had been so long, months and months, since she felt like a child with a life full of normal things. Aside from the guns, her worst fear was the sickness. Cholera. She knew you could catch it very fast, and it spread through the watery pupu and vomit shooting out of the sick ones, sucking them dry until their skin went grey. She had to stay away from it. As long as she wasn't sick she could walk. And as long as she could walk, she could find her mother and brother.

Someone opened the door at the end of the third day. No light entered because it was night-time again. Instead, cool fresh harmattan air rushed in. It woke her from sleep. When she looked up, one of the rebel boys was standing over her with a cutlass.

The room was dark but she knew who he was. The door had opened three times on the second day. Three of the boys had come in, twice to drag out bodies that had stopped moving and once to put down a big dish of rice with palm oil. She had only managed to get one handful, and as she had wolfed it down she had noticed one of the boys looking at her with strange eyes. She had known what it meant. Her mother had told her what everything meant, just before the fighting got terrible. When the boys had left, she had told herself to be brave. She had crawled to the nearest body and rubbed herself with the stinking mix of fluids all over the person's clothes, closing her mind against the smell.

'Finegeh, whah your name?' The boy put down the cutlass and dragged her to her feet.

He was old, but not *old* old – maybe five years older than she was, like her brother. Boys that age thought they were men. They loved to tell you what to do, and give you punishment when you didn't. Quincy smiled when he pushed her around. This boy wasn't smiling.

She didn't answer. Her body felt light, like there was no ground under her. It needed food, but she didn't care any more if she never ate again.

'You nah get sick, ehn,' he said. He flinched at the dried filth all over her. It wouldn't stop him. Everybody had seen everything. With unsure fingers he reached out and rubbed her chest, groping over her T-shirt with heavy fingers. Big women had breasts, but she had nothing.

'Don't touch me.' Tears on her cheeks, she shrank from him. Her foot tripped over something; her body was too light to stop its fall and she tumbled backwards.

The boy knelt beside her. Her fingers scrabbled on the ground until they closed around the cutlass. She drove it up and hit something solid. The boy's face changed. Warm liquid spurted onto her skin. The door was open, inviting her …

Something alive tickled Vee's neck. She jerked awake and scurried away until she hit a wall, choking on a yelp as her head knocked against a wooden surface. The world, or what she could see of it, swam and sharpened back into focus. Pain struck up a marching band inside her cranium.

'It's me,' came a whisper a few feet ahead of her. 'It's Chlöe.'

'Chlöe?' Vee saw two disembodied arms flailing around as they moved closer, until they wrapped around her in relief. Wonderful. She was stuck in a dark hole, phoneless and clueless as to where she was, and the only hope of getting out was trapped in here with her.

'What happened to you?'

Vee rubbed her aching neck. 'I was coming out of the hospital and got knocked out. Corniest trick in the book but it worked. Can people find somewhere else to hit me, 'cause my fucking head is paper-thin from all this abuse. Long story short, I woke up in here.'

Chlöe shook her head. 'Not before; just now. You went vacant, your eyes disappeared right in front of me. It really freaked me out. Where did you go?'

Vee tottered to her feet. Accomplishing anything with a limb that was effectively dead weight was going to be impossible, even with an extra pair of arms. Gingerly, she lifted the sling, passed her head through it and tossed it off her shoulder. She flexed her hand. The muscles felt sore through the vice of the splint-glove, but it would have to do.

'I must've passed out for a li'l bit.'

'It wasn't like that,' Chlöe quivered. 'It was like a trance, and you were muttering shit I couldn't understand ... like that juju stuff you told me about! What happened?'

'Jesus Christ.' Vee took Chlöe's face between both hands and gave her head a little shake. She didn't think it was possible for Chlöe to get any paler, but her skin was positively glowing in the dark. Vee's fingers resembled streaks of muddy face-paint against her cheeks. 'Chlöe Jasmine Bishop. This is not the time for crazy talk about juju and mystical trances, all right? It's not going to help us.'

Vee felt Chlöe's tears trickle down her palms. Chlöe swiped them off with the back of a hand. 'Then what's going to help us? I'm sorry I'm freaking out, but–' her voice cracked. 'How come she *did all this*? What's she planning to do to us?' Her eyes darted, bouncing around the cramped surroundings. 'She was the same one, right, that …'

'Yes, it was Rosie,' Vee said. 'Rosie did all this shit.' Hunted and knocked each of them down in turn, put them in the back of a car with her hoodie over their eyes, drove them to wherever this dungeon was and locked them in. Biggest cliché of the century.

Feeling like an utter fool wasn't going to help them either, but Vee figured that a minute to wallow was appropriate.

39

The hammering on the glass partition of the security booth startled both Etienne Matongo and Marlon Cloete, one of the junior guards on night shift. Etienne nearly spilt hot coffee onto his uniform and Marlon jerked out of his slumber like a man on puppet strings, his chair perilously close to upending him until he braced with one foot. The two men squinted out of the brightly lit cubicle into the rain, surprised at the commotion on such a slow night. The silhouette outside resolved into a young woman, soaked through, her eyes crazed.

'Jissis, man.' Marlon rubbed his eyes. 'Where's the fire? Why's everyone so nuts during the full moon?'

'It is raining. There is no moon,' Etienne responded in a level voice. The younger guard gave him a 'you know what I mean' shake of the head. Etienne turned back to the glass. His chest expanded painfully when he made out the face. It was Serena Fourie.

'Go and have a break,' he ordered. Marlon opened his mouth, and Etienne fished a twenty out of his pocket and pressed it on him. 'It has been a long night. Have a break and I will handle it.'

Marlon studied his boss as he got to his feet. Etienne was as calm as a bay on Sunday; he didn't flip moods like the security chief. Etienne met Marlon's eyes. He knew he wouldn't disobey. Etienne knew the other guards respected him as an understanding guy, one who projected a quiet authority out of every inch of his considerable height. He was the only senior guard, for instance, who would let a man have a guilt-free nap. Etienne would let it slide, as long as it was for short periods under his watchful eye when there were others on patrol. So he wasn't surprised when Marlon took the money without a word, only casting a quizzical glance over his shoulder before he left for the hospital cafeteria.

Etienne closed the office door behind him and joined Serena under the protective canopy covering the booth. Hard rain drummed on the tarpaulin over their heads. Shivering, Serena seemed to dance to its rhythm as she hopped and rocked from one foot to the other. Her hair hung to her shoulders like lengths of curly seaweed. She barely noticed when Etienne removed his coat and draped it around her shoulders.

'It's Rosie. She did it again. I ... I ... I ...' Her chin trembled. 'I tried to watch her. *I tried*, but she sneaked out. I couldn't find her ... the nightmares have started again, and she's been acting crazy ...'

Etienne dropped his head and cursed in a low voice. He had known sooner or later this would happen. Nothing stayed buried forever.

She seemed to take his silence like a slap in the face. 'I tried! I did everything you told me!' she wailed, tears running freely down her cheeks, mixing with rain. She spun away and wept, her back hunched. Etienne let her pour it out, everything she had guarded and fed until it had become too much for her young heart. At last, she gulped down the last of her sobs and straightened up. She slapped the tears off her face as she looked out at the storm, as if only in its chaos could answers to her turmoil be found.

'What has she done?' Etienne watched the back of her head. It shook dejectedly, like she was shaking off the nightmare, peeling its talons back to release the hold it had on her. Her seaweed tresses swung from side to side.

'She took two people,' she whispered. 'She took them and locked them up … somewhere.'

Etienne swore quietly. He wished the hands of an angel would come down and cover his ears so he wouldn't have to hear, to participate in this any longer. He thought of the young girl whose memory he had helped betray for two years, and of his own family, who stood to lose everything through his actions tonight.

'Those two girls from the magazine, the ones investigating—' Serena sucked in a deep breath and it gurgled in her throat.

Etienne's heart, a father's heart, melted in the face of Serena's desperation, as it had once before in the past. 'Where are they? Where is Rosie?'

Serena whirled on him. Her face had aged, its muscles haggard with strain. 'No, no, no,' she shook her whole body in vigorous refusal. '*No*. You can't be involved in this any more. I can't let you. I was wrong to ask you the first time. We were both so wrong.' She reached into her sodden jacket and pulled out a thick, crumpled brown envelope. 'It's to help. Please take it and go. Go now. Before the police get here and ...'

Etienne backed away as if she were brandishing a python. 'Serena—'

'Think of your wife and daughters. Do it for them,' she pleaded. 'It's mine, my savings. It's not a fortune, but it can help you start over. Please, Mr Matongo. Don't risk everything you have left for us.' The package wobbled in her outstretched hands, sobs rocking her body. 'Do it for your daughters.'

Etienne couldn't move. Serena wriggled off the jacket he had draped around her and wedged the money into its side pocket. She pressed the jacket against his chest and held it there, waiting for him to take it. Still, Etienne didn't move. Serena flung herself onto his chest and put her arms around him, squashing the jacket between them. Etienne embraced the weeping child that was not his, comforting her in a way she had long wished her own father would.

Serena pulled herself together and wiped her eyes.

'Please forgive me. Forgive us,' she said, stepping off the pavement. She flipped the hood of her sweatshirt back up and tore into the rain.

40

'I think we're gonna die in here. This isn't how I saw myself going,' Chlöe said.

Vee ran her hands along the cold plastic walls, groping her way around the small space. There were no weaknesses or breaks in the thick material. It had to be industrial-grade stuff. They had tried to rip through it with their hands, but getting traction was impossible, the damn thing was so smooth. From what she could tell, all the walls were lined with it, right up to the roof. The only exception was the bald rectangle outlining the door. They'd tried to kick it down, but all it did was rattle at their efforts. At least they weren't getting rained on.

The darkness was dispiriting. Vee moved along the walls while Chlöe skulked in a corner, her disembodied voice throwing ink bombs into the already gloomy atmosphere. As long as Vee kept moving, the fist of strangeness that built up in her chest when she was trapped in dark spaces would stay back. There had to be a gap somewhere, and she'd find it soon enough. Something that felt like a spider scuttled over her wrist. She brushed it off with a gentle flick.

'Nobody's dying anywhere, so stop being melodramatic. All we need to do is find a way out or let someone on the outside know we're in here.'

'Oh, find a way out or send a rescue signal, why didn't I think of that? You mean signal Rosie the murderer to rush in here and kill us even faster? Like, 'Yoo-hoo, crazy bitch ...''

'Look, cut that snarky shit out. Now, I know this is hard and scary, but focus on a way to help out.'

'I'm not scared,' Chlöe grumbled under her breath. 'And I told Richie to call the cops, so I don't know why no one's come yet. Even SAPS isn't this slow. It's been over two hours! Maybe ... Jeez, he wouldn't be such a selfish shit to turn his back on us to cover his ass.'

Maybe the police, like us, don't know where we are. Vee kept the thought to herself. 'Who's this Richie, now?' she angled to change the subject.

There was rustling in Chlöe's corner. 'Just this guy I know. Forget it.'

Vee paused. 'Wait, is this Richie the hacker, the one who's been getting us all the 'inside' information? As in The Guy guy?' She laughed. 'Is he your boyfriend? What's his last name?'

'No, he's not,' Chlöe spat. 'Look, just forget I said anything, okay? It's nobody.'

Vee shrugged. 'So if the guy called Richie has no last name ... guess I should just call him Guy Richie. Lot better than just The Guy.' She strained her eyes enough to see Chlöe forcing a wan smile.

'Your sense of humour sucks in here. And will you stop all that pacing up and down? It's driving me nuts and it won't help us think faster,' Chlöe said.

Vee dropped her arms. 'Sorry. I'm bad in dark rooms.' Her flesh writhed, trying to crawl off her body. She tried standing still and was surprised and relieved when her focus sharpened. The outline of Chlöe on the floor, hugging her knees to her chest, was off to her right, in the corner with the highest concentration of light. The other centres of light were the door and the ceiling. Darkness pressed back throughout the rest of the space. There had to be another exit, and some kind of implement to help them break through it. More carefully this time, she pressed herself close to the wall and began tracing it, using every inch of her skin to find a snag.

'I'm gay, you know,' Chlöe blurted. 'That's why it sounded so ridiculous when you asked about a boyfriend. I've never had one and wouldn't know what that was.'

Vee dropped her arms again.

'Girlfriend, I do have. Had. I got dumped. *She* cheated, and then had the nerve to dump *me* and throw me out of the flat we were sharing. Which is why I had nowhere to stay until my brother let me live at his place. And *that's* why we stopped at my parents' house in Constantia that day, so he could give me his spare keys. He's staying with them temporarily to give me time to figure things out.' Her face was a tiny oval moon beaming sadness up from the region of the floor. 'I'm sorry if this is a lot to take in right now. It just sucks that I couldn't be completely honest with you from the start, 'cause I wasn't sure how you'd handle it. But seeing as we're trapped in here and might not make it through the night ...'

Vee cast her eyes heavenwards. Good gracious, the theatre was missing this child. 'You don't owe me any explanation about your personal life, Chlöe,' she said quickly, before the silence got awkward. 'But thanks for trusting me.' Her hand turned a corner and she started along the next wall. 'I know all about being dumped and pathetic; my story would give yours an ass-whupping any day, no contest. And to be honest, I was kinda fifty-fifty on whether you were or weren't. My gaydar's horrible.'

A giggle drifted from the corner. 'Really? You're one of the most bizarrely observant people I've ever met, and I'm pretty obvious for the most part.'

'Ah. Put it down to ... cultural conditioning, if you will. Personally, I only care who I'm messin' with. Everybody else can watch their own backs and mind their own business.' Vee flexed her arms to loosen out the kinks. She couldn't keep this up all night.

'Well, from what I hear you're fucking half the city, so. No wonder you're so duh about other people's sex lives.'

Vee picked up the first object she could get her hands on and threw it. Chlöe squealed, laughed and threw it back, missing by a mile.

'My life's no secret, anyway. My dreadful sister found out about my relationship, outed me to the rest of my family and my parents banished me like some medieval outcast who'd shamed the lineage. She and Mum talk about me to everyone as if I joined the bloody circus.' Chlöe chuckled sourly. 'I'm like a celebrity among the more old-school lot in Constantia.'

Vee felt a protrusion in the wall. It didn't flow right around in one continuous rectangle. She doubled back and probed again, letting her fingers bump up and down against the side of the lump. It felt like a rectangle within another rectangle, a cupboard built against one end of their cell.

'I've just got one question,' she said.

Chlöe sighed. 'It's not just a phase.'

'No, not that.' The door, if that's what it was, was all rough wood, with no covering. Vee didn't know how she'd missed it. She popped at it with the heel of her palms, careful to avoid splinters. It was about two metres in width, maybe three in length. With any luck it would turn out to be another doorway. 'You're twenty-three, with a good degree. Why the hell were you still living with your parents?'

Sensing the excitement of a breakthrough, Chlöe scrambled over to help. 'Are you kidding me? My parents are loaded. I had everything: credit cards, a great ride, practically a whole floor to myself in the house. Now I'm living at Jasper's and driving his hand-me-down.'

'Rich pipo problems, right,' Vee replied.

They leaned their shoulders into the wood and the door groaned open. An array of objects fell out, clattering onto the floor.

Vee picked one up. 'I think I know where we are. This is some kinda tool shed. See, this is a rake, and some iron rods for Lord knows what, and ... wait a minute, this must be a drill–'

'Yay!'

'You need a plug to operate a drill. Definitely no power outlets in here.'

'What kind of tool shed is this? Why doesn't it have a tractor or something, so we can crank it up and mow down the door?'

'It's not a shed in a Steven Seagal movie, that's why. But I've got an idea.' Vee gripped one of the iron rods in her fist, weighing its heft.

They went around the floor space one more time, both clutching a metal rod and tapping it against the walls. Chlöe held up her hand when she heard a change in timbre that indicated glass. She drove her rod up until the sound of cracking turned into shattering. They held their breath, waiting for the door to burst open. Nothing. They switched out the rods for the longest and sharpest of the tools, ripped away enough plastic to make a sizeable hole and poked out the rest of the juts of the glass studding the rim of the frame. Wind and rain whipped into the shed. Chlöe whispered 'window' like a wanderer who'd stumbled on buried treasure.

'I think I know where we are.'

'You said that already. In a tool shed.'

'No, where the shed itself is,' Vee said. She couldn't see much through the tiny window, but there was enough light now to inspect their prison. Her best guess had been a storage container or empty garage on the Fourie property, but that couldn't be. This gear was way too boutique for a family garden shed, plus smuggling two hooded women, in two separate trips, into a backyard in a suburb was too risky.

'These are construction materials. That's what this shed is for. It's reinforced with plastic so the tools don't get rusty. We're still at the WI, at the construction site at the back!'

Chlöe looked sceptical. 'Rosie could've taken us anywhere else, where no one would ever think to look, and she chose *here*? Screw it. I'm done asking questions.' She scraped glass away with her foot and pushed her skirt up her thighs. 'The quicker we get out of here, the better.'

They piled every solid, non-sliding object from the cupboard as close to the window as possible. Thigh muscles shaking as she tried to keep her balance, Vee climbed on top of the junk heap and hoisted Chlöe up. It made sense that the smaller and shorter ought to go first. It was also pretty clear that should their captor return and catch one of them, it definitely shouldn't be Bishop.

Chlöe shot through the window like a human projectile. Vee winced, listening to the thumps and splashes coming from the other side. She waited out the thuds and spray of cursing that followed. Rain pattered into her eyes through the busted window. 'You okay? Sorry, I think I pushed too hard,' she said.

'I'm okay,' answered Chlöe's voice, strangled with pain. 'Landed on my hands. I think something's broken. Jissis, that hurt!'

'Sorry, babe, but we can't stand around making chitchat. Can you see anything?'

Vee heard her footsteps squishing through mud as they moved away. Seconds passed. The footsteps came squishing back.

'You're right, we're still at the WI. Not sure where. I think it's at the back, where they're building the sports and gym section.

There's a tennis court further down and that ugly, big-ass hole they're turning into a pool.'

'Find your way back to the main building. Get to a phone, a security guard, the first person you see. Just get help. Don't stop—'

'Wait, I'm coming around to let you out first.'

'Chlöe, just go, don't—!'

Too late, Vee heard her take off. She held her breath, prayed and waited. The storm and reinforced walls of the shed dulled every sound coming from the outside. Two full minutes ticked by. Her heart sank. The shed was the size of a doghouse; it was thirty seconds max for a blind man on crutches to go around it at full speed. She swallowed and found her mouth was dry.

★

Seven minutes.

Still nothing.

Seven and a half.

Vee looked up at the window, wondering whether to damn it all to hell and follow anyway. She was taller than Rosie. Not by a helluva lot, but yes, taller. True, for a teenage kid Rosie was built like a prize steed, but Vee could put up a decent fight. It was that or sit tight and wait, and inertia was not her friend right now. Anything could be happening to that little numbskull. Terror tightened a noose around her heart at the thought. Anything could be happening to Chlöe …

She scrambled atop the heap. Her fingers froze on the sill. A scream carried on the wind. The metal catch on the main door ground as it drew back. Vee jumped and almost lost her footing when the door flew open.

Serena pushed in first, carrying a huge flashlight. In its glow, her face looked terrified yet eerily calm. Chlöe stumbled in after her, her hair wound up in the fist of Rosie, who brought up the rear. Rosie shoved Chlöe into the middle of the room, twisting her ponytail so hard she screamed and staggered to her knees.

'Rosie, stop that,' Serena hissed, sounding like a mother chastising an errant child for smearing her best dress with ice cream. 'Could you come down from there, please?' she called up to Vee.

Vee realised her mouth was hanging open and quickly snapped it shut. The fact that Rosie was behind this was taking an appreciable amount of cerebral gymnastics, but she hadn't expected to see Serena here. Vee felt like an idiot the second the thought crossed her mind. Of course Serena would see to cleaning up her sister's mess; she'd probably been doing it their entire lives. Vee felt doubly stupid for not seeing it earlier. Rosemary Fourie was an unmitigated mess, fifteen years in the making. And unlike Lucas, the most innocuous of them all, Rosie was a powder keg begging to be lit. Little Rosie the overgrown baby, tamped down and boxed in, mollycoddled and insulated by everyone around her. Vee remembered the blaze of rage Rosie had unleashed in the street the first time they met and, looking into her eyes now, it was obvious the kid was a breath away from tipping into the void.

'Serena ...' Vee began, and stopped. Serena what? How could you do this? Why help your crazy little sister? How could you let it go this far? What choice had Serena had?

'You have one more year before you graduate. You can still have a bright future,' Vee told her quietly, which was all she could think of. 'This isn't going to fix anything.'

Serena agreed with a distracted nod. 'I know what I have,' she said flatly. She looked and sounded exactly like her mother in that moment – dutifully proud in her defeat.

'Let Chlöe go. This is way out of hand as it is, and she's nothing but a clueless brat that follows me around. She's not a part of this ...' Vee spoke fast, ignoring the incredulous whimper that rose from where Chlöe lay on the ground. 'The three of us can talk, but if anything happens to her ... if any white people get hurt, everything gets *so* much worse. You know how this works.' The sound from the floor changed to something suspiciously like muffled laughter.

'Nobody goes anywhere, so shut up!' Rosie's breath was a blast of sour air. Watching the dance and twitch of individual muscles in her face, lit by the glow of the flashlight, was almost mesmerising. 'She stays, you stay, *shut up!*'

Serena pulled her shaking sister to heel and drew an arm around her. 'Ro, please, *please*, sweetie ... she has a point ...' Her tone was so measured and reasonable that, if not for the quavering, Vee would fully believe her capable of headshrinking all of them out of their debacle.

'Noooo ...'

'Sweetie, calm down and listen to me—'

A copper-tipped missile streaked through the narrow doorway and out into the night before it dawned on anyone that Chlöe was making a run for it. Rosie roared, elbowing and squirming out of her sister's grip to pursue her. Serena and Vee leapt to restrain her, wrapping their arms and legs around her body. The sheer force of her struggles nearly brought the three of them crashing to the floor.

'For Chrissake, will you stop it … Rosie, listen, just – ow, shit! Stop it or I'll *klap* you!'

It was like trying to restrain a bronco. Serena wrapped her arms in a vice around Rosie's torso, linking her hands to close the hold. Vee held onto her legs. They bucked and keened in time with her struggles until slowly the fight in her died down. Rosie began to sob.

'They ruined everything,' she quailed. 'They screwed it up, I screwed it up. Why does this keep happening?'

'Bad things happen, Ro. It was an accident. This was all an accident. No one blames you,' murmured Serena. On the floor, Vee writhed into a better position to catch Serena's eye (*no one blames you?!*) but Serena kept her gaze resolutely turned away. Vee understood – this was her baby sister, she had to say something.

'The police should be here any minute. We heard them coming on the road,' Serena said, stroking her sister's hair. 'We'll wait here with you.'

A shriek tore out of Rosie's throat, so loud and visceral it sounded like she'd torn a vocal cord. She unfurled like an explosive blossom, her shoe kicking Vee in the neck and elbow knocking Serena down flat onto her backside. Before they could recover and make a grab for her clothes, she shook the two of them off and lunged through the door.

Vee gulped in shock and swallowed a mouthful of icy rain as she hit the outside. It took a few seconds – too long – for her vision to adjust to the darkness. She caught movement up ahead and ran towards it, in the direction of the streetlamps and unfinished sports centre. She nearly crashed into the wire fence that ringed the unfinished pool before she realised it was there, skidded and grabbed on to steady herself. Panting, she looked around again. Serena ran up behind her.

Things happened like a series of shots fired.

A streak blurred past the corner of Vee's eye off to her far right. It coalesced into Chlöe, who zipped right into the mesh, dropped to her knees in the mud, and squirmed through a fresh opening in the fence. Chewing up her trail like a creature possessed was Rosie. Chlöe pulled her foot through to the other side just as Rosie rammed into the mesh, scrabbling for her legs through the hole. Rosie wriggled through the gap after her. Chlöe sprinted, screaming, pellets of rain bouncing off her face. Her boots skidded on the smooth, wet cement near the lip of the pool and her heels crunched as she braked. Her arms pinwheeled as she fought to keep her balance. Rosie charged again. Chlöe swayed and fell backwards, landing on the right side of the world. The rocket of dark that was Rosie flew past her, her look of rage crumbling into one of shock and terror as gravity pulled her into the unfinished pool.

The splash was louder than the thunder. They all stood slack-jawed, watching Rosie dip below the surface and bob up again, her mouth filling with brown water each time she surfaced. Trembling, Chlöe looked over the expanse of the crater and through the fencing at Vee. Vee, breathless and blank, looked to Serena. Serena wrapped her arms around herself, opened her mouth and released a wail of anguish, heaving under the force of her sobs.

They stared back and forth at each other for what felt like eternity, their eyes communicating the worst: none of them knew how to swim.

Somewhere in the background, police sirens struck up a tardy redemption song.

41

'You got any idea how ridiculous two black people in a pool look? You know how the joke goes.'

'Not so crazy when one of them used to be a lifeguard. Who cares anyway? There's not a soul here to see us.'

'I bet you love that.'

Laughter. 'Yeah, I do actually.' Titus paddled up behind Vee and gently spanned her waist. The heating hadn't kicked in yet, so his hands felt warm compared to the tepid water. They always stayed warm, no matter how long they stayed in. He pressed close and ran his cheek past hers to her neck. Vee shivered and pressed her back to his chest.

'I'm never going to learn anything like this. You go round molesting all your students like this?'

'Only the very, very special ones.' His palms came to rest at the small of her back. Slowly, he began to guide her body forwards. 'Before you learn to swim, you gotta learn to float. Once you can stay afloat, you can start to move through the water. Remember what I showed you last time?'

The floor started to disappear from underfoot.

'Titus ...'

'Don't worry, I won't get your hair wet.'

'It's not my hair I'm wo– whoo! Aaay mah pipo, don't let me drown. Don't let this crazy man kill me today.'

'Don't worry, I got you. Now move your legs. Slooowly, don't thrash. Make circles, and concentrate on keeping the circles in one direction. Good, that's great. Now use your arms ... get your arms and legs to move together. I'm just gonna back off a little bit now. I'm not leaving you ...'

He let go. She didn't sink.

'Ha! I'm doing it! I can do it, I can swim!'

Titus chuckled. 'Yeah, you can swim. You're a natural.'

Voinjama circled around a small area, paddling her limbs like a joyful frog. Swimming was easy. Why had she been scared? 'When will you show me how to save somebody from drowning?'

'Let's get you from one end of the pool to the other without dying. Then we can talk about saving other people's lives.'

42

Vee dived into the pool. The tide of brown water closed its hands over her head.

She blinked into the murk. She couldn't see shit. She stretched her toes out, reaching for solid ground. There was nothing; she was too far out. The dimensions of the pool came screaming to the front of her mind, and she fought a burst of panic. Her arms arced through the water in a basic stroke, and her heart dub-dubbed in triumph as her body moved forward in response. She took a few more strokes, coasted, lost her air and pushed to the surface.

Spluttering, she looked around until she glimpsed Rosie, thrashing up a vortex of panic. Vee doggy-paddled nearer, gulping down huge breaths and bracing for the worst the closer she got. Rosie's hand smacked her all over the face, desperate for a hold on anything that would keep her from sinking, and finally latched onto her shirt.

Always remember: a drowning person is desperate. They can't swim, but survival instinct means they'll try, even if it means wasting all their energy and oxygen.

Rosie whinnied, her eyes darkening with terror. Her kicks and struggles got feebler as she clung to Vee, her weight an incredible drag with each passing second. Vee gulped some more, ballooning her lungs and forcing herself to relax and resist fighting back as Rosie wrapped both arms around her, pulling them both under.

That also makes them dangerous. By the time you make it to them, they're practically worn out. When they grab on to you, don't fight. You'll both drown. It's tough, but just go down with them.

They sank.

Lumps of dark matter floated past. Vee hastily squeezed her eyes shut, sparing herself the trauma of watching her last moments go by in what was essentially effluent.

Hold your breath for as long as you can. When you feel the person go limp, grab on tight and swim to the surface.

Pulling Rosie was like hauling a small barge to shore with one finger. Vee's burning lungs nearly ruptured in gratitude when she hit the surface. She paddled and breaststroked the best she could with one arm. Within a couple of feet of the rim Chlöe and Serena splashed in, grabbed them and dragged, the four of them trundling towards the edge like an unsteady raft.

'I don't know CPR!' Serena screeched.

Rosie saved them the trouble, vomiting on the concrete. Drained, sodden and panting, they huddled near the edge of the crater, listening to the sound of a siren in the distance. Vee didn't want to think about which of them would eventually have to hobble to the front entrance to bring in the cavalry, but she had a feeling she already knew the answer. She rolled onto her back and stretched out her legs, catching her breath first.

'It's stopped raining,' Chlöe observed softly, looking up at the sky in wonder.

'Yeah, it has.' Wheezing, Serena followed her gaze. 'Fucking Cape Town.'

43

A procession of warm bodies tiptoed in and out of the private room on the recovery ward. A junior doctor flexed Vee's arm and clucked her tongue in reproach. A male nurse asked her a string of incomprehensible questions in Xhosa as he hung a drip next to the bed. A confused octogenarian wandered into the room and managed to pee on the floor before two orderlies steered him away. Vee could barely keep her lids open long enough to register most of it. She crashed once her head hit the pillow, slept for ten straight hours and woke the following day in time for the lunch rounds with arid nostrils and a raging bladder.

Her first visitor was Bronwyn Abrams. Afternoon visiting hours hadn't quite begun but she'd been waiting for over an hour, so the nurses took pity and let her through. Bronwyn's soft, quiet eyes were rimmed crimson from crying, her face drawn and puffy. The toddler she had in tow bounced around the room, entertaining himself with a toy airplane while she talked. Bronwyn gripped Vee's hand as she sat next to the bed, breaking into a fresh bout of blubbering every time she went over another emotional part of the story she'd already spent the morning telling the police.

'I feel so guilty. I didn't know,' she sniffled, fresh tears running down her face. 'I swear, if I'd known it was important I would've gone to the police two years ago. I wish I could take it all back.'

Vee patted her hand. 'What's done is done. At least now you know what your friendship meant to her.'

Chlöe poked her head in as Bronwyn was on her way out. Vee watched them whisper in the doorway before Bronwyn scooped up her son and gave her a grave nod goodbye.

'The minute we were rescued, I called her to go straight to the cops and give a statement like you told me. I have no idea what her part in this is, but I reckon you'll tell me. And look, I've got war wounds, too!' Chlöe proudly brandished her arms, bandaged up to the wrists in a detachable splint much as Vee's had been. 'Of course, you're the real hero, which is why Portia the Proud is coughing up for such a nice room. And it's *not* at the WI, thank heavens. After this, I don't think I could ever let those crazies give me a Panado.' She gave Vee a playful pinch. 'How're you feeling? Your swimming skills saved a life, bru!'

'My what skills? I got lucky ... If that had been a real pool, last night would've ended differently, trust me. A long time ago I had three whole lessons with a great instructor and lost interest. Let's just say, when it comes to bodies of water, I know how to ... not die.'

'Whatever. You saved the person who tried to kill us, so that makes you a double badass.'

'Okay, *tried to kill us* may be embellishing a little, Bishop.'

'Excuse me? I felt decidedly in peril, so speak for yourself.' Chlöe took away the dry sandwich Vee was forcing herself to chew, tossed it in the bin beside the bed and moved the food tray to the side table. 'I'll buy you real food in, like, five minutes. I already know Sergeant Mthobeli filled you in with Rosie and Serena's statements so you have the full picture now, right? So tell me, tell me, tell me!'

Vee was overjoyed when Connie breezed in, laden with goodies: chunks of meat floating in *peppe* soup, a glistening cheek of fufu and sliced mangoes. Chlöe backed away from the eye-watering hit of chilli. Vee teared up in gratitude.

'You the one encouraging this girl to act crazy all around town and get herself killed?' Connie demanded from Chlöe as she dished up, eyes glowering. Chlöe was about a head taller, but she shrank away, throwing Vee a worried look.

'I've always found she hardly needed any encouraging,' said a voice behind them.

Titus filled the doorway, tentative of grin and armed with a goodie basket. Behind him stood Joshua, unburdened, his hands nestled in his pockets. If Vee knew him at all, there was something in there. She craned her neck, anxious to meet his eyes as the room bustled with bodies exchanging niceties and shuffling for room to sit. At last, he met her gaze and tossed her a smile that was all eyes.

Vee felt her shoulders unknot. 'Damn.' She was surprised at how relaxed – no, *buoyant* – she felt. Maybe the IV bag running into her vein contained something surplus to requirements, a dash of mood enhancer thrown in with the fluids and electrolytes. 'I *feel* stupid, if this is what it takes to get this much attention. Too bad I'm being discharged this evening.'

'You should feel stupid,' Titus said, perched next to Chlöe on the empty bed opposite.

'You're the stupidest person in the world,' Joshua added, his rump parked on the window ledge. Vee noticed they couldn't have been further apart than if she banished them to separate corners of the planet.

'Whatever, whatever!' Chlöe bounced on the mattress, brimming. 'Ooh, this is just like the mystery books, when the great detective gathers everyone in the drawing room and–'

'Chlöe.'

'Ag, then for fuck's sake, *spit it out.*'

44

Vee leaned back and got comfortable. 'We were both wrong. We had our reasons, solid ones, but we couldn't have been more off base. My biggest mistake was assuming this had to be a man's crime. If I'd paid closer attention it would've clicked from the outset this had nothing to do with the adults; they were mere bystanders. It began with Sean, and sucked Jacqui in. Serena and Lucas were satellites.'

'But you were onto something with Bronwyn too, right?' Chlöe asked.

'Which I couldn't figure out,' Vee replied. 'And if Rosie and Serena had got rid of us last night, we would've died never knowing how Bronwyn or a lot of other things added up. But I'll come back to that later.

'Like I said, it started with Sean and Jacqui, and that's more or less how it ended. Had I simply paid attention to the dates on which they both died – in the same week, only in different years – it would've clicked that the death of one led to the death of the other. When Sean died all the grown-ups died too, in a way. Everybody made so much noise about how incredible this kid was, I wanted to off him myself. Ian and Carina took it the hardest, and Adele's guilt about Jacqui's role in the transplant fiasco made her open to allowing her daughter to nurture ties with the Fouries, at least at first. It'll torture her for the rest of her life, wondering if it would all have been different now if she'd cut her losses and moved on.

'But I didn't examine the kids thoroughly. The star player was dead and the others just faded into non-entities. The kids grew up knowing that, accepting it. What Sean's death broke, no one ever wanted repaired, and they didn't dare taint his memory by learning to be happy again.

'Rosie herself said the baby of the family doesn't count. She hurt just as much as everyone else, but her grief was second-hand; she hadn't earned it. Not to mention, she's the outcast. Big girl, awkward and overly sensitive, not easy on the eye like her sisters. She's aware of it, too. Seeing the effects of Sean's death made her want to make sure that nothing would ever break her family up that way again.

'I imagine she started hanging out with Jacqui to size her up. The parents had their misgivings about another kid muscling into the fold so soon after the loss. The one smart thing Rosie realised, which no one else did, was that by hook or crook Jacqui intended to make herself part of that family. In Rosie's warped mind, she was the gatekeeper. Jacqui would have to go through her. And since the doctors raised their kids to believe that being a Fourie was the highest honour – extra fuel. Rosie went in, Jacqui wooed, and Rosie fell. For once she felt noticed and accepted for who she was. A feeling she didn't get at home, what with Serena and Lucas patronising her. Jacqui became sister and friend.'

'That was the trigger,' Chlöe interrupted. 'Serena and Lucas warmed up to Jacqui and stole her away from Rosie.'

'Exactly. Shoplifting and bunking school are out of character for Rosie, but Jacqui was a rebel. Rosie knew they got up to no good together, but screw it, she had a partner. Then Serena swooped in, Jacqui found Jesus and, ironically, everything got worse. Rosie got benched again – the baby who would never grow up – and it pissed her off. She felt betrayed. But I'll swing back to that, too. The church angle may've had nothing to do with Rosie, but it brought in a new person, or rather an old acquaintance, in Bronwyn.'

'You're a terrible storyteller,' Connie grumbled.

'Yeah, you need to explain about Bronwyn because I'm in the dark there.' Chlöe scratched her cheek. Connie and Titus frowned, only just hearing the bulk of the tale. Joshua tilted his head, the crease between his eyes deepening.

'Bronwyn came by earlier with her sixteen-month-old son. Her grandmother's very sick and they've been with her in Worcester all this time, and she wasn't taking calls. Which is why she only hit me up last night when she got back in town.'

'Wait a minute,' Joshua said. 'This Bronwyn, she was one of the two friends your missing girl was close to, right? I remember you mentioning her.'

Vee nodded energetically. 'Yep. Like Ashwin, she was one of the last to see Jacqui alive.'

'And her son is sixteen months …' His expression came alive like a comet entering the atmosphere. 'The kid, the money scam … God, she should've contacted you sooner. This could've been over weeks ago.'

'What? I don't get it.' Chlöe shifted round on the bed to glare at him properly. 'I've been working on this from day one and I don't get *any of that.*'

'Let me back up a li'l bit and explain this relationship,' Vee said.

'Please. Because I'm in the middle of this spider web of people like a fly with a serious headache,' Connie said.

'Adele Paulsen and Bronwyn's parents are old friends and their girls grew up together,' Vee explained. 'Their nickname was 'J&B' when they were younger because they were so close. Bronwyn's shy and from a strict religious home, and after Jacqui moved to Little Mowbray they drifted apart. Fast forward some years later. Jacqui catches the Holy Spirit and joins Serena's prayer group. In all that Bible study and choir practice around town, Jacqui and Bron reconnected and jump-started their relationship stronger than ever. Even though they went to different high schools, Jacqui always invited Bron to mingle with her other friends to bring her out of her shell.'

'Which explains Tamara and all her bitchiness,' Chlöe said. 'She did *not* like sharing her best friend with some mousy competitor.'

'Apparently, Bron busted too far outta that shell and got pregnant. She was sketchy about details of the father, but suffice it to say he lied her panties off, knocked her up and then played dumb. Same old, same old.'

'It's always the Christian girls,' Titus muttered.

Chlöe sucked in her breath. 'No way. Ashwin?'

Vee shook her head. 'I thought so too, but she swears not and I believe her. He's not her type, and Jacqui would've known. It's some average Joe she knew. Anyway, needless to say she freaked out and turned to the one friend she had who knew a thing or two about such matters. Getting an abortion was against Bron's beliefs, but it felt like the only choice. Jacqui tried to talk her out of it but Bron wore her down, threatening suicide and all sorts of craziness.'

Connie looked confused. 'A woman can get an abortion at practically any facility. She doesn't even need parental consent, as long as it's within the first twelve weeks. Why didn't Bronwyn just get it done at a state hospital?'

'She was hysterical. She admitted that had she done that, things would've taken a different tangent. But we're talking about two teenagers. They'd know how badly young women requesting abortions get treated, or, worse, the horror stories of backstreet procedures. Bronwyn was also terrified she'd run into someone from her neighbourhood or church, or even one of her relatives, and she'd be busted. Both she and Jacqui agreed it had to be somewhere posh and discreet if her parents were never to know.'

'And *that's* where the informal business came in.' Chlöe sighed, relieved to be on the same page. 'Jacqui had given up all her naughty tricks, and she'd blown her savings on expensive goodies, so they couldn't afford it. She tried going back to selling, but that didn't last long before she got caught and suspended from school. And still they didn't have enough for a proper doctor.'

She flagged. 'And I'm stuck again. How'd it get to Rosie? Wait, don't tell me ...'

'Jacqui decided to ask for it. She could've stolen the money from either of her parents or somewhere else, but that kind of behaviour was behind her. She was already grounded for so many other things, she figured she had nothing to lose by asking for the rest. The worst answer she could get was no.'

'So she went by the Fourie house after tennis practice that Saturday to make her case,' Chlöe said.

'First she went to see Bronwyn, who lived over in Woodstock back then. Bron was about nine weeks in, praying it wouldn't be noticed. She called Jacqui every day. That Saturday she was inconsolable, so Jacqui agreed to stop by after tennis. Later on, she told the cops that Jacqui had been with her for only a half-hour, but admitted to me it was actually two. When the case went crazy, she wanted to change her story but was scared, and didn't think the extra time mattered either way. Like everybody else, she thought Ashwin was responsible.'

Joshua asked, 'So what happened to the cell phone?'

'It got lost, or more likely stolen, like you said. Jacqui took the train from Newlands Sports Club to Woodstock at about one thirty, and Bronwyn remembers her saying she got jacked on the way there. Jacqui ended up chilling with her for a while and making plans about what to do, which accounts for the missing time we weren't able to explain. Two hours sounds about right to calm a friend down. Jacqui promised she'd fix it but didn't say how, and then she left when it was after four. After that, I'm just filling in the gaps. We know she saw Ashwin and they fought. I'm certain she went to press him for some cash, but they got into it the way they always did. She must've realised it was a dumb move, especially when he was still hung up on her. That's when she made the biggest mistake of her life, turning to the Fouries as a last resort.'

'But *why Rosie*?' Chlöe looked completely floored. 'What set her off enough to kill her own sister? The rest of us haven't heard her statement yet, but you have.'

Closing her eyes for a second, Vee tried to visualise the scenario in her mind, tempted simply to doze off. She was spent. Gratitude to be in one piece after her ordeal was all fine and well, but she needed some major downtime.

'Jacqui took the train to Pinelands and got there after six o'clock that evening,' she said finally. 'This time of year it still gets dark early. She was phoneless, hadn't checked in with her mother or anyone else as to where she was, and was no doubt in a feral mood. Pinelands is a quiet suburb and likely nobody saw her. No witnesses came forward to say they had.

'Nobody was expecting her, either. That Saturday was the twenty-second, the beginning of school holidays. Ian and Carina were grinding even harder back then than now, putting extra hours into the WI. The maid was long gone. Serena and Lucas didn't live at home any more. The only person there was Rosemary.'

She switched, paraphrasing from memory what Sergeant Mthobeli had recounted from the sisters' statements: 'Rosie refused to let Jacqui in. Jacqui had ditched her, and she was angry and suspicious. She wanted to know why Jacqui had come to the house, but Jacqui only said she needed to talk to Ian urgently and would wait around until he got home. Eventually, she lost her temper with all Rosie's prying, told her to go to hell and started to leave.

'Rosie said she *knew* Jacqui was pregnant, that she'd suspected it for weeks until Jacqui supposedly confessed it. Once she heard that, Rosie reached her own conclusion about who the father was.'

'Lucas.' Connie's mouth fell open. 'Ag no man, her brother and sister were going to have a baby together!'

'But Rosie was wrong,' Vee said. 'She'd known for a long time about Lucas's feelings, and remembered how Jacqui had been avoiding him. She jumped to the wrong conclusion. I think in her anger Jacqui admitted to wanting her father's help with *a* pregnancy, Bronwyn's pregnancy, but Rosie got the wrong end of the stick.

'Jacqui stormed off down the driveway. I can only imagine what went through Rosie's mind watching her go, what she was feeling. This girl was supposed to be the new sister they'd welcomed into their lives, but she was going to destroy everyone all over again, just like her mother had. After the devastation of Sean it would finish the family, her parents' careers, if that kind of scandal broke. She must've been revolted at the thought of what her siblings had done. She must've felt rejected that the one person she'd come to love and count on had just spat in her face. That's when she lost it.'

'And we've seen Rosie lose it,' Chlöe said. '*She ... flips ... her ... shit.*'

'Jacqui was over at the electric gate waiting to be buzzed out. Carina's car was parked, and Rosie blindly grabbed the keys and jumped in. She was thirteen and couldn't drive beyond the basics. I don't even think it dawned on Jacqui what was happening until the car crushed her. By the time Rosie came to her senses, Jacqui was dead.'

The air conditioner thrummed over the thick silence, pumping extra chill into the air. Subdued, Vee reached for the remote and switched it off. The beep it gave winding down felt like a sad punctuation mark to a long, harrowing chronicle spanning weeks.

'How did she get rid of the body?' Titus asked quietly.

'She called the sister she thought she couldn't count on, and Serena came through for her. She drove from campus in a borrowed car, which they used to dump the body. The police are conducting a search for the car and remains as we speak.'

Chlöe's bandaged hands clapped over her mouth. Her face slackened and blanched. 'Oh my God.'

Vee shook her head. 'I know. It's unbelievable, but people have died for less. A moment of madness and that's it. I read in the morning paper somebody got stabbed to death over a bag of groceries in the township yesterday.'

'No, no, no, I just remembered that I forgot to tell you something. About Serena's old roommate and the car ...' Chlöe dropped her hands, her eyes tiny blue planets popping out of her skull. 'Ohhhh fuuuuck ....'

ANATOMY OF A MURDER
Just do it

'Is Dad here?'

'Nope, working late as usual. What're you doing here?'

'I really need to talk to him.'

'Can't you come back tomorrow? I don't know when he'll be home.'

'I need to see him tonight. It's urgent.' Pause. 'You gonna let me in?'

'No one else is here. Mum says not to let people in when we're alone in the house.'

'Yeah, *people*, like strangers. She knows I've been here a thousand times. I'm not a criminal.'

Awkward pause. A cough and shuffling of feet.

'If I'm a criminal, then so are you, so don't play innocent victim with me. Now stop messing around and open the door. It's cold out here.'

The two girls glared at each other for a long time through the crack in the door allowed by the security chain.

'Ag man, Rosie, if you don't open up, I swear–' Jacqui slapped the door over and over and it rattled. 'Why d'you always have to be so *dof*?'

'Okay, fine. But I'll come outside. I don't wanna get in trouble,' Rosie whined.

'Fine.'

They stood on the front veranda, carefully avoiding each other's eyes, pretending the falling dusk was the most interesting phenomenon they'd ever seen. Sucking in her breath, Jacqui bounced up and down on her toes as a breeze picked up.

'What do you wanna see Dad about?'

'Important stuff.'

'Yeah, you said *important*. You didn't say *secret*. What's up?'

'It is secret, so mind your own business.' Jacqui rubbed her arms briskly.

'Tjo, it's cold. Thought it was going to rain today for sure.'

'Me too. We all thought it was going to rain, but it didn't. That's what always happens.'

'Mm-hmm.'

'Now there's all this wind. I don't get it.'

'Yeah. Who knows?'

Rosie rubbed her arms, too, mimicking her sister. She had on a jersey but it didn't matter. Jacqui had slender, nice arms and pretty fingers. She wished she had arms and fingers like that.

'Last day of school was yesterday, *finally*. Now I'm free. I didn't do anything today, got sooo bored. I can hang out with you guys.' Rosie blinked. One blink, two, three, four in rapid succession.

'I don't think that's a good idea, Rosie.'

'Like, when you go for tennis practice I can come, too. I'm good at tennis. And touch rugby.' Giggle. 'I kick *ass* at sports.'

'Don't swear.'

'Sorry.' Sniff. 'Don't know about basketball, though. It's complicated. But I can learn. You can teach me. You're like a real pro. We can go to the club and make teams–'

'We're a lot older than you, Rosie. You have your own friends, don't you?'

'Yeah.' Shrug. 'But they're, you know … boring sometimes. You guys are cool.'

'We're supposed to be the boring ones. We do church activities most of the time. Why would you want to hang out with preachy types when you can have fun with your own friends?'

'I like the church stuff; it's not that bad. I used to go with Serena before *you*, remember?'

'Yes, I remember.'

'So. Anyway, Dad says it's good to be well rounded, so I can do cell group and tennis and learn basketball and you can show me—'

'Rosie. Look, can you …' Jacqui's hand went up. 'Can you just shut up for one minute? Okay? Just keep quiet and let me think for a minute.'

Another pause. 'What's your problem, anyway?'

'I've got a lot on my mind. It's been a long day. And, no, I do not want to talk about it.'

Silence again. 'You used to tell me stuff.'

'What? Stop mumbling. I can't hear you.'

'You used to tell me your secrets. We used to talk and do stuff together.'

'Rosie …' Sigh. 'You're a *laaitie*, all right? I know we used to hang out, but you're still a kid. And I only told you the kinda stuff that wasn't important to me. Sometimes you have a big mouth. You spill your guts to your mother about everything.'

'Not *everything*! I so do not tell her everything. Whatever you tell me, I'll keep my mouth shut. I won't even tell Serena.'

'That's exactly what I mean. Wh—'

'I won't say anything, Jacqui, I swear!'

'Seriously. This is personal, and you're too young to understand. Leave it alone.'

'I'm not, *I'm not!* Tell me, please, I promise—'

'Jesus, will you calm down!' Jacqui grabbed Rosie's meaty arm, held it tight and shook. 'Stop it. Stop carrying on like a big, stupid baby. You always do this. What's *up* with you?' She released her breath. 'Listen, you don't want to know about this, anyway. It's really terrible, grown-up-type stuff. You'll freak out. Only Dad can help, and maybe even he won't want to. So just forget it, okay? It doesn't matter.' Her eyes were desolate as she surveyed the settling dark. 'Maybe you're right; I should come back tomorrow. I gotta get home.'

'Wait, Jacqui, wait. I know grown-up secrets.'

Jacqui scoffed. 'Good for you. I gotta go. Mum's really gonna kill me this time.'

'I know about ... you know ...'

Jacqui stopped on the front steps and turned, only to find Rosie pointing a finger at her midriff and blushing heavily. 'I know about you, and Lucas ... and that.'

'That *what*? You think me and Luke, you think that *I'm* ...' Scornful laughter rang out. 'You really are nuts. You think you know my *big secret*, huh? You think so? You're kinda right. It's a filthy secret–'

'Stop that. Stop touching me.'

'–about shagging and humping and cumming and making babies. You know anything about that? You know about naked bodies and men's penises–'

'Stopitstopit!'

'No, you stop it. Big baby. Big ridiculous baby, what d'you think you know?' Jacqui raised a finger and jabbed it into Rosie's forehead. 'Idiot. I'm out. Tell Dad I was here.'

'I know Daddy can't stand you.' Rosie's spit flew and landed on Jacqui's cheek. 'He can't stand your coming here and pretending to be one of us. He *hates* you. He wished he never made you. He hates you and your mum and he thinks you're *cheap*.'

Jacqui barked a sharp 'ha'. 'No, he doesn't. He'd never think that.' Shrug. 'Maybe your mum does, but he doesn't.'

'Yes, he does.'

'*No, he doesn't!* And I'll tell you what else *your* pathetic mother thinks.' Jacqui stuck her nose inches from Rosie's. '*She* hates *you*. Maybe she can't stand me, but it's *you* she hates. Wanna know why? Because you let her precious little Sean die. You were supposed to save his life and you didn't.'

'N-nnn-no, that was you, that was you.'

'It was *you* first. After the first time he got sick, they decided to make you, specially, to save his life. They were gonna grow their own brand-new factory and cut bits and pieces out of you to fix Sean. But you turned out to be a loser, as always. You weren't even a match for his big toe. But I was.'

'That's not true!'

'*That's not true*,' Jacqui mimicked. 'It hurts, doesn't it? Believe what you like. Maybe it isn't true, who knows? Who cares? Nobody tells us anything, Rosie, not you and not me. Live with it.' Jacqui smacked the pad of her fingers on her stunned sister's cheek. 'Now open the gate.'

'I–'

'Open the bloody gate.'

Rosie slunk inside and closed the door. Her heart was thumping. She licked her lips and tasted sweat. Her whole mouth tasted of sweat and blood. She groaned, low and anguished. Blindly, she grabbed a set of keys from the hook near the door. She ran outside.

The car's engine purred as it started. Jacqui glanced over her shoulder, squinting up the drive. She turned around and walked back, towards the car, her laugh getting louder and louder. Her lips were moving but Rosie's ears felt numb. Her head throbbed. She couldn't see straight. The car lurched forward. Jacqui's face melted, from teasing to fear and then to horror. She started to run, and got two steps before the bonnet ate the back of her legs. The car reversed and went over her again.

Rosie sat quietly, sucking in gulps of pine- and leather-scented air. It felt like hours before she could see and hear again. The taste of blood and sweat was gone. Her heart was still screaming at her.

*

'Serena ...'

'What's up? What's wrong?'

'I did something bad. I don't know ... I ... Serena ...'

'What's wrong, what happened? Are you hurt?'

'Nn-n-no, I– it's Jacqui. I hit her. She's not moving. Ohmygod Serena, she's not moving! I can't ... I don't know. I can't ... Pleeeaaase ...'

'Where are you?'

'Home. Come come please come, are you coming?!'

'Shut up and calm down. Stay there and don't move. Don't call anyone. I'm on my way. Just stay where you are and don't touch anything.'

'Don't leave me by myself, *please*. I can't! She made me ...'

'Ro, listen to me! Calm down. Shut your mouth and breathe. Let me think, okay? Let me– I'm coming. Stop freaking out, I'm coming now.'

'Hurry. I'm scared, Serena. What if–'

'Ssshhh. Breathe and stay calm. Don't move, and don't let anyone see you. Don't call Mum and Dad! Just wait till I get there. Don't freak out, okay? I'm coming to you right now.'

45

'That's so … despicable and sad.' Chlöe had her hands over her neck. The room had emptied out. Connie had gone back to her shop, and Titus and Joshua had stepped outside to give them privacy to wrap up. 'They were just two stupid sisters having a typical, stupid, sister argument. When I think of all the crap I've said to mine … But was it true?'

'I doubt it. Carina was already pregnant with Rosie when Sean first developed leukaemia, so she couldn't have been conceived for spares to save him.' Vee sipped her juice. 'They tore into each other and it spiralled out of control. Sean was always *the* most sensitive topic. We really should've looked more closely at what was right in front of us instead of chasing our tails. Rosie's *face* is literally a suicide note. Flip the coin the other way and she could've easily been tipped into murder.'

'Wow. This is *not* how I saw this ending.' Chlöe massaged her temples. 'I hate myself for forgetting to mention the conversation about the car to you. After I heard about the hit and run, my brain blanked out. That was so crucial. I'm such an idiot.'

Vee waved her quiet. 'Ah, bygones. We've both had a lot to deal with lately. Now that my car is evidence, maybe you can make good on your promise of being my driver.' She chuckled. 'It's unreal knowing I've been connected to this case all along.'

Once Chlöe had got past the gravity of her oversight and recounted her chat with the rosy-cheeked Isabella, another piece locked into place. Serena had borrowed her roommate's Toyota Corolla to get rid of Jacqui's body. Knowing full well it was up for sale and that the trip likely wouldn't be remembered or linked back to her, she returned the car and hoped for the best. Her prayers bought her two years and a twisted coincidence. The car was sold to a used car dealership, and driven off the lot a year later by Vee. Currently, it was being impounded, to be swept for evidence later. Forensics was no more hopeful about finding DNA in it than they'd been about Carina's Mercedes. But Vee had a strong feeling there was something to find. Jacqui may have gone out lying down, but she wasn't going to settle for not getting her final say. A part of her was somewhere in that car and the geeks would find it. Vee felt chilled to her marrow knowing she'd been driving around in a mobile casket for all these months.

'When I offered Rosie a lift home that day, she looked like she was about to have a stroke. I think she even recognised the plate number. It didn't make sense at the time.' Vee remembered the amazement on Rosie's face, like life had pulled the cruellest prank on her. 'I thought it was because she was scared of being in my clutches. But she recognised the car, or probably can't stand any model that looks like it. Must've been like reliving her worst nightmare driving in it again.'

'That's super *creepy*. Maybe that was your subliminal motivation for the investigation. You had premonitions, or felt these supernatural vibes in your soul …' Chlöe made an eerie noise and twiddled her fingers under Vee's nose. 'Jacqui called out to you from the dead, 'Veeeee…''

'Stop it! Don't joke about shit like that.'

Chlöe dropped her hands. 'Whoa. Shem man, sorry. Didn't mean to … but I get why you're sensitive about it. All this time, the same car … But it's a crappy coincidence, that's all. You know that stuff's not real, right?'

Vee mumbled something and fussed with the bedcovers. Every day without the visions, every day without another crushing attack, was a joyful one. She hoped to heaven it lasted. 'I hope they find the body. Adele needs that real bad.'

The police were not optimistic they would find Jacqueline's remains, even after the Fourie sisters had given them broad directions for where they had dumped her. The system of sewage pipes and waterways that drained into the Black River was convoluted, and after twenty-four months the body had surely moved.

'They all need to move on, though God knows what they'll be moving on to now.' Chlöe cocked her head. 'This'll be the blow to destroy them forever. Serena and Rosie have screwed up their whole lives. And Carina …'

She and Vee shared a look. The fate of the girls before a criminal court looked bleak. Their mother's was less certain. It was unlikely Carina would face serious criminal charges, but the impact on her psyche and career would be irreparable.

Once the statements collected from the Fourie sisters revealed that Rosie was indeed the hit-and-run driver, Carina's motives for taking the fall became crystal clear: she wanted, *needed*, to protect her daughter. Ever since Jacqueline's disappearance, Rosie had suffered from nightmares, and her monsters had come back to torment her when Vee had started poking around. The morning of the jogging incident marked an escalation. Convinced that Vee pumping her for information about Ian was actually a ruse to expose her, Rosie had taken matters into her own hands and gone after her the same way she'd gone after Jacqui. After the ordeal, Rosie had driven home behind the wheel of her mother's battered car, witless with fright, and thrown herself into her mother's arms. She had confessed everything and Carina, who had not played favourites among her children since Sean died, threw herself under the bus to protect the child she had always paid the least attention to.

'Once Carina knew that Rosie had killed Jacqui, she went ride-or-die for her baby. Accident or not, she wasn't going to let another one of her children perish because of yet another deeply unfortunate incident connected with Adele. Her mother bear instinct kicked in, but I think it was also the principle of the thing, not to let her daughter go down for Adele's daughter.' Vee dusted off the last of the mango. 'Then you got Serena, who'd been protecting Rosie all along. And even Lucas, who, in his scatterbrained way, was trying to help. I don't know if 'destroy' is the right word to use. The Fouries may be a lot of things, but they're strong. They'll cope,' Vee said. 'Call me crazy, but the person I feel the most sorry for is Etienne

Matongo. He lost so much in the DRC, only to rebuild it here and lose it all again. He had a home and now he has nothing.'

The deputy chief of security was AWOL. Security camera footage was missing from the WI's surveillance system, and so were he and his family. Their home had been vacated, packed up hurriedly, and friends and neighbours were suspiciously lacking in helpful leads.

Chlöe looked floored. 'How can you say that? He's implicated in a murder enquiry and he did a runner. Serena's refusing to implicate him in anything they did, so who knows how involved he was? If you ask me, he's as guilty as they are.'

'It's not that simple, Chlöe. He struck me as a kind man who got sucked into this bullshit and put himself at risk to help those girls. We won't ever know now, but that's how I feel.'

'Hhmmph, whatever you say. All I know is, we now have an article to write and it is going to *slay*. The madness has begun.'

Vee groaned and pulled the covers up to her chest. 'Finegeh, no shop talk, please, ibekyu. I need one more week of rest.'

Chlöe rose. 'I'll take the hint. Should I call your boyfriends back in on my way out or ...'

'Okay, get out.'

Chlöe raised her hands in surrender. 'Hey, no judgement. I knew you were a dark horse. Just make sure I get all the deets afterwards.' She leaned down and hugged Vee, then straightened up and cleared her throat. 'And um, thanks for everything, especially being there for me and taking all the hard knocks. It's really been a great opportunity—'

'Oh, shut up with the opportunity speech. Stop worrying. Portia owes me, owes *us*, in a big way, and this time I plan to milk it. You're not going anywhere if I can help it.'

Chlöe's face was sunrise as she sashayed out, already placing an excited call as she slipped out the door.

'You look exhausted.' Joshua came in, dragged the unoccupied chair as close to the bed as it could go without crushing his knees, and sat. He leaned on her, arms crossed on her hip, chin resting on his forearms.

"The supreme art of war is to subdue the enemy without fighting.' Or something close to that,' she said. 'Sun Tzu's *The Art of War*. That advice you gave me.' He raised his eyebrows in a 'not bad' salute. 'You look worried.' She caressed his head, letting his hair wind around her fingers.

His eyebrows went a notch higher. *Should I be?*

'I said a lot of things. Before. About how friends should always be cool with each other because of how valuable friendships are and blah blah blah. Then we went and ... you know ... we misbehaved in a way that was the opposite of cool ...'

'Graphic misbehaviour.'

'Yes. And now ...' She huffed. 'It sounds ideal, but this kinda thing rarely works out. Rule number one, don't screw your friends or screw them over. If–'

'Hey. Whoa.' He straightened up. 'I get it. I'm the one who had a build-up to this. We don't have to draw each other a map. It'll be okay.'

'So ... Then ...' *Do not be the one to ask what are we,* Vee warned herself. She waited.

He rooted through his jacket pocket. 'Here.'

She jiggled the set of keys in her palm. 'You've lost your Americanness. It has to be a whole rigmarole before you hand over keys to your place to a woman. I'm ashamed you're this easy.'

'Pipe down. It's to somewhere you can be invisible for a while and relax, without worrying about people beating down your door for favours and interviews.'

'Peace and quiet. Sounds awful.' She beamed. 'Can I have visitors?'

'Whomever you please. Unrestricted access.' A little tightness pulled at the corner of his eyes, but he kept his tone light.

She was slipping under when he left. She battled with her slumping eyelids, trying to keep them open as Titus went through the same motions, adjusting the chair so he could sit comfortably with his legs stretched out. Vee rested her eyes for a second. She felt like a fading icon that half the world was coming to pay their last respects to.

'How're you feeling?'

'Exhausted.' She plastered on the last smile she could manage for the day. 'Alive and grateful.'

'Glad to hear it.' Titus stroked her hair, then took his hand away quickly, collecting himself. He averted his eyes to the wall, then turned back to her, taking both her hands in his. She kept breathing and waited. 'I don't know what more to say here. When we talked on your birthday ... okay, we didn't talk, we had an argument and I deserved everything you said to me. It doesn't change how I feel about us.'

'I can't think or feel much of anything right now, Ti. I just want to put all this behind me and get back on my feet. Let me get back on my feet.'

'Yeah, of course. I know. I'm sorry.' He nodded vigorously. He looked up at last, spearing her with a stare of liquid hazel. 'I don't mean to sound selfish but ...'

'You were never selfish,' she conceded in all fairness. 'Not until ... And I too, shouldn't have been ... well. It was what it was.'

'Yeah.' He darted his eyes around, closed them briefly as if overcoming some internal war, and met her eyes again. 'All I'm asking is for you to think about us, if there's still the possibility of an us. I have no right to ask or even hope more than that, but if there's a chance ...'

Vee felt a subtle shift in the fickle lay of the land beneath her ribcage. This was too much for one day. A yawn tried to disfigure her face; that too she fought and lost. 'Titus. I don't know anything now, and I won't lie to you. But I need to process.' She gave his arm a brief caress. 'Just don't ask me to give him up. I won't give him up, Ti. That's off the table.'

'I fucked up but he's my boy, Vee, Jesus ...' Titus's voice was husky, snagging on his pride, his hurt.

'That's on you. You two can ... settle or not settle it however y'all choose.'

He gulped and turned back to the window, his jaw muscles flexing so vigorously she expected to hear his teeth crumbling. Guilt took eager stabs all around her ribcage. It wasn't fun or comfortable watching him leveraged so easily off a long-held position of confidence.

At last, Titus relented with a brusque nod. 'Okay. I'm right here. Take your time.' He leant over her and brushed his lips over hers. Familiar strands of warmth nudged away the guilt and curled around her belly.

Vee brushed back and sank into the pillow, her eyelids pulling down the shutters over consciousness. Time was good. She needed a lot of it. Ten rice bags full and a dash on top.

46

The watcher slept.

Curled up in a ball to trap every bit of warmth to his body, the eleven-year-old boy drifted between slumber and unconsciousness. He was unaware that for days his body had been failing him, but he did know he felt really sick. His lungs had slowly filled with fluid and his temperature was critically low. Every now and then, he coughed but didn't rouse.

Under the bridge was not the best place to doss, but it offered good protection from the storm. It was dry and rarely did anyone wander by and rudely kick him awake, or chase him off their turf. No one paid attention to street people in Cape Town. Maybe their eyes brushed over them and made out the shape of a human being, but their presence didn't register. The street community was not a productive part of the city. He'd been living and begging on the street for long enough to know.

He had lain down under a stone arch, making sure his tattered polyester jacket was zipped right up to the neck and the newspaper stuffed in his sneakers was still dry. He wished he still had the blanket he took from the woman's house, the one who had given him hot chocolate. That blanket was worth more than diamonds right now. Obviously, it wouldn't still be where he'd left it. He never should have let it out of his sight. Everybody on the street knew the value of a blanket in winter, so he wouldn't be seeing it anywhere but in his dreams.

The season was about to change and he couldn't have been happier about it. This winter was harder than most. He wondered if he went back to the lady's house, if she would open her door to him again. She had looked like a good person, not afraid of him or disgusted, unlike a lot of women with nice houses. But she was probably still angry because he stole from her house.

He slept, and dreamt. He dreamt of the dying girl in the sewer, a dream that didn't want to leave him no matter how he tried to beat it back. The girl whose body he still expected to see every time he passed an open drain, curled up at the bottom. The girl whose picture had scared him to death when he had seen it at the nice lady's house. He dreamt of her arm ...

… reaching up to him, trying to bridge the distance. She was covered with leaves and discarded junk; plastic cups and bottles and paper. Her body was twisted in a strange, broken way. A red knitted cap was askew over her face, leaving her head partly uncovered. Her entire body looked to be frozen in place, like she couldn't move, but her eyes burned bright. The look in them was unmistakable. It was one of pure terror.

She was still alive. The boy couldn't believe it. Twenty minutes earlier, two girls had driven up while he was eating a chocolate bar under a tree, about to push off to a less deserted area to sleep. They had driven with no lights, and he had barely made out the car. He ducked behind the tree. The two girls got out and whispered for a long time.

The boy waited. They put their arms around each other; one of them wept and the other tried to keep her quiet. Finally, they'd opened a passenger door and struggled to drag something out. It looked heavy.

Bent double under the weight of their load, they had stumbled to the edge of an open drainage canal and lowered it. They'd patrolled the length of the canal, hissing back and forth to each other. Whatever they were deciding had taken a long time. They'd nodded, picked up the bundle and rolled it down the brick-walled verge of the pipe. The bundle had rustled, thumped and landed on the bottom with a thud. One of the girls had slid down the verge after it, holding on to the other girl as she'd lowered herself down the top half. She'd disappeared out of sight for several minutes. The other girl had drifted back over to the car and started pacing the pavement. It sounded like she'd started crying again. Or maybe vomiting. The boy hadn't realised he'd been holding his breath until the girl in the pipe gave a low call and he'd sighed in relief. The other one ran over. It had been a tussle lifting out the first girl but they'd managed. They'd scrambled into the car and driven away.

The watcher had waited for what felt like years. When he'd been sure they weren't coming back, he went down the slope, too, scraping a leg on the cement and drawing blood. He crawled in and squinted into the stretch of dark in front of him, but wasn't able to see anything. The pipe had broken in two and the other half plunged further down at a sharp angle. He'd rooted around for a stick long enough to poke around and feel his way deeper inside.

His stick knocked against the shape of something big. It looked like a human being. It made a sound when he poked it, and he jumped. He snuck closer and knelt. In the dim light he could see it was a girl, or a boy with a pretty face and too much hair. She was lying near the bottom of the slope of the broken pipe.

She tried stretching an arm out to him and he tried to reach back, but the distance was too far. He tried leaning in, one arm and leg braced against the edge and his body thrust forwards. It was no use. Tired, he finally gave up. Maybe if he just jumped in … but how would he get out? He wouldn't get himself out, much less the two of them.

The girl's whimpering faded to low mewls, and then to the sound of breath rasping in and out of her windpipe. The boy considered going to get help, but the girl gave a mournful moan when he tried to move away. The boy understood. She couldn't bear to be left alone.

Minutes passed and the body went still. The boy waited some more, listening to the sound of his own breathing. Nothing answered save the wind. Using his stick, he shifted leaves and dirt off the girl. She didn't move. Her chest and one of her arms were outside her tracksuit top. He worked his stick around, pushing the body onto its side and twisting the top off. He hooked it up the slope. It was brand new Nike and looked like the real deal. The night became less unforgiving as he drew it around his shoulders.

The boy trudged to the closest police station. The policeman behind the night-desk yawned in his face and threatened to arrest him for telling stories while high on tik. The child shrank and fell silent. Then the policeman gave him two rand and told him to piss off. The boy ran back into the street with the coin, knowing no one would ever believe him.

He tried to forget.

The watcher slept, and his breathing and circulation slowed to feeble murmurs and thrums. Within an hour, they had stopped.

47

'Is this even up for discussion?'

'It's open to negotiation. Think about it. Cheers.'

Vee ended the call and tossed the phone on top of the laundry basket. Her schedule and her mind were full to overflowing, and still she was being pressured to take on more. What the hell kind of sabbatical was this?

She rose off the edge of the bathtub and walked to the basin. It was a long and majestic walk, much longer than it took in her own house, and on much nicer floors. She smiled, feeling the tiles under her feet. Cold tile was cold tile, no matter how fancy a bathroom you got.

She fiddled with the tap until she worked out which direction got the water flowing. She wasted more time adjusting the spurt from lava hot to mountain freeze and everything in between, until she got the temperature she wanted. Three days in this place and she still couldn't work all its gadgets and mod cons. Good thing she had at her disposal a brilliant head on a capable, strapping pair of male shoulders. She grinned at herself in the mirror before lifting the toothbrush to her teeth. Screw it, she deserved her fun.

'Was that another offer?' called a male voice from the bedroom.

'No,' Vee mumbled over a mouthful of toothpaste. She spat. 'Portia's on my ass, again. She wants me to go on some women's talk show and shamelessly promote the magazine.' She shook her head. 'As if we need help with circulation after this.'

She wanted a little peace and quiet and the universe was having none of it. The police had just gotten off her back. The forensic scientists had found a scrap of evidence in her car, buried deep in a crevice of the back seat cushions – a silver earring, a cross attached to a shrivelled piece of human tissue. So far the working theory was Rosie and Serena had thrown Jacqui's body onto the back seat to dispose of it. When they dragged her out, the earring and part of her earlobe caught in the fabric of the seats and ripped out. Vee gagged every time she thought about it, driving along with a piece of another human being wedged in her car, surviving months of shampooing and vacuuming in its burrow. The next ride she would do extensive homework on beforehand, then take it apart herself and clean it top to bottom.

Now the press was hounding her for an interview about the investigation. Not to mention the blitz of emails from the WI's image consultant, demanding that she speak candidly about the incident and disperse all rumours that murderous psychopaths roamed their halls. Vee had politely refused, telling her to get closure from justice being served, like the rest of the general public. The WI still circulated a statement to the effect that their reputable facility was in no way connected with the tragic circumstances of Jacqueline Paulsen's death. The worst move they could've made, in Vee's opinion. If it doesn't stink, don't spray air freshener. All they succeeded in doing was drawing attention to themselves, by implying a tenuous link to an isolated cold case. Now the press was on the hunt and WI had their work cut out for them. The thrill was gone.

Vee rinsed and knocked her toothbrush against the sink. She had to admit, she didn't mind too much the fuss being made over her. It reminded her she still had swag, and if that wasn't enough, the job offers from a few high-flyer news agencies were damn sure an ego stroke that came with a larger pay cheque. Now the only part she hated – and she'd expected there would be something, but not this – was being hounded by strangers to look into the tragic disappearance of their relative, friend, lover, colleague or pet. Vee didn't know who put it about she was a P.I. who solved piddling mysteries or how her contact details got into circulation – she strongly suspected Charisma Mapondera and her devilry on both counts – but that problem wasn't hers for now. Let Chlöe earn her new salary fielding calls and handling paperwork.

Vee headed to the bedroom. For a moment, she paused in the doorway and took it all in. The room was done up in white and teak, complemented by the right blend of muted tones and good furniture. She felt a deep pang. Were Jacqueline Paulsen alive, she would know what kind of décor this was. It was lost on heathens like her.

'Maybe you should do it.' Joshua looked up from his laptop. 'Portia gave you something; you should give her something back. Lengthen your life span.'

Vee exhaled, exasperated. He was right, but contemplating the pound of flesh she owed and would eventually have to repay stuck in her throat. Portia the Proud, and ever strategic, had handed she and Chlöe over to *City Chronicle*. *Chronicle* was small, but its investigative beat was well worth the move. And they were one building away, where Portia would most definitely be keeping tabs on them.

'Attention like this is always short-lived, not to mention hungry and dying to feed. I'll make a fool of myself on camera to please her and have to live with that piece of history hanging over me forever. Hell no. I'll find something else to trade with.'

'Come on, you'd slay a TV appearance. You could wear that lacy bra with the pop-open front, great for ratings …'

Vee jumped behind him on the bed and wrapped her legs around his waist, and hugged his back. He smelled of clean cotton, soap and pheromones. Essence of Guy, God's gift to womankind. The sun was out in full form, as it had been for days. The picture of contentment. All the picture needed was for Monro, outside sunning himself on the lawn of his dreams, to dash in with a Frisbee in his teeth. *You're a revolting cliché*, she thought.

Vee tapped the laptop screen. 'Ibekyu, I thought you were helping me find a new car to buy.'

Joshua scrolled down the *Top Gear* webpage, awash with unattainable supercars with their monstrous price tags and impossible specs. 'My bad. Got a little carried away.'

Vee put her head back down on his shoulder. 'I've been thinking. Maybe I *should* become a private investigator.'

Joshua's shoulders arched up and dropped. 'It's not the worst idea in the world. Though personally, don't bite my head off, but I don't think you're ready. You have bigger fish to fry for a while yet.'

'Yeah. You're right.' She let it hang. 'But I should learn how to use a gun.'

Joshua stiffened. Slowly, he closed the laptop and pivoted to face her. 'Okaaay. That's huge. Firearms are a major responsibility. You have to be fully trained to handle one.'

She wanted to roll her eyes but didn't, seeing as he was in his no-nonsense mode. 'I know something about guns, Joshua. I don't take them lightly.'

He shook his head and reopened the laptop. 'If you really want to learn how to carry a piece, you should ask your boyfriend Titus.'

'Ti knows how to shoot? From where?'

'Same place I learnt.'

'*You* know how to shoot? When did my life turn into *Walker, Texas Ranger*?'

'I'm from Brooklyn, and Titus owns a farm in your rebel hinterlands. Do the math.' He tapped away at the keyboard. 'You may want to sharpen your listening skills and spend less time abusing us to your salacious ends. We're people, too.' The mouse scanned across a car dealership's web page. 'How about a Renault Laguna?'

'I'd rather walk barefoot on rusty nails.'

She left his side and curled under the duvet. 'You still haven't told me whose place this is,' she murmured.

'I bring all my women here. Don't ask questions.'

That was their new mission statement. No questions. No hope, no expectations, unrealistic or otherwise. She could smell how horribly this would end a hundred miles away. 'At least tell me what you're paying for it, so I can really feel like a kept woman.'

'Paying? Damn, you do get ahead of yourself. Ask me first if I even know whose house this is.' He got to his feet, looking round the room and scratching his chin. 'Remind me again how long it took the cops to reach you last time?' He gave her a teasing look and walked out.

Vee rolled onto her stomach and propped a ridiculously soft pillow under her head. 'Whatever, Joshua Allen. I am completely at my leisure.'

Epilogue

After days scouring the major drains and canals in the neighbourhoods around the Black River – Pinelands, Observatory, Mowbray – the search and diving parties finally found the skeletal remains of a teenage girl. Forensic evidence confirmed them to be those of Jacqueline Paulsen.

A week after putting her only child to rest, Adele Paulsen cleared her bank account, liquidated the few assets she possessed and packed her bags for Australia. She took up residence with her sister in Melbourne, making no plans ever to return to South Africa, apart from a brief visit to give testimony in a murder trial.

The handsome sum of money that landed in her Absa account went a long way towards facilitating her move. In reply, she sent a distant but cordial letter to Ian Fourie thanking him for his support, though it had come too late.

Ian didn't understand the letter. Primarily because the payment had come from his wife.

Carina Fourie placed lilies on the grave of her son, Heinrich Sean Fourie. She took Lucas's hand and together they observed a minute's silence in his memory.

She had resigned from her job in good grace and liquidated a few assets of her own. She had even consulted a divorce lawyer, but knew she wouldn't go through with it. After the hubbub had died down, she planned on returning to Germany to stay with her mother, for a while at least. There was no love lost there, but at least they understood each other.

Dr Alan Weir got the appointment as chief of the cardiothoracic and lung health unit at the Wellness Institute. Dr Ian Fourie shook hands like a good sport, congratulated Weir and wished him all the best.

Shortly afterwards, a section of the oncology unit was renamed the Sean Fourie Paediatric Cancer Trust. The subdivision included a revamped playroom and gaming centre for the ailing children.

Ian stared at the sign bearing his son's name above the door of the centre for a long time. Then he went outside, sat in his car and wept, for everything he had squandered, lost and would never have.

Ashwin Venter did a short stint in Pollsmoor Prison for aggravated assault. Upon release, he went back to managing his father's garage with his sister, Marieke.

On a night in early November, a man, woman and two girls waited at a border post between South Africa and Namibia. The man presented brand-new identity books for his family, and explained in a soft French accent that he had arrived on a provisional work visa. Minutes later, the group entered Namibia.

Acknowledgements

I doubt anyone undertaking the transition from writer to published author imagines the amount of labour involved in the process. Breathing new life into a novel years after its debut is even more taxing, and for their patience, expertise and advice I appreciate the following:

As always, I thank God, for keeping the mystery, madness and method of me going.

For the love, encouragement and material for my work: endless praise to my parents, Prof. Vuyu Golakai and Ms Inez Dunbar, and my siblings Nessie, the twins Kwame and Kanda, and particularly my sister Fasia for every push. To Mrs Erika Bülck, thank you for your loving presence. To my uncle and aunt, John T. Woods and Catherine Woods, bless you always for providing heart and home to a ragtag bunch of refugees when we lost ours.

For career and personal guidance: many thanks to the Gates Immunology team of Stellenbosch University. Especial gratitude to my work dad Prof. Gerhard Walzl and mentor Dr Gillian Black, for unwavering dedication to my education, in far more than just science. This is probably the only PhD I will ever write.

My boundless gratitude to my new publisher, Cassava Republic Press, for the exciting journey we've just begun. Bibi Bakare-Yusuf and Emma Shercliff, I am grateful and awed by the attention to detail put into this new manuscript. Thank you for your keen insight and energy invested in my book. To my 'old' publisher Kwela Books, high-five for bringing this collaboration to pass.

For language and translation, thank you to: Jekwu Ozoemene, Jite Efemuaye and Jumoke Verissimo (for Naija lingo and pidginisation), Fiona Snyckers and Roela Hattingh (for Afrikaans) and Helen Moffett, for great editing advice.

And finally, and quite absurdly, this book is (still) in part dedicated to my musical muse and crush, Chris Martin of Coldplay, without whose magnificent genius I would struggle to write a single word. Chris, my feelings haven't changed ☺…

To anyone I may have forgotten, mea culpa.

CASSAVA CRIME

Easy Motion Tourist – Leye Adenle

Guy Collins, a British hack, is hunting for an election story in Lagos. A decision to check out a local bar in Victoria Island turns out badly – a mutilated female body is discarded close by and Collins is picked up as a suspect.

In the murk of a hot, groaning and bloody police station cell, Collins fears the worst. But then Amaka, a sassy guardian angel of Lagos working girls, talks the police station chief around. She assumes Collins is a BBC journo who can broadcast details of the city's witchcraft and body parts trade that she's on a one-woman mission to stop.

With Easy Motion Tourist's astonishing cast, Tarantino has landed in Lagos. This page-turning debut crime novel pulses with the rhythm of Nigeria's megacity, reeks of its open drains and sparkles like the champagne quaffed in its upmarket districts.

The Carnivorous – City Toni Kan

Rabato Sabato aka Soni Dike is a Lagos big boy; a criminal turned grandee, with a beautiful wife, a sea-side mansion and a questionable fortune. Then one day he disappears and his car is found in a ditch, music blaring from the speakers.

Soni's older brother, Abel Dike, a teacher, arrives in Lagos to look for his missing brother. Abel is rapidly sucked into the unforgiving Lagos maelstrom where he has to navigate encounters with a motley cast of common criminals, deal with policemen all intent on getting a piece of the pie, and contend with his growing attraction to his brother's wife.

Carnivorous City is a story about love, family and just desserts but it is above all a tale about Lagos and the people who make the city by the lagoon what it is.

The Score – HJ Golakai

Voinjama Johnson and her assistant Chlöe Bishop are back. They have been banished to Oudtshoorn in the Karoo, the last place on earth to expect them to get mixed up in any danger. But no sooner have they checked into their lodge when two dead bodies crop up at a business convention, throwing them under suspicion. Once again the two women dive in way over their heads, into the I.T. world of cybercrime, corruption and a shrewd killer that drags them ever closer to a perilous edge.

Navigating a sphere of sex, drugs and empowerment, *The Score* moves with breathtaking pace over South Africa's fading rainbow.

OTHER TITLES BY CASSAVA REPUBLIC PRESS

Born on a Tuesday – Elnathan John

Dantala lives in Bayan Layi, Nigeria and studies in a Sufi Quranic school. By chance he meets gang leader Banda, and is thrust into a world with fluid rules and casual violence. In the aftermath of presidential elections Dantala runs away and ends up living in a Salafi mosque. Slowly and through the hurdles of adolescence, he embraces Salafism as preached by his new benefactor, Sheikh Jamal. But as political and religious tensions mount, he is torn between loyalty to his benefactor, Sheikh Jamal, and adherence to the Sheikh's charismatic advisor, Malam Abdul-Nur, a choice that tests Dantala to his very limits.

In this raw, authentic and deceptively simple novel, Elnathan John explores boyhood in the wake of extremism and fundamentalism. *Born on a Tuesday* delves behind the scenes of the media's portrayal of Boko Haram and tells of one boy's struggle to find a purpose.

Like A Mule Bringing Ice Cream to the Sun – Sarah Ladipo Manyika

Dr. Morayo Da Silva, a cosmopolitan Nigerian woman, lives in San Francisco. On the cusp of seventy-five, she has a zest for life and makes the most of it through road trips in her vintage Porsche, chatting to strangers, and reminiscing about characters from her favourite novels. Until she has an accident, crushing her independence. Without the support of family, she relies on friends and chance encounters to help keep her sane. As Morayo recounts her story, moving seamlessly between past and present, we meet Dawud, a charming Palestinian shopkeeper, Sage, a feisty, homeless Grateful Dead devotee, and Antonio, the poet whom Morayo desired more than her ambassador husband.

A beautifully uplifting story about ageing, friendship and loss.

Season of Crimson Blossoms – Abubakar Adam Ibrahim

A story of love and longing in conservative Northern Nigeria, featuring Binta, a 55-year-old widow yearning for intimacy after the sexual repression of her marriage, and Reza, a 25-year-old weed dealer. Brought together in unusual circumstances, Binta and Reza faced a need only they can satisfy in each other.

Through Binta, we follow the intimate daily life of a Muslim Hausa family - where life revolves around domestic disputes and divorces, friendship and whispers, and religious instruction at the madrasa. By contrast, Reza is the self-pronounced Lord of San Siro, an urban cesspit that is home to a gang of misfits, outcasts and thugs.

The situation comes to a head when these two worlds collide, with disastrous consequences. This moving novel unfurls gently, revealing layers of emotion that defy age, class and religion.

HOW YOU CAN SUPPORT CASSAVA REPUBLIC AUTHORS:

1. **Buy.** When you buy a book you ensure that an author's effort is rewarded and you help to make sure that the publisher publishes their next book and many others.

2. **Review, review review.** Getting reviews is becoming more and more difficult. Your opinion is powerful and a positive review from you can generate new sales. Spare a minute to leave a short review on Amazon, Goodreads, Wordery and other book buying sites. Be sure to tweet or email the author and publisher to let us know that you have done this.

3. **Spread the word on social media.** Hearing somebody you trust talk about a book with passion and excitement is one of the most powerful ways to get people to buy or read it. If you like a book, talk about it, Facebook it, tweet it, blog it, Instagram it. Take a picture of the book and quote from it or highlight your favourite passage. Remember to add a link to where others can purchase it.

4. **Buy the book as gifts for others.** Buying gifts is an ongoing activity for most of us – for birthdays, anniversaries, holidays, special days or thank you presents. If you love a book and you think it might resonate with others, then buy extra copies.

5. **Get your local bookshop to stock our books.** Sometimes bookshops only order books that they have heard about. Request a book at your local bookshop and wax lyrical to the booksellers about the books you like. If enough people request a title, the bookshop will take note and may order a few copies for their shelves.

6. **Recommend a book to your book club.** Persuade your book club to read this book and our other titles and discuss what you enjoy about the book in the company of others. This is a wonderful way to share your favourite reads and help to boost the sales and popularity of the book.

7. **Attend a book reading.** There are lots of opportunities to hear writers talk about their work. Support them by attending their book events. Get your friends, colleagues and families to a reading and show an author your support.